NEMESIS

A BLACK FATES NOVEL

Christine Roi

Book design by Alison Cnockaert
Cover by Natalia Junqueira

ISBN 979-8-218-20646-8 (paperback)
ISBN 979-8-218-20645-1 (ebook)

www.christineroi.com

CONTENTS

For all the girls who needed protection.
Even from themselves.

CONTENT WARNING

This story contains graphic content that might be troubling to some readers, including, but not limited to, depictions of and references to:

Intimate Partner Violence

Forced asphyxiation

Severed appendages

Murder/assassinations

Dismembered bodies

Torture

Implied Sexual Assault

Trauma

Please be mindful of these and other possible triggers and seek assistance if needed.

PROLOGUE

TWENTY-TWO YEARS AGO

Lilith, why are you not sleeping?"

"It's too dark in here."

"You're afraid of the dark?"

"I'm afraid of the things that hide in it."

He nodded and cracked the door open, letting the light pour in from the hallway. Before he could leave, I called after him.

"Nonno?" I said shakily. "Can you tell me a story?"

He sat down on the bed next to me and loosed a tired sigh. "One story and you will go to sleep." Not a negotiation, a command. I nodded my acceptance.

"A long time ago, deep in a thick and forgotten forest, there was a village. This was a peaceful village that was filled with all sorts of people. Merchants, farmers, and small families shared with each other in harmony. When they ventured into the forest, it was only for small things. They respected the forest around them and took only what they needed from it.

After the sun would set, everyone remained in their little houses, afraid of the gnarling, thrashing teeth that gleamed even in the darkness. Villagers feared that thing because it chased them to their doors, threatening to tear the flesh from their bones. Parents warned their children in hushed voices to beware of the beast that stalked through the forest. But even though it filled them with dread, the villagers didn't know that the creature of the forest cared for them.

Through the night, even after the villagers had gone to sleep, their protector stalked through the trees. The beast chased them home to safeguard them from monsters they would never see. When the sun rose, the beast laid down to rest, knowing the villagers were safe in the light of day."

"What was the beast, Nonno?" I whispered.

"A wolf, mia principessa. The wolf, now alone in the forest, had once had a family. The pack was taken and killed by the brutal beasts of the night. So the villagers became dear to it, and it protected them with tooth, claw, and blood."

"Why?"

"Because a wolf protects their family. From predators and hunger. They protect them with everything they have. Just like I'll protect you for as long as I'm around." He leaned over and kissed my forehead. "Go to sleep now."

1

NARCISSUS POETICUS

This happened every fucking time. I was actually amazed I hadn't been caught because I had once again hurled my guts up before leaving the scene. Experience had taught me to keep little doggy bags on me, just so I had something to vomit into, but this time I got lucky because there was a toilet nearby and I could flush away any evidence I was here. Another wave of nausea buckled my knees and I braced myself against the toilet as my gut worked to empty itself.

Gasping for air with sweat stinging my vision, I strained to take in the room once more. The bathroom was still clean and unused, mostly, despite my recent issues with a weak stomach. In the bedroom, there were folded clothes on the dresser next to the television and the room service menu. And the corpse of Vincent Grecco.

The bed did show signs of a struggle and, believe me, he fucking struggled. Between vomiting fits, I was still catching my breath. Usually, they didn't feel the needle. This method, the poison we called the Lullaby, was supposed to be clean. It looked natural and I could slip in and out unnoticed. Unfortunately for him, he had woken up from his drunken stupor just as the needle went in. Maybe he thought he was being bitten by something because his hand moved to swat at it. Realizing what was happening, he gave me a crack across the jaw. I planted my boot into his chest and struck the heel of my palm to his nose. None of it was going to stop what happened, only now he was going to meet his maker with a cracked sternum and a broken nose.

The air conditioner rumbled on as I stripped out of the bloodstained dress I borrowed from housekeeping and stuffed it into my backpack, along with the needle and my gloves. Hopping into the jeans I brought, I glanced at Vincent. To look at him, you would think he was sleeping. You know, except for the blood that gushed from his face. My stomach flipped again. With the mess he made, I couldn't leave him as he was. So I sent a text to the clean-up crew.

> Large Pizza. Extra sauce. The Gable Hotel,
> Beverly Hills, Room 222.

My phone pinged.

> Ready in 30 minutes or less.

I chuckled at the macabre code and pulled on the clean tee shirt that was stashed in the bottom of my bag. It took a few minutes of messing with my hair to work the wavy black strands back into a sloppy bun. Killing is a sweaty business. After returning to the bathroom, I splashed some water on my face and wiped blood away with some tissue, which I then stuffed into my backpack along with everything else. Anything with a hint of me went into the bag. Giving the room one more once over, I decided it was clear enough. Kaia was going to kill me. We rarely ever used the cleanup guys because they're expensive. They were expensive because they were infallibly effective, but we're not supposed to need them in the first place. I'm supposed to make it look natural. That's the whole point. Usually, I do. A man dies alone in his bed and no one thinks anything of it. One less bastard in the world.

I checked my phone. The clean-up crew would be here any second, so I grabbed my bag and headed out. My heavy combat boots clunked down the terracotta hallway as I headed to the parking lot. As I rounded the corner, a man with a pizza bag met my eye. Our palms grazed each other and his once-empty hand possessed the key to Room 222. Goodbye, Vincent Grecco.

My black Mercedes was indistinguishable from the hired cars parked around it. Of course, that was the idea. These cars littered the streets of Los Angeles by the dozen and were utterly forgettable. I settled into the driver's seat and started the car, just in time for the hands-free to connect with my sister's incoming call.

"You left a bit of a mess."

"Hi, Kaia."

"These guys cost a fortune, Lilith. Be more careful."

Grateful she couldn't see me, I rolled my eyes. More careful. Like I woke him up on purpose.

"He wasn't as drunk as I thought and he wasn't thrilled about me being there. I'm fine, by the way."

"Fine."

The call disconnected and I loosed a disgruntled sigh while I put the car into gear. They always called Kaia for approval before coming to me, just to make sure she was good for the money. She must have been having a hard night, maybe with the club. Maybe with Daniel. She definitely wasn't alone or she would not have been as hard on me about the money. I let my mind wander while I pulled away to make the drive back to my apartment on the other side of town. Outside, the air had just begun to chill, causing the marine layer to condense into a heavy fog.

AFTER SWINGING BY Garage Pizza to fill my empty gut, I arrived at home over an hour later. I'm not too proud to admit that my text to the cleanup crew put the idea of a hot and cheesy pie into my mind. With the pizza box wedged under one arm and my backpack slung over my shoulder, I nudged my way into my humble home. My apartment was in one of those run-down complexes with an ironically luxurious name. It was a series of tiny 1920s-style studio bungalows pushed up next to each other, all painted in a faded banana yellow. The sun-bleached sign outside the wrought-iron gate read "Le Tropical" in painted gold lettering. Each little building was different on the inside, but it was basically 600 square feet to call my own and close enough to Kaia's house in the Hills for me to be minutes away when she needed me.

My keys hit the laminate countertop as I entered my dark little den, the iron security door closing with a slam. If my odd hours were a problem for the neighbors, the landlord didn't seem to mind. I'd made him a rich man, so he probably ignored their complaints anyway. Tapping the light switch beside me, the lamp turned on in the corner. Again, it wasn't much, but it was all mine. My bed was in the center of the space, flanked by my dresser and a desk. A monstrous Swedish entertainment unit that took me two days to build dominated the opposing wall and contained most of my stuff. It was covered in a thin layer of dust, random collectibles, my framed but not hung college degrees, empty glasses, and some candles. Every time I looked at my degrees, I thought *I'll get around to putting them up* but after six years they were still there.

My black boots thudded to the floor as I unzipped each one in my entryway. Cracking open the pizza box, I grabbed a slice and padded my way to the pink-tiled bathroom to turn on the shower. My jaw ached as I took a bite. The tragically ancient showerhead sputtered and hissed as it began spraying water, and I went back to the kitchen. The only way to get the night off of me was with hot water and perhaps even a shower margarita. God knows I didn't want to go to bed drenched in a dead man's sweat. The water usually took about five minutes to heat, so I had time to shovel another slice of garlicky deliciousness into my mouth while I poured a canned cocktail into a glass. You know, like a lady.

Naked with a mouthful of pizza, I was dragging the shower door open as my phone started ringing. After glancing at the screen, I could see that it was coming from the club, which meant that Kaia must still be there.

"What?" I mumbled through pizza.

"Always talking with your mouth full," West laughed.

"You know I'm pure class. What's up?" I said, after washing my monstrous bite down with a swig of margarita.

"Your sister wants you to come in."

This was the sort of power move bullshit she pulled when she was mad at me. She made the club bouncer call me like I was being summoned to the temple by an angry goddess and I didn't have the energy to deal with her. She also knew I'd have a hard time telling my only friend to kick rocks. West heaved a sigh, waiting for me to respond.

"Man, come on. I just talked to her. I'm sweaty. I'm tired. It's almost two in the morning. Besides, I'm just getting into the shower."

"Fine." West huffed into the receiver. "I'll tell her I couldn't get you. But Lili? Come in as soon as you can tomorrow."

I mumbled my agreement as I stepped over the tub to get into the shower. He hung up as I tossed the phone onto the vanity. While lathering up, I went through all the possible conversations my sister wanted to have with me in my mind. I even did both sides of our hypothetical arguments, which is the only time I ever win fights with my sister.

Once I was clean, I put on a ratty old Nirvana tee shirt and boxers I never returned to an ex-boyfriend. I'm a bit of a relationship kleptomaniac, but my philosophy is that if you break my heart, I get to keep your shit. Between college and moving back to Los Angeles to help my sister, I'd been through a few self-proclaimed "nice guys." This one needed money, that one needed rehab and the other one needed literally everyone else in his bed. This policy has gotten me a nice television, some ironic coffee mugs, and the luxurious pajamas I was wearing. They didn't smell like him anymore, just the organic laundry soap I used. Softened from years of wear, their oversized fit comforted my anxious, racing mind enough for me to fall asleep with the TV set on Netflix streaming sitcom reruns. After all of this time, taking a life hadn't gotten any easier.

2

WISTERIA SINENSIS

The sun beamed through the blinds, casting long shadows across my faded green duvet. Based on the sun's position and the gold tones of light, I knew it was well into the afternoon. Unsure as to what time I'd gone to sleep, I checked my phone. Two PM. Counting backward on my fingers, I decided I'd gotten plenty of sleep and peeled myself out of bed while shooting a text to West.

Going to miss training today. Obviously.

His response was immediate and clearly annoyed.

You already missed training.

Padding over to the fridge, I thought about how disappointed he would be in my breakfast of leftover pizza and cold brew coffee. I'd always told him that I was a scavenger, not a cook. It was pretty late in the day, so maybe it didn't actually count as breakfast, but a girl has to eat. The cold cheese and sauce satisfied my hunger as I opened the cabinets to take an inventory of my serums, needles, and syringes, only to find I was short on everything.

After horsing down another slice and quickly placing an online order for the medical supplies I needed, I got dressed.

I wasn't really sure what Kaia wanted to discuss, but since she asked me to meet her at Muse, I knew it was business. So before I met with her, I knew I needed to get more serums going. Just in case her summons was more business than pleasure. First, I would have to stop at her house and tend to the plants in the garden she was letting me keep on her property. My bag slipped into the crook of my elbow as the unpredictable autumn weather had me wrapping a flannel shirt around my waist. Cursing myself, I made my way to the car.

WE ALWAYS GIVE flowers poetic names. Some are beautiful. Others are incredibly sad. Narcissus, Forget-Me-Not, Devil's Hand. The former greeted me as I made my way through the gate of the enclosed garden. This garden had been at my sister's house for decades. Of course, it wasn't her house when it was first planted. It had been planted for my grandmother as a birthday gift from Nonno when they first moved in.

Gardening was one of the things that my grandmother and I had in common. Her love of beautiful blooms was why wisteria blossoms dripped down the patio. It was why the front door was surrounded by luscious clouds of hydrangea. Of course, the fact that the flowers helped to hide things like security cameras and microphones was merely a bonus. As I started to clip away berries and herbs, my eyes skimmed the terrace. Our grandparent's terrace looked dreamy, shrouded with blossoms, lemons, and illuminated with trattoria lights.

The iron table still sat there, freshly coated by my sister after years of wear had aged it. It was one of the things Kaia refused to get rid of when she took over the house. The more elaborate outdoor furnishings she'd chosen looked so new by comparison. I made my way up to the granny flat above the garage to get to work.

When I first left my doctoral program, this flat was my home. Kaia was caring for her newborn son and I helped wherever I could. It was in here that I'd had the idea for the Lullaby.

When I was younger, stories of people being healed by plants fascinated me. Healing burns with aloe vera. Soothing an upset stomach with ginger. That was why I started my education in biochemistry. But it was my minor in toxicology and master's in plant biology that were the building blocks to what I do for the family.

School notes on an herbal remedy for sleep loss and its dangerously close relationship to a heart-stopping poison came together in my sleep-deprived mind. So I created a mixture of hallucinogenic and deadly botanicals that left victims in a euphoric dream state before death. They'd start in the hands of Morpheus, only to find Death had taken them away. It was the kind of end most of us hope for and one that I'd likely never get. With no sign of struggle and no visible injection point, deaths would be ruled natural. Case closed.

The first person I tested my new recipe on was a rat. I didn't catch him. Gino, one of our most loyal soldiers, found out that one of his guys was feeding information to the Russians for money. He was going to take care of him on his own, but I asked for test subjects. I'll never forget the look of dread on the man's face as the needle plunged into the vial, filling the syringe with my special formula.

He took a long time to die. Almost an hour. It took me several iterations to get the mixture exactly right. The right amount of belladonna. The right amount of potassium. I tried to keep everything separate. Mixing and bottling happened in my lab, but I kept the finished product at my apartment.

By the time the mixture came together, I'd been killing for close to a year.

Much of what was in here now wasn't there before. My plan to create an apothecary from hell came with a lot of tools and expensive equipment. A worn wooden worktable replete with drawers for small devices and bottles sat in the center of the space. The surrounding walls were lined with olive green cabinets and botanical diagrams. On top of those cabinets sat the equipment I'd need to do my work.

As I pulled off my leather work gloves, I went through the list of tasks in my mind. Some of the plants went into the dehydrator, others were to be ground with the mortar and pestle. Serums were to be transitioned from the distiller into storage. Though the flat had become my laboratory, something about it still felt like home. Maybe it was because of all the hours I spent here, but it also could be because only I had the keys and kept this place locked up tight. There wasn't anything inherently dangerous about the equipment or chemicals when they were separated, but we didn't want it to be anywhere Daniel would happen upon it. Especially the little brown bottles with labels written in code stored in the padlocked refrigerator.

While the dehydrator set to work, I took care of the other equipment. Washing beakers, various flasks, and funnels. Wiping down the table to discard any trimming remnants. Misting the terrariums of more temperamental plants that wouldn't survive the California weather. Being here always soothed me. It helped to stunt the sense of dread that ate at me as I wondered what my sister needed to discuss. What other dark assignment did she have for me?

I didn't mind the stalking and killing much. That sounds strange to say but it was the torture that bothered me. Intentionally inflicting pain on someone I've never met before. The journey from being the family's assassin to the resident torture expert was a short and slippery one. First, I was seamlessly slipping into the homes of our enemies to dispatch them quietly. Then one day, I was asked to help Gino get some answers out of a man who was skimming from one of the unlicensed poker rooms. My understanding of human anatomy and very specific knife skills earned me permanent use in that capacity whenever I was needed. Never be too good at a job you don't want to do.

With the sun hanging low, casting golden light through the windows of the flat, I knew it was almost time to leave. The materials from Grecco's demise were still in my backpack and needed to be burned before I left. My boots felt heavy as I descended the staircase and aimed for the garden incinerator can. What appeared to be a simple metal trashcan was soon to contain the ashes of Grecco's evidence, which would then find its way into the composter. Ashes to ashes. Earth to earth.

3

KALMIA LATIFOLIA

From the outside, Muse looked like a grand Italian villa. Terracotta-colored stucco and big white columns flanked the large front door. The only thing that stuck out from the theme was the sign. "Muse" was scrawled out in bright glittering bulbs that always reminded me of casinos you'd see in old rat pack movies. The building was an imposing structure you could see from a block away, but the sign was what caught your eye.

As I made my way through the giant front door, I looked down at the carpet. All the confetti from the end of the night had been swept up, but a piece or two always seemed to get wedged under the baseboard. Despite that, the deep burgundy carpet always looked clean. I dragged my fingers along the top of the wainscoting, checking for dust. Once these walls had been sponge painted to match the countryside theme, the original decorator had chosen. Kaia made sure to change that as soon as she could.

"This place was built in the time of brown paper bags and back-alley peep shows. People don't want that anymore. They want luxury. They want an experience," Kaia had said.

She was right.

Now the inside looked more like a millionaire's estate than a countryside villa. Wainscoting wrapped around every wall, each surface painted soft ivory. Rich burgundy carpet wrapped around the lower level and up the stairs to the main floor. The main floor was where the majority of the customers sat. Black stone tables were scattered around the room, with three or four chairs per top. The lower level is where we had a few elevated booths, the entrance to the Champagne Room, and the bar. I often wondered what Muse would have looked like if my father had inherited the title of Boss instead of my sister.

West was sitting at the bar, nursing a glass of water and leafing through a tattered Hemingway novel. Once an enlisted man, he now worked the door for us at Muse. I wasn't sure whether he had been Lieutenant Hale or Commander Hale, but he'd seemed a bit lost after serving in the Navy for most of his adult life. I took full advantage of that when I met him at our gym. After struggling to replace a bouncer, a man who quit after sustaining some ugly injuries, I took one look at his towering frame covered in hard-earned muscle and knew he would do the trick. If nothing else, he was visually intimidating. At the time he had also seemed relatively straight-laced, wearing his brown hair a lot shorter than it was now and without as much ink coasting over his golden skin.

He looked up from his book when the heavy front door slammed closed behind me. With a glance at his watch, he raised a teasing eyebrow at me and smiled.

"How long did you sleep? The girls are in the back getting ready to open."

"You called me at almost 2 AM. You know I was up late," I said, shrugging off my leather jacket.

"Your sister's waiting for you in her office." He tucked a bookmark into the worn-out paperback and closed it on the bar top. I nodded and walked behind the bar, shoving my jacket beneath it before pouring myself a cup of coffee.

"Rough night?"

"Yeah, you could say that," I laughed. Three tiny tubs of cream and two sugars later, I circled back around with the mug in my hand and leaned on the bar next to him. West's fingers found my chin and angled my face toward him. Moody green eyes fixed on the bruise across my jaw.

"Who did that?"

"Someone who won't be doing it again," I smirked.

He released me with a thoughtful grunt and I headed to the dancer's lounge before heading upstairs to Kaia's office. The janitorial staff was vacuuming the floor and the poles were getting cleaned. This club hadn't been the center of our family's business, but it was where Kaia started when she'd graduated from college. Nonno thought the best person to be running a strip club for him would be a woman and he was absolutely right. When he bought Muse, it was just like every other shake joint in town. Under Kaia's control, it became exceptional.

A few dancers had already arrived to start getting ready for the evening, each of them lined up in front of the illuminated vanities to coat their already gorgeous faces with thousands of dollars worth of makeup. Each of these girls was beautiful in their own way, but under the pink and blue lights, it would be difficult to see. Dark shadow was brushed gently onto eyelids and lips were overlined for emphasis. I usually tried to get them what they needed, which was more out of trying to maintain loyalty than out of the kindness of my heart.

"Hey, Lili!" Sophie smiled as she smeared primer over her cheeks. One of the more popular dancers, she gave off naughty girl-next-door vibes in the cute outfits she wore on stage. Men drooled over her. Unfortunately for them, she was in a committed relationship with the dancer sitting next to her. Maya looked at her girlfriend and then gave me an irritated glance before returning to her makeup. I sighed, unbothered by her protective glare.

"Hi," I said as I took in the other girls. "Are you good? Does anyone need anything before I head to the office?"

They all murmured their "no thank you" and I shut the door behind me. As I ascended the stairs, I could see Kaia standing at the railing overlooking her domain. I knew she'd gone to bed shortly after she called me, but she still managed to look like a goddess of the Underworld outfitted in a sleek designer dress that was all business. She always wore black to appear as though she was tough and her heart was impermeable when I knew the opposite was true. Her eyes drifted to me as I neared her.

"We need to talk."

"I figured. I'm sorry about last night. That shouldn't have happened." I thought I may as well start with an apology. I certainly wasn't going to hear the end of another bill from the cleaning crew. To my surprise, she didn't acknowledge what I'd said and turned on her sharp stiletto to walk into the office. The door was open, which made it look like part of the wall had been stretching into the hallway. Her bodyguard, Nico, waited for us to enter before shutting it closed behind us.

Aside from the pulsing music faintly sounding through the walls, you'd never know this office was attached to Muse. The walls were covered with expensive dark wallpaper with swirling images of flowers in bloom. Wainscoting that matched the main area in design surrounded the space but differed in color. Instead, it was painted a deep charcoal hue to match the bookcases that stretched up the walls behind the large oak desk. Kaia leaned on it and swirled her whiskey. Usually, she was a wine drinker, but this occasion seemed to call for the expensive stuff.

"What is this about then?" I asked, eyeing the open bottle of barrel-aged Nikka on the bar. With Kaia, the better the whiskey, the worse the situation. That bottle meant this situation was shit. A twinge of nerves tugged at my gut.

Kaia took another sip of her drink. I may have only been awake for a few hours, but the day was coming to a close for her. Her flawless face looked bedraggled by lost sleep. Had she even gone to bed after we'd talked last night? I sat down in one of the deep tufted leather chairs across from her desk and set my coffee on the side table.

"Isabelle and Casey haven't been in for a week."

"Both of them? Did they call in?"

"Would I have called you here if they called in?" Kaia snapped. She definitely hadn't slept.

"Do you think one of the other families has something to do with it?"

As the only Italian-lead crime family in town, our rivals often found a way to nip at us and test us. Since my sister took over, those tests became more frequent and more brutal.

"I'm not sure. It was something I looked into, but based on the way those conversations went, no. They're not involved as far as I can tell."

It was a moment before either of us spoke. I waited for her to give me more information, and she seemed to be weighing and measuring her words. Nerves started to eat at me as I tugged on the hairs falling out of my loose black braid.

"So you need me to find them?" I asked, finally leaving my hair alone to take a sip of coffee.

Kaia looked down into her glass, contemplatively swirling the amber liquid like it would give her the answer.

"I've had soldiers searching for them everywhere, but they seem to have disappeared without a trace. At first, I thought it was something to do with the Arawn clan, but they claimed they've got nothing to do with it. As I said, near as we can tell, they're telling the truth. The only thing we know is that they both had dates with men arranged by some dating app for the wealthy called 'Eros.'"

"Eros? How did you find that out?" I had never heard of this app, but if it was exclusive to the wealthy, I certainly wouldn't've. We had plenty of money, but I'd spent more than enough time ending the lives of such wealthy men. My mind drifted to the last Tinder date I'd had that resulted in swearing off dating apps altogether. I inwardly cringed.

"They had been talking about it with some of the girls. It's an app that you have to be invited to join. One of those exclusive bullshit marketing moves. It seems like some of the girls were invited because their representatives came by with promotional codes, but it's impossible to find out who is on the app. Isabelle and Casey both joined. Neither of them came back."

"Maybe they were swept off their feet by some sugar daddies," I laughed, taking another sip of coffee. The pulsing music started seeping through the walls. Time to open.

"Don't think I didn't explore that possibility, but we've been watching their places and they haven't contacted anyone we've spoken to. Isabelle's landlord did a wellness check and said it hadn't seemed like anyone had been there in a few days."

I considered this for a moment. They were both young women. It's not like they were accountants. They might have both decided to quit without telling us, but it didn't feel like that was true. The fact that they'd both gone missing at the same time... something about that snagged on my mind.

"Do we know the last place they were seen?"

"No one we've asked has had any useful information, but they stopped posting to social media. Isabelle last posted from Las Vegas. Casey was here in L.A."

I nodded and cursed myself for not following their profiles. Not much for posting things myself, it hadn't mattered to this point, but the information would be useful now. Most of our dancers had a social media presence and kept their content fresh, so it was unusual for both Isabelle and Casey to let their feeds go dark for so long.

"So we need to find out who their dates were and ask them. But how can we get their names without access to this app?"

"I've had Gino looking into it, and it seems that we do have an opportunity to gain further insight. Eros is a Camden Industries subsidiary, which means that we can go to its owner to learn more." Kaia drained the rest of her whiskey and walked over to the bar to pour another two fingers. I winced at the name.

"Camden, as in Benjamin Camden?"

"The same man, yes."

I shifted in my seat and sighed. To say I wasn't intimidated would have been a lie. Benjamin Camden was a man who had graced the cover of several financial magazines for being a genius with money and gossip magazines because he's a billionaire who also happens to look like a Greek god. Once upon a time, this man was just starting out. Fresh off of moving to Los Angeles from London, he came to our grandfather and asked for a loan because he couldn't get the money anywhere else. Nonno, of course, gave it to him with a steep interest rate. Also, the threat of death if he didn't pay it back. You know, mafia stuff.

Luckily for Benjamin, his business acumen helped him to make enough money to pay off his debt rather quickly. However, his early business dealings meant he was subject to the occasional visit from our people for whatever they needed. Like all of those who came to our family for help, Benjamin Camden would be in our pocket forever. If the public learned that he founded his empire on funds from an L.A. crime family like the Caccias, it would tarnish his sterling reputation. Though communication from us was rare, it wouldn't surprise him. Kaia had even invested some of her money into his businesses and grown a substantial financial safety net for Daniel.

"Did you call him already?"

"I spoke with Juliet, his assistant. She was unaware of our connection to her boss and she was a pill about it because all the clients of Eros sign Non-Disclosure Agreements, so they can't just hand over the information we need. But I was able to schedule an appointment to discuss it. You're going to meet with him at his office on Thursday to try to get him to change his mind."

Fantastic. I stood from my chair and picked up my empty mug.

"Before you go, there's something else. A loose end that needs to be dealt with."

My gut tightened as she handed me a piece of paper with an address written in her tightly coiled script.

DOJA CAT STARTED blasting through the club when I opened the hidden door again. It would be too early for people to fill the VIP area on the second floor, so no one would have seen me leave this way. On the main floor below, men were filing in. The stage held their gaze as Katie, one of the other girls, started her time. Men don't notice me in Muse. I like to believe that it's because I give off an off-limits vibe while the ladies on stage are freely on display. Not that I mind. The men who frequented our club didn't usually fall under the boyfriend material category.

As I made my way toward the front door, I noticed a pack of idiots gathered around where West was checking IDs. Having taken off his jacket, he was now standing at the door in a black tee and leather suspenders, which did a nice job of showing off his imposing figure. A herd of frat boys was trying to make their way inside and it didn't look like our well-built bouncer was going to budge.

"Come on, man! Just let us in," one slurred.

"Sorry, guys. Not tonight." West said with strained patience. This had probably gone on for a bit.

They were clearly drunk already. While it's not unusual for men to leave the club that way, it's not allowed on the way in. Drunks are more difficult to control and the safety of our girls has always been the highest priority. West towered over the group, a man standing out in a crowd of horny boys. An ugly blonde with a face full of acne at the head of the pack was large, but spent all of his time building muscles he didn't know how to use outside of picking things up and putting them down.

"Let us in and I'll make this easy on you, buddy."

West chuckled darkly and the ugly blonde rushed him. That boy was about to learn what a big mistake he made. Darting out of the blonde's grasp, he grabbed an arm and wrenched it behind his attacker's back while bracing him against the rough stucco exterior. The other three idiots took a startled step away.

"Ahhhh, you fucker!" The boy screamed.

"You feel this?" West twisted the arm again. "This is my arm now. And I don't want my arm or any of its friends in my fucking club."

The ugly blonde's friends pulled him away from West and ran back to their souped-up pickup truck. Given the way he looked, it always surprised me when someone was dumb enough to pick a fight with him. West's gaze met mine when he heard me laughing.

"Fun night so far?" I asked.

West shrugged, pushing some errant strands out of his face. "What did your sister want?"

"Have you noticed that Casey and Isabelle haven't been in?"

He nodded as he let a few men pass us by.

"Kaia wants me to look into it."

"Since when are you a detective?" He gave me a sidelong glance as he crossed his arms. I leaned against the wall behind him.

"It wouldn't be the first time I've tracked someone down," I said with a sigh. It most definitely wasn't the first time. That was part of my job. It's just that usually tracking someone down would end with me killing that someone, but that wasn't pertinent to this conversation.

"That's what you were up to last night then," he said, looking at a pair of IDs before motioning a giggling couple through the door. I nodded, rubbing at the slight ache in my jaw. "You need to get better at defense."

My stomach roared with hunger. The taqueria on the corner was calling my name. I'd been thinking about a California burrito since I woke up. Luscious guacamole, succulent carne asada, and crispy French fries, all nestled in a succulent tortilla. Just thinking about it made my mouth water. Pushing off of the wall, I made my way toward the parking lot.

"What I need is some food."

"I'll see you at One-Two?" West shouted over the crowd. "If you're not there, I'm coming to drag your ass out of bed myself."

Adjusting the collar of my jacket, I waved him off and walked to my car. I felt guilty about blowing off training with him this morning, but I just didn't feel like having my ass kicked again. It felt good to spend the better part of my waking hours in the garden and then in my lab. Something about working with plants, even deadly ones, always brought me peace.

Glancing over my shoulder, I saw West tracking me as I got into my car. A small wave of fatigue washed over me and I sat in the driver's seat for a moment to collect myself. The glowing clock on the dash told me getting food would have to wait. Based on the conversation I'd just had with my sister, it was going to be a long night.

4

RHODODENDRON

Broken glass littered the street, bigger pieces shining like stars in the moonlight. Bits of it crunched under my boots. It was the only sound in the air as I made my way through the neighborhood. The air was still and each home sat toward the back of their lots, windows looking out over the street, like a crowd of observers holding their breath. As I walked by the houses, I was reminded of that cheery song "Little Boxes" by Malvina Reynolds. The twangy, swingy guitar streamed through my backstabbing brain and made me hum it as I walked up the driveway.

Walking through little neighborhoods like this always made me wonder what it would have been like to grow up in a normal family. Maybe I would have had a happier childhood. Kids here learned how to gut a fish instead of a man. Lemonade stands and bake sales instead of loan sharks and shake-downs. Block parties. It all sounded nice, albeit a bit boring.

Our neighborhood hadn't been like this. Our old home wasn't far from my studio and I found myself walking by, sometimes to pull at the loose threads in my mind. Other times, I found myself there just to make sure my father was truly gone.

Iron numbers were nailed into a wood plank by the door frame. The seven was starting to rust at the bottom, a sign of small maintenance issues that a less busy person would have dealt with. This was the address Kaia had given me. Silently, I gave thanks that there was no video doorbell to alert the homeowner to my presence as I unscrewed the porch light bulb. It was time to get to work.

Most standard deadbolt locks can be easily hacked with enough time. Time or liquid nitrogen. I was short on the former, so I brought the latter. The tiny tools tapped against the inside of the lock until it shattered into uselessness. In an effort not to create any more noise than needed, I cupped my hand beneath the lock as I opened the door, waiting for any remnants of the deadbolt to come tumbling out.

"*Little boxes, on the hillside,*" I sang quietly. I'm not sure of most of the words, so I hummed the parts I didn't know to myself. Pocketing the bits of bolt, I moved forward and surveyed what I was dealing with. I was immediately grateful that there wasn't a dog. There might've been a cat, but I haven't encountered a single one that cared whether its owner lived or died. Of course, that might have said more about the owner than the animal.

The house was a small, ranch-style home built in the 1970s. White porcelain tile lined every space. I pulled on paper shoe covers as I looked around. A sign that said "Live, Laugh, Love" was hanging over the television in the living room. The whole place smelled like air freshener. My bag jostled against my shoulder as I tried to cross to the bedroom quietly. As I prowled through the house, I thought about how negligent this man's security was given his situation.

Marshall Hendricks, a divorced man living alone in the Valley. He'd had a long career working as an officer for the LAPD. That career was, of course, stained with decades of work for the very people his department was trying to put away. Us. Sadly, the former Officer Hendricks outlived his usefulness when he decided to go to the FBI with everything he knew. Naturally, he didn't realize he'd already been replaced by a man in his unit who was more than happy to tell us everything.

"*There's a pink one and a green one,*" I continued as I sing-whispered. As

I plunged the needle into the tiny brown vial, I peered around the corner into the primary bedroom. There he was, sleeping soundly. Snoring quite loudly. Only, he wasn't alone. Laying next to him was a blonde woman. Older than me by a couple of decades, probably, but still beautiful.

A gurgling noise was followed by a roar. My stomach. Every muscle in my body froze as I waited for the nausea to pass. Instead, it barreled down on me, covering me in a cold sweat as I tried to quietly breathe through it. It couldn't wait any longer. Every second I stood there, I risked being caught by a restless sleeper. I drained the syringe into his neck, wondering what the woman would do when she woke up. If she would cry. Call an ambulance. Try CPR.

A deep sigh came from the woman. I stiffened again, waiting to be caught. Soft, even breath continued from her side. Quiet, choked gargling sounded from the man next to her. Confident my mixture had worked, I made my way out the door and closed it quietly behind me as I ignored the familiar burn rising in my throat. Officer Hendricks would have to miss his meeting with his FBI handler in the morning.

The neighborhood was still with sleep. No nosy neighbor had spotted me. No one knew that this house now contained a dead man. Not even the woman sleeping next to him. Even if she was an early riser, the effects of death would have hours to take hold. He would definitely be in rigor mortis. Hell, Officer Hendricks would be dead before I left the neighborhood.

It wasn't until I was getting on the freeway that I sent Kaia a message of confirmation.

Lullaby and good night.

The drive back home was difficult to manage between waves of nausea. Silently, I cursed the officer for living so far from my home. A chill rattled through me and pushed my nausea over the edge. The late hour meant only a few cars passed as I wretched on the side of the highway. Gravel pressed into my palms and denim-covered knees as I braced myself, trying to catch my breath before the burn of bile started again.

The rest of the drive home gave me plenty of time to think. My mind decided to fixate on Casey and Isabelle. Most of my thoughts weren't helpful or even constructive. Just reimagining the last time I'd seen them both.

Casey and Isabelle had become friends because they worked the same nights at Muse, but they couldn't have been more different. Isabelle was the kind of girl you'd never want to stand next to in photographs. Even though her breasts, lips, and hair were all bought, they always looked natural on her. She was the Malibu Barbie dream that men crawled over themselves to touch.

That much was clear based on all of the followers she had. Isabelle treated her social media feed like her second job. She even got some regular sponsors. Free makeup and clothes in exchange for posts. She really wanted money but took what she could get from smaller brands.

Casey. Well, she had an entirely different approach to living life. While friendly and open at work, she was far less social in her daily life. Or at least that's what I had gathered from our polite friendship. After a particularly crowded night at Muse, I noticed her tired expression.

"Being around other people's energies is really draining. I mostly like to hang out at home."

That didn't explain how she got mixed up with that good-for-nothing shitbag musician she was dating. A malicious part of me enjoyed hearing that Casey had joined a dating service. Perhaps she had finally come to realize she deserved better than Tyler. I'd told her that at least a dozen times.

I looked at the clock and decided it was still too early for breakfast. When was the last time I'd eaten? My mind filled with the thought of a luscious tortilla wrapped around pillowy, soft scrambled eggs with savory potatoes and succulent bacon, all drowning in salsa and cheese. I looked at the clock again. Nope. Still too early.

The streets were lined with the vehicles of other residents, so I circled the area until something opened up. Eventually, a man scurried out of an apartment with a hit-it-and-quit-it sort of exit and vacated the space right in front of my apartment. Once I got inside, I decided to just take a shower and get into bed. The shower was always necessary. Always. When I dressed for bed, I put on Cowboy Bebop for a little background noise. As my head hit the pillow, I imagined I was tucking myself into a warm tortilla.

5

LANTANA CAMARA

I made my way past the poker tables, eying the small marks and worn edges that had accumulated over the years. Cigars and cigarettes clouded the air with their smoke. Every once in a while, I caught the musty scent of marijuana coming from the men here and there. Each table was packed with players. Lush green felt and blood-red chips were the only real color in the dimly lit room.

Sure, if you wanted to gamble, you could easily go to a reservation and take your chances at a casino, but this was where big money was made. Every table had a buy-in of ten grand. If you walked away a winner, you got to keep your cash without having to pay the tax man.

That's what got these schmucks in the door. Tragically, what kept them coming back was the idea that they could win their money back. It's a perfect system. We let enough of them win so they think they have a chance. Every so often, there's a big payout, but the House does in fact always win.

My eyes skimmed each table as I passed, assessing every player. For every five players, a sixth plant at the table. When you're picturing the guys who work for us, you're probably picturing someone like Al Pacino or the cast of the Sopranos. There were some guys like that early on, but the truth is that mafiosos don't look any different from regular people. You probably even know one or two, depending on where you live, of course. Made men don't exactly look like the cast of a Scorsese movie anymore. Our generation didn't take to things in the same way our fathers did, choosing instead to carve our own paths. Do things our way. When you look at them, you don't think "wise guy." You think "Instagram model."

With seven tables to watch, our pit boss had his work cut out for him. I sidled up next to the man who held himself far too casually for so much responsibility. The olive bomber jacket and black jeans did a good job of disguising the weapons I knew he carried. The men stationed at every corner were equally strapped.

"Hey, boss," Sal drawled. I'd told him repeatedly not to call me that.

"Not the boss. How's it looking tonight?"

"Well, some of these guys have been grinding for a while."

"Oh?"

"I wouldn't worry about it too much. We already have one big winner here tonight, so there won't be any others. Probably two little pots."

I looked around at the tables again. Our fixed games were so obvious that the gamblers never bothered to notice. Guys who were almost always here, winning big on a regular basis. It never occurred to them that they'd been planted by us to win when things got too big. Either that or they were too afraid of us to question it. On top of the games we fixed, the dealers always raked the pot. Winner, winner.

"Can I get the deposit?" I asked as I watched one of our dealers collect dead cards.

Sal reached into his jacket and pulled out a small manila envelope, thick with bills from the night before. His Caccia tattoo peeked out from under his sleeve with the motion. Men who work for the Caccia family are given a specific tattoo. On every man's forearm, an arrow stretches halfway down the outside and pierces a crown. Every soldier gets it as soon as he becomes part of our organization. It's a rite of passage.

"Don't spend it all in one place," he chuckled. He always made that same fucking joke. I gave him my usual annoyed smirk and checked the contents of the envelope.

After tucking the cash into my bag, I looked around the room again. I'd be seeing a few of these faces down the road. There were a few who would certainly seal their fates this night, and the night was still young.

MUSE MAY HAVE been my grandfather's office location and the place where he did most of his business, but Bootlegger is where I felt his spirit linger. The old steakhouse was a fixture in Hollywood. Movie stars who had been household names for decades came here to eat beef and shoot the shit with each other for hours on end.

I always chuckled when I saw actors from classic mafia movies gathered in our deep leather booths, talking about this and that. Have you ever seen a frail old film star eat a Caesar salad? I have.

After stalking in through Bootlegger's backdoor, I took myself through the kitchen. Most of the staff had been here for at least ten years, some far longer than that. Only the bussers rotated through on a regular basis. My mouth watered as I watched a baked potato drowning in butter go out with a pair of sizzling ribeyes and Parker house rolls. The kitchen was humming with activity since I'd arrived just in time for the second dinner rush.

Only a careful eye would notice the two rolls I snagged before walking into the back office. It didn't belong to anyone in particular, but management used it to do all the administrative stuff you'd expect a restaurant to deal with from day to day.

What the staff wouldn't have been able to tell you was that there was a safe in the floor below the desk, nestled below a tile. They also wouldn't have been able to tell you about the books we kept for people indebted to the Caccia family in that safe. I sat down in the old banker's chair at the heavy wooden desk and took down my purloined rolls, enjoying every buttery bite.

Between mouthfuls of fluffy bread, I looked around the room. Framed photos from years gone by hung all over the walls, leaving no space left un-covered. Some of them were black and white photos of my great grandfather and his original crew, including the big boss man Bianchi. Others were of milestone birthdays and movie stars. My parent's wedding reception was held here and the bridal party photo looked like a biblical feast. The one photo that always grabbed my eye was the one of my mother on her 30th birthday.

Bootlegger is famous for serving inhumanly large slices of Brooklyn Blackout cake. A slice is sitting in front of my mother with a sparkling candle, ready for her to make a wish. The red dress she has on dips low enough to show a large swath of the delicate olive skin my sister and I inher-ited. Her smile is incandescent as she holds back her thick waves of black hair and squeezes her eyes shut. Black hair she passed on to me. Though my jaw was softer than hers. Her body was from something out of a fashion magazine, where mine had larger curves and defined muscles. I'd also not inherited her tall frame. Even in my memories, she towered over me. Though the photo has lost its color with age, her image looks timeless. I could almost hear her laughing.

The butter and flaky sea salt came off of my fingertips after I popped each one into my mouth to clean them. Before I could squat beneath the desk, Tony, the restaurant manager, walked through the door.

"Ms. Caccia! I'm sorry, I didn't realize you were in here." I could tell my presence made him deeply uncomfortable. He scanned the office, looking around for something out of place that I may have noticed.

"It's alright, Tony. I was just stopping by," I grinned, trying to ease his tension. "Did you need something in here?"

"Honestly, no. I wanted a minute away from-" he stopped himself from finishing his sentence.

"From what?" I prodded.

"Well, there's a high-maintenance customer who keeps complaining and it's become sort of exhausting."

I laughed, sympathetic to his plight. If I had been dressed like a professional, the way my sister always was, I would have gone to confront the issue. Since there wasn't really anything I could do about the customer, I could make him feel better. Leaning over in my seat, I dragged open the bottom drawer of the file cabinet behind me. A bottle of Old Forester and two tumblers appeared on the desk in front of the frazzled Tony. He sighed with relief as I poured him a drink.

We chatted for a minute about Tony's kids. One was going to be starting school soon, while the other was just out of diapers. I smiled and nodded, having had only the barest of experiences with either of those situations while helping Kaia with Daniel. A waiter poked his head into the room looking for his manager and was equally surprised to see me sitting at the desk.

"I'm sorry, sir. Ma'am. Tony, there's a guest who would like to speak with you."

"The same one?"

"The same one."

I gave Tony a sympathetic look as he sighed. Finishing off his drink before heading out, I told him I'd see him around. After he and the waiter vacated the room, I locked the door and ducked under the desk. A small button snap loosed the hunting knife on my belt into my hand and I wedged it under the tile to lift it out of place. The green face of the safe looked up at me expectantly. Soft metallic clicks rang out as I dialed in my grandmother's birthday.

Three green ledgers sat in the open safe. Each one represented a different aspect of the family business. People who owed us money from loans or debt, back alley deals we'd made, and records for our legitimate businesses. The legitimate business records were far out of date since we'd switched to using accounting software, but I insisted on keeping the ledger in the safe as a record of our Nonno's handwritten accounting. The cover was far more worn than the other two and far older. I picked it up and gave it a sniff before taking out the loans and debt record.

It only took a few minutes of crouching under the desk with my phone flashlight lit before I found the entry I'd needed. My hand blindly scrambled across the desk as I searched for a felt-tip pen. The little plastic cap disconnected from the pen as I gripped it with my teeth. A long red line went through Vincent Grecco's name and the remaining fifty thousand dollars of the very large debt he'd incurred with us.

Feeling a little uneasy about the money we would never see from Vincent, I flipped through the other names in the book. Most people paid their debts and the corresponding interest. They knew that if they'd let it become lax, they would pay with their lives. When you come to the mafia for money, it's understood that you're most likely out of options, so a threat to your life is little more than a good motivator. Suffice it to say, late payments were a rarity. My brief survey of the ledger had shown me that not only were people paying their debts, but we had also made a substantial sum in interest. Hundreds of millions of dollars.

The number wasn't new but always affected me. My lifestyle didn't require a lot of money to maintain, but I never hurt for cash. Everything I had was paid for, which was a rare thing for someone in their twenties. The apartment I lived in was cheap, so I paid the rent upfront through the next several years. My Mercedes was paid for in cash, all the bells and whistles included. Kaia told me that I lived like a bum, but haunting dark corners and maintaining order in the underworld didn't exactly lend itself to living a normal life.

As I slid the books back into the safe and turned the combination lock, I thought about her son and wondered if that was the kind of change my lifestyle would require. Before Daniel was born, Kaia worked on a near-constant basis. Her son was what had forced her to slow down and live like a human. It was what prompted me to protect our legacy.

"I can do it," I had whispered to her that night six years ago as I laid out my formulas before her. "I won't fail us."

Rough calculations circled through my mind. Millions. Many millions, many times over. There were several different accounts. Some were on the continental US. That was to keep the IRS off of our backs with the accounting for our legitimate businesses. That money kept everything operating smoothly. Others were on distant islands or in the lush green hills of Switzerland. Hell, there were even flour bags of money tucked away in my sister's pantry.

Between Kaia and me, we seemed to be doing a good job. Her head for numbers and leadership meant the businesses were doing well. Our less-than-savory dealings had thus far flown under the radar with the police, a situation that may have been improved with sizable donations to the LAPD and city council member campaigns. Aside from a bad apple or two, most of the team appeared happy with my sister's rule. With the sum of money I'd just seen, Kaia's little boy would never have to work a day in his life.

6

CONVALLARIA MAJALIS

I sat up suddenly, covered in sweat. Again. Usually, I could escape the nightmares that waited in the wings for me by having some sort of background noise going when I went to sleep, but I'd fallen asleep scrolling through the social media accounts of Casey and Isabelle. My feet hit the cold floor as I walked a hurried pace to the kitchen. The tiny neon clock on the microwave read 3:04. *Deep breaths. Deep, cleansing breaths.* That's what I repeated in my mind while I poured myself a glass of water from the pitcher in the fridge. Each sip felt like a rock going down my throat. I could still feel a knee holding me down while his hands were around my neck. Squeezing.

I am your blood. You can't escape me.

Flashes of his cruelty found me as I continued to wake. My sister's broken arm. The curses my mother screamed at him before she was knocked unconscious. My wobbling knees as his rage rained down on me. His anger was a wild and dangerous thing. Its shadows still darkened the corners of my mind.

Tremors kept the water sloshing around in the little glass as I leaned against the counter and surveyed my darkened apartment. Currents of fear still jolted through my nerves. I told myself that he was long dead. He couldn't hurt me anymore. But as sleep found me every night, the terror he left behind curled up in bed beside me. It was always hardest to come back from these nightmares when it was still dark out. I turned on the light in my bathroom and walked back to my bed. It would be easier to go back to sleep if there was a light on. The monsters couldn't get me that way.

Sweat had soaked through the shirt I was wearing, so I tossed it into the laundry basket and climbed beneath the covers. The remote on my nightstand was within easy reach. Still taking deep breaths to steady myself, I searched for something to fall asleep to. When I found Steel Magnolias, I set the sleep timer and lay back against the pillows. Something about Dolly Parton always made me feel safe.

THE SLEEP TIMER was about to click the television off when Sally Field was screaming at her friends in the cemetery. Even though I'd seen the movie more times than I could count, that part still made me cry. I couldn't believe I watched the whole thing. I blinked at the clock. It would be dawn soon. Clearly, I wasn't going back to sleep.

There was only one thing to do at this hour. Sitting up from bed, I pulled on a pair of pants and put on my boots. I wanted something more comfortable than my usual leather jacket, so I tossed on an old Berkley sweatshirt and rearranged the bun on top of my head.

Normally, it wouldn't be wise for a woman to walk around Los Angeles in the small hours of the morning by herself. As I locked my door behind me, I chuckled to myself at the idea of some poor schmuck trying to best me for my wallet. Wrong woman, pal. The thought was quickly followed by the wish that I'd be able to teach all women what I knew about how to make men fall to their knees and beg for mercy.

The thud of my feet hitting the ground at a slow pace was the only sound filling the surrounding air. Marine layer mist hung heavily in the air as the sun started burning through, giving everything a haunted look. Looking around, I realized I'd strolled right into Los Feliz. I hadn't come here on purpose, but once I realized where I was, it was clear where my mind had wandered.

The windows on the second floor of our old house always looked like a pair of eyes to me. Even in darkness, they looked like they were staring out at me like a startled owl. I stood there, hands stuffed into my pockets, and gaped back.

The scared little girl inside wanted me to leave. Urged me to walk away because I'd be taken inside at any moment. Fingernails dug into my thighs as I tried to usher away the thoughts. The memories. Despite its happier blue exterior and refinished front door, the house would never be rid of the stench of fear that emanated from every crevice.

The house used to rattle with wrathful screaming and mournful cries. Dishes smashing and the thick sound of flesh hitting flesh were only slightly muffled by tightly shut windows. As long as you were on the sidewalk, it couldn't be heard. The neighbors either heard nothing or ignored it. Our pain wasn't their business. They worked hard not to hear the screaming. My father was a dangerous man and a smart man would know better than to insert themselves into his affairs. Still, it's difficult to forgive them for their apathy even now.

While the worst of it was happening, I was spared because of my sister. Too little to be considered worthy of the attention of a grown man. He focused most of his energy on her. During what could only be described as a hurricane of rage, I would find a hiding place in a dark corner and pray he didn't find me. My only other option was to creep out of the house and find the same peace our neighbors had grown accustomed to.

Not much else had changed. The craftsman-style house had been grey when my father owned it. The front porch hadn't had any furnishings on it then. My father claimed that he didn't want anyone stealing it, but it was more likely that he'd thought it would give the home an inviting sensibility that he'd abhorred. The trim was still stark white as it had been then, but now looked fresh next to the periwinkle siding.

As I looked over the home again, I noticed a figure in one of the windows. Startled at first, I reasoned with myself. Certainly, it wasn't a ghost. This house wasn't haunted. A woman stood in the bedroom window and looked out at me with a frightened expression. Her frightened look urged me to give her a polite but cursory nod and move on. The last thing I needed was a scared homeowner calling the cops on some strange woman lurking in front of her house.

Even though the sun had risen, I decided to go back to bed. With my stride taking on more purpose, it wasn't long before I was back home, where I laid down for a few hours to catch up on lost sleep. Before I dozed off, I decided to send West a text asking him to meet me at the gym at our usual time. A hard workout that allowed me to beat the hell out of someone was exactly what I needed.

7

XANTHIUM STRUMARIUM

K-pop thumped through the late morning air. Dancing around in dinosaur print undies, I dusted every surface I could see. Cleaning helped me think. So I scrubbed the grout in between every pink tile of the bathroom. Something about scrubbing stains out of grout clears away the roadblocks in my mind.

The floors were swept and then mopped. Kitchen counters got wiped down after each avocado green dish was cleaned, dried, and put back in its place. My big finish was always stripping and remaking my bed with fresh sheets. After completing that task, I stripped and hopped into the shower to scour the dust and sweat off of myself.

Water fell into the pink tub with loud slaps as I squeezed it out of my hair. The bath towel started to slip off of me, so I wrapped it around myself again and tucked the edge against my generous breasts. They always made the towel slip off if I bent over the wrong way. As I did that, my phone rang its 80s video game tone. I answered it without looking at the screen.

"Hello?" I huffed while pulling my fingers through my hair.

"Lili? Where are you?" West.

"I'm at home. Why?"

"You were supposed to be here twenty minutes ago."

"Shit! Shit. Shit. Shit. I'm so sorry. Time kind of got away from me. I can be there in ten minutes." Hanging up on him, I quickly pulled on one of my several pairs of black yoga pants and a matching sports bra. Socks. I had no clean socks. I shoved my feet into my trainers and ran to my car. My shoes felt odd against bare feet, but they'd have to do until I got to the gym.

AFTER INHERITING THE keys to the kingdom, my grandfather started buying businesses he was interested in just for the sake of having them to escape to. The old dog bought Muse to create the ultimate strip club experience, and he spent countless hours in his office there, but it wasn't his first business. That honor was for One-Two, the boxing gym he purchased in the 1960s.

Nestled in the heart of Los Feliz and not too far from my apartment, One-Two is my favorite of all the businesses. It's one of the few places I can still feel my grandfather. He worked out here with Lupo, his old bodyguard, for as long as he could. Lupo still ran it for us. He was hired around the same time my dad graduated from high school and Nonno always treated him like a son. His sons Dante and Nico were basically my brothers. I've known Lupo for my whole life. He always treated me like I was still just the twelve-year-old girl who played rough with his boys, but I'd be lying if I said I didn't enjoy it.

When I arrived, West was leaning against the ropes of the ring. His hair was pulled into a bun, but the strands that had fallen out alluded to the training he'd done before I got there. The gym was empty, as it usually was at this hour. Even Lupo took long walks with his dog Remus around the neighborhood to pass the time. A few days a week, there were classes offered to the public. Some wanted to learn to fight while others just wanted to tone up. Still, One-Two didn't really need that money. Prize-fighting boxers and underground bare-knuckle events kept the doors wide open. The last bare-knuckle match I'd seen landed management about six figures but left one of the fighters in a halo brace.

"I'm so sorry," I groaned. "You're going to make me suffer, aren't you?"

"Sorry, champ. You gave me a half hour to think about all the little ways I'm going to punish you."

"Don't threaten me with a good time, West," I grunted as I shucked off my shoes and tossed them into a locker with my bag. He laughed. The ropes clapped against each other as I squeezed myself between them and joined him in the ring. He straightened and walked to the middle.

"Alright. Pushups. Sixty."

The canvas groaned under my weight as I lowered myself to do the dreaded pushups, and I groaned like an insolent teenager with it.

"No whining. You made me wait. Pushups."

Counting quietly, I pushed myself up and lowered myself back down again. The burn started to heat through my pectoral muscles and shoulders. Ugh. Working out was usually fun, but when West wanted to make me hurt, he committed to it like it was his mission in life. It seemed like it was going to be one of those days because commands for different conditioning exercises came in rapid succession until I was aching for another shower.

West pushed my knee into the ground as I leaned toward him, into the glute stretch. Muscles tightened before they released like a plucked guitar string. Breath hissed past my clenched teeth with the release of tension.

"Sorry I was late." I groaned as he pushed to deepen the stretch.

"What were you doing?"

"Cleaning."

"Something on your mind?" Motioning for me to turn over, I rolled and pulled up my other knee. This man knew me too well. Deciding not to share the nightmare I'd had or the subsequent walk down memory lane, I went with talking about work.

"It's just really strange that both Isabelle and Casey would go missing in the same week, even if they were both using the same dating app."

"It might be a coincidence."

"There's no such thing as coincidence."

"Okay, Sherlock."

Finishing the movement, I lay flat on the ground and looked up at West. He sat back and pulled absently on his beard as he considered what I'd said.

"Did either of them say anything to you?" I asked as I propped myself up on my elbows. He shook his head. Flopping down again, I sighed.

"Hungry?" He asked.

"Starved. My trainer was a real dick today."

An amused chuckle rumbled out of him as he helped me off of the mat. I threw a shirt on over my sweat-covered body and sighed. West pulled his shirt back on and slid his gigantic feet into sandals as he picked up the worn green duffel bearing a HALE patch on the side. Most of the time, I was disgusted by men's feet, but there was something nice about his. Or I was just used to seeing them in training. At least he kept his toenails trimmed. Between his ragged shirt and long hair, I sometimes had a hard time picturing the clean-cut ex-military man I'd first met.

Investigating the girls' disappearance was already proving to be a lot of work. Keeping an eye on our targets and locating them was different than finding women who'd vanished out of thin air. As we rounded the corner to Mexicali Taco, I worried I wasn't cut out for the job. We were still early enough to beat the lunch rush and took up a small table outside as we waited for our order. I let the breeze cool me as I leaned my head back and shut my eyes.

"You're going to find them, Lili," West said after a moment.

"Yeah," I muttered, only half sure I believed him. Closing my eyes again, I took a breath and enjoyed the briny scent of the ocean hanging in the air.

The door swung open and the cashier came out with armfuls of food. I took a swig from my water bottle as I looked over the feast before us. A street taco and carne asada fries for me, drowning in cheese and guacamole. A fry crunched in my mouth and I watched West wrap his big mouth around a burrito that could choke a donkey.

"That thing is huge," I said. He raised his eyebrows at me with a cheeky grin and took another bite.

As he chewed through his next mouthful, a flock of women walked into the restaurant. A few took long looks at the man sitting across from me. One of them drank in the sight of West's arms, which were bare in the sleeveless concert tee he'd put on. Bronzed muscle and tattoos on full display. She'd found him so distracting that she almost didn't make it through the door.

The mess of brown and gold waves on his head made him look like something between a barbarian and a beach bum. It never surprised me when women noticed him. He was attractive, even by Los Angeles standards. I watched the rest of the women go inside and shoved some carne asada fries into my mouth. Something about the gawking always made me edgy. West reached across the table and wiped a blob of guacamole off of my lip with the edge of his thumb.

"You should talk. You eat like a wild animal."

I tried to bite at his hand, then licked my lips and grabbed another handful of fries.

"What do you think I should do about Isabelle and Casey?" I said through my food. He shrugged, leaning back to think about my question. After a while, he gazed off into the distance as he replied.

"What does Kaia want you to do?"

"She wants me to meet with Benjamin Camden. He owns the company that made the dating app they were using. Apparently, I already have an appointment at his office," I grimaced. "I'm not sure what he can tell me, but it's a start. To be honest, I'm not sure I even want to meet with the guy."

West nodded as his gaze drifted over pedestrians passing us by. We finished our meal and walked back to the gym. My black Mercedes looked like a spaceship sitting next to his pale green Bronco.

"When are you going to get rid of that thing?" He asked. The alarm beeped as I approached it with my car-shaped key.

"I know it doesn't suit me, but it's just for work." I looked over the shiny black sedan and tossed him a saucy wink as I popped on my sunglasses. "You know nothing blends in around here better than luxury."

8

CELASTRUS SCANDENS

Before my parents died, I was like a wild animal. Playing rough with neighborhood boys and coming home after the street lights turned on. When I wasn't raising hell with them, I had my nose stuck in a book even though I was bright enough to do well in school without really trying. None of it mattered. I knew that my life was headed in only one direction. I would be a pawn in my father's political aspirations, just as he wanted my sister to be. Girls in mafia families were typically married off to strengthen alliances. That didn't mean I had to like it.

They started Kaia's grooming when she turned fifteen. Her trendy clothes were swapped with modest dresses. Hours previously spent talking with her friends became time for her to practice the violin, dining etiquette, and other things that would make her a suitable wife. Makeup was taken away. Men from other connected families would come over for dinner every Saturday, and my grandfather rejected every offer for her hand. To him, no one was good enough. Our father continued his crusade to make his daughter useful to his aspirations.

"She has to get married. We need her to form an alliance."

"You mean you need her. She is too valuable to be traded away like one of your baseball cards. Kaia is my granddaughter and I am Boss. It is my decision, not yours!"

"Not forever," my father seethed. "You won't be Boss forever."

Once Kaia was old enough to drive, she went to our grandparent's house every chance she could get. Like any teenager, she spent time with her friends after school. Went to the movies. The mall. Parties. No matter what time she got home, our father was waiting for her. I lay awake in bed, staring at the clock on my nightstand, willing her to come home and avoid the beating she was sure to get. Usually, I drifted off before she showed up, but their screaming always woke me. Soon she started staying at our grandparents' house several nights a week.

Her absence didn't go unnoticed. If her seat was empty at dinner, my father didn't speak. He just stared at her chair as he ate. Attempts to find her a suitable husband continued. She was nearing a marriageable age and my father wouldn't give up the opportunity to take advantage. Rage-filled phone calls to my Nonno became a daily occurrence. Until one rainy night, when my world tilted off its axis.

MY MOTHER AND father were driving through Malibu Canyon, heading home from a dinner they'd gone to for their anniversary. It was a rare rainy night in May. My father wasn't the romantic type, but it would have looked terrible to let his wedding anniversary go uncelebrated. More than anything, he cared what people thought of him. It was late and dark, and my father had probably had a drink or two when a drunk driver slammed into them and pushed their car off the road into the canyon below. The vehicle landed on its roof and was nearly flattened by the impact. Paramedics pronounced them dead on the scene. While I would remain haunted by the presence of my father for years, it was the immediate loss of my mother that plagued me.

Kaia and I were spending the night at our grandparents' house while our parents went out and were moved in so seamlessly that the transition seemed natural. Nonna had been dead a few years, leaving Rita to take care of the house and two children. Rita had been their housekeeper for close to thirty years at that point. After so much time, she was practically family herself. She cooked, cleaned, and kept an eye on the wild thing that now lived in the uppermost bedroom that had been created from the converted attic.

The first few weeks after the accident, I spent all of my time up there. Either in my room or in the small playroom attached to it, I huddled myself into the furthest corners like a bat in a belfry. I refused to go back to school, to go outside, and I hardly ate. Plates of food would appear around me and be cleared, with only a few bites missing from the serving. The absence of my mother was a throbbing ache that consumed everything. My middle school had been calling the house, begging my grandfather to send me back. After weeks of my reclusive behavior, Nonno came up to the attic to talk with me. He found me in the reading nook with a book about plants.

"La mia piccola principessa, what are you reading?"

"*Plants Affecting Human Health*, it's about using plants as medicine."

He sat down on the floor beside me, legs crossed.

"You like plants."

I nodded.

"Why?"

"Plants are easy. They're useful and nice to look at. You know, if you take care of them and stuff."

He put a hand on my shoulder and sighed.

"You know you must return to school, yes?"

"I'm supposed to start high school soon, but I don't want to."

"Why?"

I marked my place in the book and set it down in my lap. My throat tightened as I swallowed the lump of discomfort that had formed there. "The girls at school make fun of me because I dress like a boy. The boys at school won't let me hang out with them anymore because I'm a girl. I don't...I don't know where I fit in. Mama was supposed to help me." As though the heartbreak had been waiting for me to speak her name, I burst into a sob. Nonno pulled me into a hug, stroking the top of my head as I wept. When my sobs turned into small hiccups of tears, he spoke.

"First, my sweet girl, the opinions of these children do not matter. I know it feels like they do right now, but soon you'll be grown up and forget all about them." He took my face in his hand and wiped my tears away with the other as he looked into my eyes. "Second, you are a Caccia. You're not just a young woman. You're a fierce, wild thing. A force. You are not sheep like them. You are a wolf."

I returned to school the following Monday on the promise that he would help me, and he did. He taught me to channel my feelings into something constructive. My anger was redirected into training with his men. Nonno didn't want me handling guns, so I learned to throw knives and defend myself in hand-to-hand combat. Hours that would normally be spent drowning in melancholy became hours of studying.

The only peace I knew came to me in the garden he had created for me on the property. I'd planted all sorts of things just to watch them grow. Tomatoes, zucchini, and other vegetables that often graced our dining table. But even as peace and stability made their way into my days, nights were still filled with terror. I knew nothing but restless sleep. Nightmares plagued with visions of my father beating, screaming, and imposing his little punishments. Every time I woke up, my sister was there with me. She held me, stroked my back as I cried, and told me it was all over. "Everything's fine now."

Kaia had not been as visibly affected by my parents' deaths as I had been, but she grieved in her own way. Instead of sequestering herself in the house as I had, she seemed to thrive. At seventeen, she was nearly done with high school. She made good grades and had gotten accepted to several good schools. I'd even sometimes heard her playing the violin again while I worked in the garden. Without my father breathing down her neck, she finished high school a semester early and spent that time working for my grandfather.

I had been attending a private school for girls for a year when my sister started at USC to study accounting. Throughout her time at school, I had my grandfather's drivers take me to visit Kaia at the dorms. I loved visiting her there because it was the first time she seemed really happy. Surrounded by friends and always smiling. Sometimes I would even get drunk dials from her in the middle of the night. It was like she had become a different person.

That person seemed to disappear when Nonno died. Having inherited everything from him, she moved back into the house. I was taken care of, of course, but his will made clear that Kaia should have everything she needed to become Boss. Unlike my father, he had never planned to marry either of us off to men he felt were beneath us for political advantage. Instead, he trained my sister for leadership so she could take over the family business once he was gone.

What my grandfather hadn't expected was that his eldest granddaughter would be pregnant when he died. Kaia had managed to hide her pregnancy from him for months, but eventually, the game was up. The last three months were spent being questioned about the father, but she kept quiet. Daniel, who was born the day my grandfather died, was conceived while I was away at school. The father was a complete mystery to me. A small part of me enjoyed the idea of my sister having a secret romance. Like my grandfather, I spent months trying to get his name from my sister, but she finally insisted it was irrelevant and made me swear to drop the issue as I held the little boy in my arms. Whoever he was, he wasn't coming around anymore.

Daniel Matteo Caccia looked up at me with big blue eyes that were clearly from his father, but the mess of black hair was pure Kaia. I fell in love with the little bastard as soon as I smelled the top of his head.

When the house became Kaia's, she got to work changing things to her taste. I had never been very sentimental about things, so I had no problem with it. Especially because it wasn't mine. My old bedroom became Daniel's nursery, complete with a playroom that was more suited to a little boy. Everything else in the house got changed to black and white, but in a manner that conveyed classic comfort to honor the original architecture.

The house was built in 1950 in a Georgian style: massive, elegant, and white. Large cypress trees protected the house from public view and were further surrounded by tall iron gates. There was a large front yard that is impossible to see from the street and a terrace in the back with large diamond pavers that were outlined with tufts of grass. Right next to that was the lemon and wisteria-covered patio where we had enjoyed countless family dinners. While sitting at the table, you could easily see into the garden that was planted beside it.

I still crashed in the guest room occasionally when I was too tired to make the short drive home or had too much of Kaia's expensive wine at dinner. Despite living down at Le Tropical, this place still felt like home to me. Sure, I got paid enough to buy a place of my own, but I wasn't ready to put down roots anywhere.

9

COTONEASTER

Daniel shouted something from the sofa I couldn't hear over the true-crime podcast I'd put on to tune out the cartoons he'd been watching. I took out an earbud.

"What?" I asked.

"Can I have more popcorn, Zia?"

I nodded and walked to the pantry. Kaia had a meeting with Carlo and Gino, two Capos in the Caccia family, leaving me to watch her son until she got home.

My sister met with a lot of resistance trying to change the Caccia family as soon as she took control, but a change was happening in these circles whether the men liked it or not. Much like any other inherited family business, generations tend to do things differently once they're in charge. Many tried to test her because she was a woman, but those who knew her understood she was not to be trifled with. Especially when those who tried to resist were disappearing left and right. When things started to settle down, she set herself apart and shared her wealth. Our wealth.

She took a larger cut of everything, but only by a small percentage when compared to what our grandfather had taken. If one of their family members got sick, Kaia paid the bill. Kid going off to college? Caccia family scholarship. I'm not trying to make it sound like we were the good guys, definitely not, but my sister was good to those who were good to her.

While most bosses rewarded their men within a certain limit, Kaia spread the wealth around like she was running an employee-owned business. When I asked her about this, she would say that the money she earned was because of them and nothing makes a more loyal employee than being treated like an equal. As usual, she was right. The men who worked for the Caccia family would die for her.

Watching Daniel never bothered me. I loved the kid so much; I felt it in my bone marrow. It helped that he was fairly well-behaved for a six-year-old and cute as hell. Her fashionable furniture was hardly ever in danger between the two of us. Moving things aside here and there, I looked for the popcorn box. Where did I leave it?

The brown box was right in front of my face. Ugh. Picking it up, my fingers plunged inside for another bag of un-popped kernels. When I'd made him the first bag, I was so consumed with moving my serum from the centrifuge to its little brown bottles and locking it away in the mini-fridge that I had forgotten to put the box back in its regular place. Tinny sounds of bangs and crashes came from the next room followed by belly laughs. I couldn't help the smile that spread across my face.

"Alright, buddy. Popcorn coming up in two minutes."

The email alert chimed from my phone as I listened to the kernels pop in the microwave. Peeking around the corner to make sure Daniel was still occupied with cartoons, I opened it. Kaia had sent me the employee files of Casey and Isabelle. They contained all of the pertinent information about their lives. Typically, dancers just got cash and were on their way, but the secretive nature of our other businesses required we keep files on them.

IT WAS ABOUT a quarter to midnight by the time Kaia got home. Daniel had passed out next to me on the sofa before his bedtime, so I carried his little body up to his room and tucked him in. His early bedtime left me a few hours to peruse the information my sister had sent me and gave me time to set up an appointment with the landlord of Isabelle's apartment.

My head snapped up as the front door clicked shut.

"Hey," my sister said quietly from the foyer. "Is he asleep?"

Holding her heels in her hand, she padded down the black and white marble hall. The Hermes bag she carried thudded as she dropped it on the entryway table. I looked her over. The Armani suit she'd left in was only slightly wrinkled, and the black silk blouse she'd worn beneath had been unbuttoned at the neck. She never wore any other color outside of the house. I wondered what people would think if they saw her in her favorite grey sweatpants.

"Yeah, I put him to bed a few hours ago."

"Good. Did he eat?"

"He had a lot of popcorn."

"Please tell me you gave him actual food."

"All he wanted to eat was popcorn. I did manage to get a piece of fruit into him for dessert, but that was it."

Her sigh echoed out of the pantry over the rustling sounds of paper and cellophane wrapping. When she came out, she was chewing something.

"Popcorn is not a meal, Lili," she said through her food.

"I know, but it's all he wanted. I can't force-feed him. Besides, I have to stay his favorite aunt somehow."

"You're literally his only aunt."

I shrugged. Chocolate. She was eating chocolate. When she finished her bite, she walked over to the wine bottle that sat on the counter and popped the stopper off with her thumb. The movement sent it gliding across the marble top.

"What's up with Gino and Carlo?"

The bottle made glugging sounds as red wine poured into a bulbous burgundy glass. I walked over to the refrigerator and pulled out some cheese, trying not to let my sister's hypocrisy about missing meals get to me. Still, I gave her a pointed look as I put an assortment of cheese and fruit down in front of her. The roll of her eyes was all the thanks I got as she stuffed a chunk of smoked gouda into her mouth.

"Their guys are noticing a lot of eyes on our businesses. They think it's Arawn clan movement."

"So, what are you going to do?" I asked, after popping a few grapes into my mouth.

"I told them to dial up security and let me know if anything happens. There isn't anything to do until someone makes a move."

"Why not strike first? Let them know we're watching."

"Because if we strike first, that lets them know we're afraid. That we're trying to send a message. If we don't do anything, we seem unbothered. Stronger."

Specks of wine hit the countertop as she refilled her glass. I handed her a kitchen towel and wandered to the pantry, curious about where she was keeping the stash of candy Daniel obviously didn't know about. When I discovered a box of cereal that looked boring and nutritious, I knew I hit pay-dirt.

"Before you meet with him, there are a few things you need to know about Benjamin Camden."

I popped out of the pantry with a carmely, peanutty candy bar in my hand and a victorious look on my face. Kaia gave me a bored look and continued.

"He makes it seem like he came from money, but he didn't. It's why he came to the US. This country and the accent he worked hard to polish helped to elevate him to a new social status. That helped him to raise most of the funds he needed to start his VC. We provided the rest."

I sat down on a barstool and took a sip from my water bottle.

"Why are you telling me this? I'm just meeting with the guy. My goal is to get the information I need and be on my way."

"Make sure you get in and get out. He has a reputation," she said as she raised her glass to her lips. I was perfectly aware of his reputation. The man appeared in gossip rags more often than some movie stars. Girls around town talked about Benjamin Camden like he was a trophy and they were derby horses running for their prize.

"I should be careful of him because he likes fucking pretty girls?" I asked incredulously.

"Because appearances are all that matter to him. All I'm saying is don't be taken in. It's all an act."

I raised an eyebrow at her. This was a bit insane. I was just going to have a conversation with the man. There wasn't anything to worry about.

AS I GOT ready for bed, I couldn't help but wonder about the man I was going to meet. My big green duvet felt like a weight against my skin as anxiety started to take hold. It didn't take long for me to start looking him up on social media.

He didn't seem to have any presence on social media outside of an official capacity as the face of his venture capital company. Flipping through photo after photo, I started to understand the sea of raging females chasing after him. Dark brown curls, frosty blue eyes, and a strong jawline. There were dimples, for crying out loud. Benjamin Camden, the billionaire, had no right to have as much money as he did while looking like that. It just wasn't fair to the other billionaires.

Then I got started on the gossip blogs. Apparently, he was into a very specific type of woman. Statuesque women who looked like they walked out of fashion magazines were spotted holding hands with him. Having expensive dinners with him. Taking romantic walks through foreign cities with him. Most recently, he had been seeing a Brazilian model who was as devastatingly beautiful as he was.

A little gnawing feeling started tugging at me. I couldn't tell if I was a little jealous of this girl or just nervous about meeting the man who'd developed quite a reputation for himself. Either way, it was just going to be a short conversation with a stranger. I could handle that, couldn't I?

10

VERATRUM NIGRUM

Rhianna was singing about cake or something. More saying it than singing it. *Cake, cake, cake.* Still, it was catchy. I watched Sophie draw on her winged eyeliner carefully like Cleopatra preparing to be worshiped by her adoring public. Her girlfriend Maya had taken the stage a few moments before. I could hear the hoots and hollers from behind the closed dressing room door.

"Did Isabelle say anything to you about her date?"

Sophie took a sip from her water and returned to lining her eyes with precision.

"Not who she was meeting, but she said he was taking her to Vegas."

"He took her?"

"That's what she said," she croaked as she parted her lips to make her eyes stay open.

"Did Casey go with her?"

She gave an exasperated exhale, like thinking about this was tiring. I thought about what it might feel like to have two of your coworkers disappear in the same week. The leather sofa groaned under me as I stood up and crossed to the vanity. She turned to look at me with tears in her eyes.

"Do you think they're okay?" She warbled.

My face betrayed the truth of what I thought before I could speak a believable lie. I decided not to answer.

"I don't think so either," she said with a shaky sigh. I grabbed a tissue from the counter and handed it to her. Patting the offending tears away, she gave me a weak smile.

"I'll find them, Soph."

Her nod was slight. It seemed as though she summoned another personality out of nowhere because she was acting like her normal outgoing self in the next moment.

"I better get out there," she beamed. I wondered where she got the energy to do this almost every night. No matter what, she never missed a shift. Sophie always danced. Sophie always got paid. As I followed her out onto the main floor, I watched men get drawn in by her big brown doe eyes and bouncing brown ponytail. A touch on the arm here, a little wave there, and then she was on the stage. Sophie twirled like a star burning in the night sky as the opening bars to "Alien Superstar" started to fill the air.

On my way out, Maya glared at me from across the room as she danced for a customer. She was protective of Sophie. Totally understandable. I wouldn't want someone like me near someone I loved either. I gave her a nod and continued toward the door.

"Hey," said West, who was leaning against the doorway.

"Hi," I breathed. The night air was thin and crisp. Pulling my jacket around myself, I stared out at the cars passing on the street. Knowing what I was heading out to do, I ignored my growling stomach.

"Going home?" West asked, snapping me from my daze.

"No," I huffed. "Time to go to work."

Tension rippled through him. I never involved him in what I did. Never explained where I was at night or why I needed to be able to fight anyone off. Part of me knew it was because of Ethan, my ex, that I'd kept those details to myself. But West knew who the Caccias were. What the family did. He was hired as the bouncer and that's where his responsibilities to us ended. As far as he knew, I was just running unsavory errands for my sister. Partially true, but not the entire picture. Understanding marked his gaze as he said, "well, get home safe."

Tonight was a different kind of assignment. I was going to find myself on the other side of town in a hurry.

EARLIER THAT DAY, Melodie came to Kaia in tears and she called me to her office. The petite bartender had been on several dates with some guy she met on Tinder, so she didn't think anything of leaving him at their table to go to the bathroom. Little did she know that while she was touching up her makeup in the ladies' room, her date was drugging her cocktail.

The date took her home, telling her she'd gotten too drunk. Melodie couldn't say yes. She couldn't hold herself upright or defend herself. So he took advantage. When she'd called in sick the next day, she still sounded weak. The day after that, we'd sent her home. On this day, Kaia asked her to explain what happened. I leaned against the wall behind my sister and listened to her sob.

"He keeps calling me and texting me. I blocked his number and he showed up at my apartment. I don't know what to do."

"Do you know where he is now?" I asked. She looked up at me, eyes large with surprise.

"No." The word was quiet and frail.

"Give me his information," I said as I squatted next to her chair and handed her my phone. Shaking hands took the device from my grasp. Kaia eyed me from behind the desk. This was why she had asked me here. A sniffle indicated she'd finished. "His name?" I added.

"Jake Fuller."

"Ok." I tossed a glance at my sister and left the room. She returned my look with a nod, silently giving all the permission I needed for what would happen next. Jake Fuller wouldn't be bothering Melodie again.

TRUE CRIME PODCASTS will tell you that having a routine is dangerous. People can easily learn where you're going to be and take advantage of that fact. Jake Fuller was no different. He made it incredibly easy to find him. Visits to the gym were practically a religion for this guy. Based on his posts and daily videos, I knew exactly when he was going to be working out.

A small part of me felt like I should offer him a cookie or something since I knew his last meal consisted of unseasoned boiled chicken and steamed vegetables. The tiny bathroom window illuminated from within, and I heard the shower sputter on. When the sound of curtain rings squeaking against the rod reached me, I moved.

My body sometimes seemed to ready itself for taking a life. As though it knew some deaths were justified. A flush rushed through me and my heart slowed its pace. My footsteps lost their clipped stride. Instead, they took on a predatory gait. When I spoke, I rarely recognized my voice.

The shower's noise hissed through the open window, with the occasional sound of water slapping into the tub. I stalked toward the front door, knives at the ready. The clean-up crew was dialed in. My sister would be furious, but I didn't care. Men like this deserved to pay. Jake Fuller had about six inches and one hundred pounds on me. But he was tired and I was fresh, having waited for him to let his guard down. The moron didn't even lock his door.

Long showers are so wasteful. Especially in drought-ridden places like California. This was all I could think about as I sat on Jake's bed and cleaned my nails with one of my throwing knives, waiting for him to finish cleaning himself. Looking around the room, I noticed no pictures of family but several mirrors and pictures of himself flexing shirtless on vacation in various tropical locations. What a tool.

The water turned off and steam billowed out the door when he finally stepped out of the bathroom in a maroon towel.

"Hi Jake," I drolled from the bed.

"Who the fuck are you?"

"I'm a friend of Melodie's. You remember her, don't you?"

His head cocked to the side. I couldn't tell if his slow response was because he was flippant or just an idiot.

"That fucking stripper? Yeah."

"Bartender. And that's not nice, Jake," I said, arching an eyebrow at him. My blade caught his eye. Perhaps he'd figured out that I wasn't there to chat.

"What are you doing in here?" His stance shifted and his body language changed from an overly confident man to someone on the defensive. Yup, he knew.

"Melodie told me she didn't have a very good time with you, Jake."

"Did she say she was raped? That bitch says she said no now, but she fucking wanted it."

My hackles jostled at the insult, and my gut twisted at the blatant lie. I took a pointed glance at his towel and looked back at him.

"I doubt that very much, Jake." His hand was pinned to the door with a black steel throwing knife before he could argue. Big bad Jake started squealing like a pig.

"What the fuck?!"

Falling to his knees, he tried to unpin his hand from the door. I sauntered over to where he knelt and pulled out the larger, more sinister-looking hunting knife I kept strapped to my belt. As he attempted to grab me with his un-skewered hand, I took his wrist and twisted it behind his back.

"Jake. You drugged my friend. You raped my friend."

"Fuck you."

His blonde hair was so easy to grab when he was on his knees. I yanked it back to expose his neck. Tears were streaming down his face now. They always cry. Small waves of nausea roiled in my gut as my knife slid across his throat, leaving a small trail of blood behind it.

"Jake," I purred.

He whimpered.

"Do you know what a Glasgow smile is?"

THE BASTARD BLED all over my boots. I leaned over the kitchen sink and scrubbed until the water ran clear. On the way out of his apartment, I text messaged the cleanup crew to deal with Fuller's remains. It wasn't pretty. The clothes I was wearing would have to be burned later. As I stood half-naked in my kitchen, covered in someone else's blood, my phone rang.

"What the fuck happened?" Kaia yelled. "Do you realize this is going to cost thousands to clean up?"

"Take it out of my pay."

"Why did you do that? Jesus, Lili. You destroyed most of his face."

"Just trying something new."

"You're supposed to get in and get out. Do your job."

"I did my job, Kai. He's dead. I made a mess because it's what he deserved. Fucking bill me." I ended the call and threw the phone on the counter, well aware of the fact that I was the only person who could talk to her that way. She could stay mad at me if she wanted. It wouldn't change what I did as I stormed into the bathroom.

As hot water started to fog the mirror before me, I stared at the reflection. The wolf on my chest looked back at me with worry in its eyes. But my eyes, the eyes I had inherited from my father, glimmered with savage cruelty. This gaze would return to me in sleep. It always did. On days like this, I could feel it pulling me under. Killing for the family was my job. This felt like killing for pleasure. The thought sent me into a panic as I washed off Fuller's blood, and I began scrubbing my skin until it was raw.

After getting out of the brutally hot shower, I stood there in my towel. The adrenaline was finally wearing off, bringing my mind to the surface. Clenching and unclenching my fists, I tried to ground myself by looking around the room. Three green things. Plant. Plant. Duvet. Two black things. Combat boots....

My eyes landed on the little skirt suit I used to wear for college interviews, hanging on the garment rack across the room. Shit, did it even still fit? As I pulled on my old shirt and boxers, I said a silent prayer that the zipper would zip and the buttons would button. The usual grunge-chic look I sported was probably not appropriate for an office meeting at a Fortune 100 tech company with one of the wealthiest men in the world.

11

NERIUM

My heels clacked loudly through the green marble lobby. In the black skirt suit I wore, my tattoos were covered up. The dark circles under my hazel eyes were easily hidden by some concealer. I looked like just another fresh-faced employee. Kaia had arranged for me to meet with Mr. Benjamin Camden at Camden Industries. As I waited for the elevator, people walked by on their phones. Sending text messages, making phone calls, ignoring me. With people so engaged in their devices, it was easy to fly under the radar. The elevator announced its arrival with an elegant chime and I checked my sister's directions again.

Camden Industries, on Melrose and North San Vicente. 5th floor.

Images of Jake's half-decimated skull floated through my mind as I rode up to the 5th floor and made my way to Camden's office. When I arrived, a girl was waiting for me, dressed in a flawless lilac suit that looked far more expensive than mine. Standing in front of giant black doors with gold handles, she smiled as she held out her hand to shake mine.

"Ms. Caccia? I'm Juliet, Mr. Camden's assistant. He's running a bit late and would like to offer an apology. He should be along in a few minutes. May I get you something while you wait?"

"That's alright. I'm fine."

Juliet gave me another bright smile. Benjamin's assistant could have been another one of his girlfriends. She was tall, blonde, and cinematically good-looking. I idly wondered if they had ever been together romantically or if he just liked to surround himself with beautiful women. "Waiting in his office is best."

She guided me into the massive executive suite that seemed obscenely overlarge, even for the CEO of whatever. While I waited for Mr. Camden, his assistant supplied me with a glass of water from a small carafe. Looking around at the decor, I started to learn some things about Benjamin Camden's personality. A large walnut desk with a sleek monitor. Equally large black ostrich leather seat with iron nailhead trim. Across from it sat two guest chairs, both significantly smaller but crafted with the same dark walnut and leather. The office was tastefully appointed but designed for utility, which meant that he liked to impress but didn't care for excess. On the other side of the vast expanse was a set of weights, a rowing machine, and a bench. And cameras. Cameras everywhere. My eyes drifted to a lens and wondered who was watching when I decided to start asking questions. Juliet seemed amiable enough.

"Can I ask you something?"

"Of course."

"How does Eros work? Like, why is it so secret?"

Juliet chewed on the inside of her cheek as she considered my question. She placed a hand on a folder, readying herself to pick it up, but spoke instead.

"Exclusivity is good for business. It costs a lot to join Eros and the members like to know they're in good company. Especially because the members have to submit tax returns in order to join. It is a guaranteed assurance of their financial status. Because of that, we provide a covenant of privacy to all of our members."

Tax returns. That would leave me out for sure. As far as the government knew, I made about as much money as a schoolteacher. My real assets were completely off of the radar of the IRS. It was why I kept my tiny apartment and paid cash for damn near everything. Foolish gangsters who walked around in luxury always got caught. I'd decided a long time ago that I needed to look like I was hard up for money, just like most people in Los Angeles. I gave a thoughtful hum and asked, "But what about the girls? There are a lot of them who don't qualify financially, right?"

"The girls are seen as an...incentive for our wealthier members."

Something about the women being treated like door prizes unsettled me. As if summoned by a dog whistle, Juliet straightened and made a sudden exit. For a few moments, the room was suffocatingly silent. I was occupying myself by removing what looked like a tiny bit of blood from underneath my fingernail when Camden made his entrance. His stride was hurried but unbothered, taking steps toward his massive desk chair. When he took his seat, he immediately began working at his computer. He didn't even look my way. Well, hello to you too.

"Hello, Ms. Caccia. I've been told you wanted to discuss Eros with me."

He was still typing away on his keyboard, so I waited to respond while looking him over. I had seen photos of him online in my research, but they certainly did not do him justice. The man looked like a goddamn movie star. Just setting eyes on him was downright painful. He leveled his icy blue gaze at me, clearly awaiting a response.

"Yes," I blurted. "Eros. I have some questions about its clients."

"As I told your sister when we spoke, it's a confidential service. Members who join are of a certain status and need their identities protected." The words were cold but sounded polite in his London accent.

"What about when some of your members go missing? Where is your protection for them?" Thank God I practiced that on the way here because I was losing my words.

He narrowed his pale blue eyes at me and pushed a hand through his dark brown hair. Leaning back in his chair, he exhaled.

"As I stated, Ms. Caccia, I'm not able to disclose that information. If there is anything else I can do, please let me know." The last few words trailed off, showing that his attention was divided. He'd agreed to meet with me for only a few moments out of some courtesy to my family. He turned to his computer and returned to typing. I guess he thought we were done talking. He was wrong.

"Look," I said abruptly, "This isn't something we can just let go of, so if you have another avenue I can pursue, I'm all ears, but you're not going to be able to get rid of me that easily."

He rose and rounded his desk. For a minute, I thought he was going to throw me out of his office, but I stayed in my seat. He leaned against his desk and looked down his nose at me like he was going to scold me. Was he going to scold me?

"Because of the confidentiality contracts our clients sign, I can't give you their names. I'm bound as much as they are and I'd very much like to avoid being sued, but maybe I can help you meet them."

"I'm not interested in signing up for your service."

He chuckled. "The service has social events for members in different cities. It's a way for members to interact offline in a safe environment. If you would like, you could join me as my guest and meet them in person. This way I don't tell you their names. They can give them to you themselves. No contracts broken."

"That might work, but don't you think it would look strange for me to just skulk around parties and ask people for their names? How would I explain my presence there?"

His punishing blue gaze raked over me as he considered my question. My jaw clenched as I took him in again. Based on the way the fabric of his suit seemed to strain, I could tell the gym equipment in this office got used often. The expensive grey material skimmed down his obscenely broad shoulders and tapered toward his waist with barely an inch of forgiveness. His slacks fit like they had been tailored by a master but still seemed to struggle against the mass of his thighs. Crossing his arms in front of him, he hefted a sigh. It was a minute or so before he spoke again. I felt myself getting increasingly uncomfortable in the silence. *Don't offer a solution,* I told myself. *Let him offer something.* Finally, his expression went from contemplative to relaxed, as though he'd settled some internal argument with himself.

"If you're there as my guest, I can introduce you but keeping you close could be an issue. However, it may arouse fewer suspicions if we appear to have a more intimate relationship."

"Intimate?" I asked though I knew exactly what he was getting at. *Back alley trash.* Ethan's words drifted through my mind. I couldn't do this, could I?

"Yes. If it seemed that you and I were involved, no one would question your presence."

I sighed, trying not to convey the internal panic I was feeling. People love to gossip about the rich, especially when they look like him. In my research on Benjamin, I had seen the women that he spent time with in various gossip blogs. All of them tall, blonde, some models, some influencers. His girlfriends all looked like they were cloned in a lab. I mean, maybe they were. The man had a type, and it certainly wasn't me. Finally, I muttered, "I think that may still arouse some suspicion."

He smirked, as though he understood what I meant by that. After pausing for a moment, he gave me another look of appraisal as he moved toward me and leaned forward. His hands braced on the arms of my chair, caging me in.

"You've done a good job of looking like anyone else. I have no doubt you'll work to look the part."

The leather brogues he wore creaked as he stood up again and walked to his chair. Again, it seemed like we were done with our conversation, but this time I stood and gathered my bag to leave. As I did so, I reasoned with myself about the advantages of this little arrangement. Maybe I could get close to him and find another way to the information I needed. If I could get him to let his guard down without sacrificing my own.

"Ms. Caccia," He said, still looking down at his phone.

I stopped and turned to raise an eyebrow at him. Were we not done?

"Meet with my assistant tomorrow. Juliet will get you everything you need."

"Everything I need?"

"To address your concerns about looking the part. Afterward, you and I are having dinner."

I nodded. I guess we were starting tomorrow.

"THIS CERTAINLY DOESN'T leave much to the imagination, does it?" I shouted from the dressing room. Being late in the morning, the store was mercifully unoccupied as I poked my head out of the dressing room door. The sheer black dress I had squeezed myself into barely covered my ass. When was the last time I wore a dress?

"It's not supposed to."

"This looks ridiculous," I protested as I walked out to show her.

"It doesn't. It looks wonderful on you and highlights the shape of your body. You've got a nice Sophia Loren thing going on. You're just not used to the fit."

"No one could get used to this. I feel like a busted can of biscuits."

She laughed and handed me more dresses. Killing people for a living didn't make me any more comfortable with my body. I could do that job in jeans and a tee shirt. Hell, I usually did. I took the selection of dresses from her and peeled off the frock I'd squeezed myself into. Despite the abrupt behavior of her boss, I was growing more comfortable around Juliet.

"How do people breathe with these things on? Do I really need all of these?" I whined.

"All the events you'll be attending with Mr. Camden have their own dress code. You need something for each one. Do you have something for each event?"

I shook my head. There was not enough coffee in the world for this. I'm not the type to look down on shopping, but this was causing me to stress-sweat. I preferred to hoard my money and disappear into the background. I wasn't my sister. She always enjoyed nice things. When Kaia took control of the family, her wardrobe went from department store to bespoke finery almost overnight.

"Then get back in there. We don't have a lot of time if we're going to get you to the salon."

"To what, bleach my hair?" I joked, pulling at my black strands, worried about what damage she had planned. "Besides, tonight's just dinner. What dress code is that?"

"No." Juliet quirked her lips before giving me an awkward glance. "I just assumed it's been a while since you had it cut. And tonight you'll wear the black dress you just had on."

A small puddle of shame pooled in me as I thought about how obvious my split ends must've been. She wasn't wrong about the haircut. Before the day was over I had bags upon bags of clothes and shoes I would never have bought for myself, a new haircut and blowout from a pricey Beverly Hills salon, and other accoutrement befitting of a woman on the arm of a billionaire.

AROUND 5 PM, I got a text message from Benjamin Camden.

Be outside at 7 PM.

The man wasn't exactly a chatterbox. I wondered what we'd talk about over dinner. I couldn't discuss my work or my family. While pondering this, I had sorted through the myriad of options I now owned and came up with the little black dress. It did seem like the safest option for a mysterious dinner location. With it, I paired black Louboutins and prayed we wouldn't be doing much walking. A two-hour window didn't seem like enough time to become perfect, but I would do my best.

I looked myself over, giving every detail a final evaluation. The woman looking back at me in the mirror was a stranger. Long black waves framed a perfectly made-up face. I thanked the internet gods for teaching me to contour and blend. Watching the dancers get made up probably helped a little, too. After giving myself a last look, I skimmed my lip with the tip of my finger to make sure the liner was even. I locked my door and stepped outside one minute after seven to find a black Bentley with the motor idling. The driver stepped out of the driver's side and opened the door for me. I plopped myself down inside and jumped when I was met with Benjamin's voice.

"You're late."

"Sorry. These heels are practically stilts. Also, this look is more work than I'm used to."

He looked up from his phone to appraise my efforts. "Well done," he said with a half-cocked smile.

For a moment, I wondered if I'd fallen into a GQ cover. This guy was… wow. I wasn't sure I even knew how to talk to him. He was dressed in another expensive suit, but he'd lost the vest and tie. The top few buttons of his collar were undone to show a bit of skin, and the remaining buttons strained slightly against his muscles when he moved. I hadn't noticed his scent before. The man smelled expensive, like fine leather and sage. It was both masculine and refined. Juliet insisted I pick a different perfume since "people notice these things" and after smelling Benjamin, I understood why.

"Thank you, I think. Where are we going?"

"Nobu, in Malibu. Before I can take you to an Eros event as my guest, it has to appear that you and I are seeing each other."

I nodded and turned my gaze to the window. That made sense. People in Hollywood went to Nobu for two reasons. The first was to get spectacular sushi and the second was to be seen. If Benjamin was seen with me there, it would lend credibility to our little farce.

It was a long ride from my place, but I stayed quiet while Benjamin made calls to check on the various businesses under his control. Once we arrived at the restaurant, we were escorted to our table on the deck. Being wealthy and in the public eye meant that he rarely had to do any waiting, it seemed.

This is just a date, I told myself. *Figure out how to be charming and charm him.*

Benjamin carried himself in a way that seemed practiced. His walk was purposeful and self-possessed. Small sofas were on either side of our table instead of chairs in a design aesthetic that could only be described as "casual luxury." The host left our table and was quickly replaced by our server. Before I had a chance to look at the menu, Benjamin ordered for both of us. Oysters, bluefin tuna, salmon, uni, and champagne.

"Oysters and champagne?" I asked.

"You don't enjoy oysters?"

"No, I do. I was just thinking about the implication."

"I'm aware of the implication," he smirked.

I couldn't help but smile at that. As the night wore on, we did find things to talk about. Or I did. With those cold blue eyes leveled at me, I felt compelled to talk. A lot. My plan to be charming felt like it was on uneven footing with every anecdote I wove. He offered a smile or a laugh every so often but didn't say much else. As the waiter came by to refill our champagne, I shivered and kicked myself for wearing something so minuscule.

"You're cold."

Before I could respond, he moved from his little sofa to mine while taking off his jacket. He sat next to me, draping it around my shoulders. The leather and sage smell was dizzying while sitting this close to him. Or maybe it was the champagne. How much had I had? He wrapped an arm around me and pulled me closer to him.

"Better?" He asked with a soft smirk.

I nodded. This had to be for show, right? Scanning the space, I took note of the people staring at us. One or two people had their phones out. Benjamin leaned in close, his lips brushing my ear when he spoke.

"Now smile like I'm telling you a dirty secret."

I closed my eyes and smiled, biting my lip. I couldn't have faked the blush flooding my cheeks. He leaned closer, brushing his nose across my neck. I was sure he could feel me tense in his grasp as heat pooled in me.

Faking a relationship in theory was a good idea, but I hadn't considered the actual mechanics of it. Not the touching or the way it would make me feel. The last man to touch me like this broke my heart. Fuck, I might be in trouble. The server returned and cleared his throat quietly.

"Dessert?"

Benjamin lifted his head, looked me in the eye, and asked for the check without breaking his gaze. The implications of that were more clear than the oysters. The man knew how to put on a show. It was so convincing that at that moment I lost my breath a little.

Once we were back in the car, Benjamin was all business again. I took out my phone and started scrolling through social media, wanting to check on our progress. While it was fun to have dinner with a devastatingly handsome billionaire, I still had a job to do. Searching posts by location, it wasn't long before I saw my own face. Several images greeted me. One where my head was thrown back in laughter, another with Benjamin putting his jacket on me, and the grand finale captured his face buried in my neck. We had succeeded in looking like lovers.

12

LILIUM SPECIOSUM

It would have been very easy to take the official Benjamin Camden make-over personally, but the truth is that I've never much cared about my appearance. In some ways, it's because I got lucky. My olive complexion is usually free of blemishes, despite my terrible diet and insane work hours. The Caccia family eyebrows were passed on to me, which means grooming the dark arches was a task that required little effort. The only thing I did to keep up appearances was pay for the occasional haircut and I was definitely not very religious about that. Actually, I wasn't religious about anything. But when you kill people for a living, you tend to hope there won't be someone to judge you when you die.

I pulled the freshly cut ends of my hair through my fingers as I eyed the substantial collection of designer goods now hanging from a garment rack in the middle of my apartment. Valentino, Dolce & Gabbana, and several designers I hadn't even heard of hung before me. Thousands of dollars worth of clothes. Even as Juliet had laid down Benjamin's black card, I cringed. These were things I'd never buy for myself. I pictured the Saint Laurent shoes covered in blood and shuddered. The date with Benjamin had gone well, sure. But something about the disappearances of Casey and Isabelle leading to a new wardrobe of expensive designer outfits made me feel icky.

The other problem was the dubious task of taking Benjamin on as a "boyfriend." It had been a long time since I'd been in a relationship, so I wasn't really sure how to act with regular men. How was I supposed to behave in this relationship? Stroking the fabric of a silk dress, I thought about the last man I'd called "boyfriend." Being connected to a major crime family really narrows down your dating pool. You can date men who are in the family, which is unthinkable. Most of these men are like brothers to me. Or you can date regular guys and try to hide the truth about your family for as long as you can.

It wasn't until I was in my first year at Berkeley that I dated anyone at all. But I treated that school like a veritable buffet. The first guy I dated had been like a study in self-exploration. We met in a lab for a biology class. His sweet brown eyes and soft smile were immediately endearing. Seeing each other several times a week made it easy for me to get quickly comfortable with him. So I took our relationship to a physical level, experimenting with my body and with his. After learning everything that I could from him, I moved on. He'd wanted to get more serious, and I wasn't ready for that. He cried when I ended it and I still feel bad about that.

Deciding to focus more on my studies, I went on to treat the male population at Berkley more like entertainment to be enjoyed during my limited free time. I tried preppy boys, emo boys, and even a couple of the local bartenders. For me, it was easier to change boyfriends than it was to explain who my family was.

It wasn't until I was home for good that things got complicated. Still, Ethan lasted longer than most. I met him about two years after I started working for my sister. I was getting coffee before a long night of trailing a deadbeat who was in serious debt to us when our hands touched over the tiny buckets of creamer. One side of his lips pulled up when he smiled the crooked grin I'd come to know so well. He was in the middle of his shift as a paramedic and looked like a dream in his navy blue uniform. I was a goner from the start.

The entire time we were together, I felt lucky to have him. When he touched me, he made me feel like I was the only woman in the world. It made me feel like I could have a happily ever after with someone. I pretended to be normal for him. Let him believe I was a soft, lovable thing. There were brunch dates. I met his parents. We spent hours together in his bed and he treated me like a prized possession. The odd hours I kept were easy to explain away. I told him I was a private detective and he thought that was very cool.

Everything was going great until he found out about my notorious family and I found out that he was sleeping with several different nurses. I wasn't the only woman in his world. Instead of his one and only, I was one of many. He was too afraid of being murdered by the mafia to mention anything about me to the police, but it didn't stop him from calling me a liar. I thought that part was rather hilarious.

"You're disgusting," I growled at him.

"I'm disgusting? Me? Let's talk about you, huh?" He gestured to me as though my defects were obvious to the naked eye. "What you and your family do, now that's disgusting. It makes me fucking sick."

I shook my head like a dog shaking off water to get the memory of his words out of my mind.

"You're just some back alley trash. I can't believe I thought I could love someone like you."

I pulled Ethan's Nirvana shirt over my head and climbed into bed. As I scrolled through Netflix looking for a movie to fall asleep to, I thought about this arrangement Benjamin and I had made. Ethan breaking my heart was practically ancient history, but it made me terrified to get involved with anyone else in that way. Even men I knew I wanted. I couldn't even think of how long it had been since I'd been touched by a man outside of the training ring. Maybe this would be good. Like a relationship with training wheels.

KAIA CALLED ME over to the house first thing in the morning. Gnawing hunger in my gut made me resent the early meeting. The least she could do was have some food around. As she packed Daniel's lunch for school, I filled my coffee cup and briefed her on the state of things with Benjamin.

"So, what, you're just going to date him until you find out what happened to Casey and Isabelle?" Kaia asked incredulously. "And he gave you a makeover?"

"Yes, well, technically, his assistant did. It's not like the movies where the wealthy boyfriend goes with you. He's very busy and important."

She snorted as she cut the crusts off of the sandwich she'd been making. "At least your hair looks good. You needed a haircut."

"Now you tell me. Do you know how embarrassing that shit was?"

Cream swirled into the black coffee as I searched for the sugar. Frustrated, I turned to my sister.

"You're not off sugar again, are you?"

Kaia rolled her eyes and walked over to the coffee station. With an exaggerated gesture, she pointed to a tiny glass jar filled with beige granules.

"It's right in front of you. I don't know how you didn't see it."

I shrugged as I added a spoonful to my cup.

"So is that the whole plan, then? This isn't just an opportunity for you to dress up and play 'dream date.'"

"Yes, Kai. I know," I said as I took a swig of coffee and set it on the counter. "And no, that's not the whole plan. But until I can get more information on the girls, this is all I've got."

Daniel's small feet clomped down the wooden stairwell. The little guy bounded into the kitchen with the kind of energy I wished I could bottle.

"Zia! Are you taking me to school?"

"Sorry, buddy. I have to work. Nico's taking you."

Big sad eyes did their best to manipulate me. If I didn't have somewhere to be, I would have taken him. Since his brother's death, Nico had taken up Dante's position as Kaia's bodyguard. Aside from me, he was the only person Kaia trusted. Leaning down, I gave Daniel a firm hug and ruffled his curls. This kid. He knew how to tug at my heartstrings. Kaia rounded the island and handed him his lunchbox.

"Come on, you're going to be late," she said as she looked over her shoulder at me with a look that told me we weren't done talking.

I looked at the clock and realized I was going to be late for my appointment on the other side of town if I didn't get going soon. Kaia returned as I gulped down the rest of my coffee.

"Where are you going? We're not done here."

"I have to be in the Valley at 10 o'clock. I got Isabelle's landlord to agree to let me in and I need to talk to the creepy bastard."

She crossed her arms and nodded. Her face had pulled into the subtle little scowl she thought I never noticed. The one that told me she had more to say. I put my empty coffee cup in the dishwasher and grabbed my bag.

"Don't worry about me, Kai. I've got this."

13

STROPHANTHUS GRATUS

Kaia hadn't dropped any additional business into my lap, so I was free to put all of my focus squarely on Isabelle and Casey. I retraced what little I knew about their last steps before again and again. I wasn't exactly Sherlock Holmes, but I was used to having to track down men who owed the Caccia Family money or had wronged us in some other way. Sometimes that included hunting down a bad boyfriend who needed to be dealt with. Those experiences helped me become adept at sussing out certain details.

Thanks to their employee files, I already had a pretty decent amount of personal information about both of the girls. I knew their phone numbers, addresses, and social security numbers. Because of their social media habits, I was also aware of exactly when they went off the radar based on the last time they'd posted anything. After narrowing things down to a specific timeline, I went to interview their neighbors and friends.

Both Casey and Isabelle are stunning girls. They're the kind of girls that make people take notice whenever they're around. If they're gussied up for a date with fancy men from some fancy secret app, I was willing to bet they probably pulled out all the stops. If their neighbors noticed them leave, they may have noticed if they left with someone specific.

My appointment was with Isabelle's landlord, and truth be known, he kind of gave me the creeps. If I wasn't sure about her involvement with an Eros user, I would definitely be looking into this guy. He seemed like the type to install cameras in your place when you weren't home. Fortunately, his broken moral compass meant he let me into her place with very little persuasion.

After looking around the tiny place, a few things stuck out to me. The first is that it looked like she had, in fact, left on some sort of trip. Her plants had self-watering stakes in them, though they had gone dry. Her fish looked like they were finishing off one of those vacation feeders.

"When was the last time you saw her?" I asked as I added another feeder to the bowl.

"Ten days ago. Tuesday, I think. She left with a suitcase."

I tossed a glance his way to acknowledge that I'd heard him. The kitchen was relatively clean and organized for being such a small space. Opening cabinets, I wasn't sure if I was going to find anything worth noting or if I was just looking to stay busy. A Cafe Bustelo can fell off of the counter and lost its lid. Instead of spilling coffee onto the floor, there were rolls of cash at my feet. The landlord leaned further in from the front door and I hastily scooped the cash back into the can.

"Don't come in here," I shouted. "There are grounds everywhere."

He grunted and walked out, lifting his phone to his ear. Not confident this man wouldn't abuse his land-lording privileges again, I took the can and stuffed it into my backpack. Isabelle could get her money back from me, but I doubted she could get it back from that guy if he found it.

"Alright," I said as I walked out of the apartment. "That's all I need, I guess. Thank you for your help." Palming the man a hundred-dollar bill, he smiled and nodded at me.

Tossing my bag into my passenger seat, I flopped down into the car and locked my doors. I needed to get to the gym if I was going to train with West, but I opened my phone and scrolled through social media for a moment.

I had been peripherally monitoring gossip about Benjamin and myself.

Our dinner date wasn't enough for the magazines to sink their teeth into, but the gossip bloggers were already speculating about our relationship. My own Instagram had always been set to private and I had almost no internet presence, so it was no surprise to me that they couldn't figure out the identity of this new woman in his life. Of course, a short Italian woman was hardly his usual taste, so people were wondering what it was he found so appealing. That part stung a little bit.

"YOU'RE NEVER GOING to be able to get out of this," West laughed as I struggled against his thighs. I could barely hear him with my head under his arm. We had been rolling for close to an hour, and despite my having trained in Brazilian Ju Jitsu for a few years, he still managed to get me in a guillotine hold. He wrenched his arm tighter until I was struggling for air, his legs still squeezing me from the sides as I thrashed against him. Finally giving up, I tapped out and he released me.

"Told you," he said.

"You're at least a whole foot taller than me. Your reach is insane. Maybe I should train with someone my own size."

"Someone who's miniature," he laughed.

"Fuck you," I bit out, pushing him as he tried to stand up. Grabbing my wrist as he went down, his chest rumbled with laughter as pulled me to the mat. Pushing his body over mine, he straddled my hips and pinned my wrists to the ground with one giant hand. Up this close, I could see the small textured scar that cut through his eyebrow. I'd never asked him about it, but it looked like a badge of honor won from a fight.

"You're not fighting people your size, so you shouldn't train with people your size. Get used to it and stop being a sore loser."

I groaned as I struggled to get out of his hold. Briefly, I was mesmerized by the large skull tattoo on his inner bicep with octopus tentacles trailing out of its base. The rippling flex of his muscles made the tentacles look like they were coiling around the phrase "Memento mori." I shifted again, but his grip on my wrists and the smug grin on his face told me he could do this all day.

"Seriously? Come on, man. Who does this hold?" I grunted.

"Someone who's trying to kill you. Figure it out. Or you can just get nice and comfortable like you were in those pictures with Camden."

I rolled my eyes. "That's just business."

"It didn't look like business and I've never seen that dress before."

"He bought me a bunch of new clothes. Besides, what we're doing now doesn't exactly call for formal attire."

"Did he cut your hair, too?" He said, swatting at the strands in my face with his free hand. Cocky bastard. Still, I'd take the teasing over the haunted expression that occasionally crossed his face.

"Oh yeah, he's a full-service billionaire."

He grunted and rolled his eyes.

"You almost sound jealous," I laughed, straining to move my legs for some leverage. His muscled core tightened as his legs moved closer to my sides. This wasn't the first time he'd pinned me, but he always tried to change up the positions and give me more of a challenge each time. His towering frame and mass of corded muscles made him a difficult opponent.

"Yeah, sure. Jealous. Or maybe I'm worried. Be careful with him, Lili."

"I'm fully aware of the fact that he's probably not a good guy. Besides, you know me. I can handle myself." I said with a grunt, trying again to free myself.

"Can you?" He grinned down at me. God, he was infuriating. Obviously being pinned beneath his gigantic body was proving the opposite point. I shifted my hips up until I was able to get on my side against him and pull one wrist free of his grip. Striking him hard in the gut with an elbow, I pulled a leg up and around his waist to take him down. With his arm trapped between my locked legs in an arm bar, he shifted and grunted.

"I told you, I can handle myself," I mused. Wrenching my grip to inflict more pain, I waited for him to tap out.

West's fingers tapped my leg only after I lifted my hips to increase the pressure. The man was more stubborn than I was. As we lay on the mat covered in sweat, I wished I had worn a shirt over my sports bra, but it was hot as hell in the gym. The mat squeaked below me as I sat up and looked down at West. His eyes had drifted closed and his arms splayed wide.

The air in the gym could only be described as stagnant. Even in the November weather, it was unusual for a day to be so hot and breezeless. The water in my steel bottle was still ice cold, but it wasn't enough to keep the heat at bay.

"It's hot as shit in here," he finally muttered.

I grunted my agreement while taking another swig of water from my bottle. The space was quiet except for the sound of our puffing breaths. From where I sat, I could see myself in the mirror. It shouldn't have bothered me, but having the internet question my appearance got under my skin. My gym gear only highlighted my figure, but the black bra and leggings did wash me out a bit. I angled my head and the bit of hair that fell out of my braid drifted over my shoulder. Not one of those models, sure, but pretty. I rolled my eyes, annoyed with myself for even worrying about it.

"You know I'm not joking about Camden."

"I know you're not."

He opened an eye and quirked his mouth to the side in a skeptical expression.

"He's going to help me meet people in this exclusive dating service." I leaned back on my palms and sighed. "They sign NDAs, so he legally can't tell me who they are outside of the events. Everything about it is so secret that it makes me think there has to be something there. I know it's not a lot to go on, but it's something."

West smirked, eyes still closed, and blew out a breath.

"Just don't disappear. I don't think I could stand getting my ass handed to me by anyone else."

I WAS STILL covered in sweat when I got to Casey's apartment. The late afternoon sun was starting to turn to a golden haze, turning the brown stucco building a more pleasing orange hue. Her little first floor unit was one of the few apartments with a potted plant in front of it. I dug around in the dirt for a spare key.

"Looking for something?" A weathered voice asked. I twisted toward her. The woman leaned against her door frame, halfway inside her apartment in case she needed to retreat from me. Smart. She eyed me warily through thick, gold-rimmed glasses.

"Yeah, I'm supposed to water her plants while she's gone and I forgot my key. I was hoping she had a spare."

"You know her, then? What's her name?" Smart. Smart lady.

"Casey. Like I said, she's a friend."

The woman nodded and went back inside her apartment, leaving the door slightly ajar behind her. I went back to looking for a key. On top of the porch light, maybe? A light tapping on my shoulder startled me.

"Sorry," the woman muttered. "She gave me this in case of an emergency, but I suppose you could borrow it." She dropped a gold key into my palm. "Bring it back when you're finished."

"I will," I said with a nod. "I promise. Thank you."

⚶

CASEY ACTUALLY DID have plants that needed watering. Just a few succulents, but I gave them water while I looked around the place. If Isabelle's apartment said "glamourous influencer," Casey's home said quite the opposite. Bohemian decor was placed here and there, but the space was otherwise sparse.

The bedroom set was mismatched. Everything looked old, but clean. After moving her hamper to get into the tiny closet, hoping I'd find evidence of a missing suitcase or something to suggest that she'd left instead of disappeared, I noticed a bowl on top of her dresser that looked exactly like the fishbowl in Isabelle's apartment. Except the fish…Well, the fish didn't make it. I dipped my fingers into the water and scooped out the small body. Purple and red iridescent scales glinted in the light that was peeking in through the blinds.

The tiny body dropped into the toilet with a plunk. For a moment, we just sat there. This fish and me. Its colorful body stood out against the white porcelain bowl. The scales reminded me of the jewelry my grandmother was buried in. Red and purple, shining bright in sunlight pouring in through the large church windows. I shook the thought from my head and flushed the toilet.

"Goodbye, uh. Fish."

Even after I gave the little old women her key back, having pocketed the spare from Casey's junk drawer, I couldn't stop thinking about that damned fish.

14

VISCUM ALBUM

SIXTEEN YEARS AGO

When I was eleven years old, my father and grandfather had the biggest fight I'd ever heard. The rest of us had gone to bed. My grandmother and mother had both gone to sleep. I could hear the argument as I descended the wooden stairs, carefully placing my slippered steps to avoid giving myself away from a groan or squeak. My father's voice became clearer.

"They are my daughters. I'll treat them as I see fit! They're mine!"

"You are an unfit father. It's shameful, the way you treat them. They deserve better than your madness."

Peeking around the corner, I just could see into the elegant sitting room. The Christmas tree still sparkled with tiny lights. Our stockings were hung over the fireplace. My grandfather sat in the large wingback chair with his whiskey, the picture of serenity, as my father strode around the room in a frenzy.

"What of your wife, Raoul? You brutalize her as well?"

"What I do with the woman I'm shackled to is none of your business. I don't care what she told you," my father seethed.

"No one told me. No one has to be told. What happened to her arm, huh? She didn't do that to herself."

The glass shattered against the door frame so quickly that I didn't have time to move. I only gasped. My grandfather's eyes moved swiftly to mine and softened. Standing, he crossed the room to me.

"Bambina, what are you doing out of bed?"

"I heard shouting," I said quietly. Such a mistake to get out of bed. My father's stare burned into me, promising nothing but pain for this breach of his privacy. Still, Nonno took my hand and stood.

"I am taking her back to bed. We are not finished with this."

"Yes, we are." My father's words were a cold promise.

Squeezing my grandfather's hand, I sighed. I wanted to be here always. In this house. When I was here, I knew nothing would harm me. He wouldn't let it.

"Are you excited for the morning, mia principessa?"

I nodded. Christmas at my grandfather's house was the best. The whole day would be nothing but cookies and presents. We had come back to his house after mass because that was the family tradition. Nonna had gone to sleep after she and Rita finished cleaning the kitchen. The scent of shallots and wine still hung in the air. Nonno gave me a squeeze as we arrived at my bed.

"Is Papa mad at me?" A leading question. I knew the answer, but I also knew he would protect me.

"He's mad at me," he sighed. Perhaps that was the truth. My eyes started to feel heavy with sleep as he stroked my head. "Don't worry about your father. I'll deal with him."

I lay in bed and pretended to sleep until I knew he was gone. My feet were light as I placed one carefully in front of the other. The door knob made small ticks as it twisted in my hand. Just a few small steps and I was at her door. That knob didn't make a sound as I'd turned it.

"Come on," Kaia mumbled from her bed.

I shuffled quickly to her side and crawled under the covers. The bed was warm. It may have been a twin, but it was big enough for the two of us.

"How did you know it was me?"

"Because Father doesn't sneak."

My father would get upset over a small mistake my sister made or some imagined slight against him. Much like a large child himself, he would find small things to justify his rage and we always paid the penalty. When it was my turn to experience his madness, it was never quite as bad as it was for Kaia. My sister would always find a way to redirect his attention toward her. I hadn't seen his attack this night, but I'd heard it. My mother begged him to stop, as my sister only grunted in pain.

"Oh," I sighed. Her face was mostly obscured by darkness, but I could make out the yellowing bruises on her cheek. The ring around her eye had started to fade. "Does it still hurt?"

"No," she lied.

"Nonno said he'll deal with him." She put an arm around me and I moved closer to her. A hiss sounded through her teeth as my back connected with her ribs. "I heard him yelling at Father. He knows."

"It's not going to fix anything, Lili. Go to sleep," she groaned.

"Nonno won't let him hurt us. I know it."

"Nonno can't do anything when he's not around. Everything will go back to the way it was. Just like it always does."

The bedroom was dark and quiet. We were both thinking about the same thing. Christmas morning would come and Father would act like he loved us. He'd present us with gifts, hug us and smile. It was a grand act for everyone around us. People believed he was kind. They believed he was a good father. But they didn't know the way he screamed at us behind closed doors. They weren't familiar with the timbre of his voice when it cracked with anger.

Eventually, the injuries we endured left scars that weren't visible to anyone else. Our bedrooms, places that should have been a space to escape to, became torture chambers at night. While our mother slept down the hall, he would take his time forcing us to endure his sadism. He'd demand that we remain silent during our punishment. It was only at our Nonno's house that we slept soundly in our beds.

Kaia blew out a ragged breath and sniffed. I didn't have to look at her to know she'd started to cry. I grabbed a tissue from the bedside table and passed it back to her. A low laugh sounded before she blew her nose and placed the crumpled tissue on the table behind her.

"It's not going to be like this forever, will it?" I mumbled to her.

"No, it won't be like this forever."

THE MORNING WENT on just as we expected. Our father put on a good show of being a loving family man for my grandfather's guests. Lupo and his family came for brunch, as they always did on Christmas Day. He was a little older than my father, but not by much. Along with his wife, he always brought their sons. Dante was a few years older than Kaia, and Nico was younger than me. His wife brought dozens of cookies she'd made from scratch. The lemon ones were my favorites. She'd send me home with extras, but Father always ate them.

Nonna put on some stop-motion Christmas movies for Nico and me to watch. I was getting a little too old for them, but I didn't mind. Dante and Kaia sat outside on the terrace and talked. Whatever was bothering my sister, I knew she would tell him. He'd been her best friend for as long as I could remember. They would venture off whenever our families gathered for any holiday.

Christmas in Southern California was as temperate as the rest of the year. The sky was still blue and the flowers hanging over the terrace still bloomed. As Nico laughed at the misfit toys, I watched his older brother put his arm around Kaia's shoulders. She had been quiet all morning. Just as she had been the day before and every day since our father beat her for talking back to him.

My mother had thrown herself between them, trying to stop it. Every day, a part of the woman who cared for me chipped away. Grew wilder. Less tolerant of my father's outbursts. She had tried to protect us as best she could. Once she had tried to pack up and leave. She almost made it to the freeway when she was pulled over by a police officer who'd simply said, "Mrs. Caccia, go home. Your husband wants to speak with you."

My father dropped us at Nonno's house, telling us that our mother was "sick."

"She's not fucking sick. You are."

Those were the words that Kaia spat at him in front of Nonno. The words that earned her every bruise she'd gotten since.

Kaia rested her head in her hands and, as her shoulders shook, Dante's hand stroked her back in silent solidarity. Nico's loud laughter grabbed my attention as I saw his mother walking around with a tray of cookies. The lemon ones. I followed her with my eyes as she went to my mother, who sat quietly on the sofa next to my father. Wincing as she shifted her sling, she gave up and reached for the cookies with her left hand.

When the cookies came to me, I took one. As my mother sat with a cookie in her open palm, I clutched mine until it disintegrated into crumbs.

15

BRUGMANSIA

As I walked toward Pal's, I saw the shop was incredibly busy. The little deli had a line going out the door and there was hardly room to move around. People stood shoulder to shoulder to get to the counter, even though only people who had tickets were being served. Still, little old ladies had been known to draw blood for the roast beef sandwiches at Pal's.

Pal's was the first legitimate business my great-grandfather owned, after going from penniless immigrant to Niccolò Bianchi's right-hand man. A portrait of my great grandparents watched over the madness with placid expressions. They were standing in front of their first home. It was in this house that Matteo Caccia, my Nonno, was born. Giorgio and Maria worked tirelessly to provide for their family, but it never seemed to be enough. Fortunately, that was when the glitz and glamour of Hollywood started to blossom around them.

Still managing to get by with odd jobs and a functional understanding of the English language, Giorgio eventually got work on film sets. Occasionally his dark features and good looks even got him small roles as a mustache-twirling bad guy. Giorgio took every job he could get, which is how he fell in with Bianchi.

It was Niccolò Bianchi who convinced Giorgio Caccia that if he was going to make a place for his family in the United States, the only way to do it was outside of the law. Giorgio took advantage of the jobs Bianchi sent his way. At first, they were innocuous, but soon picking up packages and messages turned into delivering bootlegged liquor to speakeasies around town and shaking down people who owed his boss money. Bianchi started trusting my great-grandfather with more of his businesses until he was his second in command and the empire's reach extended over the greater Los Angeles area.

Thanks to the consistent work and connections at his fingertips, Giorgio invested his own time and money into growing his wealth. Because he married a smart woman, he did it quickly. Maria Caccia had met many men in Hollywood, desperate for their chance at becoming film legends. These men would not have looked twice at Giorgio when he was laboring on sets, but they took notice of him when he wore expensive suits and dined extravagantly beside them in restaurants they could barely afford.

It was those same Hollywood types who came around asking Giorgio for help financing their films, which they got. Whether the film was a success or not, he always got his money back and then some. It was that money that started Pal's.

People still talked about films my great-grandfather produced as they waited in line for their food. I heard someone mention one of several vampire features as I evaluated the crowd. Carefully knotted mozzarella and pillars of cured pork were ghostly silhouettes where they sat in the display case, now coated in condensation from the throng of anxious customers. I kept to the outside perimeter, careful not to upset the masses as I ducked behind the counter and made my way to the refrigerator in the back. Employees turned to ensure that no one had been bold enough to sneak behind them. Each face was relieved to find me there. The steel door clicked behind me as I let it drift shut.

"There must be a holiday or something coming because it's fucking nuts out there today," Gino grunted from under his hoodie.

"Sorry for the late notice," I said. Arranging this meeting was no more than a quick series of text messages in the early hours of the morning, but

I'd been thinking about it all night. Something niggling at me about Eros. Like pieces of a puzzle that didn't quite fit together. Gino grunted at my apology and glanced around the space.

The walk-in was cold, of course, but it was all the food that made it so distracting. Big rounds of beef, ready to be prepared for sandwiches. Salty provolone, several varieties of peppers, and Nonna's meatballs. As I eyed a tray of meatballs prepared with my grandmother's recipe, I wondered if people would be so anxious to get their food here if they knew what was happening just a few feet below them.

"I left my phone in the car like you asked. What's with all the cloak and dagger shit?"

"I need you to do something for me. You still have that MIT contact?"

He nodded. The MIT contact was a professor who had been in a bad way with his student debt and decided he was smart enough to gamble for the money to settle it. That didn't work out for him. Now he owed us. Gino shuddered as he glanced around the refrigerator, stopping to look at a prosciutto leg.

"I need him to break into the Eros server and get me access to two different user accounts. Can he do that?

"Sure, but you're gonna owe me a favor."

It was everything I could do to stifle my groan. Gino wasn't the kind of guy I wanted to owe favors to. The man knew exactly what my skill set was and had seen my expertise in action more than a few times. I knew that this favor I'd owe him would be called in quickly and it would be the kind that ended with blood on my hands. Lots of it. Still, I nodded my agreement and told him where the guy could send the information. With a slight shiver, he pulled the hood of his sweatshirt closed around his face.

"We done here? I'm fucking freezing," Gino jerked out.

"Yeah, yeah. We're done."

As we walked out from the back, I thought about the way the family used to be. When my grandfather was alive, the Caccia family was more like a conglomerate. Many more men were filling many more roles. Since a lot of those men didn't want to take orders from a girl, they turned on us. Those men eventually all got dealt with, now six feet under, and we ended up with a much smaller crew. Small batch, artisanal crime.

The crowds had doubled inside. I checked my phone. Lunchtime. I washed my hands, put on some gloves, and started building sandwiches from the order slips above the counter. I decided to stay until the crowd died down, maybe an hour or so later. As I packed deli meat into freshly cut rolls, I pictured my grandmother doing the same thing when she was a teenager. The family business had been part of the empire for decades even at that point, but my Nonna was one of its best employees. My Nonno was working hard for Bianchi. Running all over town, stealing what needed to be stolen, killing whoever needed to be killed. That is until he met my grandmother. Sometimes I wondered if my great-grandparents hired her just so my grandfather could meet a nice girl.

"The second she smiled at me, I was a changed man," Nonno had said.

Even after my grandparents married and she wanted for nothing, Nonna worked behind the counter at Pal's almost every day. Over the years, she added her own touch to things. People regularly bought her meatballs. I often brought home a tray when I was feeling sentimental.

When things had finally calmed down, I left the deli counter where my grandmother crafted a roast beef sandwich that changed my grandfather's life. On my way out, I picked up a box of cookies. Rainbow cookies, pignoli cookies, and delectable little lemon knots dotted with colorful sprinkles. I'd eaten the last of a box during some social media deep diving late last night and needed to restock. Investigating made me ravenous.

The cookies kept me company as I continued my search for any information on Casey and Isabelle's disappearance. Aside from West, Casey was the closest thing I'd had to a friend. I've never been very good at answering texts. Or phone calls. When I was working, I'd tend to tunnel into myself and float through my existence. When we did spend time together, it was always pleasant. She and her on-again/off-again boyfriend Tyler had hit the skids before she disappeared.

"He's just so possessive. I can't take it anymore," she'd said while pushing her wild red curls out of her face.

I'd thought about that conversation a lot since hearing about the disappearances. Frustrated by another dead end, I tossed my phone across my bed and got out every knife in my possession. Six throwing knives, one tactical knife. Technically, the tactical knife was a hunting knife. The floor was cool under my legs as I sat down and readied everything, flipping open the box of cookies a short, but safe distance away.

I needed to busy my hands. Do something I could control. Sometimes gardening helped. Sometimes cleaning. But my frenzied mood was sated by the cookies and meditative repetitive motion I'd submitted myself to. A lemon knot practically disintegrated on my tongue as I dragged my blade against the sharpening stone. The gritty surface made the steel sing, and my mind quieted at the noise.

When each blade was razor sharp and gleaming, I knew my work was done.

16

ACTAEA PACHYPODA

*K*eep *your fists up. You need to block what's comin' at you!" Lupo circled me, ready to strike again. I glanced down, hoping to check on my foot-work. Before I knew it, he'd clocked me in the chin. My head snapped back with the force.*

"If you were blocking properly, I couldn't've landed that."

The strike had landed brutally, but I knew he could hit harder than that. Before he was a bodyguard, he'd been fighting in the underground rings. The breeze sent a chill through me as it cooled the sweat covering my body. I forced the tears away from my eyes and huffed, raising my fists. Don't cry, I told my-self. Do not cry.

"You're just like your Nonno, you know that?" Lupo huffed. I glanced down at his feet. They were lightning fast compared to my slow little steps.

"Tough as nails?" Nonno had been sitting on the terrace, pretending not to watch as his bodyguard pummeled his granddaughter.

"Cocky," Lupo tossed over his shoulder toward his boss.

Nonno laughed. I tried to breathe through the radiating pain in my face as my grandfather shouted advice from across the yard.

"Keep your gloves up. A good defense..." he started, waiting for me to finish his prompt.

"Is the best offense, I know. I know," I snapped. He'd told me that at least a hundred times. Possibly more.

Nonno chuckled and resumed reading his newspaper. Like a lonely snare drum tapping out a lazy beat, I heard my sister practicing alone. Her knife throwing skills had improved. They were always well above mine. I would blame the weight or dullness of the blade, but there was only one simple truth. She was better. Thud after thud, the knives buried into the wood target with ferocious precision.

Eventually, I would be taught how to throw knives, but first I had to master hand-to-hand work with Lupo. Otherwise, my grandfather wouldn't let me near the knives. The next time Lupo lunged for me, his blue eyes blazing, I blocked him and landed a blow to his ribs. A choking laugh sounded from across the yard.

"That's it, bambina!" Nonno pumped his fist in the air.

Not to be outdone, Lupo lunged again. I heard his fist whoosh beside my ear as I dodged and struck again.

"There," Lupo said. "You understand now. Let's go again."

❧

"ALRIGHT, ALRIGHT!" THE man cried out as he fell to the ground. "I don't know where she is, I swear!"

Casey's ex-boyfriend was the jealous type. Not in a cute way. In a "she better not leave the house like that" sort of way. He controlled what she wore, who she spoke to, and everything she did outside of the club. I always found their relationship unsettling. He'd never hit her, but it was only a matter of time before he escalated his behavior.

"Bitch," he muttered.

I stood over him, my hood pulled over my head, almost totally obscured by the darkness of the parking garage. After clenching my jaw through the entire conversation, my head was starting to ache. He stared up at me with fear and anger in his eyes, which had started to go black from the broken nose I'd just given him. The pounding in my head would subside. Eventually. My knuckles would probably bruise a little.

"Ok, Tyler. I'm going to ask you one more time. Only once because I really fucking hate repeating myself. When was the last time you saw Casey?"

"Two weeks ago, when she fucking dumped me."

"Language, Tyler," I smirked as I watched blood drip from his nose. It was oddly satisfying. Was he trembling?

"Fuck you!" He cried as he spat at my shoes. My boot met with his gut in a swift but soft thud. For being such a gangly guy, he had a soft belly. The blow jolted him hard enough to make him gag. I looked down at the sniveling creature at my feet. Tyler was a typical variety of man, moving to Los Angeles to pursue his dream of being a musician. A Black Keys listening, Arcade Fire plagiarizing asshole. Staring down at him, I couldn't really understand what Casey had seen in the worm, but it hardly mattered now.

I squatted down to him as he retched in the fetal position beside his car. Pathetic. But I wasn't done with him. I loosed my knife from its sheath and scraped the blade against his pathetic hipster beard. The animal in my head growled, *punish him*.

"If I find out that you've lied to me, Tyler, you will regret it. You can't even imagine the ways I can make you suffer." I leaned in close to his ear. "And I will enjoy. Doing it."

The puddle of man made a confirming whimper. I stood and walked toward my car, cell phone in hand, dialing my sister. The speakers connected to my phone as I sat in the driver's seat.

"Apparently she and the boyfriend broke up two weeks ago." I started, clipping myself in with my seatbelt.

"You believe that?" Kaia queried.

"I guess. We should still keep an eye on him, but the pool of piss he made certainly smelled like he was telling the truth."

Kaia chuckled on the other end. "You know, I think I would have liked to see that."

I laughed my agreement and started the car, noticing Tyler begin to push himself up. A twinge of cruelty tugged at me as a nasty little idea took hold.

Revving my engine, I sped the short distance to him and stopped suddenly near his long legs. He yelped like a trapped rodent at the near-miss.

"What did you just do?" Kaia sounded more stern.

"Nothing," I righted the car and drove off, looking at the shaking man in my rearview mirror. I couldn't help the smile on my face when I noticed him collapse into sobs. "Just entertaining myself. Are you at home?"

"No, I'm at the club."

THE POUNDING BEAT of M.I.A. sounded through the club as I made my way to Kaia's office. Teal and red lights painted Maya's face and made the white mesh bodysuit beam against her skin. Hoots sounded from the men throwing bills at her as she climbed the pole. It was always hard not to watch her. She made dancing look like art, even if that wasn't why the customers were there. I'd always respect her for that.

As I reached the second floor, I saw that the VIP booths were full. Several meetings were happening at once. Some men were arguing, others were drinking. I saw one executive woman sitting among them, looking more uncomfortable by the minute. In a moment of pity for the poor woman, I grabbed a waitress and had a bottle of champagne sent to the table. If she had to be here, she should at least be drinking the good stuff.

I pushed on the bit of wall that hid the office entrance and went through the short antechamber to her office. Nico was sitting on the sofa, relaxed but tracking me with his hand on his gun as I came through the door. Kaia had her feet up on the desk and a glass of wine in her hand.

"Ozzie was just here," she muttered as a means of explanation. I picked up the bottle on the bar. It was near empty.

"Do you need a ride home?"

"Nico will drive me."

I nodded. As if on cue, the dark-haired man made his way across the room with a glass of water, stopping to set it in front of my sister.

"She needs some sleep," he said to me. Even though Nico was practically a brother to us, he knew better than to give Kaia commands. Kaia swallowed the last of her wine and sat up suddenly, only to fall back into her chair.

"Jesus, was the meeting really that bad?"

My sister glowered at me with an angrily arched eyebrow.

"You know that man questions me every chance he gets. It seems I'm not doing enough to strong-arm the Arawn clan into submitting to us." Waving her hand along the empty glass like a genteel lady, she grinned. "Obviously, I don't agree."

"What does he think we should do?"

"Why does it matter?" She shouted her question at me. This wasn't a conversation for tonight. I shrugged.

"I guess it doesn't. You're in charge. He should trust your judgment."

Kaia nodded and quietly hiccupped. It was time for her to go home and sleep it off. The fact that she'd climbed this far into a bottle was bad. My sister always told me she hated feeling drunk. To lose control of her thoughts at any time was dangerous as a boss. But it was always dangerous to show any type of weakness. It was why we never hugged in public. It was also why Daniel only got affection within the confines of their home. We knew better than to show our hearts to the world.

Nico slipped his arms under my sister's and lifted her from the chair, pressing the water glass into one of her hands. Gulping down, it took only a moment for her to compose herself. I knew what she was thinking. As drunk as she may have been, she couldn't be seen stumbling out of the club. Watching her pull herself together was quite a sight.

"Pop wants you to come over for dinner soon," Nico said as we watched Kaia carefully navigate the stairs to the main floor.

"I will. Text me," I said. Nico nodded. In this light, he looked just like his father. A square jaw and sharp blue eyes that didn't miss a thing. Just like Nico, Lupo was practically family. I wouldn't deny that man anything. My sister's walk to the parking lot was an act of pure grace. She pulled off the guise of sobriety as though she'd never touched a drink in her life, even though she reeked of cabernet.

"She's safe with you," I said to Nico. Not a question, but a promise of pain if anything happened to her. He nodded, understanding my meaning.

As I watched Nico load her into his car and drive off, I resolved to swing by Tommy's and grab a burger before heading home. Still riding the high of beating Tyler into the ground, I needed to blow off some steam before I could go to bed. Glancing down at my hands, I noticed a little of his blood had stayed on my slightly bruised knuckles. I'd have to wash that off before I ate. Who knows where that guy had been?

I turned and saw West leaning against the wall. He'd been there the entire time, but I was too consumed with getting Kaia home to notice him. The cold night had him in his shearling-lined jacket, a book sticking out of the pocket. His hair was pulled halfway up, which told me he had been playing with it recently. That hairstyle had a way of disappearing after only a few minutes.

"Forget something?" He asked as his eyes drifted to my hands.

"I just, uh, need to wash up." I looked down at my hands again. Tyler must have bled on me when I cracked his septum. West looked at my blood-stained knuckles, then back at me.

"I take it that isn't your blood."

"You should see the other guy," I joked as I shook my head and stepped back into the club.

17

TOXICODENDRON VERNIX

The lobby of Camden Industries was completely silent at night. Few people worked late. Even fewer did so at the office. As I walked to the elevator bank, the sound of my stilettos clicking against the marble filled the space. I'd been invited to a company dinner. Not a prospect I looked forward to, but one I couldn't pass up. Or at least, it was implied that I couldn't when Juliet mentioned it over the phone. The opportunity to slip into the offices was too enticing to miss. I just needed to find a way to slip away unnoticed.

I shifted in my heels as the elevator brought me up to the top of the building. The simple white sheath dress was comfortable enough, but the shoes were pinching my feet.

When the doors slid open, I was presented with a large space. The room was illuminated by the warm glow of an LED ring chandelier that hung over the massive brutalist dining table. Aside from the dining table and severe-looking chairs that surrounded it, there was nothing else. Each wall was made of glass, all looking out over the city. On one side, the wall was tilted open to offer guests access to the terrace. I would have enjoyed the view if everything else hadn't been so cold. Quietly, I was musing to myself that it reminded me of a Bond villain's lair when Benjamin sidled up next to me.

"Beautiful, isn't it?" he asked as he wrapped an arm around my waist.

"Uh, yes. It's a spectacular view."

He nodded. It was beautiful, really, but it would be difficult not to be taken in by the city lights. We rounded the large table and he escorted me to my seat. There were no place cards. Either Benjamin took whatever seat he pleased or everyone sat in the same place every time. Neither answer would have surprised me very much as I looked around at his associates.

These men were not used to intelligent conversations with women. I hadn't said a word in over an hour. Neither had any of the other women in attendance. I looked down at my plate, pushing around the meager portions as Benjamin and his associates discussed market dynamics. Or something. Honestly, I wasn't listening. Instead, I took in the other guests and tried to guess things about their personal lives. Things no one would know.

One of the financial advisors had a rope burn on his wrist that he was trying to conceal with an expensive watch, which meant that either he had recently survived kidnapping or he was into being tied up. He made furtive little glances for approval to the woman he'd brought, which meant that she was probably the one tying the knots. Neither of them wore rings, which meant that either they weren't spouses or their spouses weren't here.

The president of the company did not want to be at this dinner. Both he and his wife kept looking at their watches. If they both had somewhere else to be, it was probably at home. They had matching sets of tired eyes that ruled out any other after-dinner plans. The early hour indicated that it was most likely because of a small child they wanted to tuck into bed.

Benjamin's cracking knuckles brought my attention back to the conversation. I was far from a behavioral scientist, but even an expert would be able to discern that whatever he'd just been told had upset him.

"I'm sorry, Mr. Camden, but we're just not seeing the kind of return we expected."

I took his hand and pulled it under the table. I didn't know much about

Benjamin. I didn't know much about business. But a lifetime spent around men like my grandfather taught me that showing your hand in a room full of people was never a good idea. Benjamin's eyes narrowed at the touch, glancing at me for just a moment, and returning to his financial advisor. As though he understood my silent plea, a poisonous smile spread across his face.

"Well, I'm sure you'll find a way to make it work."

His hand felt warm in mine, but still tense. As his financial advisor continued speaking, the tension in his fingers increased. I let myself look at him, trying to maintain a neutral facial expression. The thick, dark furrow of his brow was straining against the rest of his features. The perfect, easy smile didn't quite stretch wide enough to show the dimples he possessed. Cold blue eyes wrinkled at the corners to indicate polite amusement, but seated beside him, I could see the tick of muscle in his jaw. Coupled with the eyebrows, I knew that this was a man on the edge and that smile was a trap.

Without thinking, I rubbed the toe of my shoe against his ankle. He didn't look at me, but an eyebrow quirked up. As if in response, his leg brushed mine under the table. I'd started the game, but I couldn't finish it. A chill rushed under my skin and I bit into my lip to prevent yelping at the sensation. Touché, Camden.

After dinner, men milled about the room, swirling liquor in tiny glasses while discussing this and that. I wandered away after one man brought up his golf handicap. It felt like the perfect opportunity to sneak off until I felt a hand on my shoulder.

"Come with me," Benjamin whispered as he guided me toward the elevator. He had been about to say something else when the company president stepped on board with his wife.

"Heading home, Camden?" The man asked. His wife gave him a reproachful nudge.

"No, more work to be done. You?"

"Sadly, yes," the wife said. "Company dinners are about as lively as things get for us since Liam came along."

I did a tiny victory dance in my head. Benjamin only nodded. The doors slid open on our floor and we said goodnight to the tired parents as we stepped off. Benjamin took my hand and lead me toward his office.

When we took a right turn as I was ready for a left, I got confused. Instead of going into his office, we entered a small room I'd not noticed before. The lights flicked on at our entrance and I realized he'd taken me to the kitchen. Benjamin dropped my hand and strode toward the refrigerator. I looked around the room and wondered if it was there only for him or if the receptionist and his assistant were allowed to use it, too.

"Here," he said as he presented me with a spoon. In his other hand was a pint of ice cream. When I raised my eyebrows at him, he explained. "I'm always hungry after those things."

"You didn't seem to eat much," I said as I hopped onto the counter. Every moment in those point-toe shoes was agony. He tilted the pint toward me and I dipped the spoon in for a bite.

"Eating isn't really the point."

"What flavor is this?" The ice cream had a familiar herbal quality to it and I'd just bitten down on something like a cookie.

"Earl Grey and shortbread," he said as he stole the spoon for a bite.

"God, you're so British."

He laughed and shook his head as he spooned more ice cream into his mouth. I grabbed the spoon back and chased a chunk of shortbread around with the tip.

"Thank you for your help tonight."

I shrugged and dug out a chunk of shortbread. As the cool, creamy treat dissolved on my tongue, I debated telling him about all of the practice I'd had in de-escalating situations as a little girl. Instead, I just smiled and took another bite.

SOMETIMES WHEN PEOPLE die, their family feels an obligation to exaggerate their good qualities. They speak about them in a reverent and loving manner. Kaia and I were never like that with our parents. Our mother faded away from us well before she died, and our father...His end was such a relief to us that we never spoke of him. Almost as if we were afraid of invoking his presence like Bloody Mary or the Candyman.

My parents were buried next to each other, but their graves looked like they belonged to strangers. Their headstones matched. Both granite, both engraved. Each with a flowery epitaph. But one was dusty and forgotten. The other gleamed with years of tender love and care.

Adriana Caccia. Beloved wife and mother. That was all her life boiled down to. The fact that her identity would always be tied to my father's made my stomach turn. To look at it, you would never know how smart she was. Or brave. I squatted to pick leaves off of her grave. The flowers I'd left last week were already dried and brown. I came here every week, but I could only get Kaia out here on her birthday.

Neither of us bothered with my father after Nonno died. Looking over it, sometimes I wondered if I should be angry with him or pity him. He was gone. He couldn't hurt us anymore. His last moments were painful, and it was what he deserved. But so were hers.

I hardly visited Nonno, but he wasn't buried here. When Maria died, they built a mausoleum for her. Heartbroken, Giorgio soon followed. My grandfather was entombed with his parents, along with his wife. The structure wasn't far from where I sat, but it felt like miles away. Still, Kaia and I would leave a wreath of poinsettias on the door every Christmas, along with a few powdery wedding cookies. Animals probably ate the cookies, but it was our tradition.

The black stone looked stark against the green grass. My mother would have preferred something softer and more natural looking. I thought about all of the flowers she used to keep in the house as I replaced the wilted blooms I'd left the week before. Fresh, bright sunflowers stood out like triplet suns against the starry darkness of the granite. She'd like that, at least. My knees protested as I sat down before her headstone, crossing my legs like a child in a reading circle.

"Do you like my haircut?" I asked the stone with a laugh. "It's for work."

I sighed. For a moment, I just sat there and toyed with the zipper on my jacket. Some weeks, I'd chat away about a problem I needed to work out. Other times I'd just sit silently. As the zipper clicked through the metal teeth, I wondered if she were alive, would I call her every day? Would she pester me about settling down? Maybe she would have wanted grandchildren. I chucked to myself at the thought.

A soft breeze stirred the leaves on my father's grave. This was a nice cemetery, so the groundskeepers wouldn't let things fall into too much disrepair. Compared to my father's grave, my mother's was immaculate. I loosed a sigh at the sight and started fidgeting with my jacket again. I spoke before I knew what I was saying.

"Sometimes I think I might be more like him than I am like you."

Saying the words out loud made my eyes sting. A shaky breath blew past my lips as tears threatened to stain my cheeks. It wasn't something Kaia had to worry about. Every time I watched her with Daniel, I saw the loving mother she had become. When she was doing business, she was every bit our grandfather's rightful heir. My sister would never follow in my father's footsteps because she was the best person I knew. The thought that I'd be such a disappointment to my mother strangled me. I pulled my jacket further around me to ward off the thought.

"I guess since I'm worried about it, I shouldn't worry about it, right?"

The air grew colder the longer I sat there. I stayed until the sun started to go down. Until the thought that always drove me from here slipped into my mind. How many people are buried here because of me?

18

DIGITALIS

Social media was like a little time capsule. I was scrolling through Isabelle's feed again, trying to get any detail about her last few days online. Reclining on my bed with snacks I'd picked up from the gas station on the corner, I stuffed another couple of Hot Fries into my mouth and crunched.

It had been a long day. Like, a really long day. First, I had to bring Daniel his lunch at school after training at One-Two. That involved going to Kaia's to pick it up and then dropping it off. I had been a little disappointed to not see his curly mop when I came by, but the school made me leave it in the office for him. Then I had to swing by a few of the businesses we owned to pick up deposits. That money was then deposited in our legitimate accounts. The money from our other ventures got deposited into an offshore account after getting laundered through our online gambling company, which was based out of New Jersey. By the time I was done with all of that, I was fried. Picking up junk food at the gas station down the street was all I had in me.

I sucked the red dust off my fingers and continued scrolling through each and every post from the week of Isabelle's disappearance. This girl had been addicted to Instagram. Outfits, dinners, spin classes, brunches, and dates. Everything got a post. Every post got a lengthy caption and dozens of tags. It wasn't until I'd gotten to the bottom of my snack that I found something. She had gone to Vegas and had a very expensive dinner with a man who was not tagged in the post, but she did drop his first name. Isabelle had a habit of writing the world's longest captions for her photos. Missing it before had been sloppy. A wave of self-loathing crashed over me as I realized my mistake. I sat up and took a sip from my water bottle to wash down the spicy snack.

"Who the fuck is Henry?"

TORTURE IS AN interesting thing. It's not a skill that everyone can possess. First, you have to understand how the human mind works. While I didn't study it in school, I did learn a great deal from the human anatomy and physiology courses I'd taken. The rest I learned from the men who worked for my grandfather. Second, you have to have a strong stomach. I don't really have a strong stomach, but torture didn't make me vomit the way that killing often did.

It didn't happen all at once, my aptitude for torture. At first, I was just doing small jobs. Quick, quiet killing. Then the guys were told about the truth serum, a simple concoction made from angel's trumpet I could administer. That made me a regular fixture at interrogations. I watched the men exact their methods of torture and couldn't keep my mouth shut.

I'd say things like, "You know, it would be easier to remove the finger if you separate it from the joint."

They got so tired of my unsolicited advice that some would dare me to try it if I thought I could do better. So I did.

It was well after midnight and I had arrived exhausted. Carlo leaned against the wall and rubbed his eyes. Gino and Carlo had been working this guy over for hours, but they gave up and called me in because of my chemical expertise. I had known it wouldn't be long before Gino called in his favor. Unfortunately for me, his favor involved me driving all the way out to the Valley in the middle of the night. Pinching the bridge of my nose, I tried to force away the headache that was forming behind my eyes.

"So," I muttered to Carlo. "It's going to be about ten more minutes before the scopolamine takes effect. Then you can ask him whatever you want and cut him loose."

"Oh, we're not cutting him loose," Gino chuckled darkly. The three of us were standing in the dimly lit storage unit in the middle of the night. I suppose I shouldn't have assumed they were going to let this guy go. Thousands of dollars went missing from the Bootlegger's safe, and it had been pretty easily traced to the guy sitting in front of me. The walls and floor of this room were lined with black plastic sheeting. A single utility bulb hung from an extension cord that had been threaded from a beam. The small metal folding chair that this poor schmuck had been zip-tied to creaked under his weight when he struggled against his bindings.

I looked him over again. His face was already swollen and his broken nose was weeping blood onto his shirt. Wheezing and rasping let me know that these guys had probably broken some ribs. While it was an effective tactic most of the time, these guys had no finesse. Glancing at my phone, I determined we had six minutes left.

"What's this guy's name?" I asked.

"Kyle Stevinson," Carlo replied.

I nodded and took out my phone to start searching the internet.

This would be a lot easier if they had some leverage. These guys knew how to beat information out of men, but they didn't know how to scare it out of them. After a few minutes of scrounging for information, I had what I needed. Gesturing to the other guys to stay put, I kneeled before the battered man in the chair.

"Kyle," I purred. "This isn't going to end well for you. But you know that already, don't you?"

He whimpered. I turned my phone toward him and revealed the photos I'd found.

"It doesn't have to end badly for her, does it? Look at her. Look at that smile. She can move on. Find love. Maybe start a family. But if you don't tell us what we need to know, I'll hunt her down and pull out every single one of those pearly white teeth."

Kyle started to weep. I watched as tears and a running nose flooded his face, trailing through the blood that had begun to dry there. Gino stood, presumably to give him another beating. I put my finger up to indicate that I needed a minute and smiled as I pulled up the next photo on the girlfriend's social feed.

"Poor Madison. Oh look, she has a dog. Kyle, what's the dog's name? Guys, look at this." I held my phone up to Carlo, who nodded politely.

"His name is Pickles," he bit out with a jaw that was probably broken.

"Pickles! That's adorable. Guys, the dog's name is Pickles." Gino and Carlo chuckled. "Pickles is going to need a new mommy, Kyle."

"No, please. I'll tell you. Please."

I pocketed my phone.

"Yes, you will."

WHEN I GOT home, it was nearly dawn. Again, I'd stayed out all night. Exhaustion seeped into my bones as I stared into the middle distance. The floor felt like it was sinking and taking me with it. Down, down, down my mind went hurtling toward the familiar darkness. In a blink, I was back. *You need sleep;* I told myself, but first I needed to wash up. Kyle Stevinson was a bleeder.

As I watched the water cloud with his blood and curl down the drain, I could still hear the mournful cries of someone in agonizing pain as they'd been taken apart, bit by bit. This was all that was left of the young man who'd wronged the family in some way or another. In the steaming sterility of my shower, I couldn't remember the details. Didn't care to retain them. It was just another dead man. Instead, I'd watched as Gino and Carlo went to work on him. Bile rose in my throat.

Quickly turning off the water, I sank to my knees in front of the pale flamingo-colored toilet and erupted. There was the cold-hearted woman who'd watched that man get taken apart, piece by piece, and there was me. The woman who watched cartoons with her nephew. The woman who took care of her sister. Somehow, vomiting helped me feel less connected to the first woman. Like I was purging her from my system.

The spiral was consistent, but it never lasted long. Shaking in the bathroom, the space chilled by the early hour, I stood on the bathmat and collected myself. Goosebumps covered me from head to toe and the sun started to suggest its presence with a dim purple glow. Pulling on the old Nirvana tee shirt and a pair of briefs, I padded to my bed and threw myself into the messy nest of sheets and pillows.

For a while, I stared at the ceiling. Not sure what to do. I felt exhausted, but every time I closed my eyes, I saw Kyle's bleeding wounds. His detached limbs. I stayed like that for an hour before deciding to turn on the TV and put on a movie. Something animated. Something comforting. Something I could easily fall asleep to.

Shaking myself out of that state was becoming more difficult. It wasn't disgust or regret. Cold, unyielding fear gripped me and turned my gut every single time. Because if I was being honest with myself, really honest, then it wasn't because I was afraid of what I'd done. It's because I was afraid of who I was becoming.

19

ACTAEA RUBRA

I was still wet from the shower I'd taken after a particularly brutal work-out when an email came through from Juliet. It was a travel itinerary and suggestions for what to pack. Apparently, I was to appear on the arm of Benjamin Camden at an event at the Chandelier bar and we were flying private. I guess it paid to be the fake girlfriend of a billionaire. I sent a text to Kaia.

> Guess who's taking a private jet to Vegas tomorrow?
>
> It better be me.
>
> I'll be there for a few days.

I sent a winking emoji and responded to Juliet, letting her know I'd received the email and that I'd meet them at the airport. A small chill rolled through me as I thought about how much I hated to fly.

"Focus," I told myself. "One problem at a time."

It wouldn't take me long to pack since it was only for a few days, but I wanted to make sure I had everything I needed. Clothes for Lilith Caccia, Benjamin Camden's new fling, as well as all of the gear needed to hunt my prey.

WHEN I BOARDED the jet, Benjamin was on the phone. He was sitting on the leather sofa, wearing another expensive grey suit with his jacket neatly folded beside him. The vest was fully buttoned and covered most of the blue-striped Winchester shirt he had on. The dark brown waves on his head were neatly combed to one side. His steely blue eyes tracked me as I sat down, though he didn't say a word to me.

Flying from Los Angeles to Las Vegas felt like a waste in such an elaborate jet. While I was sure Benjamin excused the expense with some internalized value of his time, it felt excessive. Of course that could have been because of my distaste for flying in general. I'd been picturing a small charter plane, but this looked more like an executive lounge with wings. The large leather seats cradled us as a flight attendant brought around a high tea service on gold-lined china that felt impossibly delicate in my unrefined hands. A tapping fingernail against the teacup was the only sign of discomfort I'd allowed.

It wasn't until we were in the car, on the way to our hotel, that he'd even spoken. Even with his posh London accent, he seemed tired and agitated.

"Thank you for coming, Lilith. I trust that you have all the details for tonight's event."

"The Eros event with members, yes. I have everything."

"Good. We'll have time for you to get ready, but not much." He looked up from his phone to confirm I'd heard him.

I nodded my understanding and stared out the window. The signs on the Strip were glowing in the early evening light. Tourists packed the streets and refused flyers from men standing on street corners. I hadn't been to Vegas in a little while, though the Caccias did have some businesses here. Carlo handled that end of things for us. Our visits to Sin City were always brief, usually flying there and back in a day or we'd end up staying in someone's golf course adjacent home out by Lake Las Vegas. It was always tough talks with wise guys, never glad-handing businessmen.

BENJAMIN WAS ON the phone again as we entered the suite. He entered a bedroom and shut the door as I walked around the space. There was a wet bar to my left, stocked with everything we could ever need. To my right was a luxurious and modern sitting area with a large flat-screen TV. Huge glass doors lead out to the wraparound terrace that overlooked the fountain at the Bellagio and it was hard not to watch as the water danced to the music.

As I went to find my bedroom, I was met with a gigantic bathroom with marble fixtures. Pretty. Then a coat closet, but no other bedroom. I circled the suite, wondering if I'd missed it. I stalked toward the living room and examined the sofa, hoping for a sleeper. Nope. Just the one bed, then.

Great.

"Everything alright?" Benjamin said from the doorway. How long had he been standing there?

"There's only one bedroom," I muttered.

"Yes."

"I guess I didn't realize we'd be sharing the bed."

"Does that bother you?" He leaned against the doorway with a bemused look on his face. "Women I'm sleeping with don't usually want separate accommodations. I thought it would look odd."

"You think people are watching us that closely?"

"I think I'm watched that closely," he said as he rolled up his sleeves. "I've got some work to do before this evening. You can have the bedroom."

I tried not to look relieved.

THE PARTY WOULD be my first public appearance in our arrangement. While the dinner with his business associates required little of me, meeting strangers as Benjamin's "girlfriend" was going to be more of a challenge. As we rode the elevator down to the Chandelier bar, nerves started to get to me. Squeezing my hands into tight little fists didn't seem to be helping at all. The billionaire stood next to me in a startlingly deep blue suit that brought out his eyes. His hair was still perfectly coiffed and he'd swapped his pale blue shirt for a crisp white one. It was impossible for anyone to look that perfect.

I looked over our reflections in the elevator doors. Next to him, I looked like a different person. My black hair was tamed into waves and the rose gold cocktail dress I was wearing made the gold in my hazel eyes stand out. This girl wasn't someone I recognized, but she was beautiful.

"Are you ready?" Benjamin asked, seeming to ask himself more than me. I nodded and gave a tight smile.

"As ready as I'll ever be. I shouldn't talk much, right?"

"Just smile and laugh. It's what most of these men are accustomed to."

"Huh." I blew out a breath. This was going to be a long night.

"Lilith," Benjamin crooned as he placed his hand on my lower back, his voice lower than before. I turned to look at him, his face only inches from mine. "You're stunning."

The doors opened and he escorted us out of the little box, toward the cascading crystals of the Chandelier bar. We walked past the velvet ropes and guards, my escort needing no introduction to the formally attired guards at the door. Everything in the room screamed "touch me." Brilliant blue and fuchsia lights caught on the beads and illuminated the faces of everyone in attendance. Every person looked like a millionaire or a model. No one could look bad in this light.

Deep blue sofas were nestled in every alcove and perched upon by different Eros members. Two silver mirrored boxes were spaced evenly apart from each other in the space. It seemed like we'd arrived in time for the show to begin because as we entered, two girls took their places on top of the boxes. They were clad only in pearls and pearl-embellished undergarments. As they mounted the boxes, the lights lowered slightly and the music turned up in volume. The party had officially started.

Despite the perfect fit of my dress, it still felt like I was wearing someone else's clothes. Walking in someone else's shoes. Living someone else's life. I could feel eyes on me. Women around the room narrowed their eyes in jealous stares, leaning in to whisper to each other. I knew what they were saying.

Fraud.

Whore.

Gold Digger.

As far as they knew, I'd captured the golden god of the tech industry and would take him for all he was worth, just as any of them would hope to do. They didn't know I could buy and sell any of them ten times over. They also didn't know that I spent most of my time watching the life flicker out of the sort of men they were trying to catch. I was here to blend in with them. A fox in the henhouse. No. Not a fox. I smirked at the thought.

The luxuries that surrounded us were obvious, and if I'm being honest, unimpressive. My family has had money, plenty of it, for close to a century. From a young age, I learned the difference between artistry and opulence. Fine craftsmanship doesn't always come with a designer label. Some of these people wouldn't know craftsmanship if it slapped them in the face.

Benjamin's warm hand steered me toward the bar to retrieve a serving of champagne from the tower of glasses. It took all of two seconds for us to be hounded by Eros members who were anxious to talk to my date. Men wanted to talk business with him and women ignored me while trying to get the attention of the most attractive man in the room. I wasn't surprised by either. After a few minutes of women elbowing me out of the way, I'd had enough. Turning back to the bar, I ordered a whiskey.

"That's what I like to see. A girl who can hold her liquor."

A salt-and-pepper-haired man leaning on the bar gave me a carnivorous grin as I turned to him. The glass of whiskey skated across the marble bar top and I batted my eyelashes at the stranger. Fighting my introverted nature, I knew I had a job to do. I was going to smile, laugh, and flirt with the other men at this party for the information I needed, and this man was going to be my first victim.

"Well, I appreciate the finer things. Especially when they've got a little age on them."

"If that's true then, honey, you came here with the wrong man." The salt and pepper man leaned more closely and gave my whiskey-bearing hand a stroke with his knuckle, sending a shiver through me.

A hand pressed to my lower back and I flinched, not expecting the touch. Benjamin had joined me at my side and gave me a knowing look. My flinch had been a mistake.

"I'm afraid this one is spoken for, Henry. This is Lilith Caccia. Lilith, this is Henry Johnson. He's an investor in Eros and a proud member."

Henry lifted his glass to Benjamin, looking slightly dejected. A proud member of Eros. Henry. It couldn't be this easy, could it?

"A proud member, huh? Are you having a lot of luck with Eros ladies?"

"Not tonight," he laughed. His dark eyes raked over me and lingered on the more exposed areas. I started to wonder what his face would look like with a broken nose. "But I've had a few good dates so far."

"Well, they were lucky ladies. Maybe Las Vegas just wasn't their scene. Do you live here, Henry?" I asked, trying to sound as innocent as possible. I leaned into Benjamin, who was scanning the room.

"I do, most of the time, yes. Though I do divide my time between Los Angeles and New York as well. Also, the Bahamas when I'm lucky."

I gave a breathy, well-aren't-you-charming laugh and touched his arm. The woman seated at the bar next to him smacked her lips around a crunchy croquette, wet squelching noises falling out of her mouth. It was a little unpleasant, but Henry's face began screwing up as though every second was agony.

Interesting.

"Maybe I can lure you from Camden for a little getaway. I bet you'd look good on a nude beach."

Ugh, I groaned internally.

"Careful, Henry." Benjamin snarled. He was doing a good job of sounding jealous. A bubbly laugh was all I could do to break the tension as I gave him a reassuring peck on the cheek. Seeming to remember himself, Benjamin asked Henry to join him for drinks the next night.

That gave me enough time to find out as much as I could about this Las Vegas millionaire.

AFTER GETTING ONTO the elevator alone, I rubbed my jaw to unwind the muscles strained from a night filled with empty-headed smiles. All of that socialization had made me tired. Pretending to be someone I wasn't made it exhausting. I said the names to myself again and again, willing myself to remember them accurately despite the champagne. These people drank more in one night than I did in a week. I took my phone out of my Chanel clutch and typed the rest of the names I could remember into my notes. None of them were as interesting as Henry.

It took about 30 minutes to get changed out of my cocktail dress and completely cleanse the makeup from my face. Benjamin's very tidy dopp kit sat beside the opposite sink. A leather monogrammed bag, stainless steel straight razor, and lather brush for shaving were lined up in perfect symmetry. Beside his toothbrush and toothpaste sat a tiny black bottle of cologne. As I rinsed off my toothbrush, I wondered if his scent was thanks to that little bottle or if it was some mixture of that and something that was just, well, him.

All traces of Benjamin Camden's girlfriend were tucked away for the night. My physical exhaustion wasn't enough to send me off to sleep. Tossing and turning, I spent about an hour scrolling through social media. More photos of Benjamin and I were circulating on the gossip feeds, and it was more than a little unnerving. The plan was working. No one I met thought I was there to be anything other than his arm candy, a fact that still amazed me. The sleep thing didn't seem like it was going to happen, so I decided to get some water from the kitchenette.

"You're not sleeping."

My heart nearly jumped out of my chest. I hadn't heard him come in.

Benjamin stood next to the open refrigerator with a bottle of water in his hand. He was still dressed, though his suit jacket was draped across the island and his shirt was unbuttoned. The waves of his hair were disheveled, as though he had just run a hand through them. My toes curled slightly at the sight of him.

"No, I'm a little too wound up. I was coming out for, well, water."

He reached into the refrigerator and grabbed another bottle. I padded over to him and hoisted myself onto the countertop, thanking him as I took the bottle from his hand.

"You and I have a problem, I think."

"Oh?"

He turned and faced me. The tips of his fingers brushed my leg and I tensed.

"You have to get used to me touching you. If we're in mixed company, you can't flinch. This needs to look legitimate. My girlfriend would want me to touch her."

His hand grazed my knee and rested on my thigh.

"No, I do. I mean, I know that. This is just...it's new to me. Relationships like this aren't exactly in my repertoire."

He stepped closer and his hand slid up slightly. His fingers squeezed. My breath suddenly felt trapped. This man smelled better than he had any right to.

"I'm sure you've been with other men. This is just like that."

"It's not exactly like that. I don't think I'll end up heartbroken at the end of this."

"No?" His hand slid up further, his fingertips skimming the end of my shorts. The touch sent electricity through me. He took the hem of my boxers into his grip. "Who did these belong to?"

"Someone who didn't deserve them back."

"Someone who didn't deserve you." His voice lowered an octave. The fingers on my thigh had started making small strokes against my skin.

"Maybe..." I started. This was stupid. The next thing I said was going to be *very*, very stupid. "Maybe we should practice kissing."

"I don't need practice," he chuckled darkly.

"I mean, you said I should be comfortable with... touching. We should look comfortable doing that, shouldn't we?"

He nodded, stepping between my legs. His fingers moved up to grasp my hips.

"Try not to flinch."

His mouth slanted over mine, lips sensuous but closed. I wasn't sure what my goal was when I suggested this, but then I leaned into it. It's just kissing. I could stop at kissing, but I knew no one was going to believe something so chaste. Responding with my mouth, I opened and licked his upper lip. Soon my tongue was tangled with his as his hands gripped my ass. The brutality of his tongue made my body go weak. He was warm and tasted like the whiskey he'd been drinking all night. Smoke, a hint of orange, and money.

He pulled me toward him so our bodies were flush, his hard length rubbing against my stomach. The feel of him mixed with the leather and sage smell caused my self-control to combust. My fingers gripped his shirt as I writhed against him. Small and warm, need was curling through my body and I almost forgot he wasn't mine. The small groan he made into my mouth snapped me back to the present. I pulled away, unwrapping my legs from his hips. When had that happened? His head fell to my shoulder as he huffed out a sigh.

"Something wrong?" He murmured against my neck.

"No," I said, peeling his fingers off of me while hopping off the counter. "That was good. Good job. Well done. Goodnight."

I am the most awkward idiot on planet Earth.

Dangerous thoughts clouded my mind as I practically sprinted into the bedroom. Barricading myself in the adjoining bathroom, I tried to pull myself together. If I couldn't sleep before, I definitely wouldn't be able to now. The heat that had built in me was hard to ignore. This man was the very definition of a distraction. How was I supposed to keep doing this? I wasn't some international super-spy who can sleep with whoever the hell I wanted, consequences be damned. That thought didn't stop me from wanting it.

Not mine. Not mine. Not mine, I told myself.

Daring a glance out of the bathroom door, the bedroom was still empty. I tucked myself into the farthest edge of the bed, hoping to provide some distance. I must have drifted off because about an hour later, he came to bed. While I pretended to be asleep, I heard him arrange himself on the couch. Maybe he thought making our involvement physical would be as bad an idea as I did. Listening to his breath become slow and measured, I wondered how often billionaires slept on hotel sofas.

20

DATURA DISCOLOR

The rustle of a newspaper woke me. Wearing navy pajama pants, Benjamin was sipping a cup of tea and reading the Wall Street Journal while he sat on the sofa where he slept the night before. He didn't notice I was awake, so I took in the sight of him as I tiptoed into the room. His dark brown hair was thick and tousled from sleep, with a lone curl resting gently against his forehead. A shadow of stubble had grown where clean-shaven skin was the night before. Blue eyes skimmed the words on the page before they noticed me staring.

"Good morning," he said as he took a pull from his teacup. "Did you sleep well?"

I nodded. How he looked this good first thing in the morning, I had no idea. Folding the paper in his lap, I got the full view of the version of Mr. Benjamin Camden that women all over the world probably dream about. The tufts of dark chest hair curled across his chest and trailed down his torso, where they dipped below the waistband of his pants. I'd hoped my appraisal had gone unnoticed, but I was met with a raised eyebrow and a half-cocked grin curled on his lips.

"I have some business I need to attend to today. Will you be alright on your own?"

"Of course." This couldn't have worked out better if I had planned it. He nodded and walked to the bathroom. I may or may not have tracked every step.

When the shower sputtered on, I opened my phone and started digging as I paced around the room. Of all the men I met last night, Henry Johnson stood out the most. Now that I'd met a Henry here, a Henry who was an investor for Eros as well as a member, I had a lead.

Making my way back into the bedroom, I opened Isabelle's social media accounts again. She disappeared the day after her "romantic dinner date" post. The restaurant was tagged in the photo but not her date. I'd looked into security footage at the restaurant, but it yielded no results. Isabelle had entered alone. Several men had also entered alone. I sent a text to Kaia.

> Can you email me the security footage from the hotel?

I heard the shower turn off, threw myself back onto the bed, and clicked away from Isabelle's profile. Benjamin stepped out of the bathroom with a towel wrapped around him. It took every ounce of self-control I had to keep my gaze fixed on the phone. He walked into the closet and closed the door behind him, his incredible scent still hanging in the room.

An email alert bobbed onto the screen before me. Kaia sent the file with no note and no subject line. I chewed on a hangnail as I looked at the email. Because of Henry's proximity to Benjamin, I needed to keep my suspicion of him quiet. I had a feeling he wouldn't be pleased if I made an investor disappear.

Benjamin emerged from the closet looking like he'd walked off of the cover of a magazine. He fastened his Patek Philippe watch around his wrist and looked over at the fake girlfriend lounging in bed.

"Alright, darling. I'm off. Please don't stay in bed all day."

"What, no time for a kiss goodbye?" I said with a laugh.

He smirked. "Not today."

The door clicked closed behind him. I peeked out of the bedroom to make sure he'd really gone. Belly-flopping onto the bed, I opened the video and watched. And watched. And watched. It was unmistakable. Isabelle entered Sear at 9 PM. Followed closely by Henry fucking Johnson. While I was grateful that I didn't have to track him down, I did know I couldn't lure him out myself. Letting myself be the last person seen with him alive would be a huge mistake. Especially when we were now both publicly connected to Benjamin. But I knew someone who could help.

Fortunately, I had the presence of mind to pack some regular clothes. The girlfriend of Benjamin Camden would have to stay in this hotel room. She would draw too much attention in her flashy designer clothes that showed a lot of skin. Luckily for me, going unnoticed is something that I know how to do very well. I dug around the bottom of my bag and pulled out my boots, some jeans, and a tee shirt. The little ping of a text alert sounded from my phone on the nightstand.

Getting a man like Henry Johnson alone wouldn't be very difficult. All I had to do was lure the old dog into a tempting situation. Normally this would be something I'd do myself, but since he's a relatively well-known person, people would notice his disappearance quickly. That's where Ashlee came in.

Waiting to leave the hotel room gave me time to get my plan together. With Caccia associates scattered around Las Vegas, I pooled resources with text messages as I showered and brushed my teeth. You'd be amazed at how easy it is to get access to an empty warehouse in the middle of a business district for just one night. The thought made me chuckle as I made my way past the expensive shops down to the main floor. The casino was humming with the steady thrum of slot machines, only interrupted occasionally by chimes for winners.

LUCKILY FOR ME, prostitution was legal in Nevada and very attractive sex workers were easy to come by. In fact, they make good money. When I text messaged her, Ashlee was game to meet me for coffee and a walk down the strip. Once upon a time, she was a dancer at Muse and decided to leave us for a club in Las Vegas. Dancing turned into seeing men on the side and eventually she decided to do it full-time.

People-watching is one of my favorite pastimes. I'll pick people from out of a crowd and try to guess their story by little details I pick up from their appearance or mannerisms. This is what I was doing while I leaned against the railing in front of the Bellagio fountain. For being in the middle of the desert, it was a relatively temperate day. Tourists walked by this area in droves. My eyes searched the crowd for Ashlee as I took another bite of my pistachio gelato. Her iced oat milk vanilla latte sat sweating on the pillar next to me and I kept almost taking sips out of it. Bouncing blonde hair caught my eye. As she approached, I couldn't help but notice that Ashlee seemed to be doing quite well for herself. Clad in a pale pink Chanel tweed suit, she looked like a Park Avenue princess.

When she got close to me, I nudged my sunglasses back up my nose and fell into step beside her. She took her coffee from my grasp and had a sip. While she drank her coffee, I explained my plan. Nodding along, she only asked the odd question here and there. When I was finished, she agreed.

"I guess I kind of owe you."

"You don't owe me anything. You'll get paid for your time by him and by me, so consider it an opportunity to double your profits." I held out a small vial that she quickly pocketed.

She laughed and took a final sip of her coffee before tossing the cup into the trash.

"A fucking dark opportunity, if you ask me."

AS BENJAMIN AND I got ready for our dinner, I text messaged Ashlee to make sure she would be there. Henry was supposed to meet us for drinks before our reservation so that he and Benjamin could go over the loose ends from the event we attended the night before.

Ashlee was going to run into Henry Johnson as we were leaving and pique his interest. Coax him into staying. Get him nice and drunk. Lure him to a hotel room where he would pay for her services. Then she would leave as soon as he passed out from the sedative I'd given her.

Walking to the bar in stilettos had me thinking about the boots I had stashed in a rental car, along with a change of clothes more suited to my kind of work. Johnson sat across from me and kept touching my thigh while making bad jokes to Benjamin. I imagined shattering my wineglass, the broken stem like a stiletto in my hand as I plunged it into his throat. It was clear from his occasional nervous laughter that Johnson was not the man in control here. It was the one whose grip on my shoulder increased by the minute.

My eyes saw the blonde bombshell enter the room before Henry did. My fingers went up to my shoulder to meet Benjamin's hand, squeezing me there. Under the guise of getting him away from this perceived annoyance, I looked up at Benjamin sweetly.

"Baby, I'm hungry. Is our table ready?"

Benjamin nodded and extended a hand to Henry.

"If you'll excuse us. Goodnight, Henry." Benjamin said as he took my hand to escort me to our table. "Thank you," he whispered as we walked away. "I couldn't take another one of his idiotic jokes."

I glanced over my shoulder to see Ashlee sitting down next to Henry at the bar in a red dress. A siren ready to use her beauty to lure a man to certain doom.

21

ATROPA BELLADONNA

Behind closed doors, everybody breaks and I was ready to do some shattering. It was pretty easy to get access to everything I needed for the night. Flying private meant I could bring my tools with me without having to worry about getting through airport security. I'd left Benjamin claiming that my sister needed me to check on some business across town. He'd barely looked up from his laptop. The hardest part of this night was going to be getting the information I needed.

All of the hotels in Vegas, at least the nice ones, have comprehensive security feeds. I knew from watching them myself. So getting Henry, unconscious and drooling, out of Ashlee's rented room unseen took some coordinating. Fortunately, housekeeping's laundry bins were large enough to fit a grown man and all of the bedding it took to cover him. The extra help I'd called in arrived in time to help me lift him into the trunk of my car, where I drove him out to our little hideaway.

It's really quite astonishing how much you can learn about a person from the internet. Personal details are so easy to access now. Henry Johnson was what you would call old money. His ancestors made millions and their millions eventually turned into billions. Behind closed doors, Johnson liked to get his kicks by hiring women to dress up like little girls and perform sexual favors for him. The man was a walking, talking cliché. Unfortunately for this married family man, some of those women liked to talk.

After spending some time with the old bastard, I discovered that he had misophonia. This aural idiosyncrasy that makes every little human noise grating would be incredibly useful.

Damon Roma, my help for the evening, was one of the most successful underground fighters ever to step foot into the ring. I wondered how much money we'd given him over the years as I watched him idly spin a large gold signet ring around his pinky finger. I hadn't been foolish enough to think I could handle Henry's weight alone, so he helped me heave him into the trunk. Damon was as much covered in tattoos as he was in muscles, which, when paired with the wild glint in his eye, made him an intimidating figure.

When Henry finally started to come to, I was finishing up a frosted snack cake from the gas station. Benjamin's dining selection had subjected me to painfully small portions of elegant food all night. Once I was out of sight, I grabbed the first junk food I could get my hands on. *No wonder his girlfriends are so thin*, I'd thought as I stared down at my plate with a fake smile on my face.

Once I realized Henry was awake, I winked at Damon as I stuffed gum into my mouth. It made damp, loud squishing noises. Watching my captive squirm against his restraints was incredibly satisfying. Especially because I made the knots extra tight. My boots squeaked against the epoxy floor. I opened my mouth while I chewed and moved closer to him.

"Mr. Johnson, my friend and I have some questions for you. If I like your answers, this will go easy. If I don't, well..."

I leaned close to him while and luxuriated in blowing a large bubble, smacking and squishing on the gum once it popped. He groaned into his gag, eying Damon warily.

"Now, I'm going to remove this. Of course, you could scream, but no one will hear you in here." I laughed. "You know, I've actually never gotten to say that to someone before. That's fun."

Johnson didn't waste time with silence once his gag was off. Damon leaned against the wall and watched. I'd promised him he wouldn't have to actually do anything, but Henry didn't need to know that.

"You're just a little girl. I'm not afraid of you."

"I didn't ask," I said around another bubble. "Now shut up, so I can ask my questions. Where is Isabelle?"

"I don't know who that is."

I leaned into his ear and popped the bubble. Johnson squirmed against his restraints.

"Oh, Henry, I know we don't know each other very well, but you should know that I hate it when people lie to me. Where is Isabelle?"

"I don't know any Isabelle."

"Wrong. Look, Henry, I'm trying to be nice to you. Really. My friend here can make this painful for you. Very painful. And see that bag over there? I'm not using it on you yet. You don't want to know what's in my bag of tricks. So I'll ask you nicely one more time. Where is Isabelle?"

"I don't know. I don't know where she is."

I considered his response. He went from not knowing her to just not knowing where she is which meant that he knew more. *Of course he knew more.* It's why I was here. I wasn't joking when I told him I hate lying. I didn't fucking like it when people lied to me.

"Alright Henry, where did you last see Isabelle?"

"I told you I don't know where she is."

"But you knew where she was. You were with her two weeks ago at Ceasar's Palace. People saw you. Security footage saw you. I saw it with my own eyes. Did you leave together? Where did you go?"

"We went to my room," he stammered. His eyes shot to Damon again, worried about what his answers would bring upon him. The fool didn't know it was me he had to worry about.

"And?" The word roared out of me.

"And nothing! We went to my room. We fooled around. She wasn't supposed to," he stopped himself.

"Wasn't supposed to what? What, Henry?"

He started crying. My patience was about to shred like wet tissue. God, what a useless sack of shit. When the waves of rage reduced to small swells, my stomach dipped as realization washed over me. He was about to tell me Isabelle was dead.

"Alright, Henry. Alright. Don't cry." I stood up and retrieved my bag. I was tired of doing this the nice way. Whatever had happened to Isabelle, she definitely got less consideration than this asshole was getting from me. My little leather medical bag was prepped and ready for the rest of this interrogation.

"Henry, are you familiar with biochemistry at all?"

"What?" He sniffled.

I held up a tiny clear bottle. This bastard was going to tell me everything.

"Biochemistry, Henry. Try to pay attention."

I freed a needle and stabbed it into a bottle, pulling up the plunger as it filled with liquid.

"This is scopolamine. A rather large dose of it, actually. It's most commonly used as an anesthetic, but it has another use."

The syringe dropped a bit of liquid onto Johnson's shirt. He whimpered as a dark stain spread across his lap. Old Mr. Moneybags was pissing his pants.

"Aw, Henry. I thought you weren't scared of little girls like me. Now, listen up. This next part pertains to you."

The needle disappeared into his neck and I drained the syringe. My lips moved close to the shell of his ear.

"Scopolamine is also used as a sort of truth serum," I murmured. "This is my own recipe. Made from flowers in my little garden. So here's what's going to happen: I'm going to ask you my questions. You're going to tell me everything. If I'm satisfied with your answers, I'll let you live. If I'm not, you'll get to meet my other needle. Trust me when I tell you that the other needle is far less friendly than this one. Are you ready to start talking?"

THE WAITING. SOMETIMES it was my job to get information out of men. To squeeze it out, quietly. Every time I do, I have to wait for the serum to do its work. The Lullaby waited in its amber vial. I held it and looked at the milky white substance.

The drugs took a while to take effect, but it didn't matter. Johnson spent most of his lucid minutes crying. I'm not one to shame a man for crying, but it was very difficult to feel sorry for him. It took not a small amount of effort to fight the disgust that flowed through my veins like ice water. Leaning against the work table I'd prepared, I nibbled at bits of a hangnail. I know it's not a very ladylike habit, but it's been twenty-seven years and I still haven't broken it. Normally the late hour would have me flagging, but my desire to know exactly what happened to Isabelle was stronger than a Vietnamese coffee. After a while, I scraped my pocket knife under my nails to clear away debris. Since Damon wasn't the loquacious type, this interrogation had gotten incredibly boring. Breathing out an exasperated sigh, I hopped off the table.

"Ok. You said that Isabelle wasn't supposed to do something. What wasn't she supposed to do?"

"I thought we were having a good time. She seemed like she was having a good time."

I rolled my eyes. A small ache was starting to build behind my eyes. "Did you hurt her?"

"No! No. I didn't hurt her. I didn't mean to. She just... I don't know what happened."

"So something happened," I said through clenched teeth. "What? What happened?"

"She died."

My patience had been skating far too close to the edge before. Now it was falling off of a cliff. Another surge of rage pulsed through me. I slapped him hard enough to make my bones rattle. Damon flinched.

"People don't just die, Henry. How did she die?"

"She told me to do it. She told me to!"

"Told you to what? To kill her? That's pretty fucking hard to believe." I didn't recognize my voice as I screamed at him.

"No," he said with big, fat, self-pitying tears rolling down his bronzed and withered cheeks. "She told me she liked breath play. Like being strangled. I didn't know what I was doing. I didn't know that would happen."

My head started pounding. Isabelle was dead. Henry Johnson had strangled her to death. I thought about how many people engaged in play like that and walked away from it. People don't die from something like that. Not unless their partner wants them to. Henry wanted her to. That was pretty clear. The sinking feeling returned to my gut. I pinched the bridge of my nose and squeezed my eyes shut.

"Alright, Henry. Do you remember what happened afterward? What did you do with her body?"

He sobbed. The mistake wasn't killing the woman. It was that he'd been caught. My head was throbbing and my stomach churned. If he didn't know what was coming next, my body did. It was why I rented the car. It was why I asked Damon to come with me. It was also why there was a large rolling suitcase, gasoline, and kitchen matches in the trunk. The leather medical bag was still open on the folding table. The Lullaby was ready for him.

"The men at the hotel took care of it for me. They told me it happened all the time. They told me not to worry about it. I'm sorry. Fuck, I'm so sorry!" He wailed.

Of course they took care of it for him. A wealthy man killed a stripper and no one blinked. They just got rid of her and moved on. She didn't matter to them.

On the other end of the truth were two possible endings. The first was I could let the guy could walk away. That wasn't an option. He'd seen my face. He didn't know enough about me to be afraid to run to the cops. The last thing I needed was for Johnson to run and warn his friends about Camden's girlfriend.

I picked up the little brown bottle and swirled it in the light, making sure all the ingredients were well mixed. Johnson sobbed like a little boy lost in the grocery store. It would be easy to feel sorry for someone like that, but all I could think about was my friend Isabelle probably laying in some unmarked grave in the middle of the desert. The syringe swallowed the formula into its cavity, ready to bite.

Damon rolled up his sleeves and grabbed the car keys off of the work table. With a nod, he went to prepare for what was coming next.

Johnson's head drooped, shaking with his sobs. My stomach lurched as I approached him. With a steadying breath, I circled his back and stroked the top of his head. He sighed at the soothing contact, and his shoulders sagged. This time he didn't feel my needle. It would only be mere moments before he'd never feel anything ever again.

22

NICOTIANA TABACUM

TWENTY YEARS AGO

It took me about a year to find my groove as an assassin. Wet worker. Hit woman. Whatever you want to call me. I still had a bit of imposter syndrome about it. There isn't a school for assassins. It's not like you can take classes at a community college or watch a tutorial on YouTube. But all of my years earning diplomas and degrees made me a dedicated student.

Creeping through the night took practice. Tracking people down was a skill-set best honed over time. Lessons were learned the hard way. One time a guy woke up right as I was about to jab him with a needle and I got him in the eye. We both screamed.

If you're following someone, you have to assume that they're consumed by their own thoughts. Situations that require all of their attention are good for getting close. My favorite places to get near a target were at the grocery store or at the mall. They're usually lost in their thoughts or routine and I could pick up some snacks. I'd learned not to eat anything spicy on nights I was going to bump someone off. 'Flamin' Hot' anything feels as described when it's shooting out of your nostrils.

Our father and grandfather both did their fair share of killing. Nonno had taught my father everything he knew, just as he would eventually teach me. While Nonno was practically a surgeon with his blade work, my father took that knowledge and used to it inflict as much pain as he could.

I'd heard my grandfather's men talk about my father. They'd say that he had true darkness in him. They said it in hushed voices, looking over their shoulders for him like they were watching for a bogeyman. They weren't wrong. His soul, if he'd had one, was as black and dangerous as the La Brea tar pits. I'd understood the darkness he unleashed upon our family, but I wasn't familiar with the man that they knew. Not until I saw his work myself.

When they were doing business, my father listened to my grandfather and behaved accordingly, but behind his obedient expression was a wild thing stalking about in a cage, waiting for release. Often I'd wondered why I had no uncles or aunts like other children do. It was rare for men like my grandfather to sire only one child. But then I'd see that look in my father's eyes. The one that told me he'd been born different from my grandfather. Born broken. He thought that someday he'd get to rule over his father's empire, but that day would never come. A world ruled by Raoul Caccia was a terrifying thought.

I'd seen my father kill several times. He always seemed to enjoy it. While every time he'd killed a man in front of me would stay with me for the rest of my life, the first time was the one I thought about most often. Nestled above the Bootlegger's office was a small storage space. We'd gone to the restaurant to celebrate Kaia's birthday. When my father disappeared before dessert, I went looking for him and found him there. Only he wasn't alone. The lamp lit only the man in the chair, but I could see him stalking around in the shadows. Lurking like a beast in darkness. Huddled on the attic stairs, I peeked over the edge of the floor and watched my father work.

"Raoul, please, I swear to god. I don't know shit!"

"Mr. Caccia."

"What?" The man blinked sweat out of his eyes.

"When you address me, you call me Mr. Caccia."

He stepped into the light, but only slightly. I could see it reflected in his eyes, the gleam of his teeth as he smiled like the carnivore he was, and the knife. The knife I only saw for a second before it was deeply embedded in the man's thigh.

"Do you know where the femoral artery is?"

The man whimpered.

"That's the artery right here in your thigh." My father tapped his signet-ringed pinky finger next to the bleeding wound. "If I twist this blade, it gets cut. It gets cut and you're fucked. If you tell me what I need to know, you go free."

And he did. The man told him everything. Tears streamed down his face. My father's second wiped drool from the man's mouth with a hand-kerchief. When the man was done, my father knelt before him and thanked him. Then he twisted the blade.

Cruelty came just as easily as killing to Raoul Caccia. Men who stood in his path were soon eliminated in the most ruthless way possible. Unlike the methods his father espoused, Raoul would take his time ending lives. He relished the opportunity to draw pain from his victims, savoring it like a vampire drinking down blood from a vein. Our father was a master of torture. Sometimes I could still hear them beg for mercy.

"I guess that was bullshit about letting him go."

"It wasn't bullshit," my father said as he lit a cigarette. "Now he's free as a bird."

Smoke plumed out of his mouth as he leaned against the wall, watching the man in the chair bleed out. Blood pooled on the uneven floor beneath them, trailing toward the open stairwell. Toward me. I watched it creep across the floorboards, thick and red. When I looked up again, I saw my father's face. His eyes were fixed on me and an apex-predator smile glinted in the light. I could see every ravenous tooth.

The man's blood had leaked on to my shoes. Little red footsteps followed me to the ladie's room where I heaved up my dinner. It was the first time I'd seen a man die so brutally at my father's hands. The image was still with me, twenty years later. It was what drove me to my knees after every kill. Not the blood. Not the screaming. Just the darkness in his eyes.

When I returned to the table, my mother asked me where I had gone. I told her my stomach was upset and I'd gone to the bathroom. A half-truth. Concern marked her face as she looked me over. After all, what little girl wouldn't want cake? When my father rejoined our table, we all sang the Birthday song to Kaia as they brought her the gigantic piece of chocolate cake.

My father's stare burned into me with a cold smirk. It was as though he'd wanted me to learn this truth about him. The depth of his cruelty. The truth of his capabilities and the wicked nature that lurked behind his eyes. Eyes that he'd given to me.

23

ABRUS PRECATORIUS

Henry Johnson was a fucking heavy bastard. After spending the better part of my evening helping Damon cram his urine-soaked remains into an extra large pink suitcase, we rolled him back to my rental. The gas can I'd filled sloshed when we finally managed to heave him into the trunk. Sending the fighter home seemed like the logical thing to do since I didn't want him to know where Johnson's remains would end up. Also, the drive out to the desert gave me a lot of time to think. It seemed only fitting that Johnson's body would be disposed of in a way that matched Isabelle's end. My stomach had churned and ached as I waited for Henry to die, but it didn't lurch. Something about this felt right. It felt like...I couldn't think about that now.

Despite what I did for a living, I've never had to dispose of a body on my own before now. I knew what would make identifying Johnson's corpse unlikely. Sipping on the coffee I'd ordered with a corpse in my trunk, I slapped my thumbs against the steering wheel as "Sugar Daddy" played on the radio. The highway was almost deserted at this late hour and the city lights were well out of viewing range. I was far enough out of town, so I pulled the car over and unloaded my suitcase. Jacking the car up on one side to make it look like I'd gotten a flat, I dragged this man's bloated ass as far away from the highway as I could get on foot. I ticked down the list again in my mind. This felt like a final exam with really high stakes.

Between the drive out of town and digging the suitcase-sized hole in the ground, I'd left Benjamin for well over three hours to handle some "emergency family business" for my sister that I had been pretty fucking vague about. At least gardening had made me an efficient digger. The dirt and sweat on my face were starting to get in my eyes when my phone rang. It seemed my vague excuse had run its course on believability.

"Lilith, where are you?" Benjamin asked with a tinge of concern in his voice.

"I got a flat on my way back in. My ride should be here any minute. I'll be back soon enough," I lied. I looked down at the suitcase I'd just doused with gasoline and the gaping hole I'd dug with a cringe. Under the cover of night, no one would notice the smoke from the fire and I was far enough away from the highway that there wouldn't be much of a glow. The last thing I needed was for him to come looking for me.

"Alright, well I'm going to bed. Please drive carefully."

After he ended the call, I idly wondered if he'd waited up for me because he wanted to chat or if he'd wanted to continue what we'd started the night before. It didn't matter now. I took a match out of the box and struck it against the gritty side. The match ignited the pyre quickly. It took about an hour to burn Henry's body to my satisfaction. He wasn't completely gone. The fire would never be hot enough for that, but he was burned enough that he would be really difficult to identify. Even by experts.

His phone rang inside my bag, causing his wedding ring to vibrate against it. The wallet sat next to them quietly. I would dispose of it later. The cash was a welcome addition to my pocket, otherwise, I'd have no use for it. Henry certainly didn't need it or his watch anymore. A wealthy man threw away a woman like she was garbage, tossed away himself, and burned like trash. An eye for an eye, indeed.

THE HOTEL ROOM was dark and quiet upon my return, except for one light dimly illuminating the bedroom. Soft snoring increased in volume as I approached and noticed Benjamin asleep in the bed with a book resting on his bare chest. His dark curls were mussed with sleep, his face slack with relaxation. It was tempting to climb into bed next to him, but I knew I couldn't sleep without having a shower.

Like going to church every Sunday with Nonno, the shower helped me feel clean again. Desert and ash swirled down the drain as I washed the night off of me. The water was almost hot enough to melt the flesh of a human man, so it was the perfect temperature. Steam billowed out of the glass enclosure as I stood under the spray and let the hot water wash away the lingering scent of death.

Entering the bedroom again, I noticed that Benjamin had shut off the light and rolled over to go to sleep. I could sleep on the sofa. I should sleep on the sofa, but I wanted the soft luxurious bed. Digging had worn me out, and the fluffy pillows looked so tempting. The man, well, he looked tempting too. I climbed into bed next to Benjamin after I turned off the light and put his book on the nightstand.

"Long night?" Benjamin mumbled, his refined accent bedraggled with sleep. "Everything alright?"

"Yeah, it is now. I just need some sleep." I settled onto my stomach and nuzzled into the pillow beside his. "I promise I'll stay on top of the covers."

Benjamin hummed his acknowledgment and rolled to face me. I lay there in the darkness, looking at his powerful features now slackened against his pillow. The dark curl played gently over his forehead, tempting me to brush it away.

AS THE PLANE took off from the private little airstrip, I looked out at the desert and wondered where Isabelle's body might be. I thought about how it must have felt to have the life squeezed out of you, a little bit at a time. Did she know she was dying? All of the times I'd had hands wrapped around my throat, I thought that would be the last time. The one that killed me. But maybe there was a feeling beyond the burning pain and need for air. Like darkness swallowing you whole.

Though the flight from Las Vegas to the private airstrip had been a short one, I'd enjoyed several cups of coffee from the staff to make up for the late night. I threw my bag onto my bed and went straight for the bathroom because being trapped in traffic from the airport made me really have to pee. As soon as my cheeks hit the seat, I heard my phone ringing and cursed. Whoever was on the other end would have to wait. Satisfied with a now empty bladder, I washed my hands and dug my phone out of my bag.

1 missed call: Kaia.

Foraging in my refrigerator, I kicked myself for not buying anything to eat on the way home. Hunger and exhaustion nibbled at my patience as I closed the door and dialed my sister.

"I need you at the club. Now." Her words were clipped. Not good. This would not be good. "Bring the Lullaby."

"On my way," I said, gazing longingly at the bed. A low growl slipped from me as I picked up my car keys and headed back out the door.

THE CLUB WAS at capacity, which wasn't much of a surprise. Theo, our other bouncer, was always less discerning than West. Bass thudded through the air like everyone in the room had a unified heartbeat. The lights were low, everything covered in a pink glow as two girls I didn't know danced onstage. A man seated beside the stage threw fanned-out bills in the air. His friends patted him on the shoulder, handing him more bills to toss away. Bachelor party, then.

Kaia nodded at me as I entered the office. Nico stood behind her, casual to the naked eye, but years of training beside him told me he was on edge. Ready to fight. Seated in a guest chair across from her was a man I didn't recognize, but the hands bound to each arm told me this wasn't a friendly visit. Also, she'd asked me to come armed. If his lilting Irish accent wasn't enough to give him away, the smoking skull tattoo on his right hand did it for him. He was an Arawn man.

"Start again from the beginning," my sister commanded in her even, frost-bitten tone.

"One of your boys is a traitor."

"And I'm supposed to just take your word for it."

I took my place, leaning against the wall to his right. Behind him, but close enough that he could register my presence if he was at all worth his salt. Other families didn't know who Kaia employed to do her dirtiest jobs. All they knew was that her revenge, her justice, was dolled out swiftly. As silent and elusive as a shadow.

"I'm not blowing smoke up your skirt," he said as he glanced at Nico nervously. "Someone in your crew is spilling your secrets. Someone who has a lot of fucking information."

"But you can't tell me who," Kaia said. Not a question.

"All I know is that Ronan has been meeting with someone. Someone Caccia. He won't say what he knows or who it is, but they're making a lot of money we don't have from it."

"So you're telling me that one of my men is giving your boss information about our family? I can see you're an Arawn. You're not a young man, so I can assume you've been with the family for a long time. There will be consequences for your betrayal, I'm sure. I can't help but wonder why you're here, Mr. Wilde."

"Well, I thought it would be valuable information."

"And what value did you think this information had?" My sister leaned back in her chair. Her eyes drifted to me. An almost imperceptible nod was her silent command.

"One million dollars."

"One million dollars? That's it? One million dollars is all it takes to purchase your loyalty?"

The man stilled as he felt the stroke of my finger tracing down his neck. A quick death was a privilege in this world. In our world. It was a mercy my sister bestowed on this blackmailing turncoat because sending him back to the hands of his brethren meant unyielding pain he would never have survived.

"I'll consider it," she lied as the needle slipped beneath his skin. Nico winced slightly at the movement.

His body mass required a heavy dose, but he was out quickly. It was rare for me to do this in front of anyone else, especially my sister. A strange look crossed her face as Mr. Wilde's body relaxed into a state of sleep. Waves of nausea had begun to hit me before his breathing became infrequent, stopping altogether after only a few minutes.

"He could have been full of it. Just trying to shake us down," Nico said, piercing the silence we'd fallen into. My sister's eyes drifted to me, silently asking for my opinion.

"Is that what you think? He was lying?" I asked, unsure.

My sister took a steadying breath and stood from her seat. A few steps had her at the bar cabinet. Nico and I exchanged a look as she poured whiskey into a tumbler. As she raised the glass to her lips, she breathed an uneven sigh.

"No, I don't."

WITHOUT ANOTHER WORD, I left Kaia and Nico to deal with Wilde's remains. Thoughts of who the traitor might be plagued me with every step. Identifying the information being sold would narrow the field significantly, but until something happened, we would be in the dark. Just because this guy knew who Kaia was didn't mean that he knew our chain of command. The traitor could be some power-hungry grunt looking for a payout, but he'd have to be an idiot to toy with someone like Ronan Arawn. Maybe the problem would take care of itself.

As I made my way through the club, I noticed the bachelor party had dispersed. Some were seated at the bar. Others were still sitting by the stage. Then I saw the others moving toward the Champagne Room. Our Champagne Room was the dark sibling of the main space. No poles. No tables. Just separate little nooks where lonely souls came for a little company. The bachelor got tugged toward the room by one of the new dancers, who accepted the cash his friend slipped to her as she passed.

The ladies' room was empty when I entered. I thanked my luck for the small mercies as I locked the door behind me. My heaving and retching gasps were drowned out by the mix of pop and dance music. Four songs started and finished before I was able to pick myself up off the floor again.

24

URTICA DIOICA

Screaming split the silent night.

"No! Please! I'm sorry - I" Kaia's pleas washed over me. "Please!" She sobbed.

"Which one?"

She wept.

Mother swept into our bedroom, surprised to find me awake.

"Sh...bambina." She put her delicate hands over my ears. Too late. The blade connected with flesh and bone before the thick thud it made into the kitchen table.

After our father stormed out, going wherever he always went, my mother called the family surgeon. I sat at the table, watching him reattach the tip of Kaia's pinky finger.

I lurched up from bed, covered in a thin sheen of sweat. The studio was dark and silent, but my father's presence hung like smoke in the air.

THE LATE AFTERNOON heat insisted upon the gym. Lupo's new boxer was punching a bag, filling the room with a slapping rhythm of leather hitting leather. I tried to stay focused and let my breathing steady me. Drops of sweat tapped onto the mat as I held the plank position. Burning pain lashed through my core.

"Wow, three minutes," West said when my knees finally hit the floor.

"Okay, what next?" I breathed face down on the mat.

"Maybe you should take a break."

"I don't need a break," I snapped.

"Then I'm taking one," West grunted as he walked to our water bottles. As he drank down gulps of water, I walked over to him and begrudgingly picked up my bottle. The cool water went down in jagged gulps. West eyed me warily.

"What's up with you today?"

"Nothing."

"It doesn't seem like nothing."

I picked up my wrist wraps and started covering my hands. West remained quiet as if waiting for an answer. After finishing the wraps, I walked over to the speed bag and started pummeling. All I wanted to hear was my breath and the bag. Counting strikes helped to quiet the word I'd been thinking since Johnson blubbered his truth to me. Failure. I'd failed her. It filled my ears, louder than the beat of the bag. So much so that when West spoke, I didn't hear him.

"Is this about Camden?" He asked again, stepping into my line of sight.

"No, it's not about him. Actually," I stopped myself before going on. He didn't need to know what was happening between us. I didn't know what it was, so I could hardly explain it to anyone else. I sure as hell didn't want to talk about Isabelle. How I kept picturing her death with two hands wrapped around her neck, squeezing the life out of her until it was me who was getting strangled. It had clouded my nightmares until everything was dark and all I could see were hazel eyes, my eyes that followed me like a bad omen.

"Actually, what?"

"I have a date with him later."

West's brows furrowed as his lips pressed into a thin line. His hand snapped out and grabbed the speed bag before I could hit it again.

"That's enough."

A frustrated sigh escaped me as I tossed him an angry look. He picked up a pair of punch mitts and motioned to my gloves.

"Put those on."

The gloves slid over my wraps as I kept my eyes on him. West steadied himself and waved me over.

"Alright, give it to me," he said as he raised the mitts.

"What?"

"Everything. Right here."

BY THE TIME I was done punching those mitts, I couldn't feel my fingers. I couldn't feel anything. From the way West shook out his hands afterward, I knew I'd done a little damage. The need for a shower outweighed every emotion. The swirling eddies of anger and shame had ebbed. I was still catching my breath when I threw myself into my car and dialed Kaia. She needed to know what I knew.

"Hi," she answered.

"Hey, I need to update you on something."

"Okay," the word dragged out of her mouth.

"Isabelle is dead. Henry Johnson killed her. They had a date. Things got out of hand and he killed her."

"Okay." This time the word was more firm. "Is there anything else?"

"Henry Johnson has been dealt with."

"Good. Have there been any developments with Casey?" She asked tentatively. Daniel's voice filled the background, asking for something. Her response was muffled, as though she was holding the phone to her shoulder. "No, mio figlio. Not right now."

"No. Nothing yet. It's like she just vanished out of thin air."

25

AETHUSA CYNAPIUM

Casey was all I could think about as I accompanied Benjamin to another Eros event. It felt foolish. Foolish to think that this would lead to finding her alive and well, but some part of me had needed to believe it. I hoped that I'd find one or both of them living out a sugar baby's dream, sipping cocktails by the pool at some expensive resort. Not buried in an unmarked grave.

As we made our way onto the terrace of a beachside hotel in Santa Monica, I felt the cold night air nip at my skin as the breeze caused the silk slip dress I was wearing to flutter against my legs. Though the affair wasn't as extravagant as the Las Vegas event, this party was luxurious in its way. Ice sculptures were carved in the shape of different Greek love stories. I recognized the sculpture of Eros and Psyche right away. That one had always been my favorite. Everything looked as though it had been touched by Midas. Gold fabric covered all the tables. Gold flatware brought bites of food to the injected lips of every guest. It was so elaborate that it started to feel like a parody.

Benjamin's hand was at my back, guiding me through the space as people fell over themselves at the chance to meet him. This may have only been my second Eros party, but I was starting to notice that the app catered to a very specific sort of man. Scattered around the room, there were more than a few faces I recognized. Movie stars, politicians, and other millionaires. Most of them had their age in common. I'd gathered that this service was for women looking to snag a rich husband. The men who used the app were only interested in having women served to them on a platter. Not a single one of them seemed like "husband material."

The night went by in a blur of names and faces. Taylor Bishop, entrepreneur. Donovan Keats, musician son of a bank owner. David Roth, producer. To the naked eye, I was just another bored airhead scrolling through her phone. As I hastily jotted down names to research later. The hope that any of them had encountered Casey still smoldered like an ember in the back of my mind.

Every woman at the party looked perfectly coiffed, painted, and polished. Gleaming white smiles flickered like camera flashes. I idly wondered how many thousands of dollars worth of teeth I'd just seen. As Benjamin introduced me to various partygoers, I tried desperately to pay attention. Names were typed into my phone as quickly as I could manage. But as the night wore on, I grew bored. Benjamin's social stamina was astounding. How could anyone keep up this level of energy?

As he carried on in a conversation with one of the many stuffed shirts he introduced me to, I watched various attempts at romance. One movie star seemed to grow increasingly uncomfortable at the ferocity of female interest. I laughed to myself as I watched him leave after a woman's second attempt to catch his attention turned into a pink cocktail poured down the front of his white shirt. The movie star hurried into the building, probably to escape for good, and passed a woman with familiar-looking red curls. Casey?

"Well?" the man asked, looking at me. Had he asked me a question? Benjamin looked at me expectantly. Yes, I had been asked a question. I glanced back to where I'd seen the tangle of red hair, but it was gone. *Shit*. After glancing around for her, trying to disguise my hunting gaze as mere disinterest, I looked down into my champagne. I needed to get out of this conversation. As though he could feel me getting ready to walk away, Benjamin gave my hip a squeeze and spoke for me.

"She's an accountant."

"An accountant?" The man looked me over like he couldn't believe someone dressed like me had a brain. What an asshole. The accountant part was a lie, sure, but I knew my IQ was far higher than his purely based on the neanderthal slant of his forehead. Benjamin looked at me and painted that disarming smile on his face.

"Hard to believe, isn't it? That someone so beautiful is also intelligent."

I took a sip from my glass, trying not to let my thoughts control my facial expressions. Maybe that hadn't been Casey, but what if it was? Why would she not come to work if she was in Los Angeles this entire time? Why had she not been home? Questions nipped and prodded at me as I tried to manage my patience with the people around me.

"Enjoy your evening," he said, guiding me away from the train wreck that was that conversation.

"These men are insufferable," I muttered, wondering if Casey had just been a figment of my imagination. Wishful thinking, perhaps.

"Yes, well, they pay me a good deal of money. I suffer their company as a result."

Out of the corner of my eye, I noticed a familiar blonde. Juliet. Not as elegant as I'd seen her when we met. Her hair was becoming shaggy with sweat. The man who took her arm seemed insistent that she accompany him to his next destination. The way she wobbled on her heels told me she was in no condition to make that decision.

"Excuse me," I said as I smiled politely at the man, eyeing the way his fingers gripped Juliet's elbow. "She doesn't look well."

"Yes, that's why I'm taking her home."

"You know each other?" For all I knew, maybe they did know each other, but I doubted it.

"Of course we do. Don't we, Mary?"

Nope. Didn't know her.

"That's not her name," I said, making no attempt to hide the ice from my voice. "I don't think my escort would be too pleased to hear the way you've been treating his assistant."

Some men only see a woman's value when it's been related to another man. This man's beady black eyes got wide when he realized I was talking about Benjamin Camden. His diamond watch glinted in the gold lights as he released his grip.

"I was just trying to help," he stammered. I slipped my arm around Juliet's waist and started to lead her inside.

"I'm sure you were," I said through a tight smile. I swiftly lead her away from the bar. "You're okay."

My heels clacked loudly on the marble floors as I made my way to the front desk with Juliet in tow.

"Hi," I smiled sweetly at the receptionist. "Do you have any rooms available? My friend and I want to sleep it off."

If I were just another party girl, I'd take her to the hospital. They'd ask their questions and maybe everything would be fine. But they could easily call the police and I couldn't have that. Juliet's steps became heavier and less sure as we plodded down the hall, passing lacquered door after lacquered door until we got to the room I'd rented. Given how quickly whatever he'd put in her drink was hitting her, I assumed it was GHB. That meant that she could have a violent reaction, like a seizure. It meant she needed to be watched. It also meant that I needed to make her throw up.

"Alright. Juliet, can you hear me?"

She nodded weakly.

"I'm going to get you some water. Then we're going to stay up and talk. Like a sleepover. Okay?"

The hotel could charge me twelve dollars for a bottle of water. I looked around the mini-bar for what I needed. Nice hotels like this usually had a small selection of medicines available. The tips of my fingers dragged over each little thing. Instead of their usual packaging, they had cute labels that said things like "my head hurts." It took me a moment before I found "my tummy aches."

"Okay, Juliet. I need you to drink the water." I held the bottle up to her lips. She reluctantly drank the water, too drunk or drugged to protest. This next part was going to be awful for her. A flicker of pity fluttered through me.

Juliet vomited so violently that her bladder emptied with her first few heaves. The scrunchie I'd used to hold her hair back came loose and her blonde blowout was completely ruined with sweat. Between retches, she cried.

"It's alright," I said as I stroked her hair. "The bad part is almost over."

Once the heaving died down, I got her in the shower. She was mostly lucid at that point, but I sat on the toilet. Her clothes were covered in urine and vomit, so I wrapped her in a robe when she got out and tossed her clothes in a plastic bag.

I stayed up all night to keep an eye on her. Every few minutes, I took her pulse to watch for irregularities. By the time the sun started to come up, I was confident she was going to be fine. Probably nauseous still, but fine. I scratched out a note on the pad next to the phone, leaving it on her pillow so she'd see it immediately.

> *You were drugged last night. You are safe. No one has harmed*
> *you. Please eat something if you can.*
>
> *—Lilith.*

I tried to help the door shut quietly as I left. The sweatsuit I'd purchased from the gift shop for Juliet seemed so cozy that I got a set for myself. Even as I waited for the car I'd called, I felt grateful for the soft pink joggers and hoodie.

HAVING SPENT MOST of the night making sure Juliet didn't die, I was both exhausted and wired. After scrubbing the night off of myself, I was able to unwind enough to take a long nap. I couldn't remember the last time I'd gotten a full night's sleep. Every day that passed without sufficient rest chipped away at something vital inside me. The face staring back at me as I brushed my teeth didn't show the exhaustion that lurked just beneath the surface. I thought a little prayer of thanks for the small mercy.

My restless mind wouldn't let me settle on a single task, so I resorted to aimlessly watching television and scrolling through social media simultaneously. The show I'd been half-watching ended, so I was flipping around through different channels, stopping on the news while I got up to grab another slice of pizza. The anchorwoman's voice was loud and clear from across the room.

"A disturbing series of disappearances in the Los Angeles area has women worried for their safety. Women visiting nightclubs in the area have been going missing before their companions have noticed they've gone. Taylor Johnson, a student at UCLA, was visiting the popular nightclub Siren with her friends this week. After being separated from her party, Johnson disappeared from the club and hasn't been seen since. This is the tenth disappearance of this kind in the last month. Commissioner Warner of the LAPD states that young women should keep an eye out for each other in public settings and be wary of anyone trying to get them alone."

Where did you disappear to last night?

I debated telling Benjamin the truth but knew it'd be best to let Juliet decide whether she wanted to share that information with her boss. It was more her business than mine. Would she get in trouble for leaving? Had he noticed?

An urgent issue needed my attention. I'm
sorry.

Make it up to me.

I rolled my eyes at the terrible advice the police department was giving young women. I looked up the other disappearances. Taylor Johnson was twenty-one. She looked quite young, almost childlike, with a layer of baby fat on her freckled cheeks.

Make it up to you?

I had to explain why my beautiful date abandoned me. Meet me for a drink later. The Misfit in Santa Monica.

26

TAXUS BACCATA

The screams and laughter of children played through the air like music. The tinkling tones of the century-old carousel carried along with them. Benjamin wrapped his arms around my waist and pressed his face into my shoulder. He'd insisted on taking me here. I wasn't sure why, but I also wasn't going to complain about him being wrapped around me.

"When I was a child, my father would take us to Brighton on holiday. We'd stay at a dodgy inn near the pier and eat fish and chips. Somehow, even when we had nothing, he found a spare quid so I could ride the carousel."

I nodded and continued to take in the sights. Happy families and young couples surrounded us. My eyes drifted to a father and mother holding their child steady on a galloping white horse. The thought of a tiny Benjamin riding the carousel made me smile. He squeezed my waist and pressed a kiss to my neck, making my cheeks flush.

"Sometimes, when I feel alone, I come here to remember them."

His words made me ache with envy. He had happy memories of his parents. Standing there, I struggled to think of my own parents in this way. My father was a lost cause, but my mother...small good things were still there. When researching Benjamin, I didn't come upon any information about his parents or anyone else. I didn't ask what happened to his family, though I was tempted. The details didn't matter, because I knew from the tone of his voice. It was the same tone I would use when I spoke about my mother. The soft and resolved tone we use when we speak about having lost something that will never come back to us. He loosed a warm sigh against my skin.

"Do you want to take a walk?" I asked.

He murmured his agreement and took my hand. The warmth of his body faded away from me as we stepped out into the cold. People passed us by, some turning their heads to look at the towering man next to me, while most ignored us. I gazed up at him. In his dark blue pea coat and grey sweater, he looked just like any other man who had spent time carefully picking his clothes for a date.

"Did you buy this coat?" I asked, taking the soft fabric between my fingers.

He laughed. "Of course I bought it."

"I mean, did you go to the shop, pull it from a bunch of other coats, and take it home?"

"Oh, no. I haven't bought clothes for myself in ages. A shopper has my measurements and sends things for me to try. Then a tailor fits them for me."

"That explains it then."

"Explains what, exactly?"

"Why you look so perfect all the time."

A chuckle rumbled from him. It was true. This was the sort of man that women read about in romance novels. The dark brown hair was tousled to perfection. When he smiled at me, all his teeth stood next to each other like porcelain soldiers. I kept telling myself that this was an act. Someone like him would never have a genuine interest in me. He was too beautiful. Too perfect. He pulled me toward the stairs that lead down toward the beach.

"Let's go where we can hear each other."

We walked away from the pier, down the dark and unoccupied beach. With my shoes in one hand, I felt my feet sink into the cold sand and move between my toes.

It was strange. Walking down the beach, I felt little pieces of the wall inside me fall away. The enormous dam-sized wall I'd put up because of Ethan. It might take a lifetime for it to come down all the way. Tiny cracks started to form with every stroke of Benjamin's thumb across my hand. But the questions were still there. If someone could know me, all of me, could they still want me? Was I someone somebody could want? That question illuminated within me like a lonely prayer candle in the dark. I squeezed Benjamin's hand at the thought.

"How long has it been just you and your sister?"

"Our grandfather died about six years ago. He took us in after our parents died. I was fourteen, she was seventeen."

Benjamin nodded and went quiet again. The ocean made its presence known with booming crashes of waves and whispers of water pulling away from the shore. As we passed the lifeguard tower, he stopped and sat in the sand. I set myself down beside him. For a while, we sat there and just listened to the water.

"I wasn't a well-behaved child," he said after several minutes I didn't track. "School didn't come to me naturally. Only trouble, so that's what I made. I lined my pockets with the other boy's money won in card games, making bets, and stealing when the opportunity presented itself. I got ahead in business because it's just gambling with higher stakes."

Benjamin stared at the crashing waves. We were both pretending, but he was far better at it than I even knew.

"I made good grades in school." The words tumbled out of my mouth like a confession.

He looked sideways at me, waiting for me to continue. Anyone worth their weight in the tech industry could search for me and come up with everything I was about to tell him, but I felt like saying it out loud. I hadn't told this truth to anyone in some time.

"I thought I was going to do something more significant with my life. Almost got my Ph.D."

"Why did you leave school?"

"My family needed me." A half-truth, but as much as I'd share with anyone. "My grandfather died and Kaia needed my help, so I left."

"What did you study?"

"Plants."

"Plants?" The surprise in his voice was genuine. I guess his research on me hadn't been that thorough.

"Yeah, plants." I laughed. "Chemistry. Biology. That sort of thing."

"Brilliant and beautiful." He said more to himself than to me, like he was commiserating with an unseen confidante. Turning toward me, he brushed an errant strand of hair out of my eyes and cupped my face with unfamiliar tenderness. "You continue to surprise me, Lilith."

"Well, if we were dating, you would have learned this stuff on our second date," I said, trying to ignore his compliment.

"Are we not?"

"Not what?"

"Dating," he said with a smirk.

"Not really, right?" I asked as my chest tightened. "I appreciate your help. I do. And this time with you has been..." The words died on my tongue as his fingers dragged down my jaw. "Unexpected."

Benjamin's touch trailed to my neck and laced through my hair. With a slight tug, he pulled me toward him and pressed his mouth to mine. The weight of his body forced my back into the sand as he continued our kiss. His tongue brushed against my upper lip and I sighed at the touch. He didn't hesitate to move in and taste me. The friction of his tongue against mine sparked an electric current that went down to my toes.

Selfish. It was so selfish of me to be here with him when I should be looking for Casey. By now she was more than likely dead. Images of that red-haired party goer were little more than my guilt manifesting as fantasy.

My fingers curled around his sweater and pulled, needing him pressed against me as his coat obscured us from the world. Settling between my thighs, his mouth moved to my neck. As heat built low in my belly, thoughts of Casey poured out of my head. All I could think about was his heat, the taste of his mouth, the warmth of his scent, and the weight of his body.

"If we're not dating, why do you make me feel like this?" He rasped against my throat as he pressed his rigid arousal into my hips, the motion wrenching a small moan out of me. The grinding length against my center did nothing to bring me back to Earth. I felt my mind drifting further away from me, leaving only thoughts of what it would feel like to have his skin against mine. My hands grazed beneath his clothes, savoring the warmth of his skin against the biting air. Tufts of hair tickled my palms as I pushed lower, seeking.

Fingers flicked the button of my fly open and moved the zipper down. It was clear his thoughts were as filthy as my own as he slid his hand over my panties.

"So fucking wet," he panted as his fingertips drifted along the cotton seam.

My mind and body were at war with each other. Each touch, each kiss, each breath between us fueled the fire in my core that had been nothing but embers for so long. In moments like this, any stolen intimate moment with a man, I heard Ethan's voice telling me what trash I was and it doused any desire I had. Not tonight. Tonight Benjamin burned through me. My hands gripped his waist as my hips rose to meet his touch.

Still, there was a small voice at the back of my mind that tried to make his attraction to me make sense but couldn't. Why? Why did Benjamin Camden want me? Pictures of his perfect girlfriends played through my mind, bringing me back to reality. Temporary. This could only be temporary. Hell, he was probably well-practiced in extracting orgasms from women. Seeming to feel me drift from him, Benjamin's teeth sank into my ear and tugged.

Fuck.

Maybe it was going to burn out, but I was beginning to wonder if that would be so bad. Soon this thing between us would be over, but it shouldn't stop me from enjoying it while it lasted. Right? Like scratching an itch. We could take from each other and move on. Based on the way his hips rutted against me, it certainly wasn't stopping him. Teeth dragged along my neck before he nipped at my jaw. His lips brushed against mine in a breathless kiss.

"You're coming home with me," his demand was rough and filled with hunger. As if it would sway me to agree, he increased the pace of his fingers. "Come on, pet."

I wasn't sure if it was a plea for me to go home with him or if he was urging me on, but release was threatening to barrel through me. Simmering in my blood, waiting to boil over. All of my little muscles started to tense up. Realizing we were still very much in a public place, I buried my face in his shoulder and bit my lip. I would not scream. Not here.

"That's it," he urged. And that was all I needed to fall over the edge. My ears were ringing from the sudden rush, so I didn't catch what he'd said next. Then I realized it wasn't my ears. It was his phone.

Still poised on top of me, he answered it. As I lay there watching him listen to whoever was on the other end, I wondered how much sand I had in my hair. When he told whoever he was talking to that he was on his way, I knew the evening was over. Relief and disappointment churned in me like oil and water. He reached down to help me up as he stood. Moving his hands through my hair to right it again, he kissed me softly.

"You have no idea how sorry I am to cut this short."

"It's alright," I sighed. I couldn't admit that I was terrified of going home with him. "I should be getting home, anyway."

Benjamin sent me home in a town car and drove off to handle some business that was happening on the other side of the planet. Apparently, when you own an international business, that means working at all hours of the day. On the ride home, I scrolled through social media looking for pictures of us rolling around in the sand together, and felt thoroughly relieved when I came up empty.

Still shaking sand out of my hair, when I walked through the front door, I went over to the shower and turned it on. My phone chimed with a text message from Kaia.

Come over tomorrow morning?

Sure. Pancakes?

Obviously.

THE LIVING ROOM was bathed in sunlight, which was streaming in through the large Georgian windows. As Daniel laughed at an exploding coyote, I remembered all the days we sat in that room with our grandfather. The furniture wasn't modern or covered in off-white, airy-looking canvas. Instead, everything was ornately carved, as if brought directly from a palace in Italy. Nonno liked to remind us of our humble beginnings as he sat on silk or velvet upholstery.

The sizzle of butter and batter always made me feel at home. Daniel watching cartoons in the living room, still in his pajamas, even though he'd been up for hours made me feel soft. Less animal. Kaia flipped a pancake and looked over her shoulder at me.

"How are things going with Camden?"

"They're fine," I said while sipping my coffee. "I want to get access to the Eros server. Gino said the MIT guy should be coming through any day."

"That's good, but that's not what I meant."

Adding more coffee from the pot to my empty cup, I raised an eyebrow at her. "Oh, really? What did you mean, then?"

"Don't get too attached."

"I'm not getting attached." I was. "It's fake. All for show."

Kaia sighed and shook her head as she plated the finished pancakes.

Batter poured out of the ancient mixing bowl onto the griddle, sizzling as it connected with the hot surface. She strode over to my side with her phone in hand and turned it to face me as she set down the plate of pancakes.

"This doesn't look like it's for show, Lili."

I looked at the photo. There we were, strolling down the pier. He's holding my hand and I'm looking up at him with bright eyes and a smile on my face. I clicked on the link and read the article.

BILLIONAIRE MIDAS IN LOVE?

Technology comes easily to Benjamin Camden. Love is even easier! Camden has been seen jet-setting around with Lilith Caccia, great-granddaughter of legendary film producer Giorgio Caccia.

Though the two haven't been together long, they're heating things up all over town. A source close to Camden says that the venture capitalist is "very serious about Caccia."

A little flush went through me as I skimmed the article. There we were, holding hands at the boardwalk. Dining together at Nobu. Feeding each other in Las Vegas. I said a silent prayer of thanks that there weren't more graphic photos of us on the nearly abandoned beach. Even though I knew everything was manufactured, there was still one real thing in those photos: my smile. I did look happy. While a small smirk tugged at the corner of my mouth, I wondered when I'd last looked like that.

"Because I'm smiling at him? Should I be frowning? It's supposed to look real, Kai."

"Ok. I get that, I do. But it would be easy to forget it's not, right? He's handsome and intelligent, and he's giving you lots of attention. I just don't want you to get hurt."

"Just let me do this," I said with an agitated grunt.

I stared down into my coffee cup as I added cream and sugar, letting the stirring take my ire away. She wasn't saying anything I didn't already know. We both knew that. It didn't make it hurt any less. I thought about the way his mouth felt on mine. The way his hands felt when they grasped at me, pulling me closer, touching me in ways that made me forget myself. When I finished stirring, I looked up. My sister had returned to the pancakes, but she stared at me as she told Daniel to come to the table.

DESPITE THE MAPLE syrup I was still licking off of my lips, I was in a rotten mood. Usually investigating dirt bags skipping out on their debts didn't take this long. If Casey owed us money, the ink would already be dry on her obituary. It would have talked about how she died alone in her apartment and she was too young to have gone so suddenly. Finding out what happened to Isabelle had been easy enough, but Casey seemed to drop off of the planet. Still, it was her mane of red curls disappearing into the crowd that scratched at my thoughts as I scrubbed the grout in my kitchen with an old toothbrush. Then my phone started playing its 8-Bit ringtone. The voice on the other end was frail and shaky.

"Lilith?"

"Yes." Juliet.

"I, uh, got your note."

Setting down the toothbrush, I leaned against the counter, humming to let her know that I'd heard her. The silence felt uncomfortable. I chewed off a hangnail as I waited for her to continue.

"Well, I just. I guess I just wanted to say thank you. For helping me."

"Juliet," I breathed as I examined the rest of my nails for other imperfections. "It was nothing."

"No, it wasn't." Juliet's tone dropped to an angrier octave, but her voice immediately changed back to the one I had gotten to know over the last few weeks. "Mr. Camden would like for you to accompany him to a special event that's coming up in a few days. This one will require the formal attire we selected. I'll be sending you the details via email."

"Ok," I tried to keep the surprise at the change in subject from my voice. "Juliet?"

"Yes, Ms. Caccia?" She must have been walking through the office, based on her voice and the clacking sound in the background.

"Are you alright?" A moment passed before she answered.

"Yes, Ms. Caccia, I am. Thanks to you."

27

RICINUS COMMUNIS

Gino's guy was sweaty. It was distracting how sweaty the man was. I worked to keep the grimace from my face as he explained to me how he was able to get me logged into Casey and Isabelle's profiles and personal accounts on an untraceable smartphone. My eyes followed the drop of sweat that fell from his glasses to his cheek. It was hard to believe that he was this intimidated by me, but Gino bracing the door of the janitorial closet shut couldn't have been helping much.

"The number belongs to the corporate-issued phone of a dead man whose service was never discontinued."

I nodded, trying not to look bored. Burner phones were nothing new to me. Look, I appreciated technology and all of his hard work, but I had things to do and the lecture wasn't doing anything for my current level of exhaustion.

"Explain to me how this isn't just a burner phone again?"

"It's not a burner phone. It's..." the professor let out a flustered sigh. "The phone is like a parasite. It attaches itself to the nearest phone and uses signals from other devices to operate, making it completely untraceable."

"And it can't be tracked because of the case you put on it?"

"The case blocks positioning systems from being able to track any location, but signals can get out and in. However, when a signal is identified it will be whichever other device this phone attached itself to. Not this phone."

"Alright. Thank you." I looked over my shoulder at Gino and thought for a moment. "Dr. Forester? I know this may be a wild request, but would you be able to trace the location and activity of a cellular phone if I gave you the number?"

"If it's dead, I can't. I can only tell you the last location."

The man stared at me like a scared rabbit. Minus the sweat, he wasn't unattractive. With his glasses on, he had a Clark Kent thing going on. The sweater he had pulled over his button-down looked too warm for this weather. It made me wonder if he'd known his sweat was going to be a problem. I pulled a piece of paper off of the little pad in my pocket and wrote down Casey's phone number, hoping that knowing her last recorded location would help me to make some progress.

"Get me all of the information you can on this number and do it as soon as you can."

He nodded as a bead of sweat slid down his temple.

"Gino, tell Dr. Forester that his debt to us is paid, provided he remains available for this sort of work."

Gino cocked an eyebrow. I hadn't told him my plan for keeping Forester at our disposal, but he knew better than to question me in front of the man.

"In fact," I added. "I'd like to start paying you for your services. I'm sure I don't have to tell you that your new contractor's fee, which will be a generous amount, will include your discretion."

"You heard the lady. Now get out of here."

Dr. Forester packed up his wares and hustled out of the closet. The bass thumped loudly through the room as the door briefly opened and closed.

"Kaia told me you found Isabelle."

"Not exactly," I said as I toyed with the phone settings. "I found the guy who killed her."

"Killed her? Shit."

I looked up from the phone to see a look of regret on Gino's face. The guy may be one of the most violent people I'd ever met, but he had a soft heart.

"Yeah, strangled her to death and the goons at his hotel got rid of the body. I don't know where she ended up, but I doubt we'll ever be able to find her."

"Do you think the same thing happened to Casey?"

"Honestly, I don't know right now, but that would be a pretty big coincidence." A sigh loosed from my lips as I thought about how little I knew about Casey's whereabouts. The boyfriend didn't know anything. She wasn't in the hotel security footage I'd gotten of Isabelle in Las Vegas. I had also searched Isabelle's social media feed for any mention of Casey the week she disappeared, but she hadn't shown up there either. I wasn't even sure that was her I'd seen at the last Eros event, but I knew I wouldn't let the woman slip away so easily at the next one if she appeared.

Gino and I left the closet together, but he veered away to go out the back door. He had other things to handle. Other men to brutalize. Two girls were spinning around on the main stage poles. Muse was packed with men. Bills were flying through the air at the girls, making the scene look like a music video for the Cardi B song that was playing about money.

I headed upstairs to grab my things. When I'd gotten here, Kaia was getting ready to go home. Daniel's school was having an open house. I wondered what the parents of his classmates thought his mother did for a living. She'd been wearing a suit, so I'm sure she gave them some vague corporate-sounding job title and left it at that. The truth is that most people aren't really interested in learning more about strangers. As long as they feel safe with the person, they're comfortable with not knowing details.

The wall popped open with an easy push. I sealed it shut behind me and walked through the main door. The elegant office was empty. My bag was still sitting on the sofa that was pushed against the wall. The urge to take a moment to rest overtook me as I sat down on the supple leather upholstery.

With my head tilted back, I stared at the ceiling. Every time I let my mind wander away from work, I was on the beach with Benjamin. His hot words against my skin. His lips on mine. His touch making me shatter beneath him. I knew it was wrong. All wrong. Kaia had warned me that he couldn't be trusted, but he and I were just doing this for show. He was helping me. This relationship was just a key to getting behind the closed doors of Eros. A workaround. But everything that happened when no one was looking was something else entirely.

I dozed off. The clock on my phone told me that Muse was closing up, so I stood up and gathered my things. Girls were counting their money at empty tables and the bartenders were polishing freshly washed glasses. West pretended he wasn't watching everyone work as he sat at the bar. Prepared to leave everyone to their business, I started to make for the door and tossed my goodbyes over my shoulder.

"How was your date?"

My eyebrows furrowed in confusion as I turned to face West, who had asked me the question since he was the only male voice in the room.

"What?"

"You said you had a date. How was it?"

"Oh," I felt my cheeks flush as the memory of Benjamin pawing at me on the beach flooded my thoughts again. "It was fine. Just a business thing. Nothing very important or interesting happened."

The expression that flashed across West's face was odd. In my dazed condition, I couldn't identify it. The late hour had made my nap hit me hard. Trying my best to keep sleep from my eyes, I yawned.

"Okay, well. I guess I'll see you later for training."

"Let's do it on the beach."

"What?" I blinked.

"Train. Let's go for a run on the beach. It's been a while since we did that and I bet you could use it. I'll pick you up."

28

DELPHINIUM

The sand made running so much harder. Hot air scorched my throat as I tried to keep up with West. Southern California didn't have seasons. It just had hot and slightly less hot. And sometimes cold from out of nowhere. Today was a hot day. Still, it wasn't fair. His legs were so much longer. He was taking fewer steps. That had to be it. But he ran like a gazelle as I trailed behind him.

Finally, he stopped at Point Dume and I braced my hands on my knees. Was it possible to die from running? West looked down at me and laughed.

"Don't laugh at me," I said between desperate gasps for air. "I'm taking way more steps than you."

"Here," he said as he raised my arms to put them behind my head. "You'll get more air if you stand up straight."

"You're barely winded. It isn't fair," I croaked.

"Don't blame me if you've been slacking on your cardio."

"You're my trainer. Slacking on cardio is your fault."

Sweat slid down my spine. I cringed at the feeling and prayed for a breeze as I gazed out at the crashing waves. The middle of the week left the beach devoid of tourists for the most part. While I caught my breath, I took in the people walking around us. A young mother was entertaining her baby away from sunlight, under a tiny tent cover where her partner napped in the shade. Across the dunes, an elderly couple was laughing and holding hands as they ambled toward us.

My fingers laced together beneath my thick black ponytail as I turned to look again at West. He shielded his eyes from the glare coming off of the water but watched the surfers take turns on incoming swells. With his shirt tucked into the waistband of his shorts, all of his hard-earned muscles were on display and gleaming with sweat. The gold-tinged ends of his hair were tucked into a dark bun on top of his head. I angled my head to the side like I was taking in a sculpture. He was an objectively good-looking man.

"Do you have a girlfriend?" The question just fell out of my mouth. I never asked him about his personal life. I wasn't sure why I was starting now. He shrugged, shaking his head.

"Why not? I see women notice you all over the place. Don't you want to be with someone?"

His shoulders tensed, seemingly irritated with the line of questioning I was throwing at him. Why was I doing this now? Even I didn't know. He blew out a breath.

"It's complicated, Lili."

"Come on, we never talk about you. Are you gay?" I had a feeling he wasn't, but it seemed like a good enough reason for him not to have mentioned a girlfriend.

West gave a small laugh but remained tense. "No, I'm not gay." I shrugged, not sure how else to respond. He glanced at his watch. "Come on. Neptune's Net is open."

"Good, I could use a burger." I glanced down at my sweaty stomach, which had started growling and gnawing at me with hunger. Whatever was keeping him from dating clearly was complicated enough for him to shift the subject at breakneck speed. I wasn't an idiot. I knew when someone was trying to distract me, but I didn't mind if it was with food. I also didn't want to continue a line of questioning that was clearly making him uncomfortable.

The short drive to the restaurant was silent. At first, I made small attempts at starting different conversations but had no success. After a while, I just gave up and drummed my fingers on the door. When we got to the restaurant, it was more of the same. We ordered, went out to the patio, and started eating. He hadn't said a word since we ordered our food. Usually, our silences were comfortable, but this was not that. His energy was off and the silence was eating at me.

The sun bathed the beach in its late afternoon glow. Deep sapphire waves turned aquamarine as light filtered through their cresting peaks. On days like this, you could almost forget it was fall. I smelled the salt and fried fish on the ocean air, remembering sitting across from Nonno like this.

"You know, I used to come here with my grandfather," I started. West finally looked up from his food. "He was fixing up this old Chevy. It took him years. It was kind of his only hobby. When he would take it out for a test drive, he'd take me with him. On good days, we made it all the way out here."

He nodded and picked up another fry. I pressed on.

"If I behaved for the entire drive, we got lunch. He got the patty melt and shared it with me. Days like that made me feel... normal." After a few more minutes of silence, I had given up on the conversation and took a gigantic bite of my burger when West finally spoke again.

"What kind of Chevy was it?" He asked through a mouthful of food.

"It was a 1967 Camaro. Convertible. It was painted this beautiful ocean blue with big white racing stripes. Creamy leather interior. Beautiful chrome details. That thing looked like California on wheels. I think about it all the time."

A smile spread across his lips, and the sour look disappeared from his face. Relief loosened the tension in my chest.

"What happened to it?"

"I don't honestly know. I always thought maybe he sold it while I was away at school," I said, looking out to the ocean again.

"Damn shame to lose something that beautiful."

WHEN WE PARTED ways, I felt a little better. Unsure as to why I would even push him on a subject I'd never questioned him about. Part of me wondered if it was because I was feeling guilty about being closer to Benjamin. Even as my closest friend, I never involved myself in West's personal life. He had his business and I had mine. Just because I felt the need to pour my heart out to him didn't mean that he felt the same way. Our relationship was uncomplicated and I wanted to keep it that way. At least, I thought I did.

As I showered the sand and sweat off of myself, he was all I could think about. We'd met just after I started working for my sister. When he wasn't working at Muse, he was training at One-Two. It seemed like he needed a friend, so I asked him to train me. Little did I know that he wasn't just a good fighter. He was a great one. Still, after years of training with him, I knew little about his life.

The sun had baked a glow into my skin and I regretted not applying more sunscreen to my slightly burned face. While toweling off, my phone lit up with two alerts. One text message was quickly followed by another.

> **KAIA:** Come to the house.

> **BENJAMIN:** Echo with me tonight. Wear something tempting. Car will be there to retrieve you at 10 PM.

I quickly did the math and decided I could do both.

WHEN I WALKED in the door, I was met with the delicate scents of baby shampoo and fresh laundry. A few quick steps took me to the kitchen, where my nephew sat patiently. The little body seated at the island made my heart clench in my chest. Daniel's dark, curly hair hung in soaked ringlets around his face.

"Did someone just have a bath?" I laughed. The dripping mop whipped toward me as the mouth beneath it pulled into a wide grin.

"Zia, Mama's making me macaroni and cheese. Nonno style."

He'd never met our grandfather, but I knew that was who he meant. Daniel, whose middle name was Matteo, popped a piece of pepperoni into his mouth. I looked over at my sister, who was dutifully standing at the stove, watching the pot and waiting for the water to boil.

"You know what they say about watched pots."

I walked over to the stove and saw a small cup of white puree that looked like ricotta next to the pot, but it certainly didn't smell like it. It was conveniently placed out of Daniel's eye line. My sister's eyes snagged on mine before I could say anything.

"I'll get the pepperoni," I said as I smirked at my sister.

Glancing again at Daniel, who was now distracted by a cartoon playing on his tablet, I elbowed Kaia.

"Is that cauliflower?" I whispered.

She nodded.

"Sneaky."

His pin-straight grin and familiar dimples always scratched at my brain, but never enough to ask my sister about his father. I'd done so in the hospital and she screamed at me. So loud and filled with fury that the nurses escorted me out, worried about upsetting the new mother too much.

"THE ARAWN CLAN is going to move on us."

"How do you know that?"

"Some new information on Stevinson came to light. As it turns out, we had an Arawn man in our employ for quite a while."

"Shit. He told me that the money went to his family."

"And technically, it did."

I looked down into my bowl of macaroni and speared noodles onto my fork. Did that mean Stevinson was the rat? How much information could he have possibly had? Questioning him had felt fruitless and Arawn's guy had told us Rowan was getting a lot of intel on our organization. Something wasn't adding up. Memories of Stevinson's dismembered corpse chased away my appetite.

"So you're telling me that we're basically funding a war against ourselves?" I said after a beat.

"All-out war against us would cost much more than that. They're making a statement."

I raised my eyebrows at her, prompting her to go on.

"How do you eat an elephant, Lili?"

"One bite at a time."

29

ZANTEDESCHIA

I've never been a nightclub person. They're not for me. Especially the part that required me to wear sky-high heels and a tiny black bustier dress that looked more like underwear. At least, that's what I was telling myself as Benjamin escorted me into Echo. The club thumped with atmospheric music that was halfway between having a melody and just being noise. It slithered through the air in low, pulsing beats. Painfully attractive people filled the space and eyed us with thinly veiled interest as we passed. Suddenly, I felt like I was a freshman in high school again. Only instead of sheep, these people felt more like coyotes.

L.A. was filled with places like this. Little secret dens of seduction and villainy. If I'd found my way into one or another, it was always for business. Bodies would writhe to the beat as I looked on from the shadows, waiting for someone I'd been tracking so I could follow them home. Never any time for dancing, drinking, or finding someone to fall in love with on the dancefloor. Tonight I felt the vulturine eyes set on me as I walked through the room with a billionaire on my arm. Having shed his jacket, Benjamin wore only a solid black button-down shirt with his grey slacks instead of his usual bespoke suit. His black boots thudded with his weight as I hustled to keep up with his stride.

The green velvet booth we'd been escorted to was empty except for a small placard on the table that said "reserved" in a scripted gold font.

"So," I said, leaning back against the booth as I sat. "What are we doing here again?"

"I thought we could use another night out. If we only went to events together, it'd look suspicious. Besides, I enjoyed getting to know you better."

I ignored the flutter his smirk stirred in me.

"I guess you really do think people are watching you that closely."

Benjamin sat down next to me, resting his arm on the seat behind my shoulders, and scanned the room. He'd unbuttoned his shirt and rolled up his sleeves, showing swaths of golden skin and muscular forearms that were usually covered.

"As I told you, Lilith. They're always watching."

"Well, when you look like you, sure."

His gaze returned to mine, his mouth lifted slightly in an amused smirk.

"Shut up. You know you're gorgeous." I said, waving him away as I felt my cheeks flush. Between his stare and my dress, I felt far too exposed.

A waitress saved me from further humiliation when she came to take our order. Benjamin asked her for a bottle of Veuve Clicquot, the French name rolling off of his well-educated tongue. She seemed used to the order and she hustled herself away. Benjamin turned toward me again, his focus undeterred by the surrounding revelers. I scanned the room and found several pairs of eyes on us, but his eyes were only on me.

"So," he turned my face toward him. "You were saying?"

"You don't really need me to stroke your ego any further, do you?" I breathed a half-choked laugh. Something about the way he was looking at me stole the breath from my lungs. Like he was a starved animal and I was dinner. He leaned back again but lowered his mouth to my ear.

"I can do the stroking if you like," he purred. A finger traced along the silky bust of my dress, causing my breath to hitch. My eyes connected with the waitress, who had placed the champagne on the table. I watched her fill our flutes and set them down. Benjamin gave her a cursory nod and leaned forward to grab the glasses.

"Champagne?" He asked with a quirked eyebrow, his eyes still marred with a predatory haze. I nodded. The fizz crackled on my tongue as I took a long pull from my glass.

The room was surging with people. Everywhere I looked, attractive Angelenos were dancing or talking. A stunning blonde woman started walking toward our table. Blazing green eyes looked at us with rage. Her long limbs made the distance between us disappear. Something about her felt familiar. Noticing her at the same moment I did, Benjamin stiffened.

"Ben, baby. What are you doing here? You said you were going to be out of the country," the woman said. Despite the thick accent, it was easy to hear that every word dripped with malice.

"Hello, Alexia."

The accent and name clicked together in my mind like puzzle pieces. This was the Brazilian model he'd been seeing before, well, me. I took another pull from my champagne glass.

"Who is this?" She gestured to me. Rage surged in her face. I wondered if her stilettos could kill me. Compared to the chiffon skirt that curved around my waist, the binding dress she had on probably wasn't very good for mobility. If I had to, I could take her.

"I'm Lilith. You are?" I drawled blandly. Screw it. I could be a jealous girlfriend, too.

"His girlfriend," she snarled. I wondered if he had bothered to break up with her before our little charade. Of course, men like him probably had their assistants break up with women for them.

"Not anymore," Benjamin said through clenched teeth. "You and I are through. You know that."

"I got your little note. You can't break up with me like a man?"

I looked away, trying to stifle a chuckle. Internally, I prayed that his "note" was actually an email.

"Alexia." He scolded. Before he could say another word, she tossed her drink in his face and stomped away. I gave him a pitying look and dabbed at him with a cocktail napkin.

"At least she was nearly finished with that before she threw it," I laughed. "It seems like I'm getting in the way of your social life. I'm sure she was entertaining."

"She has her moments," he said as he put a hand through his hair. "But I have a better time with you."

Unable to meet his gaze, I straightened his collar, dragging my fingers tips along his skin.

"Lilith." Benjamin's voice had gone low and graveled. He inclined his head toward me but kept his eyes moving about the room.

"Hm?"

"We're being watched."

I looked around and took another swig from my glass. It was true. Some cast us casual glances while others tried to grab sneaky selfies with us in the background.

"Should we leave? That was enough of a spectacle, I think." I asked. A stupid question. This was why we were here. To be seen. Of course, I didn't know how good that interaction would look for him. He still had an image to maintain, and public displays like that were hardly complimentary.

"I think I have a better idea. We can give them something else to talk about. You'll have to play along." He turned to face me again, this time the arm that was behind me slipped behind my back to wrap around my waist. Suddenly, I'd understood exactly what he wanted to do.

"I guess we practiced for this, huh?" I joked. He brushed my hair off of my shoulder and tilted my chin up with a smile that was purely animal.

"I told you I don't need practice," he said as his mouth brushed over mine. My eyes remained open for a moment in surprise, seeing phones raised to capture the stunning billionaire and his latest conquest sucking face in the corner booth. Knowing this, I closed my eyes and kissed him back. I let my hands drift up his thighs, to his hips, around his belt to pull myself closer. *Just pretend this is real*, I told myself. *It's just kissing. You planned for kissing. Act like he wants you and you want him.*

"Good," he murmured as his lips moved to mark their presence on my jaw, down my neck, to my bare shoulder. A shiver surged through me as he nipped the bare skin, his hand slipping up my exposed thigh. Gazing over his shoulder, I saw every set of eyes pinned to us. Public displays of affection were not my thing. Not like this. His breath warmed my collarbone as he said, "I think this dress is my favorite so far."

"Benjamin," I whimpered. I couldn't do this, could I? Logically, I knew that our relationship was fake. That it was for show. But my body didn't know that. The heat building in my core didn't know that. A soft moan escaped my parted lips as his knuckles brushed the lace front of my panties. Tiny muscles clenched, aching with want as a small voice inside me whispered *no*. The urge to close my legs battled with the desire to let him continue.

Fuck, I thought. *This is a mistake. A real mistake.* Discomfort expanded and coiled in me as I thought about how much of me other people could see and wondered how far this was supposed to go. So many people were watching. People with cameras. Fooling around in private, in the dark, away from crowds was one thing, but I was not ready to be his this way. I raked my fingers through his hair and gave it a slight tug.

"Stop," I begged.

Teeth grazed my collar before he looked at me again, but his face had a tighter expression. He was angry with me. I swallowed my own anger down and tried to smile at him, even though his hand was still clasped uncomfortably high on my thigh, the tips of his moving fingers inching down to just within reach of my center. People were still staring.

"Is there a problem?" He asked with a slight edge in his voice.

"No," I panted with an uneasy laugh. "I just...Can you slow down?"

His feral grin returned as he took his hand out from under my skirt and pushed his fingers through his hair. "Sorry, pet. I suppose I got a bit carried away."

I poured myself another glass of champagne and it slipped down easily as I tried to collect myself. Benjamin looked at his watch. He straightened in his seat and removed the arm from around my waist. Whatever scene the people in the bar had just witnessed, it was over now. A little part of me cringed as I imagined what the photos would look like and found myself grateful my grandfather wasn't alive to see them. I glanced at my date again. Business Benjamin seemed to be back. Cell phone in hand, he was having a back-and-forth via text message.

"I need to go," he said abruptly. "I'm having a car pick you up to take you home. They'll be here in a few minutes."

Stunned by the sudden change in plans, all I could do was nod my agreement and pour myself a third glass of champagne. Benjamin motioned to the waitress for the check. After giving her a few bills, he finished the champagne in his glass.

"Goodnight," he said abruptly as he stood up and left before I had the opportunity to return the sentiment. Even as he parted, eyes remained fixed on me. Some hands drifted up to mouths to shield whispered conversations about us away from me. Maybe some were judging me. Certainly, none of them were judging him. I adjusted my dress and swallowed the last of the champagne. The heat that was coursing through my blood gave way to frigid hostility as my stomach clenched with embarrassment.

IN AN EFFORT to erase the shame that coated my skin like oil, I made the driver take me to Muse. It was my domain. A place I could go and feel like I was in charge. Kaia wouldn't have been there, but I didn't want to go home. Nothing was waiting for me there but the opportunity to keep reliving Benjamin's hasty exit. No. I needed to block it out. Erase it.

The parking lot was remarkably full, which meant the inside was packed. No one else would be let in and it was late enough that there was no line at the door, but it was still being guarded by West. He was wearing a white t-shirt and black jeans, his blue denim jacket draped over the stool behind him. When the driver let me out, my step faltered a bit in my stilettos. I corrected my posture and adjusted my dress as I thanked the driver, heading toward the door.

"Lili?" West looked at me with surprise as his eyes took in my glamourous girlfriend getup. "I almost didn't recognize you."

"Yeah, I had a thing with the billionaire playboy but it ended kind of abruptly. I didn't want to waste this dress on drinking alone, so here I am." I tossed my hair over my shoulder and walked toward the door.

He opened the door for me, flashing blue light greeting me as I passed. "Slumber Party" was thumping on the sound system and men howled at the stage. Two women were moving seductively to the melody, practically swimming in the hundreds of bills that littered the floor beneath them. Several pairs of hungry eyes tracked me as I walked to the bar. The bartender smiled at me and grabbed a glass.

"Hey Cari," I said as I sat down.

"Lili! You look amazing. That dress! Oh my god. You look so naughty."

I laughed. "Yeah, well. You can borrow it. I've got a few like this. Can you make me a gimlet?"

"Sure!" She said as she got to work on my drink. A few men had been sitting around the bar, staring at our bartender. Long strawberry blonde curls bounced as she shook the cocktail shaker. It wasn't hard to understand why they sat here instead of over at the main stage. Her smile was magnetic and probably earned her more tips than some of the dancers. Still, it was always entertaining to watch her let them down easily. She placed the beverage in front of me and winked. The cool lime and botanical flavors of the gin slipped down easily. She made me another.

Feeling the effects of the champagne mixing with the gin, I turned in my stool to watch the ladies on stage. One dance turned into another as I started working on my third gimlet. My gaze drifted to West, who was leaning against the wall across the room, eyes fixed on me. Something about his gaze made my chest tighten. Then he was tracking something else. I felt a hand on my knee.

"Hey, sweetheart. What's a little girl like you doing in a place like this?" A half-drunk man who was a bit too old and too patronizing for my liking squeezed my leg.

"Don't touch me," I spat, turning away.

"Hey, hey, hey, don't be shy. You're not dressed like you're shy." He slurred and leaned in close enough that I could smell his cologne and what he'd been drinking. I cringed away, tired of being pawed by men with no boundaries. Taking advantage of my new angle, he squeezed my ass. "Come on, sweetheart. Let me buy you another drink."

"*Stop it,*" I snapped.

"Hands off," West growled. I looked up to see his hands under the arms of the lascivious businessman, dragging him away.

"Hey!" He shouted as he was hurled out the door. A swell of laughter erupted from men at a nearby table. They lifted their glasses to West as he passed by, and headed back to where I sat. Cari poured a glass of water and handed it to him as he leaned against the bar next to me.

"You didn't have to do that."

"It's my job, Lili."

I shrugged and finished my drink. He motioned to Cari for another glass of water and gave me a look of appraisal. She put the glass down in front of me with a sympathetic smile and I took a sip. I was being cut off.

"I don't need a babysitter," I snarled.

"I'm taking you home," West said.

"I'll call a car. It's fine," I declared. "Besides, you still have like an hour left before closing."

"I'm not letting you out of my sight like this."

"I'll take care of her," Cari volunteered. "Come with me."

I followed Cari to the dressing room where dancers were taking off their makeup and getting ready to go home for the night. The large leather sofa was empty and inviting.

"Keep drinking the water. Westy will drive you home when it's closing time."

Garbled protests tumbled out of my mouth, but I found it difficult to resist once I was fully reclined. Little sips of water and the soft murmur of dancers chatting sent me off into a light doze as I said a little prayer that I wouldn't get the spins.

A large, warm hand brushed my hair out of my face and squeezed my shoulder. West looked down at me, his head cocked to one side. My eyes adjusted to the light of the room and took him in. I always forgot how large he was. I'd curled into myself, hardly warm enough in what I was wearing. He held his jacket and his keys in one hand as his other extended to me, ready to help me up. I sat up slowly and slid my shoes back on. Before I could protest, he draped his jacket across my shoulders. It was gigantic on me, but warm and comfortable.

"Come on," he said with a tired smile.

The big green Bronco felt like it was miles away, even if it was only a few drunken strides from the door. Black asphalt was shining from a light rain that must have happened while we were inside. West rounded to the driver's side after helping me into the seat. I pulled his denim jacket further around me and enjoyed the warm cedar and eucalyptus scent on the soft shearling lining.

A soft drizzle patted against the windshield as we made our way to my apartment. I leaned against the chestnut leather seat and watched him steer us home. The hostility that Benjamin had stirred in me had melted away as I'd slept in the club. Instead, I let affection for my friend take hold as I took in the sight of him. His long brown hair was loose around his shoulders, rumpled from an anxious habit of putting it up and down and up again. The deep yellow streetlights highlighted strands that had become bleached from sunlight and illuminated his tanned skin, catching occasionally on his dusky green eyes and the dog tags swaying gently on the rearview mirror.

Before I knew it, we were pulling up in front of my little bungalow, not noticing I had again fallen asleep on the drive. He hopped out of the car and walked to my side before I could set my feet on the ground. A hand extended to steady me as I got out and walked carefully across the grass to my front door.

"Thank you for rescuing me," I said as I unlocked the door, finding my-self suddenly wondering how clean I'd left my apartment.

"The rescue is free. The ride comes with a price." West said with a smirk. I raised my eyebrows in surprise. "Can I use your bathroom?"

"Yeah," I laughed. We walked inside and I pointed him to his destina-tion, praying he wouldn't judge the overwhelmingly pink space too harshly. Or spend too long looking around. Or go digging through the cabinets. But only because these are things that I would do. I'd never entered a bathroom without at least peeking inside the medicine cabinet. He'd never been inside my place before. Outside, a few times. I was amazed he remembered where I lived. Being a responsible drunk adult, I trudged to my kitchen to fish out a glass and fill it with water from the filtered pitcher in the fridge. "Can you grab me some aspirin while you're in there?"

Setting my water on the nightstand, I sat on the bed and took his jacket off, folding it gently. I may have also taken a moment to hold it to myself and give it another sniff. It smelled so good. Exiting the bathroom, West walked to the nightstand and placed two pills next to my water.

"How are you feeling?"

"I'm fine," I said as I sleepily took pins out of my hair. "I'll be fine, I mean. It was just kind of a bad night."

"Let's get these shoes off and you can go to sleep," he suggested, kneeling in front of me as I slugged down the water and aspirin. His right hand slid up my calf and under my knee, lifting my foot out of its shoe with his left. The touch was gentle and warm, tingling through me as I became aware of every place his callused fingers connected with my bare skin. The soft glow of streetlamps cast the apartment in quiet darkness and I could just make out his face. His eyes had gone dark as he repeated the motion on the other side, brushing the thumb gently over my knee. The scrape of rough skin against my soft flesh felt... The silence pressed in on us as I gave in to the urge to lean slightly toward him.

"Go to sleep, Lili," he rasped, abruptly standing and taking the empty water glass to the kitchen to refill it. I scooted under the covers and shimmied my dress off. As I let my eyes drift shut, I listened to him rustle about for a few minutes before he left. Something about the sounds of his puttering helped me relax enough to fall asleep. It had been a long time since anyone else had been in my place. It felt nice.

When I woke up, I noticed he'd taken his jacket and left more aspirin by the glass of water. As I took the medicine, I realized that despite the fact that I didn't have movies or television to chase away the nightmares, I hadn't had a single one.

30

ARISAEMA TRIPHYLLUM

The morning hadn't been too bad, despite the wretched hangover that made my brain feel like it was being fed through a meat grinder. I looked around my apartment and noticed that the kitchen counters had been wiped down. Recycling had been emptied. Trash was taken out. West had actually tidied up a bit.

A small laugh burst through my lips. Without thinking, I typed out a text.

> Thank you for cleaning. I should have you over
> more often.

A soft knock sounded at my door. I eyed the knife on my counter and looked at the doorbell camera feed on my phone. Flowers? I opened the door to retrieve the arrangement that had been placed on my doorstep. Sprays of lilac, snapdragons, fluffy pink peonies, lavender and anemones. A beautiful assembly. An expensive one. My fingers fished out the card nestled amongst the blooms.

Forgive me. - B

The flower petals felt velvety soft under my touch. Leaning in to smell the flowers, I thought about the comforting scent of West's jacket. I'd felt off-kilter when Benjamin and I parted last night. Something about a night of restful sleep balanced my thoughts. I lifted my phone to send Benjamin a thank you and was met with West's response.

I'm surprised I didn't wake you. Are you feeling alright?

Good. Well, good-ish. It feels like a parade is marching through my head. Too many sugary drinks.

Get some food in you. You'll feel better. No training today.

Though I was physically relieved at not having to tumble with him in this state, a small part of me felt disappointed. Padding over to the fridge, I went in search of coffee. The empty cold brew pitcher sat on the counter, mocking me. *Shit*. I poked my head into the refrigerator hoping that by some miracle I had some leftovers to eat. *Double shit*.

An idea started to take root. Fresh air would do me good. Probably a walk, too. I pulled on my jeans and threw a tee shirt over my head. Slipping on my boots, I grabbed my keys and wallet while I pocketed my phone. The perfect juggling act for a girl on a mission. A mission for coffee and food.

WHEN I ARRIVED at a local coffee shop I'd come to love, all I could think about was the chorizo burrito and an oat milk latte. Tragically, there was a bit of a line. It took only the growl of my stomach for me to fold and step obediently into the queue. People passed by with their breakfasts. Some in groups clad in immaculate athleisure. Others were alone, enjoying their beverages as they ignored each other while focused on their devices. Rocking back and forth on my feet, I noticed an attractive girl sipping coffee on one of the patio chairs just outside the wide-open sliding doors. A little fuzzy mutt pawed at her, desperate for attention while she scrolled through her phone. I tilted my head, wondering where I'd seen that dog before. The ambiguous feeling tugged at me when I got to the head of the line.

After placing my order, I walked outside with the newspaper I'd also purchased and took up the table next to the girl while I waited for sustenance. Though I tried to ignore her by reading an article about another missing girl, this one's parents were offering a reward for information on her whereabouts, I was distracted by my inability to place the girl. Or the dog. Where had I seen this face?

"Cute dog," I mumbled to the girl, hoping I'd figure it out before she left. Maybe if I spoke to her?

"Thanks," she said tightly. "Come on, Pickles. Let's go."

Fuck.

Kyle Stevinson's girlfriend and her adorable dog were walking away from me with a macchiato for her and whipped cream in a cup for the adorable mutt. As I glanced over my shoulder at her, I thought about Kyle. About how I'd watched him weep and beg as he bled to death on a meat hook. How Carlo and Gino cut him up like a side of beef and carried him in pieces to the unmarked white van. Those pieces of Kyle had drifted down to the bottom of the Pacific. My stomach lurched. It was at that moment I was presented with my coffee and burrito, suddenly not hungry anymore.

THE WALK BACK to my apartment was long enough for my thoughts to wander away from the gruesome end of Kyle Stevinson. Instead, I tried to piece together the evening prior. Benjamin manhandled me within an inch of my life. In a public place. Based on the flowers this morning, Benjamin knew he had acted inappropriately, even for our little arrangement. It felt foolish to let his behavior bother me. He wasn't actually my boyfriend. Sure, it was all just an act, but I wasn't sure how far I was willing to take it. We never discussed boundaries. We'd kissed and fooled around, so it was possible I was sending mixed signals. At least, that's what I was telling myself.

When I got back to my apartment, I started the shower. The long walk in the late morning sun had the booze from the night before practically seeping out of my pores. Looking around the bathroom, I couldn't help but chuckle to myself when I noticed that West had straightened up a little in here, too. Then my phone pinged with a text message from Kaia.

> Emergency meeting at Muse. I need you here
> in 30 minutes.

This had to be about the Arawn clan. When compared to the dynasty of other mafia families, the Caccias legacy was relatively young. In Los Angeles, we were at the top of the heap, but there were others. The Yakuza run their own games through town, though they did most of their business out of San Francisco. And the Irish, well, they've been coming for us since day one. The Arawn clan, as they like to call themselves, caused trouble wherever they could.

The whole family was being called together. That meant this was important and it was most certainly not good news. While I was in the shower, I tried to imagine anything else it could be. Kaia needed me there to show her strength to the men in the family. They all knew what I did. They all knew what I was capable of. So I would show up for her as I always had. Her weapon against all of them. Her wolf.

Getting ready for the meeting didn't take long. I tossed on my clothes and pulled my hair into a bun. The bulk of my preparation was focused on weapons. I checked every throwing knife before packing them away. The blades were clean. Ready. I tucked them into their holster and rolled it up. After stuffing the roll into my bag, my larger knife got clipped into the sheath at my hip. It was time to go.

31

OENANTHE

The room was silent except for the sound of a scratching pen. Once, when she was 12, my father broke all of the fingers on Kaia's right hand. She had to learn to write with her left. I imagined all of the fingers in their angry blue hue, slightly out of line in one way or another, as she scrawled a note to herself. Every man who mattered was here, waiting for Gino to update her on the situation. I glanced at the note.

Books.

Sitting in the large leather chair behind her desk, Kaia quietly waited for her second-in-command to continue. Her fingers were now steepled in front of her mouth, easily conveying the quiet power that emanated from her dark brown eyes. I leaned against the wall to her left and looked around. This was uncomfortable.

"The Bootlegger burned down."

"Yes, I knew that part," Kaia said cooly. "Tell me exactly what happened."

Gino sighed and scrubbed his hand down his face. It was clear that this was the last thing he wanted to be doing, but he had asked my sister for a meeting with the administration, so here we were. I took a look around the room. Carlo was seated in the other guest chair across from the desk. Antony, her consigliere, was leaning against the bar. Ozzie, another capo, was standing with his arms braced on the desk next to my sister. Each man had two bodyguards with them, most of whom were sitting in the VIP area just outside of the office. My eyes took apart their faces, looking for the microexpressions that would give away a hint of betrayal.

"It was a message from the Arawn family. We don't know what for. Nothing got stolen, as far as we know, but they killed two of our guys in the process. They're out for blood."

"This has to be retaliation for Stevinson. But he seemed to be relatively low-level. The blowback doesn't make any sense," Kaia said, more to herself than anyone in the room. My sister was wearing her usual black, but the dress had little plates of metal sewn into the bust. It looked more like a suit of armor. Kaia wasn't a boss doing business so much as a queen readying herself for battle.

"What should we do?" Carlo asked, chiming in for the first time since we'd gathered. A sheen of sweat had gathered on his brow. His leg bounced anxiously in his seat. It made me wonder how he got through other tense situations if his poker face was this shitty.

"Nothing." Kaia sighed, leaning back in her chair. She fanned out her fingers and curled them again, an anxious gesture I'd grown familiar with. "We can't do anything until we know what this is about. If we retaliate now, we risk bringing their attention to the other businesses. With Bootlegger out of commission, we're going to need that income."

"We do nothing?" Ozzie groaned. He'd always had an itchy trigger finger, but this outburst was ill-advised. I kept my place behind my sister but took out the hunting knife strapped to my hip and started casually flipping the weapon in my hand. I aimed a glare at him.

Men like to say women are too emotional. It's the reason a lot of men in the Caccia family so adamantly objected to my sister taking over. They screamed and spat. They shook their fists and pounded tables. Emotional. That was the difference between us and them. The Caccia women. Our anger wasn't boisterous. It never announced itself.

The motion of the black steel blade caught his eye. It was important to remember who was in charge here, because it sure as hell wasn't him. I couldn't be sure what Kaia's face was doing, but it couldn't have been good because he piped down very quickly.

"We. Do. Nothing. Is that clear?" Kaia said, this time with enough force to send a chill through me. The boss had spoken.

"We can get extra guys on the other joints," Gino offered after a minute of tense silence. Carlo took a pull from the whiskey he'd been nursing and nodded. Ozzie stiffened. Something about that made him uncomfortable.

"That might be all we can do for now," he muttered.

"We keep an eye on the other businesses, but we do not engage. Not yet." Kaia commanded. Standing from her seat, she turned toward me. She had been blindsided by this information, that much was clear. Only I got to see the uncertainty she felt. A flex of her hand, the scar on her pinky stretching with the movement, was her only tell. Her vulnerability was reserved only for me, but I knew what she was thinking. The Bootlegger had been in our family for over sixty years. It was a Hollywood institution. Now it was gone. I wondered if the picture of our mother on her birthday was among the ashes.

When it was obvious that our discussion of the fire and the Arawn family had ended, the other men brought their business to the table. This person wanted a loan, and that guy brought shame on the family. We needed to bankroll a new construction project downtown, but we were having problems with a city councilor. A new soldier had to be initiated. I wasn't sure how Kaia managed it all, but I wouldn't trade places with her if my life depended on it. As she discussed what seemed to be a complicated financial issue, I left her side and poured myself a glass of whiskey.

Nico took my side at the bar. Even in a room full of men I'd known for years, I knew he'd be the only other person with whom I could be truly honest. I raised an eyebrow at him, waiting for the question I saw brewing in his sharp blue eyes.

"You think this stuff with the Arawns is serious?" He asked me in a hushed tone.

"Everything with them is serious," I said with a shrug. "I'm sure Kaia's right though. We shouldn't do anything until we know more about the situation. It doesn't make sense. There's always been tension, but this is… There's something we don't know."

Nico nodded and crossed his arms, now watching Carlo discuss things with Ozzie, who was gesturing wildly. I looked at the tattoos on Nico's forearms. The Caccia mark took up the largest swath of skin, followed by wrist wraps to honor his father's brief boxing career and his own training. On the other arm was his brother's name in a scrolling font.

My eyes shifted back to Kaia, who was still discussing finances with Antony. He was leaning over her laptop, which was now open, probably looking at a spreadsheet she'd drawn up. If my sister knew anything better than these guys, it was money. We always had it. She always knew where it was going and how she could make more of it. All these guys had to do was take their marching orders. When she was done explaining whatever it was she was talking about, she tilted her head in a way that silently asked Antony if he'd understood her. He agreed and pocketed the notes he'd been taking.

It was about six by the time we'd finished. Kaia had that tired look in her eyes but maintained a stern expression until all of the soldiers and their bosses had started making their way downstairs. After the office was clear of others and it was just us, I looked at Kaia. The boss mask had started to slip and I could see the strain of worry pull her eyebrows toward each other.

"K? Are you alright?"

"I need you to do something for me," she said as she closed the door. When she was sure no one was coming, she walked me over to the portrait of Nonno between the bookcases. Pushing on the frame, it popped away from the wall like a small door on hinges. Behind the photo was a safe. I looked at her with raised eyebrows. This was not something I'd seen before.

"If anything happens to me," she said as she punched a code into the lock, "take everything in this safe, get Daniel, and leave."

"Nothing is going to happen to you, Kaia."

"Just listen, Lili. Do you understand? Everything you will need is here. Promise me," she begged as her teary gaze burned into mine.

I nodded. With everything going on, it made sense to have a contingency plan, but her fear was a new layer. It unsettled me. "What's the code?"

"Mama's birthday."

A FEW MEN were hanging around, talking to the dancers who were arriving for their shifts. It wasn't that surprising. Some of them had even dated. I leaned over the railing and heard pop music blasting from the dressing room. It was time for the girls to get ready.

West was arriving at the bar as the rest of the Caccia men were leaving. Some of them he knew, others rarely set foot inside of Muse and hadn't crossed paths with him before. A wary look crossed his face as he observed them. As I descended the final few steps of the staircase, I realized I hadn't seen him since he left my apartment. My foot hung in the air as I hesitated at the bottom step, not sure what to say.

Torn between acknowledging the confusing moment we had in the darkness of my apartment and wanting to get past the embarrassment of being that drunk in front of him, I decided to be a mature adult and just thank him again. He disappeared behind the bar, bending down to store his jacket. I was before him when he stood up again. I stuffed my hands into my pockets and rocked back on my heels. So much for behaving like a grown-up.

"Thank you for taking me home," I said quietly.

"Sure," he said, looking at me but not looking at me. A smoke bomb of shame went off in me. Maybe I had imagined something that wasn't there. He had only done me a favor as a friend. I should have just had the driver take me home after the club. Rocking awkwardly on my heels, I tried again.

"You and I are still on for training, right?"

He nodded.

"Okay, well, I guess I'll see you soon." I couldn't do anything but stare at the carpet as I hurried out the door. God, that was humiliating. Why was that so hard?

32

STRYCHNOS NUX-VOMICA

To the untrained eye, Councilwoman Barton had fallen asleep at her desk. Blind-covered windows separated her office from the rest of her floor in City Hall, illuminated only by the green banker's lamp on her desk. After turning out the lamp with a gloved hand, I pulled the needle out and placed it in the biohazard bag. As with everything else I'd touched, it went right into my bag. The office was dark and quiet. All of the other city employees had gone home for the night.

Like some other public servants, Barton had become a problem for us. She did things like getting in the way of liquor licenses and helping the local police to bust trucks moving our stolen products. It was when she got in the way of a two million dollar real estate deal that her fate had been decided. I'd killed others for far smaller sums. Kaia sent me a message earlier in the day. Luckily for me, public figures are pretty easy to track. They have regular schedules. Their social media feeds are updated by interns. It took me only a few hours to figure out where and when she would be alone.

The councilwoman hadn't noticed me in her office when she returned from the bathroom. At first, she was startled, but then polite while remarking that this was something she'd been expecting to happen.

"Of course, I wasn't expecting a woman."

"People seldom do," I said coolly.

For a while, she was quiet. As if making peace with her fate. Tight knots started to form in my stomach as it growled like an unhinged beast.

"All I ask is that you leave my family unharmed," she said as she glanced to a framed family portrait on her desk. An older woman and a little girl grinned at me from the photo.

"Our business with you is done after tonight."

That seemed to settle her. When the needle went in, she'd flinched at the pain but remained silent. Her death was the work of a moment. I looked over the elegant woman. Ash blonde hair spilled over her face and her skin had only just started to show her age. The gently creased blue eyes were now closed forever.

I WAS WALKING out into the hallway when I heard footsteps coming up the stairs. *Shit*, I thought. *No one should be here.* I had ridden upstairs in one of the golden elevators dressed in my little skirt suit with a wig of blazing red hair, but I'd changed in the bathroom. Security cameras meant I'd have to find my way back to the ground floor without being seen. A door in the hallway clinked shut and I decided to chance my exit. The hallway was wide and lined with tile, making a perfect echo chamber to give away my every move. Each step I took was gently paced on the ground, as though I expected to set off a landmine.

My ears were attuned to the space, twitching at every tiny noise. Only twenty-ish steps laid between me and the door to the stairwell. Silently, I thanked the councilwoman for not having an office in the tower portion of the building. A loud clack and squeak alerted me to an opening door.

On the lightest steps I could manage, I turned to enter the nearest room and found myself in the office for one of the city's district attorneys. Searching around the room for evidence of its resident and a potential hiding place, I found only an inactive computer, a pad of hastily scrawled notes, and an ice cold mug of coffee. Whoever was here had left hours ago.

Readying myself to attempt an exit, I listened for the guard again. As I waited for any noise to give them away, I read the pad on the desk. A list of names. All female. Curiosity tugged at my mind like a belt loop catching on a doorknob. A familiar name was all the motivation I needed to take pictures of the list with my phone. Taylor Johnson, the missing UCLA coed.

Footsteps sounded down the hallway again. The strap on my bag slid down my shoulder as I hoisted up the pocket to deposit my phone. Every tooth on my bag's zipper sounded like a tapping finger in the silence. The footsteps had come and passed the office, but I hadn't heard a door close. Whoever had passed was standing in the hall. I wondered if I had been seen or heard. As I started getting nauseated, imagining the trial of the People vs. Lilith Caccia in vivid detail, the bell of the elevator chimed. The sound of doors sliding open followed. Braving a glance into the hall, I cracked the door ajar enough to see the security guard step aboard.

The stairway was empty. I said a prayer of thanks to whoever was listening for the clear path out of the building. Unconvinced I'd gotten away without being noticed, I kept casting doubtful glances over my shoulder.

I MADE TURNS all over the city trying to lose what I thought was a police car following me. When what turned out to be a taxi made a left turn behind me, I realized I was just being paranoid. Then the nausea hit. Barely able to keep myself from vomiting in my car, I pulled into a convenience store parking lot and sprinted into the bathroom.

Squatting in front of the toilet, I tried to avoid touching anything as everything came rushing out of me. The bathroom's tile floor was more brown than white, which meant this room hardly got cleaned. My mind shot back to the councilwoman and her last words to me. Some little girl was going to grow up without a mother because of me. The thought sent another violent heave through me.

It wasn't until a minute after I set foot through my front door that I was able to breathe a stabilizing sigh.

33

CICUTA MACULATA

Every second I spent getting ready for my next appearance with Benjamin had me dabbing sweat away from my brow. Though my apartment did have a small air conditioning unit that had been cranked to full blast, I couldn't stop sweating. It had been like that since I left the gym.

Working out with West this morning had been awkward. When we met at the gym, we got right into training. No small talk. No playful jabs. Just jab-block-jab. After training was over, West told me he didn't have time to grab lunch with me and left without saying much else. I thought we had gotten past whatever awkwardness muddied our conversations, but I was wrong.

When I was finally ready for the evening's big soiree, I gave myself an evaluative glance in the bathroom mirror. With practice, I'd gotten rather good at making myself look like the other women I'd seen on Benjamin's arm. The floor-length dress hugged every curve, displaying my breasts with an off-shoulder neckline that dipped between them. I leaned down to adjust the straps of my heels and smirked. In this outfit, even I would say I looked rather beautiful, but I may have been a bit biased. I'd always preferred myself in black.

The driver nodded at me as I approached the awaiting vehicle. A small smile was the only hint that he'd appreciated my getup. Benjamin was face-deep in his phone when I sat down next to him.

"Lilith," he'd said tightly, by way of a greeting.

"Benjamin," I mocked.

He looked up and seemed startled by my appearance.

"You look perfect."

Shifting my hair over one shoulder, I pulled out a mirror and checked the lining of my deep red lipstick.

"Why, thank you," I drawled. "I was going for a sexy Morticia Addams."

The gleaming grey Bentley made its way into the heart of downtown, an area replete with old buildings. Some had been revived with love and care while others deteriorated without notice. My eyes skated across the exterior of a brick building covered in colorful murals. Our destination seemed to be coming up when Benjamin reached into the bag that was at his feet. As the car rounded a corner and approached a large hotel with an arched entrance, he handed me a mask.

"Put this on."

"Why?"

"This sort of event demands anonymity."

Nodding, I took the mask from his hand and gave it a look. A simple black domino mask that would cover half of my face that had cat-like ears and a ribbon to secure it to my head. Benjamin's was made of leather and shaped like a fox. I had my doubts about their ability to conceal our identity. It was the same sort of logic that kept everyone from guessing that Batman was Bruce Wayne. Still, I did as he asked. The car rolled to a stop at the entrance and the driver got out to open the door.

"Don't be disturbed by what you see here."

That warning chilled my blood. What kind of event was this? After a moment, I took a breath and let myself be comforted by the fact that Benjamin had no idea what I did for a living. I'd probably done things that would haunt his nightmares. It would be pretty difficult to shock me. The driver opened the door and took my hand as I exited the car. Careful not to step on my dress, I ascended the steps and waited for Benjamin to accompany me. Deftly securing the buttons of his tuxedo jacket, he stepped to my side and told the driver we'd call for him when we were ready.

AS WE ENTERED the building, I took in the space. Built during the height of early Hollywood, this space reeked of old money. Large pieces of stately furniture created intimate seating areas. Bartenders surrounded the water fountain that filled the space with its babbling. At the end of the room, two sets of stairs met in the center at the top, where a DJ played moody ambient music. For as grand as the space seemed, the room felt stuffed with people. It seemed that everyone in the grand hall was attending this event. Not one lost tourist.

Everywhere I looked, there was black finery that seemed to swallow up the light. Black masks covered the face of each man and woman. I wondered what good my presence would do here. There would be no way for me to get the information I needed with everyone concealing their identities.

Black cloth covered every table. Blood-red calla lilies oozed from their arrangements, illuminated by candles scattered everywhere. Some people were dressed in clothing as dark as pitch, but I noticed that others glittered in their garments. From the ceiling, there were long bolts of onyx tissue with dancers moving around in them. A small part of me worried for the aerialists, very aware of the stone flooring beneath them.

Benjamin guided me toward the bar with a hand at my exposed lower back. Even with his face covered by the fox mask, eyes were glued to us. The striking figure he cut was unmistakable. People probably could tell it was him just by his strong square jaw and the cleft in his chin. Unease turned my stomach as I nervously smoothed the front of my dress.

"Don't worry. No one is going to force you to do anything," Benjamin purred as his thumb stroked the skin beneath it. I was starting to guess that I knew exactly what kind of party this was.

As we stepped to the bar, I examined us in the gilded mirror beside it.

This dress made me feel wholly exposed. The bodice was a corset with a bustier style bust and the skirt was floor length but had a generous slit that came to my hip. Did I mention the slit was so high that from certain angles you could definitely see my underwear? Aside from my breasts and the tattoo nestled between them, you could see almost everything. Seeing other women in similar clothing didn't make me feel more comfortable. Only like another piece of meat for sale.

Benjamin handed me a glass of champagne, then clinked it against his own. I gave him an undoubtedly nervous smile.

"So, what kind of party is this?" I asked, after gulping down half the flute.

"Well, Eros likes to invite members to celebrate their new relationships with public displays of affection. Uncoupled members are encouraged to attend as well. It's a bit unconventional, but everyone eventually enjoys themselves in one way or another." His eyes met mine, then dipped to my lips. A man dressed in all black and wearing a rabbit mask approached us.

"Sir," the man said.

Yep, it was impossible for people not to know exactly who I was standing next to. Benjamin turned to face him.

"I'm sorry, Mr. Camden, but there's a problem with Amsterdam."

Benjamin tensed. Returning his gaze to me, he put his hand back on my lower back. A conspiratorial smile crossed his face.

"Darling, it seems as though I need to handle some business. Fetch yourself another drink and I'll find you."

I nodded and he quickly strode away. Stepping over to the bar, I asked the bartender for a second glass of champagne. Lilith, the assassin, would never drink on the job, but this girl needed another to steady her nerves. Couples and groups had formed in the small seating areas. Other people made their way into the darkly curtained halls.

While the main hall seemed like any other masquerade, curiosity took hold after a few minutes of watching people hit on each other. After brushing off one or two advances, I followed a couple behind the black velvet curtains. Shadows crowded every corner. This hall had been almost entirely cloaked from light, lit only by large iron candelabras. Gradually, flashes of the public displays of affection Benjamin had described came into view. This was a very specific sort of party.

WATCHING MEN AND women move through the covered corridors, I was reminded of the great halls and temples in ancient history. Rituals. Orgies. Human sacrifices to angry gods. As I watched a naked woman pour wine into the waiting mouth of her kneeling partner, I wondered how far we had actually come from that time. He looked up at her with pleading eyes, clad only in a black leather harness and matching sheer underwear. She placed her foot on his chest and said with quiet dominance, "lick them."

A couple sat in an armchair across from them and watched. The young woman still wore her mask, her dress pooling around her hips as her partner rocked them against himself. The scene behind them was far less gentle. I continued down the hall, away from the sounds of someone choking on their lover's cock.

Dark alcoves were nestled about in the dimly lit hall. Candlelight illuminated people who were engaging in other various sexual acts. While some were comfortable doing their deeds in clear view, others were cloaked in shadows. Some of the acts were relatively tame, and others fell outside of my personal repertoire. Whips, cuffs, clamps, multiple partners. A woman with a gag in her mouth eyed me as she gripped the plush ottoman beneath her, whimpering with every lash she received. That didn't stop me from watching. Who was I to judge?

In one alcove, there were two men taking a woman from either end. Another held several men, each of them enjoying each other's bodies. There were people pleasuring themselves or being pleasured by others, watching from armchairs and sofas dispersed throughout the hall. It was clear that the intended use for this space was to give exhibitionists a place to be seen and voyeurs a place to enjoy. The dim candlelight and haunting melodies filled the air to add class to pure bacchanalia.

Still, a feeling of unease coated my skin. Even as I walked through the party alone, I had the sense that I was being watched. My gut pinched and I shifted my gaze to the corners. While most people were involved in activities with other people, it sounded like someone was walking down the hall alone, as I had been. I saw a figure lurking in the shadows. The figure was near enough to feel close, but cloaked in almost complete darkness. I couldn't make out anything beyond a skull-shaped mask. But I felt the burn of their eyes on me.

Turning away, my breath felt shallow and nervous. I hoped that this person would not follow me as I reached the end of the hall. In the last alcove, a couple was taking their time licking and kissing each other's bodies. Compared to everything I'd seen up to this moment, it was surprisingly intimate. Their kisses were long and deep. Fingers traced along every curve of flesh. The woman turned her head and smiled at me as he took one of her nipples into his mouth, which somehow made me feel better about watching. Like a welcome participant.

My mind drifted as I watched them. It had been about a year since I'd been with anyone physically and even that barely counted. It was a half-hearted dating app hookup that didn't do anything for me. In. Out. Gone. An effort to shake me from the stupor that Ethan had left me in. This was fucking hot and I was definitely going to be thinking about this couple when I took care of myself later.

Approaching footsteps were drowned out by my thoughts and the woman's moans. With my head tilted to one side, my fingers dragged across my throat. This time I didn't notice I wasn't alone until I heard a throat clearing behind me.

Benjamin pulled up the nearest armchair and sat. He crooked a finger and beckoned me to come closer. The air around him crackled with mischief. Pulling me into his lap, he placed his hand on my exposed thigh.

"I don't think I understood what kind of party this was going to be," I said, flustered that I'd been caught gaping at the scene before me.

"I'm sorry, though you did seem to be enjoying yourself," he replied. I laughed softly, starting to feel flush with embarrassment. "I don't generally enjoy these sorts of events, but I have to meet with associates at these things. Some of the men I'm meeting later are on the board of Eros," he continued.

"Okay, I'm just not sure why I'm here. It's not like I can meet anyone like this," I said while absently touching my mask.

"Well, I felt odd about coming here alone, and bringing another woman was not an option, given our current arrangement, so here we are."

It made sense when he explained it that way. As I thought about it, I almost didn't notice the way his hand had been working up my thigh in small strokes, taking advantage of the access the generous slit in my dress afforded him. My spine straightened as his lips brushed my ear.

"It would look strange if we sat here doing nothing," he teased.

"What are you doing?"

"Taking care of what belongs to me. Will you let me entertain you?" His voice darkened, thick with promise, as his fingers reached my panties. I nodded. "Watch them."

The man had the woman's hair wrapped around his fist and was taking her from behind with one of her legs propped up on the armchair so voyeurs could witness every powerful thrust. It was clear this woman liked to be watched. Benjamin's touch had moved below the lacey fabric and directly into my damp sex. My breath hitched. Approval hummed in my ear.

"You intrigue me, Ms. Caccia."

"Why?" The word fell out of my mouth in a soft moan.

The tip of his thumb brushed against my clit as he spoke.

"You don't know me. I don't know you. But I want to find out what drives you. What makes you come undone?"

This felt public. Surrounded by people enjoying themselves, I shouldn't have been self-conscious, but I couldn't escape the feeling that we were being watched. That *I* was being watched. But everyone was watching everyone else, right? That's what this was for. *Show off your relationship. Enjoy each other.* For a moment, I wondered what Benjamin thought he was doing. But I didn't move to stop him. No, instead I let my knees part as he plunged in. He dusted kisses down the column of my neck, stopping only to speak.

"Did you know that the taste of your mouth stayed with me for hours? I went to bed wondering if you truly wanted me. But your body is telling me now. I can feel how wet you are for me."

I stifled a moan as his thumb circled the bundle of nerves that had swollen with anticipation. The delicious friction was almost too much to bear. I started circling my hips, desperately seeking relief. His other arm banded around my waist, pushing his increasingly hard length into my ass. Slowly, steadily, his touch unwound me. Bricks tumbled from barriers I'd worked hard to build. Warm breaths ghosted across my neck. The sureness of his touch sent a shiver through me. Every tiny muscle in me started to clench as heat pooled in me. I was lost. Lost in his scent. Lost in his touch. Lost in the feel of his body against mine. A long lick dragged up from my shoulder. My fingers dug into the armchair as my head sank back against him.

"Do you want me?" He asked.

I nodded.

"Good. Because I want you too, Ms. Caccia." He growled as his teeth grazed my ear. "I want to know what this beautiful pussy feels like wrapped around me. I've wanted it since the first moment I had you in my arms. You're intoxicating."

A second finger slid inside as he pressed the heel of his palm against me. Breath rasped from my deep red lips. His strokes increased in pressure and pace. Being this vulnerable was out of the question for someone like me. This much exposure while working was wildly inappropriate, but I didn't care. Everything had narrowed to his touch. It had been so long since I'd been touched by capable hands, my body felt like a sparking power line. The kiss his lips demanded felt as dangerous as as a blade.

"From the moment I tasted these lips, I wondered what they would look like screaming my name."

I wasn't far from that. Not at all. Any thoughts of being watched were gone, replaced only with his touch and everything that it promised.

"Lilith," he murmured. "Are you going to come for me?"

"Yes." I breathed.

"Good girl."

My legs began to shake as I bit my lip, stifling a whimper. The couple in front of us raced toward their mutual climax as I crashed through my own. My thighs clenched around his hand. Burying my face in Benjamin's neck, I breathed little cries of pleasure through my release. After I'd caught my breath, he pushed his fingers into my mouth and watched as I licked myself off of them. The satisfaction in his darkened gaze could not be hidden by a mask.

"Get on your knees," he rasped.

"Mr. Camden?"

The man in the rabbit mask was standing before us now. Benjamin groaned softly into my ear and adjusted himself in his pants.

"The board members are meeting in five minutes."

"I'll be there shortly," he said as he gestured to dismiss him. "Sorry, pet. Next time I'll take you to one of the private rooms and we can finish this properly. I promise."

As I stood and straightened my dress, I remembered I'd been followed. My eyes searched for the skull-shaped mask I had seen lurking in the shadows. They were gone. When I didn't find them, I hoped that they'd left before our little show.

34

AGERATINA ALTISSIMA

I went to see the wreckage at Bootlegger for myself. All that remained of the dining room was smoldering debris. Large leather booths that had been there for decades were skeletal carcasses with bits of flesh dangling here and there. The marble bar top was the only item that was unscathed, the mirror scorched and cracked behind it.

My boots crunched over splinters of wood and glass as I made my way to the office. The floors seemed to be in decent shape in that they still more or less existed. The door to the office, well, not so much. As I stepped through the opening, I looked around at the walls. It had started here. That's what the fire department said. Someone would have to have the security code to disarm the restaurant's system and the key to get into the office.

All of the photos were gone. My mother's smiling face was burned to ash. Kneeling next to the remnants of the desk, I pushed aside what I could and removed the heavy flooring panel. Fireproof. Clicking through the numbers on the combination lock, I opened the safe and cleared out the contents into a file box I had brought with me. As I placed the items inside, I seethed with anger. This attack felt personal. The office wasn't just the point of origin. It was the message.

AFTER I PUT the fear of God into the contractors, I went home to work on finding Casey. It had been a few days since I had made any progress and even longer since I left Henry Johnson in a shallow grave in the middle of Nevada. Before I buried him, I pocketed his phone. The beautiful watch I'd also kept was a solid gold Submariner with an onyx face. It glinted up at me as I stuffed his corpse into a suitcase. It would have been a shame to bury it.

The pizza I grabbed from Garage was making my mouth water, but the stress sweat I was covered in had started to stink. I took a shower, then set to work digging up more information. Unlike Isabelle, Casey's social media was far less elabroate. Her lack of a social circle and low-profile lifestyle didn't leave me with a lot to work with. Isabelle was the only dancer she spent time with, which explained how Casey got mixed up with Eros but not much else. At first, I thought maybe she went to Las Vegas with her, but I didn't see Casey in any of Isabelle's posts or the security footage at the restaurant. Without any other leads, I decided to stay focused on learning more about Henry Johnson.

My wet, inky black hair was making big splotchy watermarks on my tee shirt as I started digging through Johnson's phone settings. Resetting his security had been so easy. When I had taken it initially, I just used his face to open the security settings. After that, I changed the lock code to whatever I wanted. With his phone in my hands, I had access to his entire life.

The first things I searched were social media, bank accounts, and email. I'd taken to reading emails in my spare moments at home, leaving them in a locked signal-blocking box when I was away. I had already flipped through his photo albums to find pictures of his kids and his dog, but no photos of his wife. Any text messages were all business related. Henry had leveled himself up in some bubble-bursting game. I even had access to his Eros app. On the app, I saw his messages with Isabelle. He was also sending filthy messages to several other girls after he had put her in the ground. What a prick.

Between the hours I'd spent looking through his emails, looking for something that might give me more information on Eros, I got pretty good at the bubble-bursting game. Then, while I was reheating another slice of meat-covered pizza, an email alert bobbed onto the screen from someone named Stephen Bryant.

Henry,

We're moving forward with Trans-Oceanic. They want a meeting set up within the next two weeks. Location to be determined.
    We'll be in touch.

SB

Whoever he was, he had no idea that Henry was dead. This email had an incomprehensible attachment. It was a spreadsheet with a bunch of numbers and letters written together in some kind of code. Each one had what looked like a date next to it. I tried to comprehend the patterns. Tried to make sense of the dates.

First, I needed to get some food in me. Then some sleep. I leaned against the counter and chewed on the freshly heated pizza, making little cooling noises with my mouth when the hot cheese obliterated my tongue. When I finished, I put on Netflix and started watching Pulp Fiction.

It had been a few hours since I put the movie on, but it was too engaging for me to be tired. Pouring another glass of cold water for myself, I took a look at the small glowing clock on my microwave. It told me it would be morning soon, but I still had enough time to get a decent amount of sleep before seeing Kaia later. The water on my shirt hadn't quite dried yet, though my hair mostly had. I padded over to my bed and put on another movie. My phone pinged on the nightstand. A text message from West.

If you're seeing this, you need to go to sleep.

My stomach did a little flip when I saw his name on the screen. He had finally broken the silence. When I went to the gym at our normal time, he didn't show up. I had spent my entire workout wondering if I could fix whatever it was that had changed between us. Thankful he was talking to me again, I quickly sent a response.

I'm in bed now. See?

I sent a selfie along with the text to prove myself, not really caring that I was in the old Nirvana tee shirt and my bed was a disaster of twisted sheets. The text bubble with the three dots popped up and went away a few times. It was well past closing time for Muse. He was probably already at home. Probably in his own bed. I found myself wondering what kind of night he'd had. If he'd gotten into any fights. If it was slow. I watched the text bubble bob into view again and again until my eyelids felt too heavy to keep open. Before I fell asleep, I sent him another text.

Good night.

A few minutes went by. My mind drifted to Casey. The sinking feeling that I'd failed her surfaced. Trying to snuff out the thought, I switched over to a comfort sitcom on Netflix. I was nearly dozing when my phone pinged again.

Good night, Lili.

I WORRIED MY bottom lip as I crossed out another name on my list. Stephen Bryant's list of strange codes would have to wait. I needed to stay on task. I looked over the list of party guests again. The men whose names I collected were qualified for my list by a line of seemingly innocent questions I'd disguised as polite conversation.

"How long have you been with Eros?"

"Have you met anyone special at these parties?"

"Did any girls catch your eye?"

Depending on how they'd answer, most got dismissed early and I wouldn't waste my time trying to remember their names. The barstool made little clanging noises as I tapped my boot against it. Another name crossed off. Every time someone had a viable alibi, they got marked off. Looking down at my list of names tugged at the pit of anxiety and despair that grew inside me. I was starting to wonder if this path lead to a dead end.

"Don't you have the internet at home?" Sophie asked as she bounced into the club.

"Yeah," I sighed. "I just needed a change of scenery."

The laptop made a soft clicking sound as I pushed it shut. This wasn't helping. My brain felt fried. I hadn't slept much in days. I sat up, stretching my back after having been hunched over the computer for the last few hours. Sophie stopped and hoisted the bag she carried up on her shoulder.

"Have you found anything yet? About Casey or Isabelle?"

I cringed and debated how much I wanted to tell her.

"No, I haven't." Keep it short, I thought. Don't say too much. I didn't want to tell her that Isabelle was dead. I didn't want to tell her that I had no idea where Casey was.

Sophie blew out a breath and nodded, fighting tears. I debated giving her a hug, but she walked away before I could get up. The muscles in my jaw tightened as I bit back my own tears.

"Lili," Kaia called down from her office. "Come up here."

I walked quickly toward my sister. Today she was wearing her "don't fuck with me" Gucci suit. Walking up the stairs toward her felt intimidating. Like I was being called into the principal's office. When her door snicked shut behind me, I raised my eyebrows at her and waited for her to speak.

"Do you want anything to drink?" She offered.

"So it's going to be that kind of conversation, huh?"

She didn't say another word. Instead, Kaia walked over to the bar and poured a glass of whiskey. Only, it wasn't for her. It was for me.

"I need your help with something tonight."

I took the glass from her hand and tossed back the contents. The single malt burned down my throat as I put the glass on her desk and sat down. I didn't prompt her. Didn't ask follow-up questions. She would explain what she needed when she was ready, and given the way she had decided to ask, I knew what it was going to be.

"Carlo and his men tracked down the man responsible for Bootlegger. An Arawn man, as we thought. The fire started in the office, so we know that he had help. Help from one of our men."

"Where is he now?"

Kaia rounded her desk and sat. She never looked more like a vengeful queen than she did in that seat, in that suit, with that wrathful look on her face. I knew what she was going to tell me before she opened her mouth.

"He's being held at Pal's. I need you to go there and find out what he knows."

I nodded and stood, readying myself to leave. There was only one thing I needed to know before I got started.

"Does he need to be able to talk when I'm done?"

My sister steepled her fingers and looked up at me. Her expression was pure Matteo Caccia.

"He burned down a Caccia business and he was stupid enough to get caught. He's already taking his last breaths."

35

TOXICOSCORDION VENENOSUM

Basements aren't really a thing in Los Angeles. Mainly because of earthquakes. It doesn't really occur to anyone to go looking for one. When Giorgio bought the deli, he'd done so partially for the business opportunity and partially for the distilling and storage of liquor he could keep hidden from the law. It wasn't much. A utility sink on one end, and rickety stairs on the other. No floors, just sealed concrete and a drain. Sparsely lit, it wasn't suitable for much these days. Still, its usefullness had never exhausted itself.

I leaned against the stairway and watched from the shadows as our captive roused into consciousness. The wounds he'd obtained going down were still seeping, only hours old. His hands were bound to the arms of the chair in which he sat. Ankles tied to its legs.

Brian Donnelly sat before us. Not terribly high up on the Arawn food chain, but he'd been the man to light the match at the Bootlegger, and now he was going to pay, but not before giving us the information we needed. Rage still pumped its way through my blood as I approached the bleeding man before me. Prowling beneath my skin, huffing with carnal anticipation. I shook my hands out and got to work.

"I have some questions for you, Brian."

I took a breath, tamping down on the roaring in my head, praying it would quiet the howling beast within. When he spoke, his accent was so thick that it sounded like he was speaking in cursive.

"You're acting the maggot if you think I'm telling you shite."

Carlo gave me a wary look. This time, I'd left the serums and poisons at home. We were going to do this the old-fashioned way. My blades were ready, clean, and waiting. I pulled one from its sheath.

Brian watched me approach him with guarded eyes. I took his pinky in my hand and squeezed. My knife slipped through the first layer of skin quickly. Easily. Blood welled to the surface and started to coat my fingers.

"I'm going to start small, but I promise you that I will work my way up to larger things. Things that have far more nerve endings than the tip of your pinky."

His hand was sweaty in mine. It made his finger hard to grip. He kept moving it, trying to pull it away from me. I grabbed his wrist and twisted. Hard.

"You fucking cunt!" He screamed, spit rocketing out of his mouth.

I smiled at him in a way that wasn't so much smiling as it was baring my teeth.

"Honey, I haven't even gotten to the painful part yet."

With his palm facing me, I tipped the blade between the base of his pinky and his palm while holding the tip of it with my other hand. Then I severed the finger. The noise he made was part scream and part wretch.

"You said you were taking the tip, you fucking slag."

"I lied."

The first finger came off clean. Well, as clean as a disembodied finger could be since he'd struggled. The next was rougher. I'd felt the ligament give when I severed it, and a small gush of blood followed. After that, I took his right ear. I didn't usually vary my approach, but he called me a "vindictive cunt" and I felt the need to admonish him. He'd given us small pieces of information. Fluff. Nothing. Things we already knew, so I took small pieces from him.

"Our restaurant, the one you burned to the ground, had some pretty elaborate security measures. You seemed to know them all. How?"

I knelt before the man. This was it. The reason we were here. Not because of the Arawn clan. They would always be a threat, but because one of our men had to have given him that information. He looked around the room. His once stark white shirt was now drenched in sweat, revealing all of his tattoos, and stained with his blood.

"How, Brian? How did you know those codes?"

"I don't know...I," he stammered. He'd gone into shock long ago. He must have, after all of the things I took. I looked at the bleeding gash where his right ear used to be. If I had any plans for letting him live, I'd feel bad for the guy. I stood and walked back to the steel worktable, looking over the items there. Pliers, my knives, a soiled towel, and a bowl of Brian's parts. The biggest knife, my hunting knife, still had a little blood on it. Turning to face Brian, I casually cleaned it with the towel.

"Alright, Brian. You know what happens now."

"No, please. I can't!" He cried, frantically looking around the room again. He'd resorted to begging. I'd broken him.

"You can't? You can't what?"

Tears streamed down his face.

"They let me in! He -" Brian's head was there and then it was gone. It took me a second for it to sink in. Then I vomited all over his shoes.

"Jesus, what the fuck do you think you're doing?" Carlo shouted.

My eyes shot to Ozzie. The gun in his hand was still angled at the man's head. Or what was left of it.

"I don't know what happened," Ozzie said meekly. "It just went off."

Carlo started shouting at him. They argued. Carlo screamed at Ozzie about making sure the safety on his gun was locked. But I'd heard it, I thought. I heard it click off while Brian was begging. I lifted my shirt to wipe the blood and bits of Brian off of my face, thankful I'd chosen to wear black.

"It's fine, Carlo. Shit happens." I looked at Ozzie. His face was wild, twisted with something I couldn't name. I tried to keep the tone of my voice neutral. A flippant smile curled my lips. "Oz, go call the clean-up guys. Tell them we got done early."

I thought again about Brian's last words. The tiny expressions on his face. The small, thinly veiled glances. Not at his gun or even at the door. At Ozzie. I didn't miss any of it. He nodded and left the room. I waited for a beat, trying to avoid being overheard.

"Keep an eye on him. That was no fucking accident."

Carlo nodded. He had to have suspected the same thing I did. Ozzie's hair-trigger temper was infamous and reason enough to doubt his loyalty. For the number of times he'd looked at Oz, Brian may as well have been pointing at him. But I needed proof. Something beyond what I assumed because Oz was a capo. He had his own crew. Guys who would go down fighting for him. If he was a betraying bastard piece of shit, I needed to be able to prove it.

36

RUMEX CRISPUS

The metal ping and thwack sounded through the yard.

"Bullseye!" I shouted.

"Showoff," Kaia grumbled.

I pulled another knife from my belt.

"Okay, if I make this one...you owe me twenty bucks."

"I literally pay you thousands of dollars a week."

"Fine. Fifty bucks." I smirked. Kaia walked to the table and took a sip of her wine. Giving the blade a few flips, because I actually am a showoff, I steadied myself for my next shot. The wood target was splintered to hell and already heavy with several other knives. Polished steel blades had been thrown by Kaia. The more closely grouped matte black blades were my own.

The blade whipped through the air and stuck to the board, right next to its friend. A victorious laugh burst from my lips as Kaia groaned. I may have done a few dance moves just to rub it in. My sister, having had enough of my bragging, briskly walked to the board and pulled all of her knives.

"Aw, come on Kai. Don't be a sore loser."

An irritated chuckle was the only warning I had before knives started flying past my head. Six pings rang out behind me, one right after the other.

I turned to look at the board and saw a perfect circle of steel blades surrounding my black ones.

"So, what, you were letting me win?"

"No, but I was also throwing with my left hand," she said with a smirk. Walking over to the iron table, she poured herself another glass of wine. Sunlight had started to dim, making the wisteria blossoms appear more violet than purple while the scent of lemon filled the air. "We're not going to find Casey."

The matter-of-fact tone hurt more than the truth of it. I knew it too but had avoided thinking much about it. Especially after I'd told Kaia what I'd been doing, the email from Bryant to Johnson, and what happened to Isabelle. We both knew the statistics. We knew the likelihood of being able to find Casey after so much time had passed. I took a sip from the gin and soda I'd been ignoring, trying to will away the wrenching pang of guilt I felt. Kaia put her arm around me and squeezed.

"Don't let it eat at you."

"I'm not. It's just that I feel like I'm getting close to something. I still want answers. Something. She deserves an ending. Even if it's awful."

She gave me a knowing look and sipped again from her glass. The sounds of turtledoves cooing in the trees filled the silence. Twilight made this space truly beautiful as the trattoria lights switched on, gently lighting our faces.

"How much of that Camden stuff is real?" She finally asked, clearly trying to change the subject. She wasn't going to let this go. Of course, she wouldn't. I'd sworn to protect the family but she would always protect me. I laughed and walked over to the board to collect my knives.

"None of it." I was always bad at lying to my sister.

"It certainly doesn't look that way to me."

"Yeah, well, that's kind of the point," I grunted as I pulled a deeply embedded blade free from the wooden target. "He has to be getting bored with me by now."

"I doubt that very much," Kaia mumbled into her glass, trying not to spill as I punched her arm. "Lili, you don't give yourself enough credit. I can't believe I have to tell you how gorgeous you are. You own a mirror."

"Men aren't exactly beating down my door, K."

"No, you just don't notice the men who notice you."

"Well, that's vague. Thanks for that." I finished my drink and set the empty glass on the table. Kaia gave me a sympathetic smile and patted my shoulder. "Besides, aren't you the one who warned me not to get too invested in him in the first place? All that 'he's all about appearances' talk was for nothing, then?"

"No! I'm not even saying that… Just try to do better at noticing."

I nodded, not quite sure what that even meant. Kaia was the kind of woman who turned heads in whatever she wore. Of course, men noticed her. She was slender and towered over me. Her cinema-star bone structure was all our mother. Though we both got the same pitch-black hair, it took me a long time to appreciate our differences. Except for one. I didn't know if I could ever come to appreciate my eyes.

It wasn't like I thought I was ugly. My short stature isn't exactly something you can change, and my ample bosom and backside make it difficult to argue that I don't fill a dress well. Hours of training in the gym kept my muscles toned. Spending my time hunting people down made it hard to remember to go to the salon. My black strands were more messy and wavy than carefully coiffed. The clothes I wore were usually some grunge-adjacent version of the tee shirt and denim combination topped with a jacket or sweater when it was cold, and my combat boots whenever I could. My look had become almost entirely utilitarian since I left school.

Still, it was hard not to feel like an imposter next to Benjamin. When my hair and makeup were done and I donned the expensive clothes he'd bought for me, I felt like a completely different person. Like me, but wrong somehow. The version of me that people were taking pictures of was beautiful, but a complete stranger. A lie.

"Do you want to stay for dinner?"

"When have you ever known me to turn down food?" I laughed. "What are we having?"

"Something frozen or delivered."

"You're the best mom ever."

Kaia took out her phone and started to order from a food delivery app. With a sidelong glance at me, she said, "I shouldn't order anything spicy, right?"

I sighed through my nose.

"Who's on the chopping block tonight?"

"Eric Smith."

She handed over the manila envelope I'd seen and had been silently hoping wasn't for me. A ruling from a goddess to her angel of death.

AFTER HORSING DOWN a few taquitos and guacamole, I headed to my car to review the assignment Kaia had given me. She and I both knew I wasn't going to give up on Casey and I'd told her as much over dinner. We never discussed work in front of Daniel, so all I said was that I wasn't going to drop it until I knew what happened. She'd nodded her agreement.

As the iron gate rolled open, I glanced at myself in the rearview mirror. I had gotten his damned eyes. The green-ringed pupils are surrounded in gold. His angry, dark eyes. I turned on the radio, needing to blast the darker thoughts out of my mind with some girl rap. The expensive sound system almost couldn't handle the heavy bass. Megan Thee Stallion was starting to talk about being savage when my phone pinged.

KAIA: Make it quick.

An ounce of pity for a man whose fate was sealed.

37

HIPPOMANE MANCINELLA

Stalking a target is an intimate process. You learn everything about them. Things not even their partners know. I've seen wives kiss their husbands goodbye and unknowingly send them into the arms of a lover. I've noticed eating disorders and drug addictions well before they'd admit it to themselves.

I checked the time again and shifted in my seat because my ass was starting to fall asleep. It had been two hours since I left the house and came right over the hill to Studio City. My black Mercedes sat alone in the parking lot, which was dark except for the light being cast off from the buildings across the street. Eric Smith frequented this liquor store because it was convenient for him. At the end of a long day working as a security guard for a film studio if he wasn't in a bar, gambling away most of his paycheck, he would buy himself a sixer of beer and spend the night betting on sports through an online portal. Our online portal.

Most of the time, finding someone like him takes a decent amount of surveillance. I'd follow them around, go to their gym, make friends with their favorite barista, and even chit-chat with their significant others at the grocery store. Thanks to Eric's sad little routine, it was easy to track him down and even easier to figure out when and where he would be alone. First, we sent our bagman after him. Since he accepted the promise of repayment six months ago, Eric had been living on borrowed time.

Any minute now, he was going to walk out of the liquor store and go back up to his apartment to pour himself a pint.

Empty promises to pay down his double-or-nothing bets lead to this. This was his fault, I told myself as I took another swig of my coffee. His own doing. I glanced at the details again. Thousands of dollars. Debt to the Caccia family was taken seriously and it was clear he was making no effort to pay off the mountain of it he'd acquired over the last year. Like dozens of men I'd put in the ground before him, his habit was a slippery slope and he was about to plummet off of it. My stomach clenched as I got out of the car and grabbed my bag. As I shut the door, Eric stepped out of the store and back onto the sidewalk.

Careful to keep my distance behind him, I tread lightly. Stalking men is far easier than stalking women. Women tend to be aware of their surroundings because the world has always been more dangerous for them. Men, especially those who don't know they're being stalked, tend to be very flippant with their security and Eric was no different. He didn't glance over his shoulder to see if he was being watched. He was. The doors he opened were still closing as he moved on to the next, never checking to see if they were shut behind him. They didn't. When he got home, he immediately went to the bathroom to relieve himself. Too busy emptying his bladder to notice someone tucking themselves into the coat closet. Which I did.

The slats on the louvered closet door were small enough to obscure me from view, but a broken piece allowed me to take an appraisal of his home as I settled in for a long wait. The room had all the trappings of a man who never wanted to grow up. A variety of craft beer bottles stood on the tops of the dingy kitchen cabinets like trophies, each one placed equidistant from the next. A thin layer of dust coated almost every surface. There were no framed family photos, just movie posters tacked hastily to the walls. Reservoir Dogs, Scarface, and Goodfellas. It was hard not to chuckle to myself at the irony.

The half-rotted sofa he'd flung himself onto had seen far better days. Patches of duct tape were holding older parts of the leather upholstery together. Despite it being a sectional, he had his socked feet up on the wooden crate he was using for a coffee table. Professional football, college football, basketball, and even poker. He bet on them all.

After about an hour of calling bookies, gambling on credit he didn't have, there was a knock at the door. Unhurried steps moved past the closet to answer it. He'd been expecting someone. I tensed. The hinges squeaked as the door opened, followed by the crackling sound of a paper bag. He'd ordered dinner. The scent floated through the air and beckoned to me like a starved cartoon character. Was that curry? I said a small prayer to myself that Smith wouldn't hear my stomach growling over the TV.

Between the biting pangs of hunger, the urge to pee, and waves of boredom, I thought about the spreadsheet Stephen Bryant had sent to Henry Johnson. The sequences looked familiar on their own, but together they didn't make sense. All of those numbers and letters scrambled together. His email had no context clues. The document was just labeled "units." What the fuck did that mean?

THREE HOURS. NOT the longest I'd waited for a target, but environmental factors added to my discomfort. He drank his beers, shouted at the television, and placed bets. I stretched my arms and wished I had the presence of mind to pee before this. My short stature made it easy to hide in places tight spaces, but I still felt cramped and tired. The syringe had been prepared and waiting once Eric had finished his fifth beer and started to nod off. If this was his routine, I'd suggest he get some help, but it wouldn't've mattered much at this point.

I was staring into space while the TV was rattling off some football players' stats. My skin was starting to feel three sizes too small when I started looking around at the contents of the closet. A worn leather bomber and teal windbreaker were hung and pushed to one side. The floor was replete with empty boxes from various online orders. All shapes and sizes. As I stared at one label, wondering what he could have ordered from a place called "Silicone Wonderz," it clicked. A series of letters and numbers are sequenced together.

Stephen Bryant's spreadsheet. It wasn't nonsense. They were fucking tracking codes.

Soft snoring sounds were almost drowned out by the blaring television. The doorknob twisted easily under my grip. With the needle in one hand, the other hand stretched out for balance as I moved quietly from one end of the room to the other. Eric was slouched back in the sectional, mouth agape, with his phone resting on his chest. The undershirt he wore reeked of sweat and body spray. It was hard not to feel sorry for him. He was just a guy who got in too deep on a habit he couldn't break. But I knew he had put himself here. His story wasn't unique. He wasn't special. He was a man who owed us thousands and didn't pay it back.

He brought this on himself, I told myself as the needle slipped beneath his skin. Roiling nausea coursing through me disagreed. Dropping the used needle back into my bag, I let myself into his bathroom to pee and purge as quietly as I could. It wouldn't take long for the toxins to work, but I didn't need his last moments to be filled with the sounds of me not keeping dinner down.

Based on his lifestyle, people wouldn't notice Eric wasn't around until he repeatedly missed showing up for work. By then, the remnants of the toxins in his system would fail to appear in a basic toxicology report. Careful not to touch anything else in the apartment, I found his spare key and locked the door behind me after I left.

As I made my way back to my car, I thought about the rows and rows of information I had seen on the spreadsheet. There must have been at least twenty per tab. The idea of trying to comb through all of it sent a wave of exhaustion crashing over me as I waited to cross the street.

We're not going to find Casey.

It was possible. Probable, even. I knew it, and so did my sister. She and

Isabelle were our responsibility. Their safety was in our hands. Henry's confession still echoed in my mind. Isabelle's body was disposed of like a cheap toy by a married man who was looking for a little fun. The thought of failing Casey like I'd failed Isabelle enveloped my mind like an ill-fitting wool sweater: heavy, itchy, and uncomfortable. There was no way I was going to give up on her. Even if the end of the story hurt like hell, it ate at me. I needed to know.

BEFORE I KNEW what I was doing, I found myself driving back to Casey's apartment. It was just as I'd left it. Just as she had, except for a few minor things. There was a pile of mail on the floor that had been growing for weeks. Her hamper was pushed against her nightstand, as I moved it to get into her closet. The small studio still smelled like incense and patchouli. I scratched absently at the back of my neck as I took a seat on her bed.

It felt like a tomb in here now. Everything around had suggested she expected to return. Dishes sat in the sink, waiting to be more thoroughly washed. A roll of quarters was resting on top of a box of laundry detergent. She was going to do laundry. I'd flushed the dead beta fish the first time I'd visited this place. She and Isabelle must have gotten their fish together. They had exactly the same setup. Somehow, after everything I'd seen these days, flushing the fish still bothered me more than it should have.

Casey was one of those girls who believed in crystals. When I'd gotten my heart broken by Ethan, she gave me a rose quartz to attract love. The small altar on her nightstand had a few different stones on it. Some were sitting in a seashell. Others were scattered around with the jewelry there. Earrings, rings, and bracelets. All of them had gemstones of some type or another. All of them had some meaning. When she'd come in to work, she looked like she was going to tell your fortune.

My gaze snagged on a tiny black sphere. Pinching it between my thumb and index finger, I picked the pea-sized stone up for a closer examination.

Threaded through the middle was a thin gold chain. I remembered this necklace.

"Obsidian," she had said. "It's for protection."

At the time, she was wearing it to keep away the "bad vibes." The delicate gold chain was quiet as I slipped the bauble into my pocket and stood up to leave. As I gathered her mail into one of her reusable grocery bags, a small part of me wished that she had been wearing it when she left her apartment for what had apparently been the last time.

38

CRINUM ASIATICUM

ighting has always come naturally to me. Call it an instinct for self-preservation. I started as more of a scrapper than anything. Growing up, boys knew that I wasn't above scratching or biting. Everything was fair game. My fighting "lacked finesse." At least, that's what West told me the first time he saw me spar.

I walked into One-Two with my duffle bag slung over my shoulder. Lupo was overseeing a sparring session between two boxers. Since it was the middle of the day, the space was mostly empty but it still smelled like sweat. Honestly, I love that smell.

"Hey, kid!" He shouted from beside the ring.

"Lupo, I've got a sandwich in here for you," I said patting my bag. "Capicola, salami, provolone, and everything. No onions."

"You're too good to me," he said with a hoarse laugh. Remus's big, sad eyes stared up at me as I took out the sandwich. The old bull terrier was a fixture in the gym as much as its general manager.

I fished the sandwich out as he stepped down from the platform. Though he seemed frail, this man was one of the most feared of my grandfather's soldiers. Men would piss themselves whenever Lupo showed up. He was fierce, but more important than anything, he was loyal. The weathered skin that covered him was marred with battle scars. Burns, stab wounds, even bullet holes.

My eyes skimmed over his scarred knuckles as he took the sandwich from me. The white butcher paper crinkled in his fingers as he squeezed it with gratitude.

"Thank you, sweetheart," he rasped. "Your date is already here."

"Yeah?" I laughed, rolling my eyes at the old man. "He's probably getting ready to beat my ass."

Lupo chuckled and walked back to the ring.

"Come on! My mother hits better than you!" He shouted at the fighters.

The rapid thunk of a speed bag filled the room. I made my way over to the lockers to store my bag and get ready. While wrapping my wrists, I looked over to see the broad man pummelling the small leather sack. West had beaten me here and was already warming up. His long wavy hair was piled on top of his head, but coming down in little pieces of gold and brown around his face. The black tee shirt he wore had the sleeves cut off, which left gaping holes large enough to see the twisting muscle and tattoos beneath.

Cursing the old space for lacking air conditioning, I pulled my shirt off and stuffed it into my locker before closing it up and adjusting my leggings around my waist. After spotting me from his corner, he made his way over to me.

"Hey," he panted. It was easy to forget how big he was. Standing at about six and a half feet, he was over a foot taller than me. Something about the way he looked at me made me feel even smaller.

"Have you been here a while?"

He shrugged. "I didn't have anything else going on today besides work later." He lifted his shirt to wipe the sweat from his face. "Do you want to get started?"

"I'm here, aren't I?"

No less than thirty minutes into our session, I felt like I was going to pass out. We were focusing on boxing for the day, but West was always ruthless when he trained me. My short stature accounted for my lack of reach, but his instruction helped me to overcome that issue. By the end of each training session, he made me feel like I could take anyone down.

"How's the search going?" He asked as I jabbed at the punching mitts.

"There's a lot to it. I found out what happened to Isabelle, but I still have no idea where Casey is." I jerked out between hits.

"What happened to Isabelle?"

I stopped and gave him a knowing look, then continued to punch the pads. It was hard to tell if it was the workout or the thought of her rotting in some unmarked grave that made me sick.

"Fuck," he said, blowing out a breath. "Is that what you've been doing with Camden? He helped you find that out?"

My gut twisted. Telling him about Benjamin felt strange. I decided to keep the details to myself. Especially about what started to happen between us. West arched an eyebrow at me. He knew I was holding back. He always knew.

"Well, sort of. I found out about Isabelle through him. So, yeah, in his way." I finally countered.

West grunted.

"I do sort of feel like I'm missing something. But he is helpful."

"Yeah, I'm sure he is." His words dripped with sarcasm.

"What is your problem?"

He rolled his eyes. I started punching the mitts harder. Sometimes West poked fun at me to get me to work harder, but this felt different. Like I was being hit below the belt. Neither of us spoke for a few minutes and I punched until my muscles started to ache. I tried to ignore the pain as frustration boiled in my stomach, but my temper was getting the better of me. The last thing I needed was his judgment. Words tumbled out of me before I could stop them.

"You know, I'm getting really sick of this. If you have something to say, just say it."

"Do what you want, Lili. Just don't be stupid."

"You think I'm being stupid?"

"I think this guy is getting under your skin and you're not watching your ass."

"Under my skin? Like I just can't help myself? I'm not some bobble-headed bimbo gold-digger. This is business."

"Sure," he laughed coldly.

I scoffed and backed up, peeling off my gloves with my teeth. I didn't need this shit. Not when I was burning the candle at both ends. Hell, I was running out of wick.

"You don't know anything," I snapped.

"Lili!"

Stomping over to the lockers, I jammed the gloves under my arms. It was suddenly impossible to catch my breath. He wasn't out there with me. Rubbing elbows with potential murderers and risking my neck by showing my face to these elitist assholes. He wasn't the one who was sitting up all night, researching every single name, only to come up with nothing.

Henry Johnson was burned and buried in a shallow grave because of me. The smell of his burning flesh would never leave my memory. Maybe Camden was getting under my skin, but when was the last time I did something for myself? The last several years of my life had been filled with nights hunting down men just like Johnson only to end up cold and alone in my bed.

"Lili, wait."

West was standing over me with a pained look of regret. Good. He braced a palm on the locker beside my head. The air felt hotter than before. It scorched my throat and stole my breath. Leaning over me, I could see him searching for the right thing to say. The coiled snake of anger twisted inside of me and brought tears to my eyes. I hate that I cry when I'm angry. It made me feel weak, and I was *so* angry. I bit my lip, trying hard to hold on to the rage.

"I just think..." He trailed off. My lip quivered as I choked on a sob. West reached out but hesitated, his hand hanging in the air between us. Another sob lodged in my throat and I turned quickly back to my locker. I squeezed my eyes shut and begged the tears to go away. An aggravated breath blew out of him as he stormed off, a loud thudding sounding across the floor. The bathroom door slammed behind him.

A graveled laugh sounded from a seat beside the ring. The gym had cleared out. With a glance at my phone, I noticed it was getting close to lunchtime. There wouldn't be anyone else here until the kickboxing classes for the regular office job folks. While I'd usually grab something to eat with West, I had lost my appetite.

"What are you laughing at?" I asked, wiping away a tear. Lupo stood up and popped a cigar into his mouth, lifting the butane lighter I'd given him to the tip. The dog at his feet was letting out squeaking, muffled barks in his sleep. A puff of smoke billowed from his lips.

"Nothing, kid. Nothing at all."

39

SOLANUM NIGRUM

Hands skimmed up with assured grace. When they found their place, they squeezed, then stroked. He was licking me, kissing and nipping until he reached where rough hands pressed me open. Thumbs brushed against the tender flesh of my inner thighs with gentle passes. As he sucked my clit into his mouth, my hips bucked at the sensation. Keening sounds of pleasure burst from me like a wild animal.

Those hands released me as I pulled on his shoulders, begging him to meet my gaze. Begging him to kiss me. He crawled up my body with the slow and measured pace of a predator, stopping to worship me with a squeeze of my ass, a lick at my hip, and a bite at my nipple as he moved to my mouth.

I woke up with my hand stuffed down my boxers, covered in sweat. It had been a long time since I'd had a sex dream and this one was a real doozy. With my hand still between my legs, I decided to get back to what the man of my dreams had started and damn near finished himself. It didn't take long for me to get there, but I let my imagination fill in the blanks. Let the man's burning gaze meet mine. Imagined the eyes were an icy shade of blue. Imagined the hands and mouth belonged to Benjamin.

For the rest of the day, I couldn't get the dream out of my mind. I chewed on the possibilities as I made the drive to Lupo's.

Lupo invited me to dinner at his home, which, despite all of the money my grandfather paid him over the years, was still just an unassuming house in Glendale. The drive over also made me rehash my argument with West. I stewed over it and imagined what I should have said to him instead.

Sunlight started to fade from the sky as I parked and stepped out of the car. The hot day had filled the air with the scent of citrus. Heavy, late-season oranges dangled down from the trees lining the short driveway. Having heard me arrive, Lupo stepped halfway out of the front door.

"Come in, Sweetheart. I've got something on the stove."

"Can I take some of these oranges off your hands?"

"You can take 'em all," he groused.

With a laugh, I followed him into the house. The craftsman-style porch creaked under my steps as I made my way inside. Looking around, you'd never think that this place belonged to a man who'd killed dozens of men. The wood-paneled walls had family photos everywhere. Lupo holding his two boys, Dante and Nico, laughing over a board game. Playing with their mother on the beach, a kind woman who had passed while I was away at school. Dante graduating from high school.

I never could understand how Lupo handled losing his son when he was so young. He and Kaia were the same age. Just before Nonno passed, Dante got killed in a shootout with another mafia family that we had since wiped off the map. There he was, smiling next to his father and holding up his degree, dark curls falling into his face as they always did.

The scent of garlic and onions coaxed me into the small kitchen, where I found Nico slicing bread and his father standing over the stove, poking at some sausages and peppers in a cast-iron skillet. Remus perked up and started wagging his tail at me, slapping the dog bed loudly with it.

"Need some help?" I asked. Lupo waved me off with a grunt.

"Get the wine," Nico said while pointing his knife at the bottle of chianti on the counter. I leaned over Lupo and grabbed the bottle. Over the years, this place had become a second home to me, so I knew my way around the kitchen. Nudging Lupo slightly, I grabbed the corkscrew out of the drawer beside the stove. Soon, three short glasses were filled with the humble red wine. After handing each man their glass, I sat at the kitchen table and watched them work.

"You want to tell me what that little spat was about?" Lupo asked.

"Getting right to the point, huh?" I said into my glass as I took a sip of wine.

"No, no. We've got a lot to talk about. I just want to know why you were making so much racket in my club."

I shrugged and put down my glass. "I'm working on something for my sister and West is being kind of a dick about it."

Lupo and Nico exchanged a look.

"What?"

"He's protective of you. Wants to make sure you're watching out for yourself."

Nico put a basket full of the bread he'd sliced on the table with some olive oil. I dipped a slice and took a bite, then washed it down with more wine. After topping off my glass, I sighed.

"Lu, you taught me to protect myself. West works with me so I can protect myself. I don't need a babysitter."

Grunting, Lupo took the sausages, peppers, and onions off of the stove and put the skillet on a trivet on the table. The smell alone made my mouth water. Lupo gestured toward me and invited me to fill my plate, which I did without hesitation. After a few minutes of comfortable silence, each of us enjoying the food in front of us, I decided to ask. "Alright. So what do we have to talk about?"

"I've got colon cancer."

The bread I'd bitten into scraped down my throat as I forced a swallow. This was his way. Abrupt, to the point, no sugar-coating.

"What?"

"Colon cancer."

Looking to Nico for confirmation, my chest caved in at his nod. I put down my fork and leaned toward him.

"How long have you known about this?"

"I've been seeing a doctor about it for a few weeks. He says we have to move on to chemo." There was a minute of silence, then he continued. "After all these years working for your Nonno, running into bad situations with guns blazing, this was not the way I thought I was going to go."

"There's no guarantee that this will kill you. We'll get you the finest treatment available. We can afford it. I can."

"What, so they can pump me full of chemicals?"

"Pop," Nico looked up from his plate. They had clearly already had this conversation.

"Please, Lu. Please let me," I choked out. "I can't lose any more family." My eyes stung with tears I struggled to fight back. It wasn't my choice to make, and I knew it. Nico put a hand on my shoulder. My brother, not in blood but in spirit. Despite the tattoos covering his skin and his typically cold expression, he had a soft heart. He looked at his father.

"You'll stand your ground in a hail of gunfire, but you won't get stuck with some shit that will help you?" Nico said. "It didn't help Mom because she was too far gone, but you have a chance."

For a long time, we sat in near silence, birds chirping outside and my occasional sniffles were the only sounds.

"Alright," Lupo held up his hands in defeat. "I'll do the treatment if it'll shut you two up. But if I die anyway, I'm haunting the both of you."

I laughed through my tears. Lupo handed me a napkin. While I dabbed at my traitorous eyes, Nico sighed. It was clear that he'd tried to reason with his father and come up short. Lupo could be a very stubborn man. Years of training with him had taught me that. But he was a sucker for me and his son knew it. That's why I was here.

We sat and ate and talked. Nico put on a pot of espresso and Lupo broke out the cookies. As he finished his wine, Lupo gave me a look of appraisal.

"I know it's easy to ignore the advice of an old man."

I sighed and leaned back in my chair.

"Life is short, sweetheart. When you're young, it feels long. Like the world is stretching out before you. It is. But don't waste time."

Eying him for a moment, I stuffed a lemon knot into my mouth. Nico leaned against the counter and watched his father. I stood up and went to the sink, grabbing his empty dish on my way.

"All I'm saying is if you've got a chance at something good, take it. Don't hesitate. Tomorrow isn't promised."

"Alright, Lu," I said as I started washing dishes. "I get it."

An espresso cup was set down on the counter next to the other dirty dishes. Lupo walked out of the room, muttering to himself on his way out.

"He means well," Nico sighed, placing the rest of the dishes beside the sink.

"I know he does." I glanced over my shoulder at him. He looked as tired as I felt. "How are you doing with all of this?"

He shrugged. "It's hard not to think back to everything that happened with Mom, but I know this is different."

Breast cancer had taken Lupo's wife quickly. By the time they had discovered it, there was almost nothing to be done. When she died, it left them feeling helpless. They never said as much, but her absence was felt even now. Kaia was at their house almost every day, doing as much as she could to help without being asked. For her, caring for people who mean something comes as easily as breathing. Nothing had to be said.

Nico finished drying dishes and braced his hands against the counter. "Honestly, this would be easier if Dante were here. He was always better at handling stuff like this."

"You're handling it fine," I said as I hugged him from behind. "Just let me know when he goes in for infusions."

Nico nodded and I patted him on the back as I left him to his thoughts in the kitchen. The night air had cooled significantly. Fat, juicy oranges dangled down so low that I could reach them by standing on my toes. After I'd collected a box full, I put them in my backseat and headed home. The tart scent perfumed my car and left me thinking about what Lupo had said before heading off to bed.

"If you've got a chance at something good, take it."

40

DIEFFENBACHIA

Colon cancer. Lupo had colon cancer. When I closed the car door behind me, my ears started ringing. The people who were dear to me had a way of disappearing. It's funny how a bit of grief could summon every other ache, as though every past hurt was waiting in the wings. *He's not going to die*, I told myself. *I won't let him.*

I looked at the box of oranges on my passenger seat and thought about bringing some to my sister. Then I wondered if she knew about Lupo. Nico was her most trusted bodyguard, but they barely seemed to talk. Wouldn't she have told me? I dialed her number as I pulled out of the driveway.

"Yes?" she answered abruptly.

"Hey, Kai. It's me." I sniffled, trying to clear the resurgence of tears from my voice.

"I know it's you. What's wrong? Are you alright?" Her tone shifted from irritation to concern in seconds. It was amazing.

"I'm fine. I'm just leaving Lupo's. He had some news." A little sob burst from my throat.

"Lili," Kaia cooed. "It's going to be okay."

"Maybe. He has colon cancer."

"I know." My stomach dropped. She knew? I'd thought the possibility existed, but I didn't think she'd keep something like this from me.

"You knew? How?"

"Nico told me and before you start, he asked me not to say anything."

The tears I'd been crying evaporated on my scorching hot cheeks. Every ounce of grief was replaced with anger.

"How could you not tell me?"

"Lupo wanted to tell you himself."

I went quiet. My sister was just respecting his wishes. Kaia loved Lupo like I did. She would do ask he asked. He would expect that of her. The other end remained quiet for a while as I digested what Kaia had said, unwinding my fury with deep breaths.

"Lili, are you still there?"

Blinking, I brought my mind back to the present. How long had I been driving while lost in thought?

"Yeah. I'm sorry. I was just thinking about something else."

"Have you found out anything else about Casey's disappearance? Anyone she's met?"

Another wave of grief rolled through me like the rising tide threatening to pull me out to sea.

"It's, I don't know. It feels like I'm following leads that aren't going anywhere."

I heard murmuring in the background and wondered what I had interrupted. Given the hour, chances were good that Kaia was still at Muse. Maybe she was trying to decide what to say or thinking about telling me to quit and focus on our other problems.

"Lili, you're the smartest person I know. Do you know why I let you come to work for me?"

"Because I begged you?" I snorted.

"Because I knew you were a problem solver. You look at every angle to find your answers. So do that now. I know you're tired, but if anyone can figure it out, it's you."

If anyone can figure this out, it's you. The words bounced off the edges of my mind and through again until I got home. How could I solve something when there were so many pieces?

With everything shaking around in my head like loose nuts and bolts, there was not going to be any sleep tonight. For the first time in a long time, I pulled out my old coffee pot and got brewing. Before I could solve anything, I had to know everything.

I couldn't attack this problem like an investigator. I was hell and gone from that, but what I could do was treat it like a research assignment. A study. The pot sputtered as it finished brewing the freeze-dried crap I picked up. This Ph.D. dropout was about to pull an all-nighter.

A SMALL KERNEL of hope illuminated within me as I gathered every bit of information I had. My laptop had about twenty tabs open, but that didn't stop me from opening a blank document and writing down everything in bullet points. When it stared back at me, it still wasn't much to go on.

The biggest contributing factor to all of this came as I flipped through my photos while procrastinating about doing the actual task. The district attorney's notes. I had a list of names. After typing each name into a separate document, I looked up the girls online to learn as much as I could.

Lisa Booth, 21 years old. Disappeared after chatting with a man at the bar. Ella Perry has not been seen since leaving the Velvet Room with an unidentified man. She was 21 years old. Alison Booker, an art student, tragically missing after visiting the Blarney Stone. Security cameras have footage of her getting into an unmarked vehicle.

Almost every story was the same. Girl goes to a bar. Girl meets guy. Girl disappears. It was what was happening all over the city. It was what almost happened to Juliet at the Sandalwood Hotel. It could be a coincidence. Or it could be the same man. I jotted down everything I could remember about the guy. Dark close-set eyes, blonde hair, but a dark beard, and a flashy diamond watch. It was so blinding that it was difficult to remember his face. Of course, that was the idea, wasn't it? Blinding prey like one of those spooky fish in the deep, dark depths of the ocean. If this guy was taking women from clubs all over town and not getting caught, then he had a method.

IT WAS TIME to take a lap and give my brain something else to do. With a reluctant sigh, I dumped the hamper full of unfolded clean clothes onto my bed and got to work. He was a killer. Each of these girls was probably dead. Casey was probably dead. A killer. Despite everything, a small smile spread across my face. I'd certainly put in enough hours to be considered an expert in the field of murder.

Rolling all of my socks together gave me time to think about the method. Juliet had been approached while she was alone. That wasn't a surprise, but she had been drugged. Being a girl with a knack for pharmaceutical chemicals, I knew it was most likely GHB. To the layperson, GHB is liquid ecstasy. It's a clear liquid, which makes it perfect for drugging unsuspecting coeds.

After putting away my final roll of socks, I pulled on my boots and headed for the door. All-night sessions were nothing without snacks. During my walk to the 7-11 down the street, I text-messaged my sister.

Thanks for the pep talk earlier. It helped.

The cashier gave me a look I didn't love as I paid for my slush, candy bar, and goldfish crackers. My walk back was meditative. Each of the girls was alone with this guy. Running into him while out at clubs... shit. I stopped dead on the sidewalk.

"He's using the app."

No one was around to hear me. The goldfish crackers almost fell out of my mouth. Of course! It was the perfect situation. Fixate on a specific target and invite them out to get close to them. Find out personal information about them. Drug them and attack them after they let their guard down. I knew exactly how he'd do it because I'd done it to Vincent Grecco.

WHEN I GOT back into my apartment, I put on my pajamas. I'd arrived at my hypothesis. Now I just needed to prove it. I started scrolling through the Eros app on the unlocked phone again. Maybe this guy had contacted Casey? As I looked through countless messages, I tried to identify him and had no luck. None of the photos matched up with the man I'd seen, and there were over a dozen accounts with no pictures at all. Then I started looking at invitations and noticed she'd opened a few of them, one for a masquerade like the one I'd gone to with Benjamin.

I checked the time. It was getting late and I was wired, but my brain felt fuzzy. I'd had enough of research and caffeine was still coursing through my veins. I needed something to do. My eyes traced around the room as I tried to land on a task. My laundry was folded. The kitchen was clean. I didn't have quite enough energy to scrub the grout and I'm pretty sure my neighbors would pitch a fit if I started vacuuming. There was only the giant bag of Casey's unopened mail. Sure, it probably wasn't going to lead to anything, but I thought maybe there was something I was missing. If nothing else, I could pay a few of her outstanding bills. Among the stacks of credit card offers, coupons, and catalogs there was a purple envelope.

I wedged my index finger under a loose corner and tore it open. Confetti and glitter dumped out onto my bed before I could stop it. Muttering curse words, I pulled out the greeting card. A birthday card. From her mother.

Happy birthday, my sweet girl! I can't believe my youngest is already old enough to drink. Next time I visit, let's have champagne to celebrate.

XOXO

Casey had just had a birthday. A surge of guilt crested through me as I wondered if I had even wished her a happy birthday the last time I'd seen her.

A real friend would have known that.

41

IPOMOEA

After our fight, I couldn't even look West in the eye. I avoided Muse for the next few days. It was easy to find other ways to keep busy. I skipped training, opting instead to go to the gym when I knew he would be working. It wasn't just that he was overprotective. Something about his lack of confidence in my judgment bothered me. Like him thinking I was being reckless was making me crazy. Every time my mind drifted back to his words, I flinched because some part of me worried he was right.

Juliet emailed me with a plane ticket to Amsterdam that left in the morning. He hadn't mentioned this trip the last time we'd seen each other. I thought about what Kaia would say. What West would likely think. Benjamin Camden was getting far too comfortable with me. And they didn't know the half of it.

"What the hell is this?"

"I assume you're referring to the flight," Benjamin said coolly.

"I'm going to Amsterdam? With you?"

"Yes, there's an event there for VIP Eros users and board members. I assumed you'd like to accompany me, so I bought you a ticket."

"What I don't understand is the purpose of the trip, Benjamin. I can't just leave."

For a moment I could hear murmuring on the other end of the telephone. I hoped that Juliet wasn't being yelled at for my anxious phone call. I needed Benjamin to keep taking me to Eros events. Needed to find that man again. I couldn't burn this bridge. As I nibbled on the tip of my thumb, I realized this would help me avoid things at Muse and West for a few days. Where did I leave my passport?

"Alright, I'll go. I'm sorry for the freakout."

"I'll have Juliet send you the rest of the details. A car will pick you up to make sure you're at the airport in the morning."

In the morning. His definition of "morning" and mine were very different. After looking at the departure time, I decided I'd be better off not going to sleep at all, which wouldn't be a problem with all of the anxiety now coursing through my veins. Padding around my place with new nervous energy, I blew out a sigh. If I was going to be leaving with him first thing in the morning, I'd have to get my shit together quickly.

I'm going to Amsterdam in about 8 hours.

I'm sorry, what?

It's a thing with Benjamin. I'll be back in a couple of days.

Bring me some wooden shoes.

It would be difficult to look for a murderer on the other side of the world. The theory I'd had about the killer stalking Eros girls held water, but without knowing who he was, I couldn't track who he was speaking to. It's not like there's a weekly murder sewing circle. We don't all get together for cocktails and gab about the people we've killed. But there are some advantages to being outside of the law. When I caught the man, my justice system would decide his fate and the scales always tipped toward painful retribution.

THE FIRST-CLASS LOUNGE was relatively underpopulated on a Thursday morning. Not that I would know from previous experience. For as much money as I had, I rarely traveled and never did so in first class. A few tired-looking passengers were taking advantage of the hot breakfast bar. Glancing at the flight tracking board, I noted the time. Our flight didn't depart until just before dawn, but I was here an hour early. Between anxiety about getting everything packed and finding my passport, I never went to sleep.

According to the emails I received, this surprise trip to Amsterdam was related to a formal event for foreign investors, which meant I had to bring a fancy dress and text messaged Juliet about four times before I selected my shoes. After I held her hostage on the longest text chain I've ever participated in, I was able to get a second outfit thrown together for going out in town while Benjamin was occupied with work. We were only supposed to be there for two days, so I didn't have much else with me aside from the clothes on my back and something to sleep in. In a momentary wave of panic, I looked down at my suitcase to make sure it hadn't gone anywhere. Nope, still there since the last time I checked. Which was about five minutes ago.

Leaning back into the seat, I took another sip of coffee. I'd gotten here with enough time to cram some of the free food into my mouth without having to do so in front of Benjamin, but I'd only had a few sips of the coffee. The scrambled eggs and sausage were sitting like a lump in my stomach. Despite the high price tag for getting into this place, the coffee still tasted like it was brewed in a burnt-out diner pot. More cream and more sugar wouldn't help it, but it didn't hurt either.

The lounge server was making her way around to clear the tables when Benjamin walked in. As he looked around the room for me, I sat up reflexively. It took me a moment to recognize him because he wasn't wearing a suit. The gleaming metal on his expensive watch was the only hint of luxury, but it was obvious that everything else he wore was carefully selected.

Of course, it was still all perfectly fitted. The light grey jacket he wore was still cut to fit his form. Designer jeans stretched over his thighs but didn't hang or sag anywhere. Brown brogue shoes shone up at me. As I glanced down at my hastily thrown-together travel outfit, I wondered how much this man spent on tailoring. I tossed back the rest of my coffee and stood to greet him.

"Good morning," he grinned. "A bit early for you?"

"No, I'm just not fond of being late and even less fond of flying, so I didn't get very much sleep."

He nodded and looked at the flight tracking board in the lounge. We still had a little time. I was sure that with his clout, they'd hold the plane for him if he didn't show up. With a glance at his watch, he adjusted his jacket and lifted the small leather bag he carried.

"You'll be able to sleep on the plane," he said as he gave the bag a small pat. "I've got something you can take."

AIR WOULDN'T MAKE its way to my lungs, no matter how hard I gasped. Burning and starving for oxygen, I cried fat tears. Heavy, unforgiving weight was pressing, pressing, pressing down on me. No, I cried. Please.

Gold, angry eyes stared down into mine with otherworldly menace. Two large, callused hands tightened their grip around my throat and squeezed. A knee pressed down on my chest to hold me in place. The tears I cried streamed down my face, soaking the pillow beneath my head. Fear coursed through me as I felt my lungs give up on finding relief. Wrath was making way for the death that crept closer to me.

Please, I thought, please let me go.

You will never be free of me, he said as he freed a hand from my throat only to hit me with the explosive fury of his rage.

I woke with a start, the feeling of my father's hand still scorched across my cheek.

"We're still two hours from landing in Amsterdam," Benjamin said. I turned over to find his eyes fixed on me. Reclined with a book resting against his broad chest, his face wore a look somewhere between concern and curiosity. We'd been in the air for over ten hours and he still looked perfect.

"You were having a nightmare." The tone in his voice gave away his interest, like he wanted to know more, but knew it would be impolite to ask.

"Sort of," I sighed. The chairs in our suite had been made into a little bed by the flight attendants, and the pill he gave me took little more than an hour to work. Thanks to Benjamin, I'd been asleep for most of the flight after watching Silence of the Lambs for a little inspiration, but the drugs only exacerbated the nightmares that plagued me regularly. Despite the airborne luxury, I felt like a dirtbag in my leggings and an oversized sweater. The scrunchie I'd tied my hair back with had come out with my movements, making a mess of my black waves.

"You mumbled and tossed about a bit before you woke," he said, pushing a strand of hair out of my face. "What were you dreaming about?"

"My father," I sighed.

"I take it your father was not a good man."

I chuckled in the dark suite. Rubbing my eyes, I could feel the fear still permeating my flesh. "Yeah, you could say that. He wanted sons but got daughters and he made us pay for that as often as he could."

Benjamin's jaw clenched as he sighed. Marking his place in his book, he rubbed his tired eyes and looked at me again.

"Anyway," I said in a desperate attempt to change the subject, "he died when I was young, so it's just residual stress, I guess."

"Post-traumatic stress."

"Right."

"Come here," he said while holding his blanket open to me. Scooting myself across our little bed, I pushed my body into him. Letting the blankets settle over us, he stroked my back as I settled my head on his arm. He pressed a soft kiss to the top of my head and murmured against my temple. "He was weak. You're free of him now."

I nodded and let myself be soothed by his touch. It wasn't the truth, though. He wasn't weak. Waves of fear still sloshed through me, as they always would. I would never be free of Raoul Caccia. Not so long as I could dream. Laying there, the remnants of my dream clung to my thoughts like cobwebs. Blazing hazel eyes loomed over me while my lungs still felt the burn of panic.

Benjamin's fingers grazed the curve of my jaw and our eyes met again. Screw it, I thought. I needed to clear my mind and I had one of the most beautiful men I've ever seen up close holding me in his arms. Instinct would always tell me to do nothing. Let this pass and move on. But I needed to get away from the drowning feeling I was fighting. My hand drifted around his neck. Pulling his body against me, I pressed a kiss to his lips.

"Please," I murmured against him. "I just need a distraction."

I didn't need to say anything else. His mouth sealed over mine as he shifted himself over me. His massive form was a welcome weight. A strong hand drifted up my body, squeezing all of my soft curves. My upper lip felt the lick of his tongue, a sensual request, and I let him in. His hips ground into me and I could feel his hard length pressed against my core. I let out a soft moan.

"Sh...," he whispered with a dark laugh. "This suite isn't soundproof."

Anxious for more, I lifted his shirt and felt the hot plane of his stomach. Delicate hair and velvet-soft skin greeted my touch. The grinding motion of his hips caused the muscles there to flex beneath my fingers. I slipped my hand between us until I found his waistband and dipped below the fabric. He was hard and swollen with need as moisture collected at his tip. You're taking this too far, I thought to myself. This is crossing a line. But then I remembered the party. The way his fingers felt when he wrung pleasure from me. It was only fair that I return the favor. My fingers curled around him and he groaned.

"What are you doing?" He questioned against my lips.

"Do you want me to stop?"

"Fuck no."

My hands moved to open his jeans and pull down his boxers. I was sure he wouldn't want to walk through the airport with evidence of his release all over him. Without the fabric between us, I could feel the waves of heat coming off of his body. It seared into me. Bracing himself over me, one hand tangled in my hair as he panted against my neck. The other hand pushed up my sweater and squeezed my breast. It felt like an effort to steady himself as much as it was for my pleasure. He gritted his teeth and bucked against my hand as I worked his shaft, wondering all the while what every inch would feel like inside of me. When his hips stuttered, I knew he was close.

"Shit," he hissed.

Pulsing and tensing in my grip, I felt his climax. Hot, wet breaths escaped him as he shuddered against me. I looked down to see my stomach painted with him.

"I'm sorry, that was… faster than I'm used to." He said with an apologetic look and that damn curl hanging over his forehead. I smirked and dragged a finger over my stomach, my eyes remaining on his as I licked it.

"Thank you for the distraction."

42

EUONYMUS EUROPAEUS

We had enough time to clean up and right ourselves before arriving in Amsterdam. When we landed, I turned my phone back on. While the plane did have internet, being able to get away from everything for a few hours felt like reason enough to switch it off. It started pinging immediately with several text messages. Two from Kaia. One from West.

> **KAIA:** I told Daniel you're going to the Netherlands.
>
> He asked that you watch out for Captain Hook.
>
> **WEST:** I'm sorry.

I sent Kaia a joke about Peter Pan and just stared at the text from West. I knew I should respond to him. It was unlike me to ice him out like this. After sleeping on it, I knew I had overreacted to what he'd had to say. The fact that I'd cried made it worse. He had never seen me cry. Hell, I hadn't let anyone see me cry in years. Not even Kaia. Something about that knotted my insides together with guilt.

A hired car took us to the Waldorf so we could get cleaned up and ready for the event. I started and deleted five different responses to West during the short drive. I wanted to respond but couldn't get the right words together. I'm an overreactive idiot. I know you're just looking out for me. You were right. You're always right. No, I couldn't say that. Stuffing my phone back into my bag, I resolved to just stare out the window.

The second phone I carried with me chimed. Henry Johnson's phone. I wondered if they thought he'd scampered off to the private island he'd tried to tempt me with. Chancing a glance over at Benjamin, I pulled it out of my bag. He'd been copied on another email from Stephen Bryant.

> *Henry,*
>
> *Contract with Trans-Oceanic has been processed. We can begin moving product immediately. They're pressing hard for a larger profit share. Will leave meeting details with your assistant.*
>
> *SB*

Attached to the email was a spreadsheet with more tracking codes. They were also getting ready to meet with a third party. Before I could figure out why they were meeting, I had to figure out who they were meeting.

After I emailed the spreadsheet to myself, I returned to staring out the window. We went by a park filled with flowers, trees, and people on bicycles. People were smiling and eating lunch because for them it was the middle of the day. They paid no attention to the black sedan carrying a billionaire and an executioner.

AFTER A TRANS-ATLANTIC flight, I needed a bath. Sweat and sleep still coated my skin, despite the wipe down I gave myself with a warm washcloth. The suite we'd been given for the night had both a large glass shower and a freestanding tub. The choice was easy. As the water filled the tub, I cleaned myself off again with a soapy cloth. Steaming hot luxury welcomed me as I sunk into the depths of the porcelain basin and let out a relieved sigh.

Sinking into the water, my face was almost level with the surface as I thought about West. The way he looked at me as I cried was still fresh in my memory. Even thousands of miles away, I still felt the burn of embarrassment. In all of our time together, I'd never behaved so poorly. What would I even say?

"Comfortable?" Benjamin said as he strode in. The clothes he'd had on for the flight were discarded, now wearing only a well-fitted pair of black boxer briefs. I wasn't sure how much of me he'd seen, so I crossed my arms in front of my breasts. Seeming to think better of turning on the shower, he walked to the tub and placed a hand along the rim. "May I join you?"

I cursed inwardly and nodded. We'd already crossed a line. Hell, we'd crossed several. But now the line was becoming a distant memory. Especially as I watched him step into the tub. We faced each other in the small space and he extended a hand to me.

"Come here," he said as he gestured toward himself. Turning, I moved to lean against his chest and felt his hard shaft brush against my ass. For a moment, I stilled. It shouldn't have surprised me, but it did. Even though we had been circling each other like animals. Swallowing my butterflies, I rested against him. "Lilith," he hummed as his hands traveled to my core. "Do you feel what you do to me?"

I closed my eyes and nodded. His fingers had started to work at me, teasing and stroking my center. A hand drifted up, catching my nipple and rolling it. The touch inspired my hips to roll against him in seeking movements. Leaning into my ear, his voice was thick with promise as he growled. "Finish cleaning yourself."

He extended a bar of soap to me and watched as I lathered up my skin. The heavenly lemongrass smell filled the space, but I could only focus on the icy blue eyes fixed upon me. They followed the soap as I moved it over my skin, taking extra time to wash where I wanted his attention. When I finished, he took the bar from me and I watched him clean himself with the soap I'd just used. When he finished, he stood. Water sluiced down his perfect, thick form.

His body reminded me of a Renaissance sculpture. Figures like his were immortalized by the hands of great artists. The ice in his gaze turned to liquid heat below the dark furrow of his brows.

Towering over me, he extended a hand to help me out of the tub. Once both my feet hit the ground, he dried me with one of the cloud-soft towels, taking time to let the cloth drag against my sensitive regions. When he was finished, he lifted me and placed me on the counter as he pressed a kiss to my shoulder. The hot water had penetrated me to the bone, making the marble feel cold against my freshly washed ass. Benjamin parted my legs, stroking me with his thumb as he fished a condom from his toiletry kit. The length of him was so rigid that it bordered on obscene. I watched as he rolled the condom down to his base and stepped toward me.

"You're exquisite," he said in a low purr, running an appreciative hand from my chest to my stomach.

As I watched him, I let out a nervous breath. *This is crazy. This is crazy. This is crazy!* The words sounded through my mind, beating in time with my racing heart. I wanted him, but I couldn't throw this relationship away. Not with so many loose ends. The craziest part might have been that I was starting to like Benjamin. Maybe he felt what I was feeling, but the rational part of my mind explained it away as physical attraction. Just a proximity thing. There are only two people in the world who knew the real me. My sister and the man who broke my heart. Kaia had to love me because we're family, but her hands were also just as bloody as my own. Ethan was a different story. A mistake. One I hoped I would never make again.

"I'd love to do this for hours, pet, but there will be time for that later," he said as he pressed a kiss to my ankle and notched himself at my entrance. "Let's call this scratching an itch."

A half-swallowed cry burst out of me as he thrust his considerable length inside. As I leaned back to make myself more comfortable, I almost laughed at how strange my life had become. I'd gone from horrible online dates to this. Benjamin Camden, one of the most eligible bachelors in the world, was fucking me on a bathroom counter in a suite in Amsterdam. A hand pressed to the counter beneath the leg I'd had against his shoulder, while the other pressed down on my stomach. My eyes rolled back in my head at the sensation this move created, and a groan fell out of my mouth in gratitude.

Dropping my leg, he pulled my hips toward him and ground his strokes into me. The water from his freshly washed hair dropped onto my skin. It was hard not to get lost in watching this near-perfect man. The expression on his face was that of focus and determination. Abdominal muscles flexed with every stroke. That dark curl dangled over his forehead. I almost reached out to touch it. Nearing the edge of climax, I reached up to grip his shoulder. He leaned down to press his lips to mine as he instead slowed to a teasing pace.

"More...please." I didn't recognize the words coming out of me. A stream of gasps and begging. In here, we were two different people. Instead of a polished man of means, he was snarling and savage. I became utterly helpless. His mouth spread into a wicked grin as he yanked me off of the counter. The motion surprised a yelp out of me. A quick spin had me facing the mirror as he drove himself into me again. My stomach stung from the biting cold of the marble counter.

"Watch," he gritted as he wrapped my hair around his fist and pulled me against him. "Watch while I fuck you."

I'd never been so undeniably dominated. While a small zing of fear sizzled in me, everything I felt became magnified. Without having to think about what came next, I was able to revel in every delectable moment. My skin was singing with sensation, enjoying the way his dominance allowed me to set my worries aside and be present in the toe-curling pleasure of it.

His strokes returned to their steady pace as he kept his hand tangled in my hair, placing the other between my legs with savage force. Hardly able to stand anymore, every muscle tightened as I felt his hips start to lose their rhythm. Teeth playfully nipped at my ear as his touch and thrusts brought my orgasm out with a scream. He grinned at my loss of self-control. We watched each other in the mirror as I gasped for air, shockwaves of sensation still rattling my bones. His ice-blue eyes watched the color flush across my chest. Anguish twisted his features as I felt him twitch and jerk inside of me. The sound of lost breath filled the room and I looked up at his face in the mirror. The feral grin had faded to a smirk.

It took only a moment for him to withdraw. The man who took what he wanted was replaced once again with the gentleman I'd been keeping company. I felt cold as I watched him walk away, holding myself up at the counter and trying to catch my breath.

"Get dressed, pet. The car will pick us up in an hour," he called over his shoulder as he strode away.

As I got ready for the party, I kept trying to make sense of what had just happened. Tried to make it make sense, anyway. It didn't, of course. The only explanation I could come up with was that I was a thing to be played with. Something for him to amuse himself with, which wasn't the worst thing to be. Not for me. My heart wasn't a thing I could give away. It couldn't belong to anyone. But I could at least have fun.

I LOOKED MYSELF over in the mirror one more time. The dress Juliet had picked for this event screamed "less is more." Sure, its neckline was high, but created by the wrap-around fabric that fastened at the nape of my neck. The back dipped down low to show a wide swath of skin. Scarlet silk wrapped around my body, accentuating every inch of my hourglass figure, and split to float away from my legs whenever I took a step. In this dress, I felt indestructible.

My pleasure with the garment must have radiated from me because I couldn't keep the grin off of my face. When I stepped out of the bedroom, tacking my earrings into place, Benjamin was on the phone but looked me over. A small smile tugged at his lips, and I knew I had his mark of approval.

"Shall we?" He offered as he extended his arm to me.

43

DURANTA REPENS

An actual castle. A castle surrounded by a moat. A real moat. The event we were attending seemed like something from out of a dream. Strings of lights dangled over the courtyard as we entered the main hall. Large black and white marble stones paved the floor. A fireplace big enough to roast a whole human being was at the end of the space, unlit but filled with candles.

Flower arrangements spilled out of floor-standing vases in white waterfalls of delicate buds. I gazed up at the ceiling to observe the heavy beams and joists against the ancient wood panels. Servers dressed in white jackets handed out glasses of champagne and canapes to elegantly dressed guests. It felt like a real-life fairy tale. For a moment, I wondered if I was dreaming. Maybe I'd died somehow and this was where we went before we would be judged. Eying the other guests, I squeezed Benjamin's arm out of sheer discomfort. This whole event was out of my league. My gut twisted with unease as I blew out a breath.

"Relax," Benjamin whispered into my ear. We made our way around the room as people competed for his attention. This crowd was on another level. Unlike the lascivious men in my own country, the men here seemed to care only for my escort's attention. Some gave my hand a polite kiss when introduced, others merely offered a terse nod. I preferred it to the gatherings I'd been to so far. These people were more well-mannered than the American businessmen I'd met.

Benjamin guided me toward a small man with light brown hair and pale grey eyes. He'd been sweating because a small fleck of cocktail napkin still clung to his forehead from where he'd dabbed it. The man he was conversing with was familiar looking, but I couldn't see more than the side of his face.

I tried to follow him with my eyes as he walked away. As we stepped up to the small man, Benjamin made his introduction.

"This is Camden Industries' Chief Financial Officer, Stephen Bryant. Bryant, how were things in Belfast?"

"It would have been a lot easier if you were there," the man seethed.

Words failed me. This man had been corresponding with Henry Johnson about something related to Eros but seemed unbothered by his lack of response. Nervous and bespectacled, this man reeked of underhanded dealings. For someone with such a high-powered job, he was terrible at hiding his stress. I let out a soft laugh and apologized, introducing myself with an extended hand. The man barely looked at me. Obviously, he was used to meeting the vapid women Benjamin usually brought around.

"Camden, I need to chat with you. Privately." Bryant snarled with a pointed look at me. I couldn't tell if he was irritated with me or with Benjamin. Bryant closed a hand over Benjamin's arm and steered him to the door while the unease in my gut surged with a warning. The absence of my knife suddenly felt like a phantom limb. This was not a man to be trusted.

The party had been in full swing for a while and people were scattered about everywhere, having conversations about this and that. I kept an eye out for the familiar looking man I'd spotted for the rest of the night with no luck. Instead, I overheard one woman describe the breeding of her prize dalmatians and stifled a chuckle as I wondered if she'd be making a coat out of the puppies. I circulated about the room, trying not to let my curiosity get the best of me. My complete lack of comfort with Bryant was only magnified by the urge to hear what he had to say.

I gave Benjamin and his CEO a comfortable distance and did my best to try and follow them without drawing attention to myself. They had stepped outside to talk privately in the courtyard. Carefully placed footsteps moved me to the door. The gargantuan wooden panel had hinges wide enough to provide me with a large crack to observe them. As servers passed, I pretended to be distracted by my phone.

Bryant gestured wildly while Benjamin maintained neutral body language. Shoulders relaxed and hands in his pockets, he was not nearly as upset as his associate. At this distance, I couldn't quite make out the expression on his face, but it seemed relaxed. When the rant was done, Benjamin placed a hand on his shoulder and said something that seemed to soothe his CFO as he guided him back toward the doors. I stepped further into the shadows to avoid being seen.

"I need you tonight. They're not taking me seriously without you." Bryant warbled as they entered.

"I'll be there."

The two of them made their way into the hall again, and I stayed behind to avoid arousing suspicion. This Stephen Bryant seemed to be hanging on by a thread. Acting like a man who had a lot to lose. When you have a lot to lose, you tend to make terrible choices. I should know. Men like that often found their way into my grasp after gambling their lives away or making some other terrible decision that needed to be erased. Men like that, men like Stephen Bryant, were always dancing on the edge.

Benjamin was talking with some of the other stuffed shirts as I entered the hall again. He turned and smiled his gorgeous smile at me. My chest squeezed and an involuntary grin spread across my lips.

"Where did you go?" He queried, as his hand drifted to my lower back. It always seemed to drift there, as though he enjoyed having access to my body, but thought better of settling his touch elsewhere.

Standing there, I had to remind myself that this was not real. Despite the way he kissed me and the mutual attraction we felt. The way he smiled at me, eyes alight with desire and affection, was manufactured. Any chemistry passing between us was just physical. I knew that. Everything else was fabricated, just like the image we concocted. An Italian socialite who is besotted with her billionaire boyfriend. Perfect hair, makeup, and wardrobe. A beautiful lie we were telling to the world.

Still, a shiver went crawling through me as his fingers grazed the skin beneath them in a casually intimate touch. It suggested more than the expression on his face.

"The ladies' room," I lied. "This place is massive. Finding it was quite an adventure."

He excused us from the conversation he'd been having. Was I that bad a liar? He couldn't have seen me. I knew he hadn't, but maybe someone else had. Steering me toward a darkened corner, he started talking to me with a lowered voice.

"Negotiations for our venture here aren't going well, and my presence is required to smooth things over. Will you be alright alone at the hotel?"

I struggled to keep the relief off of my face and nodded. This must have been what Bryant was shouting at him about. Johnson's phone was sitting in my bag. Maybe I'd get lucky with another email. Pressing a soft kiss to my lips, he gave me a wink before walking away.

BEING ALONE IN a suite at one of the most expensive hotels in Amsterdam is just like being alone in a shitty motel. The only difference is threadcount. Bryant hadn't sent another message to Johnson. I wondered if he had mentioned the lack of response to Benjamin. Can emails have read receipts? After taking another shower to get the social anxiety sweat off of me, I changed into my pajamas and hopped into the continent-sized bed.

I lay in the large bed thinking over how insane the last twenty-four hours had been. Benjamin wasn't like I thought he would be. Well, he was and wasn't. The version of him that I'd been warned about was who I had first met at the office. The small glimpses in our private moments were entirely unexpected. The gentle way he comforted me after my nightmare couldn't have been fake. No one was watching while he put his arms around me in that first-class airline suite. Absolutely zero people were around for our athletic escapades in the bathroom.

Struggling with the time difference and the fact that I was now hunting a serial killer, I tossed around in bed while trying to find comfort. A movie occupied me for a while. When it ended, I rolled over to find something else to stream on my phone, hoping to get some sleep before our flight out the next day, but I opened my text messages and started typing.

I'm sorry too. I just need for you to trust me.

What time was it in Los Angeles? It had to be late in the day there because it was after one in the morning here. I gave up on the movie and rolled over, trying to relax enough to fall asleep. Squeezing my eyes closed and open again, I heard the metallic clack of the door unlocking when my phone chimed with his response.

Of course, I trust you. I don't trust him.

44

ALKEKENGI OFFICINARUM

My hand drifted to my side as I thought about the holster full of blades I'd left at home. The coat I had on would be perfect for hiding several weapons, but I would probably sell it when all was said and done. The expensive outerwear was waiting for me when I woke up, along with a note from Benjamin. It didn't make sense to own a wool coat in Los Angeles, even if its cream-colored fabric was soft and pretty. The sleeves were a bit too long, which gave Benjamin a challenge when he reached for my hand.

When I mentioned that I'd never been to Amsterdam before, Benjamin decided to save his work for the flight home and take me out. The autumnal cold nipped at me beneath the soft cotton shirt and thin denim I had on. I stopped to fasten the buttons of my coat. He turned and took control of my failed buttoning efforts.

"Come now, it's not that cold."

"You're talking to a born and raised California girl. My tolerance is low."

His grip remained on my coat, and I became aware of how close we were standing. A slight tug on the material had me flush against him.

"No wonder you're not cold. You're a furnace," I said breathlessly.

Up this close, it was easy to see why women lusted after him. Eyes that looked cold from a distance were like thermal pools of beautiful blue, giving away the danger of heartbreak that dwelled beneath. His nose nudged mine gently, preceding the warmth of his mouth on mine. It felt like leaning too far over a cliff; the bottom promising only pain. But I didn't care. The brush of his tongue against mine filled me with heat. My coat pulled at my waist as his fingers twisted the fabric. As he nibbled on my lower lip, I melted against him.

"Benjamin," I whispered. "Can we go back to the hotel?"

I'd climbed back into bed with him this morning and ridden him until I saw stars, but empty want still scratched my nerves. Circling my good sense until it was blinded. His attention soothed an ache I'd long ignored. But as with most chronic pain, the fear of its return, the return of my solitary existence, haunted me. He pressed his forehead to mine and sighed.

"Sadly, no. We've checked out, but we still have a few hours before we need to get to the airport. Let's walk."

The words were like ice water in my veins. For a second, I tried to collect myself and reel everything I'd been feeling back under control. With a warm flush still coloring my cheeks, I gave Benjamin a wry grin.

"Is there somewhere around here that we can go warm up? Maybe with some liquor?"

Large fingers gripped mine as he pulled me down the street to a tiny Irish pub. The locals hardly glanced at us as we took up a table in the back corner near the bar. Benjamin and I were hooking our coats to the wall when a waitress came by for our order. After Benjamin ordered a very British gin and tonic, the waitress looked at me.

"Oban, 14 year. Neat, please."

As she walked away, I noticed Benjamin's raised eyebrows.

"What? You don't know as much about me as you might think, Mr. Camden."

A soft glow had started filtering through the windows as the street lamps turned on, readying the locals for the night ahead. People filtered in off of the street to cap their workday with a drink surrounded by friends. While Benjamin sipped his drink, he answered texts and emails but kept chatting about the city. We talked about tulips and art. I told him about my love of Van Gogh's "Sunflowers" and he told me that he preferred "Cafe Terrace at Night."

"How's the whiskey?"

"It's good," I said as I took another sip.

"May I try?"

"Sure." I was ready to hand him my glass when he leaned over, framed my face with his hands, and kissed me deeply.

"Delicious," he grinned.

WE WERE READYING ourselves for the car when Benjamin excused himself from the table, leaving his phone behind. After pulling on my coat, I'd picked it up, ready to hand it to him upon his return. That was when he received a text message from Stephen Bryant.

> With your help, Amsterdam and Belfast will
> both be ready to go. Shouldn't be long now.

Stephen Bryant bothered me more than anything. After years of following people who crossed us, I discovered there were two types of people. The first was the kind who went about their business, completely oblivious to the danger they were in. Then there was the kind who knew. Twitchy. Always looking over their shoulder for signs of trouble. Bryant had the look of someone waiting for the other shoe to drop.

"Lilith."

I was startled as Benjamin reappeared at the table.

"I, sorry. You left your phone."

He nodded, but his face was marred with mistrust.

"Were you reading my messages?"

"Just the one that popped up while I was holding it. I didn't mean to. I'm sorry."

Benjamin took his phone from me and glanced at the screen before dropping it in his pocket. With a smile, he guided me out of the pub to the town car that was waiting to take us to the airport. He didn't speak again until we were boarding the plane.

"I'm sorry for being so terse about the phone. I've had some girlfriends with boundary issues. Did Juliet send the invitation to the next masked event? It's at the hotel again. Perhaps you can come over the night before?"

I nodded, not sure of what to say. It wasn't just an awkward moment. The fact that he felt the need to explain his reaction to the phone said more about it than the reaction itself. As we prepared to take off, I wondered if maybe I didn't know as much about Benjamin as I had thought.

45

DAPHNE ODORA

The entire flight home was torture. Between trying to stay awake and trying to control myself, I wanted to bust open the emergency door and leap out. Benjamin made work calls, wrote emails, and read documents while I watched movies and took strolls around the plane to stretch my legs. Most of that was to distract me from how damned good he looked. As I watched his long fingers wrap around a champagne flute, I remembered what it had felt like to have them wrapped around my ankle. Every time I thought about his lips, his hands, or his body, I took a drink to wash the thought away. By the time we landed, I'd drained eight glasses of water.

We'd parted ways at the airport after a lingering kiss that distracted me for most of the drive home. Despite following Benjamin's instructions on avoiding jet lag, I slept through most of the day. The flight home had been so long that I threw myself on top of the covers of my bed fully clothed and passed out cold. Sleep was my top priority. Maybe sleeping and dreaming about an impossibly handsome billionaire. Instinct was still telling me to stay away from him, but every other part of my body told me to just enjoy the ride while I could.

After a short power nap, I pulled out my laptop. I'd only been gone a few days, but I'd not kept up with news in the area. Maybe another woman had gone missing while I was enjoying myself with Benjamin. Thinking about how his body felt in the sheets of that Amsterdam hotel made me feel selfish and guilty. Rubbing my eyes, I returned my focus to the screen in front of me.

First, I searched the newspapers in the area for any sign of foul play. Then I hit the missing person's reports. Nothing came up about any missing girls in Los Angeles from the days I'd been gone. But something else did.

> *Henry,*
>
> *Trans-Oceanic meeting at midnight. Muse in West Hollywood.*
>
> *SB*

Another message from Stephen fucking Bryant. They were meeting in my territory, of all places. A small smile tugged on my lips. This was perfect. Stephen Bryant had secrets and that little bastard was about to tell me everything.

A cursory glance at my tactical medical box showed that my inventory of poisons, sedatives, and other serums was almost completely depleted. Empty brown bottles greeted me everywhere I looked. Shit. With an agitated huff, I performed an inventory of the ingredients I still had in case I needed to take Bryant down. There was only about half of what I needed and I was completely out of the Lullaby. There wasn't time to make more. If I had to eliminate Stephen Bryant or anyone else, it was going to have to be the hard way.

Looking at my watch, I realized I still had plenty of time to get started processing belladonna before I had to be at the club. I needed to head over to Kaia's to work in the flat and start another batch of serums. I wouldn't be able to make a batch of anything useful for tonight, but I could get things started for next time. There would always be a "next time."

After going through my nightstand, I pulled out my hunting knife. I mean, I've never actually used it for hunting animals. West had given it to me as a Christmas gift after his first year with us. He'd said it was similar to the knife he'd used in the service.

I looked at the black zinc blade. It had come in handy many times, usually when I needed to intimidate someone or when needles failed me. Nonno had insisted on training with knives when we'd come to live with him. I ran my thumb over the spine of the blade. The spine had tooth-like serrated edges that went all the way down to the hilt. This weapon was truly brutal when used against delicate flesh.

"Knives are elegant. Personal," Nonno had once said. "Killing a man with a gun is easy. Any neanderthal can do it. Taking life with a blade is art."

FRESH-CUT GRASS AND sweet flower blossoms perfumed the air as I enjoyed a rare moment of peace on the Caccia mansion grounds. The purple blooms of the nightshade plant looked almost pink in the light of the setting sun.

The air started cooling as the sun dipped below the horizon, painting the sky with its watercolor hues. Pruners clicked in my hand as I clipped away the rogue buds and put them in my bag. Back here, I felt normal. Heavy sliding metal sounded through the garden as the gates to the motor court rolled open. Kaia's matte black Range Rover crunched over the gravel as I put away my gardening tools.

Daniel burst from the backseat and ran to wrap a hug around my waist. I ruffled his long, dark curls. He needed a haircut but was probably avoiding it.

"Can we watch a movie tonight?" He asked, with his face buried in my jacket.

"Ask your mom, okay?"

"Mama, can Zia Lili watch a movie with me?"

"Yes. But nothing violent and it can't be too long."

Kaia shrugged off her blazer and folded it over her arm. Handing Daniel his backpack, she sent him into the house. Watching him slide the door closed behind him, she turned to me and observed my bag full of blooms.

"So, what are you doing now?"

"Stephen Bryant has a meeting at the club later tonight. I'm going to try to shake him down for some information. Henry Johnson was supposed to go. They're still sending him emails. I don't think they know he's dead."

Kaia's eyebrows raised in surprise.

"I know. It's all sloppy as hell, but it's happening."

"What time?"

"Midnight."

"Well, then it sounds like you have time for a movie."

"Something animated, at least. I'm going to need a happily ever after to pump me up. And some food. Definitely some food."

My sister patted me on the shoulder and steered me inside. With her arm still wrapped around me, she laughed.

"I've got a frozen pizza with your name on it, kid."

Daniel was asleep and practically drooling by the time the movie ended. His tiny body was easy to carry to his room, which was only a few steps away from the playroom we were occupying. I could have let him sleep in the giant foam pouf, but there was something about knowing he was safe in his bed that comforted me.

The space hadn't changed much since I occupied it fifteen years ago. This little bedroom was where Nonno had put me when we moved in with them.

A twin bed sat next to the window and a nightstand was beside it. Peeling down the comic book comforter, I deposited the small boy into his bed and tucked him in.

"Zia?" He mumbled sleepily.

"Yeah?"

"I wish I had an inflatable robot. We could fight bad guys together."

I smiled and brushed the hair off of his face. The grasp this child had on good and bad would land me firmly in the latter category. If he knew what his Zia actually did for his mother, I don't know if he would ever look at me the same way again.

"Good night, buddy."

He rolled over, falling asleep again. And I, the bad guy, turned out the light as I quietly shut the door.

Kaia had her laptop open on the kitchen island. Her head rested in the palm of her hand as she read what was before her, taking idle sips from her oversized wine glass. Peering over her shoulder, I could see what looked like legal documents, but I had no idea what they said.

"Do you ever stop working?" I asked, shoving another slice of pizza into my mouth.

"Do you ever stop eating? You're like a raccoon," she said, quirking a perfectly manicured eyebrow up at me.

"Trash panda at your service," I said as I sketched a bow. "Daniel's asleep in his room. I've got to go."

I grabbed a napkin and wiped my face. She nodded, her eyes again on the computer screen. After I slipped my boots back on, I walked over to pick up my satchel of berries on my way to the front door when an alert sounded from my pocket. It was an email from Dr. Forester.

Here is the last known location of the number you gave me.

The Sandalwood Hotel. That sounded familiar. I typed the name into a search engine and was immediately met with a familiar sight. The location Casey's phone had last been marked was the same beachside hotel where I attended an Eros party with Benjamin. Exactly where I'd rescued Juliet. Thanks to this information from Dr. Forester, I could confirm that Casey had likely been killed by the same man.

"What?" Kaia asked, reading the tight look on my face.

"I think I have an idea about the mechanics of what happened to Casey, but I need more information. If I move on what I've got, it could get very dangerous very quickly."

Did I have Juliet's phone number? If I could confirm with her, then everything else might fall into place. Finally, I remembered that she had called me after the party and found her number.

Juliet, how old are you?

I gave Kaia a long look. If I was right about my suspicion, this opened things to an entirely new level. This meant I would have to face off with a serial killer. Waiting for Juliet to respond felt like the air was gradually being pulled from my lungs.

I couldn't believe I hadn't seen it before. All of the parties we'd attended. All of the women I could have saved. Every man I met was under close examination, but I should have been paying attention to the women. The alert on my phone sent a jolt through me.

21, why?

"Lili."

I spun to see my sister now turned around in her seat, looking at me.

"What's happening?"

I walked back over to the kitchen island and put my bag down. My sister looked up from her laptop.

"I don't think Casey was taken by a random Eros date. I think a user is targeting girls on the app. All the girls who have disappeared lately are the same age. When I checked, I discovered that they were all users. At an Eros function, I saw a guy try to drug Benjamin's assistant and leave with her."

Kaia closed her laptop and looked up at me again. This time there was sympathy in her eyes.

"Lili, that happens all the time. How can you be sure the two are even connected?"

With a heaving breath, I threw myself down onto the barstool and rubbed my eyes. This was going to get complicated. Silence filled the space as I gathered my thoughts.

"Okay," I sighed. "Isabelle was twenty-three. She was taken to Vegas and killed by accident. That was covered up, but her disappearance and Casey's happening in the same week was most likely just a coincidence."

Kaia pushed herself out of her chair and walked over to the wine bottle on the counter. It was obvious that she couldn't have this conversation without a drink in her hand. I waited until after she poured a glass for herself before I continued. She handed a glass to me and I nodded my thanks.

"Casey was twenty-one. I just heard from Juliet, Benjamin's assistant, that she is also twenty-one. All of the girls who have been disappearing from clubs lately were also twenty-one. I think we may be dealing with a serial killer with a well-established modus operandi. He always targets the same type. Twenty-one years old, relatively slim in build. Young looking for their age. I think the guy is setting up dates with them and then killing them."

"So this is connected to all of the disappearing girls from the news."

I nodded solemnly. Kaia looked down into her glass and swirled the liquid. I shifted my weight, waiting for her to speak again. Her face was tight as she asked, "are you sure?"

"I mean, no. I'm not. There are no bodies. But why twenty-one? And these disappearances are happening fast. Maybe they haven't had time to discover the bodies yet."

"Then this isn't something we should be toying with."

Kaia stood up and drained her glass of wine.

"Kai, I've got this."

"No, Lili. You have to stop now. Leave it alone. If this is what happened to Casey, then it's a police problem."

In the moment, I didn't understand why Kaia was so concerned for my safety. Not that I don't understand her wanting to keep her little sister safe. But what I do, what I've been doing, has never been safe. Every time I disappeared into the night to collect a soul for the family could have been the last time. All it would take is one man who was ready for me. One person who could best me. Outsmart me. Catch me unaware.

"Just listen to me for one minute," I said as I took a breath to compose myself. "Think about it. I'm trained. I'll see him coming. He doesn't even know that I'm looking for him, so maybe I'll get lucky and he'll be sloppy. I know he's going to parties. I can use the parties to find him. Maybe even catch him. Now that we know this, don't we owe it to Casey?"

Kaia stared at me. The gears turned in her mind. I could always see her working. Piecing things together. After a few moments, she sighed.

"Please be careful," she conceded.

"I'll do my best," I shrugged. Dissatisfied with my answer, she blew out a breath and picked up her phone. No more time to worry about her reckless little sister.

46

LUPINUS

SIX YEARS AGO

My sister and Nonno were in the hospital at the same time. Nonno for the heart attack that would claim his life and Kaia laboring with the son she would call Daniel. The phone call I'd gotten that day set my head spinning. Since I was up at Berkeley, I took the first flight home from SFO to get there in time. I was lucky enough to be there for the birth of the baby. I had missed Nonno by ten minutes.

The first few months without him were the hardest. I'd sent for my things and moved into the flat over the garage. Kaia spent hours working hard to be a good mother to Daniel and also to be the boss the family needed, just as Nonno stated in his will. Between the little one and our grief, neither she nor I got hardly any sleep.

I spent every night in my room when I wasn't inside helping with the baby. Truthfully, I would have been in there twenty-four hours a day, but Kaia insisted that she could do things herself. Still, I kept the baby monitor going on my phone. My little flat was haunted by textbooks, journals, and unfinished papers. One night, in the stupor of a seventy-two-hour vigil, I noticed a recipe in my notebook I hadn't seen before or had overlooked. Some hastily scribbled down notes from one of my toxicology courses. It was...

"Holy shit," I whispered to no one.

I marked the page and put the notebook down on my nightstand. The full moon cast its unforgiving light down on the garden Nonno had let me plant. Surrounded by flowers and hedges, tomatoes and other vegetables grew with abandon. Most of the food was given to the men who stood guard around the house. Looking down on the fenced in garden, my garden, an idea began to take root.

It was that night that I decided to replant the garden with everything I would need. Everything my sister would need. After scribbling down my plans in the notebook, I grabbed it and jogged into the house with renewed energy. Winded from excitement and sprinting up the stairs, I stopped in my tracks to collect myself.

"What are you doing up here?" Kaia asked with a note of panic in her voice. "Is he awake again?"

"No, I..." I glanced down at my notebook. "I think I just figured something out."

Her head cocked to the side, waiting for me to elaborate. She'd not been sleeping herself.

"I know we lost Dante, but you don't have to find another fixer. I can do it."

"What? No, Lili. You have school. Also, I'm not going to let my little sister become a hitman. Woman. Whatever."

"I..." I lifted my notebook to hand it to her. "The people we need to take out. I can do it."

"What the fuck are you talking about? Lili, you're not an assassin. I'm not going to let you do that."

"Think about it, K. You know I can hold my own in a fight. If I can sneak up on the guys, I won't even have to do that. I can be smart about it. Get in and out without getting caught. I can take men out without leaving a mess behind."

Kaia sighed and sat in the window seat. Pinching the bridge of her nose, her shoulders slumped as she squeezed her eyes shut. She was tired. It wasn't supposed to happen this way, but now she was at the top. We both knew that she would have to make all the hard decisions, but I could take this weight. The unforgiving moonlight illuminated her as she leaned against the wall. For a long moment, neither of us spoke.

"What about school?" She finally asked.

"I'm not...I can't go back there. I'm done."

"You dropped out?"

"I've been here for six weeks, Kaia. I'm already so behind." I let out a breath so I could stuff down the truth that knotted in my throat. "Besides, I was thinking about leaving before...all of this happened. It's not the right place for me."

"And you think killing people for a living is the right place for you?"

"Standing by your side. For this family. That's my place. Do you remember the bedtime story Nonno used to tell about the village?" I sat down next to her and handed her my notebook. "Please, Kai. I can do this. For you. For Daniel. Let me be the Wolf."

YOU ARE THE wolf. Those were his words to me when I was grieving my mother's loss. It was also what Kaia told me when she finally agreed to my plan and I used my notes to create what we eventually called the Lullaby. It was a title that had passed from Lupo to his son, Dante. The Wolf. Sworn protector of the family.

Nestled between my breasts, the wolf stares back at me every time I get out of the shower. A starburst came out of its head with a blade situated below it. A nod to the man who had first held the position as well as a reminder of the responsibility it implied.

"The Family comes first, le mie principesse. Do not let anyone come between you. Blood is sacred."

47

CERBERA ODOLLAM

A shaken martini takes on water from the ice. Old-school bartenders don't like to make them that way. Poured up, it makes no visual difference, but the drinker can taste it. That's why Flemming's favorite spy drinks them that way. He wants to appear less in control than he is. Nonno loved to point that out. "Shaken, not stirred."

The bartenders had started cleaning glasses and putting them back on the shelves. A few idle stragglers lingered, but the place had pretty much cleared out. I glanced at my phone. Almost 2 am. Soon Muse would close for the night, which meant that these men would leave. The acidic tang of anxiety coated my tongue like bile. The music was just loud enough to prevent eavesdropping, but Benjamin's partner had Sophie perched on his lap. While his guests had seemed interested in the innocent-looking brunette, it was Stephen Bryant who offered her the largest sum to sit still and look pretty. Before she sat down, Sophie and I had locked eyes. I tugged my ear and whispered, "listen." She gave an almost imperceptible nod. Smart girl. The poor bastard didn't know that she was in my pocket, not his.

Guilt tugged at me as I watched them from the corner of the bar area, perched on a stool and slightly obscured by the barrier that separates it from the main floor. When they glanced this way, only my eyes were visible

beneath the top of my hood, and nothing else. It would be difficult to recognize me without all of the makeup, the fancy clothes, or the billionaire
Greek god on my arm, but I wasn't taking any chances.

Muse's unique atmosphere and proximity to the wealthier parts of
town made it a popular meeting spot for powerful businessmen. It was a
short distance away from Camden Industries' office, so Bryant's choice to
meet here hadn't been that surprising. I couldn't help feeling that the move
felt sloppy. Unbeknownst to him, he was being watched from the moment
he set foot inside. This man wanted to be surrounded by beautiful women
while he made deals that earned him millions. But he had been stupid
enough to do so on my hunting grounds.

West leaned against the wall nearest the door, his duties complete for the
night. Wariness flooded his eyes when they connected with mine, the curling marks of his tattoos peeking from beneath the sleeves of his black henley
as he crossed his arms. We hadn't said anything to each other since our fight,
aside from the brief text exchange that followed.

I'd come in through the back door with my key and I hadn't told him I'd
be in. Kaia wasn't upstairs, but if I had my own business to attend to that
was where I would normally be. It wasn't like me to just sit at the bar and he
knew it. I inclined my head toward the men at the table I'd been watching.
West raised his scarred eyebrow in reply.

As they spoke with each other, I looked over the men meeting with Bryant. The first guy looked like an uglier, less friendly Joe Pesci. The second
guy looked familiar. I took a sip from my drink and tried to avoid staring as
I raked my mind for any memory of the face under the terrible hat he'd been
wearing. Then the man scratched his beard and I noticed it. The watch.
Diamonds. The light reflecting on the elaborate timepiece jogged my memory. This was the man who gave Juliet the drugged cocktail. The one who'd
been trying to lead her away. If this man is the killer, the one luring all of
those girls away, what the fuck was he doing meeting with Bryant?

Not being nearly as sophisticated as James Bond, I nursed a vodka soda.
While shaken, I couldn't pounce on the man. Not in front of his entourage.

But men weren't like women. Men don't go to the bathroom together. Men don't look over their shoulders to see if they're being followed. Men stare down at their phones and ignore the world around them. Men like Stephen Bryant.

The other men at his table were engaged in an argument with each other. Confident they wouldn't be watching me and shielded by the barrier around the bar, I finished my drink and hopped off my stool to follow Bryant. West kept his eyes on me but didn't move. The snaps on my sheath clicked under my thumb as I loosed the hunting knife from my belt. Thumping bass notes rattled through my bones as I locked the bathroom door behind me.

"Hello?" A voice came from the stall.

"Hello, Stephen." I purred.

"Who's in here?" He opened the door and found me perched on the counter.

"Wash your hands, Stephen."

"Alright, so you know my name. Care to tell me how?" He shuffled out of the stall. I toyed with my large hunting knife, amazed he didn't recognize me when I wasn't dolled up on Benjamin's arm. Bile rose in my throat. This was going to be ugly. I would make sure of that.

"You can learn anything from the internet, Stephen."

"Stop saying that!" He gritted angrily.

"Saying what, Stephen?"

"My name. Stop saying my name!" He spat. Lunging toward me, I dodged him quickly. A kick swept his feet from beneath him and I heard the hard crack of his bones against the tile. Soon he was on his aching knees with my razor-sharp edge at his throat. The blade would do its work with ease.

"Who are those men with you?"

"Who the fuck are you? I don't have to tell you shit!"

"Oh, mistake. That's a mistake." I pressed the blade to his flesh and drops of blood formed against it. Stephen squirmed and gasped. A flutter coursed through me. Was I actually enjoying this?

"They're buyers! They're buying our product."

"What product, Stephen?" I yanked his head back with my other hand, exposing more of his throat to me. The killer was a buyer. That didn't make sense. Not unless...

"Please," he gritted through bared teeth. "Please, they'll kill me."

"Does it look like I'm getting ready to tell you a bedtime story? Tell me what they're buying!" I growled.

"Girls! They're buying fucking girls!" My gut gave a flip. Girls. The disappearing girls weren't being murdered. They were being trafficked. Hurling himself backward, his head connected with mine. I fell backward and he stood above me as my knife skittered across the tile. Before I could rise, he was on top of me.

Though he wasn't as large as Benjamin or West, I still struggled to get free against his weight. After telling me what he had, it was clear he couldn't let me leave. Only one of us could walk out of this room. He pressed his fingers around my throat and squeezed. My mind became fuzzy with panic. Bryant's hands became my father's hands. Their faces switched. Deep, bottomless fear threatened to swallow me whole, its maw opening wide beneath me as a scream lodged in my throat. Kicking, kicking, kicking, I struggled against him while trying to get myself free. Then I remembered West and his lesson on how to get free of this.

A calm washed over me as I shoved my hips up as hard as I could and knocked him to the ground. The air whooshed out of him as I punched his gut. Rushing to take his back, I wrapped my legs around his waist and laid backward, choking him with the crook of my elbow. Squeezing the air out of him by gripping my lapel and twisting, he couldn't take a breath to scream. His hands scratched at my jacket in hurried little gestures. Wild rage filled me. It burned and snarled in my gut whispering *make him suffer*.

I reached for the blade that had landed just a few steps away. My feet were locked around his waist and my left arm was still drawn tight around his neck. My fingers wrenched at my lapel to keep my hold. He drew in a strangled, uneven breath. The tips of my fingers brushed the butt. I had seconds. Seconds to make my move. Seconds before he realized he could free himself from my grasp. Closing my fingers around the handle, I moved my hand with fatal accuracy. A choked gurgle sputtered above me.

Releasing him, Stephen's throat opened all over the faded green tile. His hands scrambled to his wound, trying to push blood in where it would never be regained. After kicking him over, I watched him with a blood-spattered grin of satisfaction while he gaped and twitched like a fish out of water as the life drained from his eyes. Watching Stephen Bryant bleed out, I wondered how difficult it would be to get his blood out of the grout.

The heavy metal lock snicked as I turned my key, making sure no customers could enter. Scurrying over to the janitorial closet, I nodded at West to get his attention. As he approached, he looked me over and noticed Stephen's blood splattered across my hands and face.

"What did you do?" he demanded through bared teeth.

"The men's bathroom is out of order. Get someone in there to clean it up." I rasped, still panting, trying to draw in a breath.

"Lilith, what did you do?"

"Just tell Kaia we need a clean-up crew in the bathroom. Tell her I said so," I barked. He looked stunned, unaccustomed to seeing this side of me. I already knew Kaia would be furious with me for the bloodshed at Muse. Muse was supposed to be a haven away from the bloodier end of the Caccia family business. A place for us to conduct business where our potential partners and skeptical allies could feel safe. But I didn't have time to be careful. She would understand that eventually. Making a mess was necessary. "Where did the men at the bar go? The short, ugly one and the guy in the bad hat?"

"They went out the back door," West said as he eyed the burst capillaries that had surely formed around my neck, which was already sore. His eyes flared with anger.

"Make sure Sophie doesn't leave!" I snapped as I sprinted for the exit. I couldn't lose them. This lead. With Stephen dead, I'd have no other information. I hadn't intended to kill him so soon, but he would have killed me.

Even if I had somehow survived, he would have told the other men about me if he'd made it out.

Two large and well-suited men were guarding the hallway for the exit. Just looking at them, I knew they weren't ours. I recognized them from the main floor. They had been sitting a few tables away. I'd clocked them, but since they had gotten here before the rest, I'd assumed they weren't together. That was a mistake. My mistake. Adrenaline coursed through my system. "Salt Shaker" blasted through the sound system as I made my way toward them. Lights flashed as confetti rained down from the ceiling. I shrugged off my jacket and flashed them a wild grin. The end-of-the-night theatrics were another home field advantage.

They were both almost a foot taller than me and looked like they had never skipped the gym a day in their lives. But in the close quarters of the hallway, their reach didn't mean shit.

I'm at a disadvantage, usually. My reach is short because I'm short. However, their large bodies made them slow and over-confident. For every step they'd take, I'd take two. Before they could reach me, I'd planned my attack.

Stepping quickly to one side before they could grab me, I threw my jacket to cover the face of the first goon. The second goon lunged and got an elbow to his nose, blood spurting from the wound. Not to leave the first goon out. His booze-soaked breath blew out when my boot connected with his gut.

Screaming sounded from across the room, followed by a slamming door. I couldn't spare a glance to see who it came from, confident West was handling whatever it was. Mr. Nosebleed lunged for me again. Block. Jab. Right hook. I felt his ribs crack when my knee collided with his chest. His buddy staggered to his feet. I couldn't help the grin that crossed my face. Wrapping my arms around his neck, I jumped and used him as leverage to get my legs up around his friend's throat. My weight took them both to the ground. Checking to make sure they were both unconscious, I stood up and rushed toward the exit.

As I was running for the door, I knew there was a slim chance those men were still there. The goons had been left behind intentionally. An obstacle for whoever had delayed Stephen. They knew. They knew that Stephen wasn't coming back. They knew that he'd been compromised, which meant that they were just buying time to get out.

The door slammed shut behind me as I set eyes on the nearly empty parking lot. They'd gone. They'd gone and I was too late. Adrenaline pumped through me as I stood there for a minute, trying to delay going back inside, where I knew West was waiting for an explanation. The angry scream that clawed its way out of my throat left it ragged.

When I entered the club again, I noticed the hallway was empty. Shit. West sat on the stage steps next to Sophie. She adjusted her oversized hoodie and sighed. I knew she wanted to go home, but this couldn't wait. The men Bryant met with would likely change their plans if they thought the information had fallen into the wrong hands. We wouldn't give them time to scramble. Arranging myself on the stage next to them, I scrubbed my hand down my face. This night felt like it would never end.

"Alright. Tell me what you heard."

Sophie shifted, glancing down at my blood-soaked hands. Fear twisted her features. I couldn't imagine how I looked to her. To the girls, I was just an owner. Someone who took care of them. I never asked the girls to do this sort of thing. Dancers here are just like dancers anywhere else. They come to Muse for honest work, not to get mixed up in Caccia business. The only thing we have offered is protection, but if I couldn't fix this we wouldn't be able to offer that anymore. My stomach tightened at the thought.

"They kept talking about San Pedro. The skinny guy said they're moving a shipment on Monday." Sophie stared down at her almond-shaped nails, which were dipped in glittering black. West leaned forward, bracing an arm on his knee as he listened intently.

"Did they say where the shipment is going?" I asked, trying to soften the edge in my voice.

"No. But they said another shipment is gonna be ready soon."

Monday. I sighed to settle the anxiety squeezing the air out of me. I struggled to take another breath. That gave me four days to find the girls. Four days to stop this. West gave me a stern look. I text messaged Kaia.

There's a shipment leaving from the harbor on
Monday. We need to find it before then.

Sophie stood from her seat, her eyes lined with tears. "Can I go home? I'm really tired and that's all I heard."

With a nod, I reached into my pocket and pulled out some cash. I didn't want her to feel used and hoped it might make things less awkward. Still, I couldn't quite meet her eye as I handed her the money.

"I'm sorry about tonight," I said quietly. "Thank you for your help."

She pocketed the bills and gave me a faint smile before West escorted her out to her car. Seeing the tears in her eyes made me feel like a giant piece of shit for getting her involved in the first place. I hoped she would forgive me as I watched her leave. My phone pinged.

Which harbor?

San Pedro.

Alone on the stage, I stood and walked to a pole. The room had only been closed for about twenty minutes, but the smell of sweat and cologne still hung in the air. The janitor was almost done cleaning confetti off of the floor. At this point, he had it down to a science. Otherwise, the space was empty. I wrapped my hands around the pole and swung around. A nauseating lightness drowned my mind. My hands had started to shake. I needed to get some food. Or sleep. Probably both.

West marched back in and braced his arms against the stage, looking up at me with the full measure of his anger. I slid downward until my ass hit the stage and I was sitting before him. My whole body had begun to shake from the adrenaline coursing through my veins. Wrathful green eyes tracked the little squeezing motions I made with my fingers as I tried to steady myself. How was it possible to be this wired on adrenaline and so exhausted at the same time?

"The bathroom will be clean in an hour," he said with an agitated sigh. "Why didn't you tell me what you were doing here? I could have helped you. You shouldn't have done that alone, Lili. It's not safe."

"Where did those guys go? The ones from the hallway."

"They left while I was moving the girls to the dressing room. Did they hurt you?"

I gave a small laugh and shook my head. "Not as much as I hurt them. I told you that I can handle myself." He scoffed at this. "I'm staying with Camden on Friday and then we have a Masquerade on Saturday. I'll try to get as much information out of him as I can."

"You're staying with him? Why?"

"He invited me," I said as I looked at the men's room door, not wanting to meet his eye. How could I explain that I wanted to?

"Don't go," West growled.

"Stop it. I have to. You know that."

His grip tightened on the railing, knuckles going white. As his glare burned into me, he looked like he wanted to say something but said nothing else. I couldn't miss this event. Not when someone's life could be at stake. The silence was only broken by the ping of my phone.

We can watch the port. Keep an eye on anything going in or out. What are we looking for?

Women.

48

RHEUM RHABARBARUM

The bruises around my throat were starting to fade, thanks to the arnica I'd been smearing on them. A small turn in the mirror revealed the black and blue marks that marred my side. As I grabbed the ice pack from my freezer, hoping it was cool enough to resume its place on my neck, I thought about how lucky I was to walk away from those fights with so little to show for it.

Still, it was the closest I'd come to being killed so far. I could see it in his eyes. The decision to kill me had been easy for him. I was an obstacle to be eliminated. But years typing away at a computer were not kind to his hands. The grip he'd had on my throat was not quite tight enough to kill me. The paralyzing effect his hands had on me had more to do with my past than with lost air. Most people don't know that it takes a pretty long time to strangle someone to death with your bare hands.

The watery grey light of the early morning sun was peeking through my blinds. It had only been a few hours since I got home. I'd needed to clean, well, everywhere. Stephen Bryant's blood had gotten all over me. I stood under the shower until the water ran clear. During that time, I kept picturing the way West looked at me.

I never told him in so many words what I did for a living. It had been hinted at. Alluded to. He'd seen me get injured. He helped train me to fight. Because of him, I'd known how to survive the man who tried to kill me. But last night he looked at me with anger and that was new. Maybe he didn't understand what I did. Maybe he was disgusted, too.

Somehow, this line of thinking was making me more exhausted than I had been before, if that was even possible. Throwing myself down on my bed, I picked up my phone again. The clean-up crew would have finished up at the club hours ago, which made my lecture from Kaia imminent. Or so I thought. Checking the time again, I wondered where she could be as I pulled the covers over myself and let sleep take me.

It wasn't long before shadows snaked around my neck and squeezed. Gold-ringed eyes burned out of the darkness. Raoul's eyes. My eyes.

I WOKE UP with a jolt, feeling Stephen Bryant's blood splashing onto my face. It was almost two o'clock in the afternoon. Still no contact from anyone. It felt strange. I should have heard from my sister by now. She would have called to yell at me about what happened at the club. Anxiety got the better of me, so I dialed her. She didn't pick up. That was nothing new. She was often too busy to talk. But no matter what, she always calls me back.

Another two hours went by and still no contact from her. Not even a text message. I had cleaned my apartment. Laid in bed covered in ice packs watching Deadpool. The big fight scene at the end of the movie was about to happen when I turned it off. I wasn't paying attention, anyway. Where the fuck was my sister?

Panicked, I text messaged West.

> I know you're mad at me, but I need your help.

His read receipts were on. I knew he received the message and had looked at it, so I continued.

You know we're dealing with something
dangerous. Please keep an eye out for my
sister. She's not answering my calls.

A sinking sensation took hold of me. No one was getting back to me. Why? I went down the short list of people I trusted in my mind. Gino never answered the phone, so that wouldn't've helped. Lupo was supposed to be at the hospital. When I thought of who I should call, it wasn't a mistake. Carlo picked up the phone immediately.

"Carlo, have you seen or talked to my sister? I can't get her on the phone."

"Last I saw her, she was on her way to the harbor with Ozzie."

My gut twisted. She was looking into the shipping containers. Maybe bribing some guys to help us out. It was strange for her to do it herself. Not when she had other men at her disposal. And in terms of Caccia family members to be alone with, Ozzie was at the very bottom of my list. He'd succeeded his father to get capo, but he'd also been a problem ever since. Every chance he got, he undermined Kaia. Argument after argument, he always lost and it showed in every subsequent interaction. Ozzie may have been one of our guys, but in name only.

I remembered the way Brian Donnelly kept sneaking glances at him. At first, I'd thought it was because of his imposing figure. Ozzie was tall and bald, shaved clean so it was anyone's guess about whether or not it was by choice, and built like a heavy-weight boxer. Anyone would be intimidated by a man like that, especially when his gun had been trained on Donnelly from the beginning. A bullet to the head was by design. Of that, I could almost be certain.

As I started to pack a bag for my weekend with Benjamin, I kept checking my phone. It was difficult to care about spending the weekend with him when Kaia was alone with a possible traitor. The zipper was fighting me as I tried to close it when my phone finally pinged. It was West.

She's at the club.

I looked at the ceiling and thanked whoever was looking out for me. Looping the bag over my shoulder, I huffed a sigh as I typed my response.

Who is she with?

No one. She came alone.

Thank you.

I locked the door behind me and walked to the black sedan that idled by the curb. The ride was long. As I stepped out of the car and into Benjamin's building, I sent Kaia a text.

Stay on your guard.

Nico will be here soon. Lupo started treatment. I'll be fine at Muse.

The walk into the building gave me time to re-affix the mask I'd grown accustomed to these last few weeks. Away went the screwed-up expression of an anxiety-ridden little sister. The pleasant and neutral countenance of a society girl was fixed firmly in place.

49

CORIARIA MYRTIFOLIA

Los Angeles is all about appearances. Benjamin's hand gripped mine as we strode through the lobby of his building. You would never know people lived in this building if you were just passing by. Marble covered the floor while the walls were lined with acacia paneling. A large table with a tall orange flower arrangement was sitting in front of the brass mailboxes. The elevators were opposite them. Standing at the bank of elevators, I watched as women still drooled over Benjamin. Letting my mind focus on that instead of the uneasy feeling that had been blooming in me for hours was easy. My presence was of little consequence to them.

I made eye contact with as many of the lobby women as I could and maintained my grip on the fingers threaded through mine.

"Feeling territorial?" He said through a chuckle.

"Just looking for a little respect. It's like I'm not here."

"Well, let's fix that," he said and pulled my body against his. He planted his other hand on my ass and kissed me.

"That was a bit showy for my taste," I said with a smirk.

Stepping into the elevator, he brought my hand to his mouth and kissed it gently.

"Apologies, darling. Perhaps later I'll do better."

His words sent a thrill through me. The ding of the elevator snapped me into the room again. Without it, I wouldn't have noticed that we'd arrived on the top floor of the building. The floor Benjamin owned. As with everything he had shown me, his home was one of the most glamorous things I had ever seen. Glamorous and cold.

Appearing as a true palace in the sky, every surface finish was white marble and every fabric begged to be touched. The floor-to-ceiling windows displayed the sprawling city below. Beside the windows sat a large glass dining table surrounded by sumptuous velvet dining chairs. It even smelled expensive in here. I drifted to the table to get a better view from the window and put my bag down. The city lights glowed like scattered stars below.

The driver was moving my overnight bag to the bedroom when Benjamin cleared his throat. Turning away from the window, I found his brutal gaze pinned on me as he dismissed the man.

"That will be all. Thank you."

After saying good night, the driver saw himself out. The heavy front door slammed closed behind us. His gaze was still locked on me. My breath became shallow. It was like looking into the fucking sun. My hands tensed and released.

"I should go hang my dress up for tomorrow, I think." I managed to get out.

At this moment, Benjamin Camden took control. He took a step to close the space between us and the smell of his expensive cologne burned through me. He tilted my chin up with two fingers and dragged his thumb across my lower lip. That hand drifted down, circling my throat, as his other hand worked its way up between my thighs. A gasp burst from my lips as I braced myself against the table.

"You're not going anywhere." He growled the words as his breath ghosted across my lips.

I felt like a snared rabbit, utterly at the mercy of a predator. We were two adults who were attracted to each other. Maybe it was foolish for me to be nervous. We'd already slept together, but I was shaking in his grasp. He must have felt the flutter of my pulse beneath his fingertips because his teeth closed around my ear and tugged.

Fucking hell, I thought. *I could die from this.*

"Do you understand what's going to happen now?" The words were rough and low as he moved his icy gaze to meet my own. Before I could speak, he pressed his lips to mine. They were demanding, almost angry. His tongue swept in, taking, taking, taking from me.

"You and I are going into the bedroom. Then I am going to take my time with you, Lilith. I'm going to make you understand what it means to be mine."

The hand around my throat tightened as his fingers worked under my dress. Knuckles grazed across my panties as profanities slipped from me. Finding the fabric wet beneath his touch, he gave an approving groan against my lips.

"Eager, I see."

Stepping back, his gaze raked over my body, the fingers once wrapped around my throat now moved with it until they grabbed my hand and yanked me into step behind him. Any anxious thoughts I'd been having had completely gone from my mind. The room felt like it had entered the stratosphere, almost completely deprived of oxygen. Amsterdam had been a heated moment. This was premeditated, and calculated. A certainty.

Every nerve in my body thrummed with anticipation, buzzing like a live wire. It almost drowned out the sound of our expensive shoes urgently clacking across the marble hallway into his bedroom. That room was just as grand as every other inch of the space, but I was definitely not thinking about that. Not thinking about the California King bed and what are probably Egyptian cotton sheets. No, I was thinking about that damn feeling swirling and building low in my belly. Pulling me toward him, his arm wrapped around my waist as he trailed licks and kisses down my throat. His knuckles skimmed up my spine and swiftly down again, pulling the zipper of my dress with it.

"Off," he said in a rough whisper. "Take this off."

The soft cream fabric drifted down my body and pooled around my feet. Standing back from me, he watched me step out of it and my shoes, toward him with shallow breaths. My nipples peaked and my skin turned to gooseflesh beneath his gaze. The heat in his eyes could destroy a woman stronger than me. There was nothing left to protect me now. I kept telling myself I wanted this. I wanted him. Grabbing my hand again, I thought he was pulling me to him, but he stepped aside to guide me to the bed.

"Sit," he commanded.

The cool, luxurious cotton hit the backs of my thighs as I did as he commanded. Benjamin's eyes remained fixed on me as he removed his jacket and shirt. His cashmere slacks barely contained the urgent length of him. Stepping out of his loafers, he advanced on me and came to his knees so we were facing each other. Pushing my legs apart, he moved closer. His eyes locked on mine. If he could see any hesitation in my expression, he didn't let on.

"Lilith," Benjamin breathed. His fingers traced up my legs, pressing me open. "Let me taste you."

Too stunned to speak, I nodded. My head and my body were fighting for control of the situation, but my mind lost the battle. One of the most powerful men in the world was on his knees before me. Every second I allowed myself to forget this was fake felt like holding my breath underwater. Beneath the surface, everything glistened with permeating light. While my mind enjoyed the numbing silence, the rest of me burned with the need for air. His icy blue eyes looked as lightless as the bottom of the sea as his head dipped between my thighs while he pushed me flat against the soft duvet.

Without pretense, he dragged his tongue across the cotton gusset of my panties and let out a low growl. I jerked at the sudden contact and let out a squeak. The hand at my waist moved swiftly to my hip and pinned me while the other pushed the cotton aside. Another lick dragged across me and I whimpered, squeezing the duvet between my fingers.

"Look at me."

I looked.

"Watch."

I watched.

His eyes locked onto mine as his tongue teased my clit in languid circles. Pleasure wound its way through me, dragging its nails through every doubt and loose end in my mind. Not satisfied with simply holding my panties aside, Benjamin tugged the offending undergarment down and tossed them away. Returning to his assault, he plunged two fingers into me and moved until he found his target.

I tried. I tried so hard to keep my eyes on him. He had all the power. All of it. I let him take it because the loss of it was too delicious. A strangled moan slipped from my throat as I raced to the edge. Tension twisted within me and my hips undulated beneath his grip. A ragged gasp burst from me as his tongue stroked me through my climax. He let out a low laugh.

"*Fuck*," I panted.

While climbing up from the floor, one hand worked off his slacks. I moved up the massive bed to make room for him as he knelt between my legs, covered only in black boxer briefs. Palming himself through the fabric, those devastating blue eyes remained fixed on my body as I took him in. With a rugby player's build, he was inexplicably large and covered in golden, muscular flesh.

The other men I'd been with started to float through my mind. Boys. They had all been boys compared to this. Benjamin knew what he wanted and he fucking took it. Right now, that thing was me. He was going to swallow me whole. I bit my lower lip as he discarded the boxers and revealed the immense length of himself to roll on a condom. I'd seen it before. Felt it before. But the sight still sent a shiver through me, like remembering the taste of a desert that was so sweet it made your teeth ache. There was only a moment to take in the view before he moved to cover my small frame with his massive form, settling between my thighs. Nose to nose with me, he grinned as he nudged the breadth of himself against my opening. My breath stilled at the contact.

"Don't worry, pet. I think you're ready for me."

His hips pushed forward, a tempting shallow taste from the inside. A soft groan was the only evidence of his weakness, stopping as he braced one arm at my side to collect himself. I sat up and kissed him softly, an invitation to keep going. The sound that escaped me was strangled as he plunged inside.

Even as my body took him and enjoyed it, I could only think about what a mistake this was. A horrible, delicious mistake. Since I'd had my first taste of him, I knew two things. The first was that I'd wanted it, this, again. The second was that I knew he would never love me because he didn't know the real me. He loved a facade. A girl who looked like luxury, just like his expensive suits, his Bentley, or any of his designer watches. But he had shown me kindness in my weaker moments and held me when I was afraid. It was possible that maybe he did feel something for the real parts of me I'd shared.

Moving in a torturous assault as he bit at my neck, I could feel every inch of his skin slide against mine. Licking the mark his teeth left behind, his attention shifted to my breasts. Each nipple bitten. Each nipple licked, then sucked. The man was all teeth and tongue. I raked my fingers through his dark curls, lifting my hips to meet his. His lips quirked as he looked down at me with a glint in his eye.

Maybe, I thought, *maybe I can be that girl for him. I could belong to someone.*

Pressing himself down over me, he took my lips again. Though his thrusts were slow, his kisses were urgent and demanding. I moaned against his lips and the sound urged his pace. Teetering toward the edge again, I wrapped my legs around him. The movement pushed him to his end. I cried out as his wild thrusts took me with him.

His dark brown hair was a mess and his skin glowed with sweat. Even disheveled, he looked like he'd descended from Olympus. Between breaths, he chuckled softly. Standing quickly from the bed, he walked to the bathroom to clean himself up.

THE TANGLES OF his dark chest hair were soft beneath my fingers. As though every stress had emptied from his mind, he'd found sleep quickly after giving me a lazy smile. Unfortunately, my mind wouldn't let me find the same peace. Traitorous bitch. I wouldn't stop thinking about how to make this work because, despite rational thought, I did want him. Against any sort of reason, even when I knew the truth.

If we had met sooner or somewhere else, he would not have looked twice at me. Hell, in his dealings with the family, it was possible he had already seen me and ignored me. His women were elegant and statuesque. Women like Alexia. When he stood next to them, they looked like a set. A pair. I was only masquerading as a woman worthy of him. The mafia princess and the billionaire. The idea of it was laughable. Next to him, I looked like a misplaced pepper shaker next to a candlestick. We both knew that this was going to end. It had to.

Slipping out of bed, I went to the bathroom and washed my face with his expensive products. Then I stepped inside his closet. Everything was sealed off behind mahogany doors. Drawers were filled with neatly folded undershirts, socks, and underwear. Then there was a drawer filled with pajamas, all of them navy, all of them embroidered. I grabbed a shirt from the pajama drawer and wrapped it around myself, watching the wolf disappear as I buttoned it up. The damn thing smelled so good. I took a sniff as I entered the dining area.

This time I milled around the space more casually. The whole penthouse felt odd. Unoccupied. There weren't any personal photos around. A large framed painting of a sailboat cresting over stormy waters hung over the living space. Despite its sleek frame, the painting looked out of place amongst the modern furnishings. It felt staged.

Tip-toeing over to the dining table for my purse, I dug around for my phone. I hadn't checked it since I had left home. Four missed calls. No voicemails. All of them were from Kaia. I sent her a text message.

I'll call you in the morning.

The slumbering billionaire snored softly, his broad body sprawled across the expansive bed. As I sat there, sipping water, I admired every curve of muscle and the soft curls of his hair. I had intended to tell him about the secrets that Bryant and Johnson were keeping from him. Everything I'd discovered about what his partners were doing right under his nose. But tonight I would let him sleep.

50

ILEX VERTICILLATA

Benjamin Camden needed to buy groceries. As I poked through his sparsely stocked pantry, I wondered if he even lived here.

"We have to stop meeting like this."

The man himself was leaning against the counter. The lights beneath the cabinets were on with a flick of his wrist, casting the grand marble kitchen in a soft glow.

"Sorry, I was just…"

"Hungry."

"Yes," I sighed. "When you keep the sort of hours I do, food is more readily available than sleep."

The shadow of his stubble looked darker in the low light. His steely blue eyes were fixed on me as I pulled odd items out of the pantry for a closer inspection. Steel-cut oatmeal, flavorless protein powder, almonds. Yuck. Good lord, this man was devastating to look at. But had he never heard of snacks?

"Why do you keep such odd hours, Lilith?"

"Well," I breathed. "I have a lot of jobs that I do to help the family. To help-"

"Your sister."

"Yes," I said as I poked my head into the refrigerator. Eggs, cheese, milk. "You have no food."

"What are you talking about?" He approached the refrigerator with a laugh. "I have food."

"No, no. I see ingredients. I do not see individually edible items." I pulled each item out to articulate my point.

"I'll make a deal with you." He stepped closer and wrapped an arm around my waist. "I will make you a delectable, succulent, mouthwatering omelet." He paused and pressed a kiss to my shoulder. I sagged against him as his warmth leaked into me against the cold of the open door. Fingers traced up my thigh to squeeze my hip beneath his shirt. "But you have to tell me about the real Lilith Caccia."

I turned to face him, a small pit opening in my stomach. The way he looked at me, with a small smirk and cocked eyebrows like we shared a private joke, was completely disarming. He tilted my chin up and brushed his lips against mine. The soft, sensuous press of his mouth clouded my mind as I thought about what I should share and what needed to stay hidden. Then Ethan came to mind. If I had just been honest with him, maybe I wouldn't have been so devastated. His hatred of me hurt worse than his betrayal because it felt like a black mark against who I truly was. Maybe things would have been different with West, too.

"Please?" He groaned into my neck.

"Alright," I said, as his kisses moved to my collarbone. "You've convinced me."

"Good. Start talking."

Benjamin pressed a quick kiss to my mouth and picked up the eggs. Then he fished out a bowl from under the counter. The eggs were cracked into a bowl as I started spilling my guts.

"My father was in line to become Boss, so he wanted a legacy. Boys to follow in his footsteps. Nature got in the way when it gave him two girls instead of the sons he always wanted. He made us pay for being born girls as often as he could."

Benjamin leaned against the counter as the pan heated over the stove. I climbed up onto the counter opposite him and settled in. With a deep breath, I tried to quiet the anxiety roiling in me before sharing things few people knew.

"Go on," he prompted.

"Being four years older than me, Kaia got the worst of it. She trained relentlessly, hoping to prove that she was worthy of taking on the family business, just as she would have been if she were a boy. No matter what she did, all of her hard work didn't seem to be enough."

The eggs sizzled as they hit the pan and Benjamin's attention shifted to the dish. I decided the tougher things would be easier to share with his back to me.

"I was able to mostly avoid his attention by staying buried in school-work. Our mother would keep me occupied and out of the way, but I got my fair share of it anyway. Kaia always found a way to get his attention away from me, though. That's why I do what I do now. I owe her."

Without turning to look at me, he asked the question I'd been dreading. "What do you do, Lilith?"

"I protect the family."

He stilled at the stove and I stopped breathing. The only sound in the room was the gentle sizzle of the eggs.

"You kill people."

"Not randomly," I blurted. "Not just anyone I feel like. She's Boss and gives me assignments. But you know what my family is. What we are. I'm a part of that. I take care of the loose ends. The people who get in the way."

After pulling a plate from the cabinet beside him, he flipped the omelet out of the pan. I sat quietly as he opened a drawer and brought out a pair of forks.

"Alright," he said as he brought the plate to the dining table. His shoulders had tensed, but he was acting casual. Negotiating his acceptance within himself. "How? Do you shoot people?"

"No. Most of the time I drug them. Sometimes if there's a fight, it's more violent than that, but it's usually quiet."

I hopped off of the counter and grabbed a bottle of sparkling water out of the refrigerator before joining him at the table. He sat at the head and I took the seat beside him, tucking my feet under myself. Silently, he handed me a fork. The steaming eggs sat between us, so I took a bite. Salty, savory, cheesy. Everything I wanted.

"This is so good," I said as I speared another bite for myself. He gave me a half-cocked smirk. Not quite a smile. "I'm sorry."

"For what?"

"I know it's a lot. Too much."

Benjamin placed his hand on my thigh and leaned forward. He looked at me thoughtfully, seeming to debate what he wanted to say.

"Lilith," he murmured. "I knew about your family. What you do is just business. We both do things we dislike for the sake of an empire."

The relief I felt surged through me. It made me kiss him. He'd understood. I hadn't shared that with anyone. Everything I do to protect the people I love. To repay the insurmountable debt to my sister. That wouldn't make him run from me. A tear slid down my cheek.

"Don't cry," he whispered against my lips. "Now finish this omelet so I can take you back to bed."

51

DATURA STRAMONIUM

In the faint glow of the early morning light, I sat on the terrace. Benjamin was snoring softly when I woke, so I snuck outside to call Kaia away from where he could hear me. The early morning chill was no match for Benjamin's robe. His leather and sage scent felt good wrapped around me. I'd felt a little guilty leaving him there. His business partner's death was still unknown, but they spoke every day. It would be difficult to keep it from him for long.

"Yes?" Kaia said roughly. She must have gone to bed. "For someone who was desperately trying to get in touch with me, you took your time calling me back."

"I was busy with something. I'm sorry to wake you. Did you find anything?"

"Nothing yet, but we left some guys behind. They're being as thorough as they can be with all of those locked shipping containers. There are hundreds, Lili."

"They sail on Monday morning. Did the clean-up crew keep Bryant's phone?" I asked as I pulled the robe around myself more closely, not sure if the chill I'd felt was from the air or rising anxiety.

"I don't know. I'll ask. Lili, I don't like this." The concern bled through her already tired voice.

"We're already in it, Kai. I'll watch my back. And you watch yours. Especially around Ozzie. Hug Daniel for me. I love you."

"I love you too," she murmured as she hung up. Clearly, she was going back to sleep.

Cold bit into my bones as leaned back against the seat and looked out at the rolling hills of Los Angeles. This high up, there was very little noise. The city hadn't yet woken up. At this hour, everything was peaceful. Marine layer mist curled around nearby buildings, making it look like we were in a floating metropolis.

"Good morning."

I jerked with surprise. Benjamin leaned against the frame of the door, which I had forgotten to shut. Navy blue pajama pants were still slung low on his hips, revealing the vee of muscles that dipped below them. Wondering how long he'd been standing there, I feigned an innocent smile.

"Good morning. Did you sleep alright?"

He nodded and crossed the terrace to where I sat. Kneeling before me, he braced his arms on the seat to cage me in. That intoxicating leather and sage scent enveloped me as he leaned forward.

"I thought you'd left," he said as he planted sensuous kisses against my jaw.

"I was just checking in with my sister. She called me last night, but I forgot to get back to her. I guess I got a little distracted."

He grinned and placed a hand on my knee, pushing the robe aside to expose more skin. His thumb traced along the inside of my thigh and a shiver followed in its path.

"Come back to bed," he demanded, looking down at where his fingers idly lingered.

"Okay," I breathed. It was possible that he hadn't heard me on the phone. He could have only been there for a moment, looking for me because I had been missing when he woke.

The blackout shades in his bedroom were still drawn, cloaking the room in darkness. I shed the robe and climbed back into bed. The mattress sank with his weight as he curled himself behind me. With only his pajama pants between us, his rigid shaft pressed against my backside.

The warmth of his body seeped into me, unwinding all of the uncertainty that had been there moments ago. Soft, wet kisses pressed to my neck as I sighed. Last night, I'd laid myself bare over a plate of eggs. Any man would have gone running. But here he was, holding me close. Benjamin Camden, the billionaire playboy of Los Angeles, was spooning me.

"You're unlike any woman I've ever known."

The hand that had pressed against my stomach coasted down between my thighs. Apparently, we had not come back to bed for rest. I wasn't sure what he'd said could be construed as a compliment. The ministrations of his hand stole any rational response from me. Instead, I rubbed my backside against him. When I pushed his pants down, his length sprang free. The hand that had been working me moved down to lift my leg and make room for him. I let out a quiet gasp as his tip brushed against me. Thrusting himself against my sensitive flesh, I writhed in his grasp. Teeth nibbled at my ear.

Everything narrowed down to him. His touch. His hands and the way they moved over my skin. The way he breathed my name into the dark strands of my hair. The grip of his fingers on my hip. It was so difficult to think. Deft little flicks of his fingers unbuttoned the pajama shirt I'd borrowed, exposing me to the cool darkness. When he was around, all I wanted was for him to touch me. Taste me. I wanted to hold on to this feeling, this alive feeling, because I knew it could fall away like so many grains of sand.

Then he stopped for a moment and moved away from me. I looked over my shoulder to see where he'd gone. Kicking his pants off, he gripped the base of his shaft, which was now armored and ready for me.

Aligning himself behind me once more, he pushed inside, his size filling and stretching almost to discomfort. I let out a whimper as he nipped my shoulder. Every second his hands were on me destroyed me a little bit more. Grazing my ear with his lips as he spoke, his voice was rough and hungry.

"I couldn't live with myself if I didn't have you at least one more time."

GETTING READY FOR the event took all afternoon. Since our tryst in the morning, Benjamin hardly spoke. Though a quiet peace had settled between us, it still made me uneasy. I watched him in the mirror as I swept makeup on here and there, creating the illusion, when our eyes locked. The way he smiled at me felt different. Something in his ice-blue stare was shuttered. Guarded. As I forced myself to smile back at him, I couldn't ignore the twisting feeling in my gut. Something had shifted. It was unmistakable. Before I could ask what was wrong, he left the room. Perhaps I'd been an idiot to share with him. Maybe it had been too much for him.

Growing discomfort kept my phone not far from my fingers for the majority of the day. Benjamin and I maintained silence in the car. Nico let me know he was going to his father's chemotherapy appointment and that Kaia was at the club. She must have told him I was working. My gaze traveled over the passing city as I wondered who had taken his place guarding my sister. I sent a text message to Nico.

Ask West to look after Kaia while you're gone.

I knew the hotel when we arrived. The same location as the last formal Eros party where members showed off their partners and, well, connected. Though, this time, the entrance looked different. A line of guests had formed by the front door. When we parted from the Bentley, I expected Benjamin to walk through the crowd with his usual authoritative ease.

Instead, we stopped at the door where a booth with security guards had been situated. The lace mask I wore suddenly felt tight around my eyes. It looked like people were checking in. Or handing something over. Nico's reply popped onto my screen.

He's not here. Called out. It's fine. I got Ozzie
to cover for me.

"Miss? Your phone, please?"

"I..." I stammered. Anxiety coursed through my blood, filling every space in me. "What?"

I shot Benjamin a look as the security guard again asked for my phone. Benjamin seemed to tense at my resistance.

"It's a check-in. You'll get it back when you leave. Like a coat check," the guard explained.

"We've had some issues with photos and videos getting out," Benjamin said quietly.

My teeth clenched. I wasn't armed. This was my only lifeline. The man at the desk cleared his throat, waiting for me to hand over the device. Letting out a small sigh, I shut the phone off and handed it over. The guard gave me a ticket that I stuffed into my clutch.

"There," Benjamin laughed. "Was that so hard?"

As we entered the space, I looked around. Eros had outdone themselves with the affair we were attending this evening. If I thought the previous party was elaborate, it was nothing compared to this. This scintillating event made the other look like an amateur hour. Everything gleamed and glittered. Instead of black table linens and red roses, everything was dazzling and white. Puffs of white flowers floated on silver towers. Diamonds, bone, mother-of-pearl, all sparkling in low candlelight. The warm glow was reflected in mirrors that had been placed against the walls. Ivory-clad waitstaff wore white masks and...wings. The first party we attended here felt like Tartarus. This heavenly display was closer to Elysium.

Instead of the DJ they'd hired before, a string quartet played light and breathy covers of popular music that lent an angelic tone to everything that was happening around us. My stomach twisted with unease as I mentally kicked myself for letting them take my phone. If I was somehow able to find the traffickers, I would have no way to call for help. The claim about photos and videos felt half-baked. Wouldn't he have mentioned that? Wouldn't I have seen them for myself? As though he could hear my thoughts, Benjamin grazed my exposed back with his hand in soothing strokes.

"You look like a goddess," he whispered.

The fingers grazing my spine seemed to raise my hackles. A mirror close to us caught my attention. My black waves were loose around my shoulders, and the moon-shaped earrings I wore were revealed only when I tucked loose strands behind an ear. My gown was made of soft, shimmering chiffon arranged into panels to cover my breasts, held in place by small matching cords that crisscrossed over my torso. The wolf tattoo was in full view to everyone in the room. As my gaze met with it, its face seemed tight with worry.

Benjamin and I would need to find a place to be alone together. I could tell him everything. I needed to. He could call for the large security guards I'd seen around the room. I could explain Stephen Bryant's plans for the girls and Henry Johnson's collusion behind his back. He could help put a stop to it.

Every step I took with him felt like I was wading into an ocean of unanswered questions. I thought about my sister and the shipping container and wondered if she'd been able to find the missing women. I thought about my phone locked away in that damned security locker. As we moved through the hall, I watched bodies writhe and pant in dark alcoves, light glinting off the gold and leather masks.

"Can we find somewhere to be alone?"

"Of course. I told you I'd arrange something special for you next time," Benjamin purred. "Come with me."

His fingers gripped around mine and continued to pull me down the large, dark hall. My heels clicked down the marble flooring, my footing quick but uncertain. What was the rush?

An oily sick feeling squeezed my gut. As we passed various alcoves, I felt it again. The eyes peered back at me from the darkness. I tried to school my expression as I strained to see who was there. Someone lurked in the shadows. I felt the urge to ask if we could just stop for a moment.

The dazzling, white-attired guests may have been dressed like angels, but the ethereal environment felt cold. The candlelight gave everything a soft glow. I glanced down at the wolf tattoo, almost for reassurance. It looked out at the hall with its carnivorous gaze but was no help at all. A shiver crawled down my spine and discomfort tugged at my nerves. Writhing bodies, crying out as they had before, looked more like trapped souls than lovers. I thought I saw the skull mask as I glanced over my shoulder. The stranger from the shadows I'd seen before. Everything was wrong. As Benjamin pulled me through the array of public displays, a voice in me whispered something over and over: *Run*.

Benjamin's stride quickened as he made for the steel door at the end of the hall. I wondered what sort of kinky plans he'd made that required a room away from the depravity that surrounded us. He strained to heft the steel door open and it squeaked on its hinges. Turning to face me, he gave me a broad smile.

"This is for you, pet."

The room appeared barer than the rest of the hall. In fact, it didn't even look like a room. It looked like... a utility closet. A utility closet with a chair sitting below a dangling bulb and a large bald man who looked like he'd been waiting for us. I stared into the room like a doe trapped in headlights. *Fuck.*

With cruel force, Benjamin pushed me through the door and slammed it shut behind us.

52

ACONITUM

My knees were scraped and bleeding from the fall, the hard concrete reverberated through my bones. That would have never happened in my damned boots. Having fallen out of my heels, I tried to get up quickly. A hand coiled into my hair and yanked back. My scalp burned from being pulled so hard as Benjamin tugged me up to walk me to the chair. I reared back against him and kicked up, getting the bald man in the jaw.

"Bitch!" He spat. A meaty fist connected with my head, and everything went fuzzy. Benjamin deposited me in the chair as the bald man's aggressive grip held me down in the seat.

Rope scraped against my wrists as Benjamin tied me to the backrest. The bald man in the domino mask dug his fingers into the bleeding wounds on my knees as he held them apart. His boss made quick work of tying the same rough restraints around my ankles. Cold, angry dread seeped into my bones. The moment the door closed, I knew. I knew I wasn't walking away from this. There wasn't going to be a happy ending to this story. The billionaire hadn't fallen in love with me. He'd been playing me and I was the fucking fool who was about to get herself killed.

"You're trafficking those girls, aren't you? It wasn't Bryant, it's you." I spat at him.

He ignored me and the large bald man stood at the door. People don't get out of situations like this. I should know. Looking around, I didn't see anything prepared for blood. If they were planning to kill me, it was going to be something quick. I eyed the bald man and wondered if he'd ever broken someone's neck with his bare hands before.

"Those shipping containers in San Pedro. The Belfast shipment. Amsterdam. They're full of fucking people."

Benjamin huffed a laugh as he took off his tuxedo jacket and hung it on a broomstick. Rolling up his sleeves, his gaze raked over me. The plunging neckline and thigh slits of my dress made me feel like his human sacrifice. I didn't have time to brace for his fist striking my cheek. Circling behind me again, he tugged my head back with a yank of my hair and grabbed my throat with his other hand.

"Do you have any idea what sort of mess you've created for me?"

The fine London gentleman had disappeared. Rage and indignation coated his words. Up close, I could smell his cologne. His sweat. The shaky grip on my throat tightened and I felt his freshly filed nails dig into my skin. Air was slipping away and every breath hurt. If he was planning to strangle me to death, he'd be here a while. My heart started racing at the thought.

"Mess?" I choked out. Tears welled in my eyes as I struggled for oxygen.

"I thought I could keep you away. Distract you until you gave up, but you made that impossible."

Oily regret and embarrassment seeped into me. My sister had warned me not to trust him. West warned me not to trust him. Kaia told me not to be taken in by his show. I fell for all of it anyway because I wanted to be accepted by someone. Wanted my secrets to be safe with that someone. Now it was going to get me killed. Bastard.

"Right, like you being a monster is my fault somehow."

Benjamin laughed. "Now, darling, don't be offended. You want so badly to be loved. You made it so easy. Some of it was quite fun, but I was never going to be serious about you." He practically spat the word "you" at me.

Fucking prick. The whole time I thought we were putting on an act for his partners and customers, he had been putting on an act for me. And oh god, the things I let him do to me. Humiliated was too kind a word. Anger and shame twined in my blood, like barbed wire pulling on everything inside me. I watched him with new eyes as he moved about the small space.

I wasn't anything to him. Just an obstacle. An inconvenience. He had dressed me for the altar and now I was ready for slaughter.

"Because you were always going to kill me."

"Oh no, pet. I'm not foolish enough to pick a fight with a mafia family. Lilith Rhamnusia Caccia, no. When you came calling, I learned everything I could about you. About your sister. That sweet little boy of hers. But now that you've become more than just a nuisance, I've got no choice. They'll never find you. Just like we'll never find Bryant or Johnson, will we? Poor Stephen didn't deserve to die such a gruesome death." Renewed dread washed through me at the sound of my middle name. He brushed the hair out of my eyes and cupped my face. The man had the nerve to look offended when I flinched. I couldn't believe I ever let him touch me. Leaning in with a cruel smile on his lips, his breath ghosted across my skin as he whispered. "I'll never forget the way you moaned when I fucked you."

"Ugh, if you're going to kill me, just do it," I muttered, stuffing down the raging panic his words stirred in me. I scanned the room, looking for something. Anything to get me out of this. There was nothing I could do. No one to call for help. My body shook as my knees began aching from the spill. The scraped skin bled slowly.

Benjamin squeezed my exposed thigh as he stood up. The bald man stepped forward and handed him something. A syringe glinted in my view.

"You're familiar with this particular cocktail." A brown vial was drained into the syringe. "A favorite of yours, really. How many men have been on the receiving end of your needle, I wonder?"

He knelt again and dragged the needle across my thigh, the point biting at my skin. *Fuck, fuck, fuck,* I thought. I can't die like this. As I looked more closely at the syringe, I noticed that the liquid didn't seem quite right. The mixture was too clear. That wasn't the Lullaby. Of course, that didn't mean it couldn't kill me.

"Now I get to stick you one last time." He plunged the needle in with a grin. I tried not to wince at the pain. I didn't want to give the shithead the satisfaction. "Sadly, I won't be around when you finish."

He stood and tugged on his tuxedo jacket, repositioning the mask he'd worn. I opened my mouth to speak, but only a groan came out. No last words for me. As the door slammed shut behind him, the floor felt like it was slipping out from under me. My head dropped back. It wouldn't be long now.

Cold started at my feet and worked its way up. Like a frozen ocean gradually swallowing me into darkness. Benjamin. For the last few weeks, he worked at chipping away at my resolve. The walls I'd had in place for years crumbled at his touch. Like a goddamned idiot, I let him in and gave him exactly what he wanted.

The loose ends of my life started drifting through my thoughts like tumbleweeds. The first of them were thoughts of Kaia. I'd failed her. I fucking failed. A pit settled in my stomach as I thought about her grief. She had plenty of people to help her, but who would listen at the end of a long day? Who could she let her guard down with? I was the last person on the planet who knew the whole woman, not just the boss mask or the mom hat.

And what about Daniel? He would be graduating from kindergarten soon. I'd never get to see his first day and watch Kaia try to not cry. I promised him I'd always be there. That I wouldn't be like his dad and just disappear. I didn't even have a chance to watch Star Wars with him yet. And West…

The edges of my vision blurred as everything faded into darkness. The cold I'd been feeling had spread through my limbs and dread dropped in my gut like a stone into water. I wondered what they would do with my body. Would I be disassembled and burned? Dropped into the ocean? It would be somewhere I'd never be found. An unanswered question for the people I loved.

The heavy steel door slammed again. I wasn't alone. I wondered if the large man came to watch me die. Maybe Benjamin. Straining to sit up and see who was in the room with me was impossible. All of my muscles felt useless now. Words failed me. Only whimpering gasps for air left my lips. My head lolled backward as I heard footsteps hurry toward me.

"No, no, no." A voice. "Shit."

Warm, callused hands framed my face.

"Stay with me. Eyes open. Come on, Lili. Look at me."

This voice, scent, and hands all felt familiar. I fought, forcing my eyelids up. My throat still felt tight. Only a whimper escaped from me. I couldn't speak. Smokey green eyes, a small scar... West. He came for me. His thumb stroked my cheek, drying the wet that had been there. Had I been crying? A scrape rang out from my wrists as they were freed from the rope. How was he here?

"I've got you. Eyes on me. Please, Lili. Please, don't give up on me." His voice rasped.

I strained to keep my eyes open. I tried so hard to keep him in my sight. West gave me a weak smile and pressed his fingers to my throat. Then I heard the rope drop away from my ankles. Before I could slump to the floor, warm arms enveloped me. He was so warm when everything else felt cold. So cold and heavy. As he curled me to his chest, I felt myself being lifted. Then there was nothing.

EPILOGUE

Sunlight beamed onto the grey linen-covered pillow next to me when I peeled my eyes open. The space I was in was soft and comfortable. A thick green flannel blanket lay over the top of the sheets. There was a short dresser against the wall to my right and a mirrored closet to my left. I caught my reflection and dear god; I looked like hell. My hair was a tangled mess. Thankfully, all of the makeup I was wearing seemed to have been cleaned off of my face. The last thing I remember wearing was the evening dress, which was now draped over a chair in the corner. An oversized green tee shirt covered me now.

A wave of nausea speared through me in a violent lurch. My head throbbed and my body ached, but I was pretty sure I was alive. If there is a heaven, I certainly didn't deserve to go there and this was a far cry from hell. I'd just left there.

I braced my elbows against my knees and tried to take in my surroundings. Every movement I made brought on a fresh bout of vertigo, but curiosity overwhelmed me. Deep steadying breaths helped me to keep hold of my stomach. Where was I? The space was small and warm, the smell familiar and inviting. As I moved, I felt the tug of a needle in my arm. It was set up with an IV drip dangling from a wire hanger bent around a curtain rod that clanged like a bell with my movement. This was someone's bedroom, but it had been turned into some kind of makeshift hospital.

"Hey, you're awake."

West leaned against the doorframe. His doorframe. This was his room. Based on the size of it, I was also wearing his shirt.

"I think you mean 'alive.' Sort of." I said, rubbing my temples. "Is this... where are we?"

"This is my place." Taking a swig from the enamel coffee cup that looked tiny in his large hand, he shifted his weight and looked me over. His long hair was a tousled mess around his shoulders and his beard needed to be brushed. "About an hour outside of Big Bear. You've been in and out of consciousness for almost a week."

I looked around the room again and took in little details I hadn't noticed before. A folded flag was framed atop his dresser. Next to it was a shadow box with patches pinned inside. One was a smaller flag. Another looked sort of like a Jolly Roger. The only one I could make out clearly said US Navy SEALS in bold letters, surrounding an eagle gripping a trident and what looked like a rifle. I'd known he served in the Navy, but he'd never told me this.

"I...a week?" I blinked as I glanced at the box again.

He nodded.

"How am I not dead?"

He set his coffee down on the nightstand beside the bed and sat next to me. Steam wafted from the coffee mug. West took a breath and furrowed his eyebrows, seeming to debate exactly how much he wanted to tell me.

"After everything started happening with the Arwans, Kaia had me shadow you. She wanted to make sure you were safe. Since you told her where you would be, she told me."

I narrowed my eyes at him. Shadow me? The lack of confidence in me was at war with the reality that I'd almost been killed. The spinning feeling was making this hard to understand. It took everything I had to stay focused. I rubbed my eyes and tried to collect myself. "Ok, that doesn't explain the whole me-not-dying part."

"Benjamin thought he had a lethal injection. He told his guard to wait to move your body."

"What did he actually dose me with?"

"A sedative. I'm not sure how much he gave you, but it was a lot." West scrubbed a hand over his face. From the dark smudges beneath his eyes, it was clear that he had hardly slept. "You were barely here."

I couldn't tell what was making me exhausted. Vertigo, or the fact that I'd had more than just a brush with death. I'd had a head-on collision with it.

"Jesus, no wonder I thought I was dying. Did you do all of this?" I asked, jangling the IV bag on the hanger.

"No, that was my sister. I have been changing the bags, though."

I blinked. I didn't know he even had a sister. Sitting in this cabin, it occurred to me that I didn't know as much about him as I thought.

"The men who got away at the club came back. Came back with more people. And guns. They knew about the man you killed and wanted to know what you knew...." he trailed off.

My blood turned cold. I had figured my apartment wasn't safe after I saw my medical kit in Benjamin's hands. Even the small amount of information he had on our family was enough to do real damage. He wouldn't be able to access the safe. Not even if Kaia was there. Not that he needed the money in there, but there was so much more that needed to be protected. My gut churned. The pain in my head became almost unbearable as I considered the consequences.

"What did they do to the club?" I asked, unsure I even wanted to hear the answer. The wood headboard was cool against my back as I leaned against it for support. Overwhelmed with pain, I started rubbing my fingers against my temples again. This was so bad. So fucking bad.

"I'm sorry, Lili. I'm so... I wasn't there. If I'd been there, it wouldn't have happened."

"What? What wouldn't have happened?" I asked, pressing my hands to my eyes. God, my head was pounding. Nausea burned through me like wildfire. Cold sweat covered me as I tilted my head back and closed my eyes, letting all the worst possible scenarios pour through my mind.

"The club is fine. All the girls are safe and nothing big got damaged. But Lili, they got Kaia."

My eyes popped open as I sat forward. The churning in my gut stopped. It felt everything inside me went still.

"What do you mean they got Kaia? Is she alive? Where's Daniel?"

"Daniel is safe. He's with my sister."

"West," I asked more slowly, "is Kaia alive?"

"I don't know."

The room tilted off of its axis and my body felt like it was being dragged underwater. Frost-bound rage replaced the torrents of hot fear coursing through my body. My way of killing was always clean, measured, and fast. It was the only way I could sleep after taking a life. Kaia means more to me than a clear conscience. More than an hour of peace.

Benjamin Camden may have been one of the most powerful men in the world, but he didn't understand a fundamental truth about me. That I'd been holding back. I would educate him on the darkness of true fear. He would know pain of the highest measure. I would savor every second of the unrelenting, unyielding torment he was going to feel at my hands.